Dirty Metal

Dirty Metal

A Novel

ALLISON LaMOTHE

FLATIRON
BOOKS
NEW YORK

This is a work of fiction. All the characters, organizations, and events portrayed in this novel are either products of the author's imagination or used fictitiously.

Printed in the United States of America. For information, address Flatiron Books, 120 Broadway, New York, NY 10271. EU Representative: Macmillan Publishers Ireland Ltd, 1st Floor, The Liffey Trust Centre, 117–126 Sheriff Street Upper, Dublin 1, DO1 YC43.

www.flatironbooks.com

Library of Congress Cataloging-in-Publication Data

Names: LaMothe, Allison, author.
Title: Dirty metal : a novel / Allison LaMothe.
Description: First edition. | New York : Flatiron Books, 2026.
Identifiers: LCCN 2025018654 | ISBN 9781250382528 (hardcover) | ISBN 9781250382535 (ebook)
Subjects: LCGFT: Detective and mystery fiction | Novels | Fiction
Classification: LCC PS3612.A5474324 D57 2026 | DDC 813/.6—dc23/eng/20250623
LC record available at https://lccn.loc.gov/2025018654

First Edition: 2026

10 9 8 7 6 5 4 3 2 1

I am nobody; I have nothing to do with explosions.

—SYLVIA PLATH, "TULIPS"

March 23, 1992

The platform is practically empty, as it always is at this time of day, creeping toward night. A lone figure emerges from the stairwell on the far end, puts his hands in his jacket pockets, and leans out to stare into the tunnel, the way people always do. As if that'll make the train come faster.

It's that here-nor-there time between seasons, evenings opening up but the air still carrying the chill of late winter. A few stalks of greenish weeds pinch up from the jagged rocks laid between the rusted tracks. Beyond the opposite platform rise pre-war apartment buildings strung with clotheslines, bricks dirtied from decades of subway exhaust. A restful ease has taken over, so deep in Brooklyn where the tourists don't go much because nothing much happens. Every so often, the slam of a car door. The *thwack* of a window sash. The closing of a gate.

Underground, the train barrels in with a brain-shaking clatter. But out here it comes quietly, as if running on greased tracks. You might not even notice it's there until it's zooming past your nose in a blur of dirty metal.

The only other sound is the pigeons. They roost in the metal overhang, small shadows that stir and coo and take off, one at a time, and make for the opposite side, wings bruising the satiny dusk. Every time one gets close to its destination, it wheels around and flies back to where it started, tucking its feathers into that dark shelter. Something unnerves them. Eventually, inevitably, one won't pull its about-face fast enough. Its hollow bones will hit the overhang and its body will fall, limp and lifeless, onto the yellow-painted edge of the platform.

I watch them and think, it's only a matter of time.

When you spend a lot of time on trains, you spend a lot of time thinking about them. How they manage to be in two places at once, as if they've solved the paradox of time travel. Half in the past, where you can't go back; half in the future, too far ahead for you to ever catch up.

The tracks click softly. The yellow eyes of the subway appear inside the tunnel.

A girl's scream tears through the quiet night.

In a moment, the peace is revealed for what it is: a flimsy retaining wall holding back a scrabbling force of dark, unnameable things.

Just as suddenly, my feet are pounding up the platform steps and rocketing me toward the turnstile. My mind careens, the air rushes in my ears, the pill jar jangles in my pocket, my heart darts like the small, raw heart of a bird. Only somewhere behind it all—the last clear memory I have of the evening—do I hear the train barreling into the station.

###

Then things start to muddle. The pills take hold and I can't hold them back, the ride of one too many sweeping me away on a current of chalky pharmaceutical blue. I can feel it happening: the softness settling in, the world coming at me like a series of out-of-focus photos. Reaching the street. Watching the sidewalk pavers being slowly swallowed by my feet. An eerie silence gathering on the back of my neck. The time compresses.

One block, another. And then: A body. Her body.

Pale sweetheart face. Eyes open and stunned. Dark, arched eyebrows. Long hair spilling over the pavement.

And there, on the sidewalk, glimmering—a ring. I pick it up.

1

A ring in my pocket . . .

My name is Parker Snow. I'm a person of simple needs: black coffee, cigarettes, my cat Nellie, notebook, pen, and every inexplicably terrible thing that happens in New York City. I have very bad handwriting that seems to be running over itself; it's because I'm always trying to get it down too fast. I hate the outdoors, I can't drive, I don't cook and, generally, people don't really notice I exist, a skill that comes in handy in my line of work. Not being seen is more of an attitude than a physical characteristic.

That's what seven years of crime reporting for one of the city's finest tabloid papers will do for you. *The New York Street*: the junket of junk, the talk of the tawdry, the holy *who's who* of local hucksters, scofflaws, killers, and con artists, not a few of whom are on our fine city's payroll. It'll give you the skill of invisibility, plus a knee-jerk suspicion of anyone who seems too good.

I'm on the organized crime beat now, though it's not my preference.

Too organized. I used to be just a crime reporter, no qualifiers, but you could say I got benched. Some people would say I'm lucky that's all I got.

Tonight, I'm at a Russian poker game in Sheepshead Bay. I'm counting on the games being my entrée into the Russian mafia activities du jour, which is my current assignment. This one is being held in the basement of a restaurant called the Peterhof Palace—if that isn't the overstatement of the century. The air is heavy with cigarette smoke and pregame trash-talking, recognizable in any language. Both issue from a group of men sitting around a table, t-shirts spread tight over big muscles and big guts, the faces above them lined with years of hard and fast living. I watch as one of the men gives another a good-natured punch on the shoulder that would probably knock me flat.

I'm hanging around by the door, having paid fifty dollars to the menacing-looking Slav who guards it. While I wait for my contact to arrive, I take the ring out and examine it. I'm no expert, but I'll bet my byline this is no diamond. The band is gold—plated, I'd guess—and tarnished, with a princess-cut fugazi in the middle.

Memories of the night before come back to me like they're being passed through a sieve. I went to see my doctor out in Bensonhurst. We started with our usual exchange. *How are you feeling?* he'd asked me. *Any new symptoms?* About the same, I'd answered. Always about the same. A pageantry he respected as if it were something sacred, there in that dim office with the fake name on the dummy diploma, the old exam table where no one was ever examined, leather cracking at the corners.

But then he'd veered off script. He said that I should find *more sustainable methods* for dealing with my stress. He'd been slick palmed and nervous, which in turn made me nervous. What if he was starting to worry about getting too loose with the prescription pad? But to my immense relief, he'd given me my usual and sent me on my way. I swallowed a few dry as soon as I left the pharmacy next door, right there next to that toxic box of dirty syringes they have to keep padlocked to keep out the neighborhood junkies.

When I mentioned my simple needs: I guess the pills are the other one, except that they're so much a part of me that I hardly consider them a *need.* Just the only thing that keeps me semi-functional and that I don't like to think about not having. I'd had no plans to do any more work that day, just a long smooth ride home to a pleasant oblivion. I knew there were just minutes until it would come rushing over me like high tide.

But then I heard that scream. I rushed off the platform to find its source and somewhere along the way, I picked up this ring. I saw her body on the pavement, the shock of it rippling through me slowly, a pebble falling into still water. Cop cars, red-and-blue lights, slow-moving figments of a crowd converging.

Like the subway's revolving turnstile, except the details are only going one way.

So, maybe I took a few more than a few.

"Parker." The voice, smooth and youthful and infused with Russian inflection, breaks my thoughts. "So good of you to come."

I pocket the ring and turn to see the one who invited me here: sharp Ukrainian cheekbones, sea-blue eyes, and a boyish fringe of white-blond hair. He's wearing gray slacks and a blazer over a crisp white shirt, all of which fit closely to his rangy frame—a contrast to the track suits and gold chains worn by the two muscle-bound hard boys who flank him.

"Sergei," I say. "*Privyet.*"

"An honor to receive you." *Resssss-eive.* He pronounces his *s*'s with a slight sibilance that somewhat undercuts his post-Soviet cool. "If only *in the background*, as you promised me."

"On background," I correct. "But yes, that's right. And I always keep my promises."

Sergei and I have struck up something of a deal. He'll let me sit in on his poker games and generally act as my steward of the Russian underground. In exchange, I won't print anything about his more questionable activities while using his name. I don't like to make these kinds of arrangements with sources—the next thing you know, they're giving you suggestions on your copy—but it seemed reasonable enough at the time for information I'd probably only use *in the background.*

Sergei gestures to the men seated around the table. "May I introduce you to Misha, Vasya, Pasha, Sasha, Vanya, Alyosha, and Dima."

One by one, they nod, heads hardly moving on thick necks. I nod back. "Pleasure."

Then I go prop myself on a table in the back and light a cigarette. I'm paying, but I'm not playing. I'm just here to watch.

A young woman appears from a door on the side of the foyer carrying a tray laden with green bottles. She's thin and very tall with light brown skin and jet-black hair trussed into a bun, dressed in the waitress's unofficial all-black uniform. There's a canniness to her movements: the way she approaches the table, sets down the tray, and serves the drinks, taking in and assessing everything without looking straight at anyone. She takes the empty tray and slinks back through the door, shoulder blades rippling above the square neckline of her t-shirt.

The dealer—I'm not sure if it's Sasha or Vanya—riffles, cuts, riffles, and cuts again, each maneuver made with a slight hesitation that has all the subtlety of an orange traffic cone. The pocket cards are taken into mitt-like hands and initial bets placed. Another round of betting follows the flop and the turn. What the players lack in savoir-faire they make up for in decisiveness: The pot grows bigger and bigger, chips thrown in like arcade game tokens. Scarcely ten minutes are up when the dealer thumbs out the river and it's time to show hands.

The guy across from him (Pasha?) reveals two aces and a pair of sixes. No one else has anything close.

The groans and Russian curses dissolve into growling good humor as thimble-sized glasses of clear liquid are delivered by the woman in black. She disappears again, leaving the men to toss down their drinks after a toast to the collective health they all seem very concerned about. Just a refresher until they play another hand. This will go on all night.

I've seen enough. I stub my cigarette out, jump off the table, and walk up to Sergei, who's dealing a round of slaps on the back to his merry band of suckers.

"So," he says, with a look that's halfway between a smile and a smirk. His teeth are very white and even, but a little too small and pointy. "How did you enjoy the game?"

"Immensely. I'm just glad I didn't stake any of the players, with that second deal your man pulled. Shoddy as it was." The other object in my coat pocket: a book I picked up earlier at the fusty used bookstore on the corner of Ninth and Avenue A called *The House Always Wins: Tricks of the Trade of Underground Cardsharking*. "The two-card push-off, was it? You might want to invest in a better mechanic. If any of those guys hadn't had vodka for brains, they'd have seen that top card never moved."

The smile-smirk hardens into a scowl. "So, that's how it is going to be." He takes a petulant draw of his cigarette.

"Can't say I don't do my research," I say. "Speaking of which. Are we still on for next Tuesday?"

He nods. "Two o'clock at Skovorodka." *Ssskovorodka.*

"Two o'clock." I tip an imaginary hat at him and the track suit boys, who can't decide whether or not to be amused. "*Do sssvidaniya.*"

I ascend the stairs and nod to the Slav, who silently opens the door for me. "Where's the next game?"

His thuggish face is practically immobile as he speaks. "Call for address."

"What's the buy-in?"

"Feefty."

I pass through the empty hall, the white keys of a piano glimmering in the darkness, and push the metal door open. The air feels heavier than it did when I walked in. What does the buy-in buy you? All night, I've been turning this cold fact over in my mind: A girl is dead in the Sixty-Second Precinct, and no one knows who killed her. I tilt my face up to the sky.

Fifty dollars. Feels like rain.

###

I twirl the ring around my finger, deep inside my coat, all the way home from Brooklyn. Once in a while I take it out to inspect it as the subway car bounces along the rutted track. Did it belong to the girl on the sidewalk? Who gave it to her? What price did she pay for it?

I should just give it to the police. Let them do what they will with it. That's their job, after all. But there's something buried in the back of my mind, something about the night before that doesn't quite add up—a question I can't form that this ring seems to answer.

I'll keep it until the morning, I decide. Then I'll turn it over to the powers-that-be.

I get off the train at Astor Place and swing onto St. Mark's, heading east. It's one of those March nights that's edged with the promise of spring, despite the pressure in the atmosphere. Everyone seems more alive than they did the night before, the NYU kids smoking and carousing under the green lights of the all-night bookstores and café-bars. Even the Cooper Union kids, in their black jackets and combat boots, can't hide the smiles sneaking out from behind their glowers. I pass Veselka restaurant and the Polish record store and the co-eds give way to the punks, drunks, and would-be artistes that make up my bonny neighborhood. The Lower East Side: home of cheap rents that buy you either space or heat, but not both.

As I walk, my mind keeps returning to the girl on the pavement. Who she was, what her life was like, what her death was like. Things I'd want to know if it were my job to know them. *If it were.* A rare English example of the subjunctive. Leave it at that, Snow.

Luckily, the organized crime beat has its points of interest. Getting to know these hustling Russians, for one. They're a relatively small group, a certain unsavory element spat out of the Soviet Union only to make haste for the gilded shores of Brighton Beach and get themselves into every racket they could think of. You name it, they try to sell it, steal it, or skim it. They were doing the same thing back there, where what little one had had to be stolen; here, they're kids in an astoundingly well-stocked candy store. Kind of the American dream.

Sergei's superior is Nikolai Solnikov, crime boss of Brighton Beach since he landed there in the seventies. Though he doesn't have the rap sheet—on paper he manufactures office furniture. I've never met the man himself, but when I was working my last story, I got a tip about his crooked gambling operation. Which is why I'm whiling away my evenings with Sergei and his dollar betters. It's the type of small-time bad stuff that exists in a no man's land between vice and organized crime, between the street detectives and the feebs, and so it tends to slip through the cracks.

I like the cracks.

Outside my corner bodega, Geronimo is turning in a circle around himself. He does that all day, every day, as he goes about the neighborhood, a tidy little planet revolving around a sun only he can see. Talking to him is a very lucid experience, though it tends to make one dizzy.

"Hey, Geronimo. How's life?" I ask.

"Oh hey, Parker," he says when he gets around to seeing me. "It's good, all good, everything's good. How's how's how's everything with you?" The words fade in and out as he makes his revolutions.

"So good I can hardly stand it." I nod toward the door. "Can I grab you anything from inside?"

"Oh, that's okay, Parker, that's okay," he says. "I just had a, I just had a cup, a cup, a cup of coffee."

I put two fingers to my forehead and tip him a salute before I push open the door, greeted by the tinkle of a bell and my friend Sunny behind the counter. Something about the bodega, its random abundance, never fails to bring me comfort. The pills hung on peg boards over the cash register promising power, vitality, energy, life; the crumbling, plastic-wrapped fig bars; the cigarette cabinet, boxes stacked neatly into their cubbyholes; the forest-green boxes of Chinese diet tea with the three ballerinas prancing out of a teacup, and everything under light that manages to be, at the same time, a little too dim and a little too bright. I gather my few groceries—instant noodles, yellow canister of Café Bustelo, a few tins of cat food, a solitary orange—and ask for a pack of Lucky Strikes.

The door swings shut behind me and I walk to my building, humming. I always savor the feeling of unwrapping a new pack: the peeling away of the cellophane wrapper, the sharp-cornered newness of the cardboard, the cigarettes tucked tight against each other like sleeping soldiers. I shake one out and flick open my lighter, the silver one inscribed with my initials that may be my most precious material possession.

My apartment door unlocks with a dry click. I push it open and enter, kick off my boots and shrug off my coat, and switch on the light.

It's not a bad place, really. I keep it clean, if you don't mind a thin layer of dust over everything. Real convenient, too, besides the five flights of stairs. Nellie's in there somewhere, pretending she's not. You'd think it'd be hard to keep cover in a 330-square-foot efficiency, but somehow, she always finds a way.

"Hey, Nell," I say. "Hey, girl. You can't hide under beds forever. Couches are going to feel neglected." Mine is a threadbare, off-white loveseat with carved wooden legs, abandoned on a curb one day just like Nellie. I acquired her from a church parking lot one chilly December morning when she was just a wee, one-eyed kitten. She's really come into her own since then: coat's grown out, claws've sharpened, and disposition's mellowed into a total indifference I truly admire.

I cross the living room into the tiny kitchen and set my groceries on the counter. It's the usual narrow galley with an ancient refrigerator, postage stamp of a countertop against a grease-mapped wall, and a rickety gas oven where I store all my important papers. I reason that in the event of a fire, that's where they'd be safest. There's also a little window that looks out onto the courtyard between our building and the one next door. Beyond it, you can just make out the Manhattan Bridge. I watch a train shuttle across, yellow lights bouncing off the river.

There's something else about the night before, lingering like the residue of a bad dream. I screw my eyes up hard, trying to put the feeling itself into focus. Someone in the crowd . . . Not a face, but a voice. Male. Agitated. He's talking to someone—a female cop, I think—hurling sharp sentences with a bristling energy. I can't make out his words, or the cop's response.

Is he her boyfriend or fiancé—the one who gave her the ring? Or maybe another guy, *the* other guy—the one who didn't?

That's the problem with these pills, and I'll admit it, too. Take too many, and they can wipe away your memories without even the courtesy to warn you. Sometimes they come back, but where and when is anyone's guess. I guess I got a little overexcited. Blame it on the full bottle bop, counterpoint to the empty bottle blues. I've been trying to keep them under control, but lately, well . . . There's always some "lately" coming to chase down "now." Memories resurfacing. Wispy specter of the past growing solid, hostile spark that won't be tamped down. And the sight of that dead girl's body hasn't helped.

Despite it all, what I want to know about the dead girl in Bensonhurst is everything.

I go to the phone and dial.

"Captain Maloney. Homicide." I can practically smell the cigarette smoke in his voice.

"Baloney," I say. "It's me."

There's a short pause, then a sigh. "Yeah," the voice rolls wearily over the word. "Waddaya want?"

"I'm calling about a murder that occurred yesterday in the six-two," I say. "A young Caucasian woman. Around six thirty p.m."

"Nothing to report."

"Come on, don't be like that," I protest. "It's been more than a day. You must have a few suspects by now." Then I throw in, "I know how fast the guys work under your watch."

It doesn't take. "I got nothin' for you. So, quit bothering me," he says. "Since when are you back on street crime, anyway?"

"What about the guy?" I press, speeding past his question. "The one who was hanging around, shouting at the cops? Something about him didn't feel quite right."

I hear some papers shuffling on the desk. "Victim's brother. Not a suspect."

"So, who did it?"

"Some goddamn goon, Parker!" he roars. "Some punk! Some petty criminal who killed her for her wallet. Brother said it probably had five bucks in it." His voice turns bitter as it smacks out the last four words. "Neighborhood's going to hell. Goddamn streets getting dirtier by the day."

I can picture him up and pacing now, looking at the crime patterns on the bulletin board stuck with red pins. Cigarette between his lips, brow furrowed as he looks from sector A to B to C, bleak in the pallid fluorescent light. Those red constellations follow him around everywhere, the last thing to flash in front of his mind's eye as he goes to bed at night and the first to greet him in the morning after a few blissful, unconscious hours.

I try one more time. "Did any witnesses come forward?"

"No," he says after a brief silence.

"Strange," I say. "No one saw anything on that busy Brooklyn street? A mugging? She screamed. I heard her." Maloney keeps quiet. Like any good detective, he's not going to give me anything. But like any good reporter, I have to keep trying. "If anything comes up, you call me first, okay?"

"Yeah," he says driftily. The phone clicks and I'm left with the mosquito buzz of the line.

Nellie's one-eyed gaze seizes me from the floor, her tail twitching. Murders in this town are anything but rare. Usually they get solved fast, and the killers don't get far. Gangsters knifing gangsters, husbands shooting wives. Even the randoms, the muggings and robberies gone wrong, tend to leave a trail so wide the cops can saunter right through and slap on their cuffs. No witnesses or suspects is definitively odd. And then there's that ring: the one that no mugger would leave on the ground, even if they weren't an expert in karat size.

A few fat drops plunk wetly against the windowsill—the rain that was hanging all day over this blighted island. I know what my boss, Crock, the bureau chief, would say if he heard me talking to Maloney. He'd tell me to drop it, to stay in my lane. Not my job now. Not my job.

As I tell myself this, I see the paper on top of the stack in the oven blaze up red, as if alight. A blistering reminder of my last street crime story, and my last fatal mistake.

Nellie interrupts these reflections with her best pathetic mew. She jumps onto the counter and nuzzles my hand. I open the drawer between the stove and the sink where I keep the can opener and take it out along with a squat white bottle, the one with the peach-colored pills that I keep for the evenings. Especially evenings like this.

2

Fragments of color . . .

For most people, death is a departure, an absence, a missing shape in the rooms of their lives. What they don't realize is that death is a system. It's a multi-stage event and when it's your clambake, everything stops for you, but it's just starting for everyone else: the cops, the detectives, the reporters, the medical examiner, the pathologist, not to mention the funeral director and the undertaker. Dying lonely isn't hard, but staying dead that way is.

Fragments of color and sound float above me as I sleep that night, dark figures drifting across my consciousness. When I wake up, a plan is already forming in my mind. As usual, Nellie is on my stomach, meowing for her morning can of tuna shreds and goo.

"A frugal repast," I say as I dump it in her bowl. "Sorry we can't get the good stuff. No Fancy Feast for either of us."

But Nellie doesn't seem to mind. I get myself dressed and run a hand through my hair—there's a reason I keep it cut short—and slide into the boots and coat I left by the door. I grab cigarettes, lighter, notebook, pen, and the skinny billfold that counts as a wallet, and stuff them into my pockets, along with the ring that I plan to give Maloney. My pager I leave on the desk—I hate being too easy to reach. I just tell Crock I forgot it. He accuses me of having a selective memory, but then I say I'm selecting doing my job without a bunch of dimwits bothering me.

I hoof it down the stairs and onto the avenue, where last night's whisper of spring seems to have been choked off overnight. The morning is cold and colorless, sun struggling weakly through a sick-looking clot of cloud. I stop at my usual cart on the corner for a cup of black coffee and a toasted bagel with butter—both just a little bit burnt—and nod hello to the neighbors. It seems like everyone ran out of cash all at once, abruptly cutting off the rabid construction projects of the last booming decade. Needle heads are propped up against the building sites, real estate developers are filing in to sell the units at fire-sale prices to anyone who will assume the debts, and everyone's bidding each other good morning with real bonhomie.

My walk to work is a half hour at a fast clip, which is the only clip I know, through Alphabet City and down to the neighborhood they call Civic Center, just south of Chinatown. I pass the seniors doing tai chi in Columbus Park and the jail and the bail bond outfits that line the opposite side of the street, then follow Park Row until I reach One Police Plaza.

Just off the Brooklyn Bridge, among a cluster of courthouses, prisons, and churches, is the headquarters of the NYPD. A charming locale, with a row of spindly trees as welcoming as the uniformed cops milling around outside the redbrick, brutalist rectangle gridded with windows like so many staring eyes. It's also home to what's known as the Shack, where the *Street*'s police reporters have an office, along with every other major paper in the city. That gives us the best proximity to the office of the Deputy Commissioner for Public

Information—DCPI—on the fourteenth floor. That's where we access the running ticker tape of incidents—domestics, robberies, murders, along with false alarms and workaday misdemeanors—so we can be dispatched at a moment's notice to see to the so-called "unusuals."

When I first came to the city, skin sticky with sweat and street grit after a five-hour bus ride from Providence, Rhode Island, final resting place of my short-lived college career, I knew I wanted to be a reporter. I coaxed a proofreading job out of the *Street*—I'm not sure who was more desperate—but I always had my ear to the ground for my own story, talking to anyone I could but mostly doing a lot of listening. One day a call came in over the police radio about a tenant reported missing from a Park Avenue apartment building. It was a small thing, easily missed, except for the fact that I knew I'd heard the building's address before. No one was picking it up, so I went to talk to the doorman between proofing sessions and what do you know? The tenant, Mary O'Donahue, wasn't the first. In fact, she was only the most recent in a string of women the doorman had known over the years who had mysteriously vanished.

I worked it without anyone's permission and handed Crock my draft as if it was the most natural thing in the world. He read it, and his first question (after "Who the hell are you?") was "When can you get me a follow-up?" Seeing my byline run in the next day's paper was a moment of deep satisfaction unlike any I'd experienced before. I worked that little story into a multi-part takedown of the soon-to-be-named murder mill. With all the renewed public interest, the police were forced to reopen the previous cases, quickly finding similarities with the latest victim. They were aging spinsters with few connections to follow up on their cases, all put down as lost to the city or maybe returned to where they came from. They were, frankly, women no one cared to look into much.

Not a month later, the killer was apprehended: an unassuming maintenance worker with a contracting company the building used. He was soon handed seven consecutive life sentences, which, in my opinion, was seven too few.

Maybe I got lucky. Or maybe that's what a deep and probably unhealthy obsession with the ways and means and patterns of killers will do. But I long ago decided that health was not my priority. If the body is a temple, mine's a desecrated altar to the dark lord.

I go through the metal detector, nod hello to the desk guard, and go to check DCPI for news about the murder. Suspected homicide of a Caucasian female in Brooklyn's Sixty-Second Precinct. Victim identified as Carla Russo, twenty years old. No one in custody and no suspects.

I'm about to take this information all the way down to the Detective Bureau, but then I think twice. Instead, I ride the elevator to the ground and dash out to the deli on Pearl Street. Then I make my way back up to Detective Maloney's office on the eleventh floor. I'm preparing to knock and enter, but the door is already ajar—and I can just make out the unsightly shapes of my two least favorite detectives in the history of the New York Police Department inside. Timothy Shepherd: mean little eyes set in a doughy face and all 250 pounds of him ready to beat the truth out of you, whether it's true or not. And his partner, Michael Szybist: skinny, clumsy, and dumb. Which can be just as dangerous.

"Lookie here," I say, pushing the door all the way open. "If it isn't Jack Sprat and his comely wife."

Shepherd turns. "The hell she doin' here?" He jabs a pudgy thumb in my direction.

"Just wanted to drop by and thank the boys in blue for their service," I say. "It's an honor to meet you two hometown heroes in person. But I guess I really have the Police Benevolent Association to thank that you're still out on the street. That guy you put in the hospital for not moving his car off Lexington Ave might not agree, though. Funny how that complaint just disappeared."

Maloney is sitting at his desk, evidently in the middle of briefing these two. He's a lean Irishman in his midforties, with bright blue eyes, bad posture, and an expression that always wavers between exhausted and crazed. "Parker," he says, drawing out the word like it's a net he wants to trap me in. "I *told* you I'd *call* you."

"And I thought I'd save you the trouble," I say. "Got a minute for me?"

Maloney shakes his head, exasperated, but then he says to his two juniors: "I think we're done here. Everyone clear?"

"Clear as mud, chief," Szybist says. Then they both leave, Shepherd stopping to snarl at me on the way out.

I place the chocolate chip muffin I picked up for him at the deli on his desk like an offering. I know Maloney's supposed to be watching his cholesterol, but I also know how much he likes them. "Carla Russo," I start. "I found . . ."

But then I stop. The ring is burning a cold hole in my pocket, reminding me of the nagging gaps in my memory of that night. So instead, I hear myself asking: "How much do you know?"

He picks up the plastic-wrapped muffin and starts to unwrap it without even moving his eyes. "Not much. Time of death, around six thirty. Body's at the OCME in Brooklyn awaiting autopsy, but cause of death seems clear. Blunt force trauma to the head."

Blunt force trauma. I remember the girl's face as unmarked—no blood, no bruises. "Weapon?"

"Nothing yet." He tears the top of the muffin off.

"So, what do you think happened?"

He swallows. "Someone whacked her real hard right there on the street and took her wallet. Or they abducted her up the block, did it in the car, and then threw her onto the sidewalk and drove away. Wouldn't be the first time." He has the matter-of-fact tone all detectives use when talking about violent loss of life, like they're speculating about the fastest way downtown at rush hour. "We've been questioning witnesses, everyone on the block and the blocks around it, to see if anyone saw anything. So far, nothing helpful."

"How about the tire tracks? Can't forensics look at them?"

"It's a busy Brooklyn street. There are tire tracks from here to Vancouver." He puts down the muffin and picks up a pen. "Listen, I don't have time to play Clue with you. And anyways, I have two guys on it."

"Who?" I demand.

He gives me a look. After a beat, I remember who he was just briefing—Shepherd and Szybist.

"Those two boneheads?" I exclaim in dismay. "They couldn't catch a perp if they had him on a leash."

"Don't talk that way about people in this department," he says, but without much fight in it. "And anyways, between these goddamn fires and the usual stick-'em-up crap, I gotta take what I can get."

But I don't, I think. I let the ring fall through my fingers and safely into my pocket.

I'm almost at the door when I hear Maloney's warning voice, half-swaddled by papers, at my back. "By the way, you should be careful out there. Things have changed since Gorbachev's little Christmas speech. They're a whole new crop of criminals over in Brighton Beach that we're only just starting to get a handle on."

It takes me a moment to realize what he's talking about: the organized crime beat I'm supposed to be reporting on. The words hardly sink in. I'm thinking about the one other person who might see Carla Russo as something more than another pin in the crime map—and who might have some crucial information.

###

Thirty minutes later I walk into the office of Morgan Delacroix, Medical Examiner, holding a coffee with lots of milk and sugar, the way she likes it. It's not nine o'clock and the place isn't officially open for business, but Morgan is already deeply immersed in a report.

"Morgan," I say, holding it out to her. "Tell me the truth. Do you sleep here?"

"The answer would creep you out," she says, accepting the cup.

Morgan is slight as a bird, with short, white-blonde hair framing her angular face, giving her a somewhat ethereal look that belies her inner toughness. People are in a keyed-up state when someone dies, liable to take their grief and agitation out on anyone who happens to be close by, especially if it's the one touching the body of their dead loved one. I've seen her get punched in the face at a crime scene only to pop right back up again. And it's because, unlike some of the other MEs the city employs, Morgan cares more about finding the truth than about what can be expediently added to a death certificate. She's one of the smartest people I've ever met, with an almost uncanny ability to read a corpse, to understand it at an almost cellular level that goes beyond science. Not that she lacks the science. She went to medical school, then realized she didn't have the stomach to work with the living.

"Long night?" I ask.

"Not long enough."

I'm in the Manhattan Office of the Chief Medical Examiner on First Avenue, the place where they do autopsies and IDs. Usually, regular people aren't allowed to traipse in here, but I'm something of an insider. As much as you can be while you're still warm.

"I'm looking for more information about a homicide scene I was at last night," I tell her. "Do you know anything about Carla Russo?"

"Carla Russo." She shakes her head. "Doesn't sound familiar. Manhattan?"

"Brooklyn."

"Well, that's why," she says. "Who's the ME on it?"

"I don't know," I say. "Maloney is saying blunt force trauma, but the whole case feels off. For one thing, no witnesses or suspects have come up. No weapon, no obvious physical evidence for forensics to analyze."

"Every crime leaves a trace," she murmurs. "But sometimes the only trace is the body itself. And the body typically has a lot to say. I'll look into it and let you know what I find."

"Thank you, Dr. Delacroix. I'll let you get back to . . . whatever it is you do all day," I say, standing up. "And don't forget to wear your helmet." Did I mention that Morgan rides a motorcycle to crime scenes because it gets her there faster than the OCME van?

"Wait a minute, Parker. You said you were at the scene. So, who was the ME there?"

"I don't remember," I say, not meeting her eye.

She gives me an odd look. "Are you sure you're okay? I know what happened last year at the clinic took a toll on you—"

"Hey, Tink!" a male voice yells from the hall outside Morgan's office. It's joined by another: "Tinkerbell! We got a live one! Well, not exactly." The voices dissolve into laughter. No doubt they belong to the type of brawny young men the office employs and underpays to move around bodies.

Morgan's face tightens.

"I'll leave you to it," I say.

She sighs. "Thanks for the coffee."

I retrace my steps through the sterile hallway and back out onto the street. I know Morgan means well. We've always been in the same camp, she and I—fighting to be heard, in our own ways. Morgan, quiet and methodical. Me, not so much. But I bristle every time anyone, Morgan included, brings up *what happened last year*. **PARKER FUCKED UP**, they might as well write in bold, sans serif font. And it's true, I did. The last big street crime story I wrote didn't end so well. But no one—not even Morgan—knows the full story. I keep that shut away like the papers in my oven.

No one, that is, except my editor, Crock.

I make my way back to 1PP and up to the top floor, where all the city tabloids have offices within police headquarters. Ours is rivaled only by the DMV when it comes to aesthetics: four desks in varying states of disarray, everyone's favorite bylines pinned to the walls like trophy hides. So far, the only person in is Schultz, one of the three other police reporters who think it's their job to make mine harder. Something about the fact that I don't have three days' worth of stubble on my face seems to rub him the wrong way.

He's sitting at his desk, feet spread, elbows on knees, staring down at a sheet of newsprint like it's announcing the apocalypse starts tomorrow. "Did you see this shit?" he says, looking up at me. "I mean, did you *see* this shit?"

I drain the last of my coffee and toss the empty cup into the wastebasket under his desk. "What shit might you be referring to?"

He thrusts *The New York Daily News* into my hands. On the front page is a picture of Saint Patrick's Cathedral up in flames and the words: **ISLAND ARSONIST STRIKES HOT** written in black all-caps.

"That *wood* is on fire," I remark.

The "wood"—those blazing, bleeding words on the front page of a tabloid paper, which, along with an eyeball-burning image the photographers will gladly injure themselves to get, make all the difference in outselling the competition that day. Which is the prize we play for around here.

Schultz sits back in his chair and moans. "Matchstick Murphy. That was *my* guy. *My* story. The cops told *me* and *only me* the Saint Patrick's fire was connected to the Chinese New Year fire down on Mott Street. That it was the work of the same guy. But no, *our* editor doesn't think it's good enough to be the fucking *wood* because the cops don't want to have their names on the record before they've nabbed the guy. So instead, that goddamn piece of shit Cabrera from the goddamn *News* takes my goddamn scoop!"

I pick up the day's edition of our paper, also on his desk. The front page is adorned with a nasty *wood* about a deep-seated corruption case at the DMV. Inside is Schultz's story under the headline: SAINT

PATRICK'S UP IN FLAMES. Angelo Esperanza, the *Street*'s best photographer, snapped a doozy: a portrait of a fireman in profile holding his length of hose, staring at the cathedral with his teeth bared like a gladiator ready for the next round of combat, face streaked with sweat and cinders as flames leap from the windows in front of him. "You got it in on page two and anyway, our photo's better," I say.

"Page two," he moans, covering his face with his hands. "Page two."

I flick through the rest of the local headlines. A schoolteacher was found naked on her bed in Crown Heights, set on fire. Four cops were implicated in taking bribes from neighborhood crack dealers, but the charges were dropped. A man held up a bodega and everyone almost got out alive until his gun accidentally went off, killing the owner's four-year-old daughter. And there's a new area code being rolled out, the snobbish-sounding 917, because we're running out of 212 along with apartments, water, and everything else.

I throw the paper back onto his desk. "I don't think it counts as 'taken' when you're shouting about it at McSorley's with the rest of the rabble from every other tabloid in the city."

"Speaking of which, I never see you there." He eyes me through his fingers. "What's the matter? You think you're too good for us or something?"

"We've been through this before," I say. "How many times do I have to repeat it? Yes, I think I'm too good for you."

He shakes his head and makes a noise in between a laugh and a scoff. "You're unbelievable."

I saunter into Crock's office. The man himself is sitting at his desk, poring over proofs. His desk is piled a half-foot deep with notebooks, newsprint, ashtrays, and coffee cups. He's every cliché you can think of about the hard-bitten newspaperman, and then some: paunchy belly, nicotine-stained fingers, and thinning hair held back by its own grease.

"Crock," I say. "I need fifty dollars."

"What for?" he grunts. His red pen is scratching at copy with a fury usually reserved for meting out sentences to war criminals.

"Research."

"File an expense report."

"I hate to tell you this, but the Russian mafia doesn't exactly give out receipts."

"Can't help you."

I sigh.

"Speaking of money," he says, looking up, red pen still slashing bloody marks. "I pay you to file stories. So, where are my stories?"

"You pay me?" I act surprised. "That's news to me."

"Cut it out with the smart-alecking. I don't got time for it," he growls. "Go out and look into this tip. A truck found in Brighton Beach carrying a hot load. Organized crime. That's what you report on now, remember?"

"Sure, Crock. I remember." I pick up one of the mugs. "Is it true you can tell the age of a coffee cup by counting the rings on the inside?"

He looks up long enough to spare me a livid glance. I put the cup down. "So, what's the load, anyway?"

"Chocolate."

"Chocolate?"

"Chocolate, Parker. Willy fucking Wonka." He rips a piece of paper out of a notebook and thrusts it at me. "Now *go*. Outta my face. I want three inches by tonight. And bring your pager."

"Three inches by tomorrow morning," I say, taking the paper and folding it in half. "Got it."

"Tonight!" he explodes. "Eight o'clock! Deadline! I got space to fill on page eighteen!"

"Would I argue with you?" I say. "Except this one little thing." I square myself to face him. "A young woman died in Bensonhurst yesterday. Murdered. But no one saw anything. No witnesses, no suspects."

He doesn't tell me to get the *expletive* out of his office, so I can tell I have his attention. Like all editors, Crock loves a scoop.

"I just happened to be at the scene," I continue. "And I didn't see anyone else there. No one from the *Post*. No one from the *News*. No one from the *Times*, obviously."

It's the first time since last year that I've brought him a story like this. A story like the ones I used to write. Crock's steely look seems to—almost—soften. He knows better than anyone how badly the last one worked me over, even if we've never exactly talked about it.

"That's not your beat now," he says, his voice more reasonable than insistent now. "Plus, there's enough going on in Brighton, especially with the new wave of guys coming in. If you could break a story about them, it would be a real scoop. Something none of the other papers have."

"I know," I say. "But I want to write about this."

All at once the old Crock is back, his sweat-damp face flushing red. "Goddammit, Parker!" he roars. "How many times do I have to tell you? No more getting tangled up in the goddamn yellow tape!"

"I don't get tangled, Crock," I say on my way out the door. "I duck."

3

I think about the dead girl . . .

Ten minutes later, I'm on a Q train heading toward Brighton Beach. A stalled chocolate racket. It's just the kind of offbeat tidbit the *Street* loves to publish, weird little jewel tucked under a plummy two inches about the mayor's wife's charity gala. Or an acerbic four about the mayor.

That's the business we're in. Gossip and news, critiques and puff pieces, all of it mixed up like the pulp that it's printed on. And as reporters, it's not always our choice which we get, or the space that it's given.

On the ride over I think about the dead girl, and what it would be like to feel someone's life fade beneath your hands, and why it is I always end up in Brooklyn. The scenery flashes past the train window like frames on a film strip: a yellow billboard announcing ACCIDENTS and a number to call, a tiny figure in pink pajamas folded into the checkbox of a window frame over the Manhattan Bridge, laundry flapping on either side like flags on a line, then the forlorn avenues of myth: J, M, U. Yards swim past in back of the worn matchbox houses that line the subway tracks, sun-bleached umbrellas, rows of sickly potted plants, mismatched furniture on gray concrete slabs. Faces.

The car slowly empties out. By the time the doors part at Brighton Beach station, I'm the only figure to emerge from the car. The heels of my boots tap morosely against the worn wooden floor of the elevated station, the turnstile echoing in the vacant air as I pass through. On a day as gray and unloving as this, nobody fancies a jaunt on the Brooklyn shores.

I pause to look around at the bottom of the stairs, on the corner of Coney Island and Brighton Beach Avenues. A hunched old babushka wrapped in a red printed shawl slowly pushes a cart laden with shopping bags, its wheels scraping the sidewalk. The only other sign of life is the middle-aged woman selling pirozhki from a cart in the track's penumbra. She looks at me suspiciously as I walk by. Around here everyone looks at you suspiciously.

On the paper Crock gave me is scrawled *Land-O-Fun, Coney Island Ave & Shore Parkway*. I start up Coney Island Avenue, toward the exhaust-thick on-ramps of the parkway. The sea is just a few blocks south, but on a day like this, everything hanging heavy and damp, you've never felt farther. The storefronts quickly turn into auto shops and gas stations, tired signs for a free car wash with oil change. A car painted red, white, and blue sits on the roof of a repair shop above a sign that reads GUARANTEED ALARM & GLASS.

I can tell you that nothing is guaranteed here except trouble. The last big, organized crime story I wrote, a series, was about the fuel tax racket the Russians were very hot on for a time. They call it a daisy-chain scheme because it involves a convoluted chain of shell companies designed to cheat the government out of taxes owed on wholesale motor fuel sales. Some genius decided that diesel sold for home heating doesn't have to be taxed, but motor fuel does, even though the product is the same. With these shell companies and throughput accounts, they'd make fake invoices and transfer the fuel around, then sell it to a retailer nice and cheap, showing all taxes paid, and pocketing the spare change. At the end of every tax quarter, they would just shut down the operation and open a new one. It was almost fun for them. It probably helped that the spare change added up to millions.

Eventually the law wised up and changed the rules so that oil is taxed at the rack, or the initial point of distribution, rather than at the pump. And so Solnikov and his crew gave a weary Slavic shrug and moved on to more advantageous pursuits, namely shaking down local businesses in exchange for their "protection" from rival factions, via ambassadors like Sergei. I've been trying to get said businesses to talk for months to no avail. Once in a while I get a hint, but then it goes out with the tide. This neighborhood has a way of pushing you out, so that no matter how much you walk through its thoroughfares you always wind up on the edges again.

Right where Coney Island Avenue butts up against the parkway, on the corner with Banner Avenue and across from a windowless wheel alignment center topped with menacing-looking barbed wire, is a small brick building with a green sign that reads LAND-O-FUN.

I double back a few steps to the small parking lot on the adjacent avenue. There are two vehicles parked in the lot. One is a white box truck that sits squatly against the far wall, surrounded by caution tape that ripples faintly in the breeze. The other is a light blue NYPD squad car. A fair-haired cop with a face still padded with baby fat is standing by it, looking as though he's waiting for someone.

"Police investigation," he says as I approach.

"Parker Snow, from the *Street*," I say, pulling my badge out of my pocket. He gives it a scant glance, as if it's hardly worth the effort of moving his eyes. "Came to see what there was to see about this chocolate truck."

"No press," he says with the personality of a can of Metamucil.

"No problem," I say. "But maybe you could let me in on a few details? My boss hates it when I come up empty."

"Nothing to tell," he says in the same warm tone as before. I'm really starting to feel welcome.

"But surely, officer, you must have some idea, knowing the neighborhood like you do," I press. "Like, for example, how you think the truck got here, who drove it, and why they decided to abandon it."

"Listen, we don't know anything just yet. It looks like someone ditched it here overnight." He does a double take. "Hang on a minute. Snow. Don't I know you from somewhere?"

I shrug. "Can't think of where."

I walk back to the sidewalk and turn right toward the building, where a spindly hedgerow shields me from view. Junior's now perched on the seat of the patrol car, saying something into the corded radio, a finger to one ear. I circle the building, approach the truck from the back, and duck underneath the police tape.

I walk the length of its side, hoping some clue will reveal itself. Its main identifying features are that it has four wheels, a white cab of about fifteen feet long, and New York plates. Not enough material for a bad joke.

Then something catches my eye—a sticker on the bottom of the cab next to the license plate, the text faded and worn. Hunching over, I can just make out the words "Black Sea Holdings."

"What the hell did I say?" says the cop's voice behind me. "I could arrest you for this."

"I would really appreciate it if you didn't," I say, straightening up. "My boss really hates it when I get arrested."

"Snow," he says. I cringe at the recognition in his voice. "Listen, it's for your own safety. We haven't even gotten the dogs here yet. There could be explosives inside, for all we know."

"That's very dangerous," I say. "Three ounces of chocolate can kill a fifty-pound German shepherd."

I walk back onto the avenue and wait until the light has changed and I can cross the street. Another police car pulls up labeled K-9. A cop gets out and exchanges a few words with Junior. Then she opens the back of the car and two spry-eared shepherds jump out. She leads them over to the truck and the other cop jimmies something into the lock and raises the door. Inside are cardboard boxes, stacked somewhat helter-skelter, as if they'd been loaded in a hurry. One of them is open, the glint of gold foil catching the light when the cop jumps in the truck and nudges it forward with his shoe. The dogs are straining at their leashes.

I can't count on getting much more for Crock's three inches of copy, so I'll have to fill it out with a little local color. I reach Brighton Beach Avenue and take a right as the B train rattles overhead. All the storefront signs here are in Russian: the *aptyeka* with its aisles of medicines; the *magazin knigi* with its window display of stark, unrevealing covers; the *gastronom* with its cardboard bins of cucumbers and tomatoes standing guard outside. I've taught myself Cyrillic over these past few months, plus a few words to add to the ones I picked up during my neighborhood wayfaring. I found a book at one of those ratty, moth-eaten joints selling old military uniforms and odd pieces of Soviet kitsch called *Learn to Interpret by Interpreting*. Written in the early sixties for Western businesspeople visiting the USSR, it contains useful phrases for such useful situations as *At the ball-bearing plant. Mr. Frost: I've visited a number of enterprises and have talked a number of trade-union leaders to death . . .*

I enter a dentist's office, a pharmacy, and a coffeehouse that I've visited before. I tell them again that I'm a reporter interested in learning more about the neighborhood. One by one they cast me hostile or confused glances. Either they don't understand me, or they're pretending not to. Finally, at a *parimakher*—a hairdresser—I get a few words out of the proprietor until she, too, shuts down.

I stop by the pirozhki stand and ask for one *s kapusty* and one *s gribami*: cabbage and mushroom. The woman says nothing as she plucks up the pastries and places them in a wax paper bag, handing me my change with a glare underneath her gray ushanka hat. I make my way south via Brighton Sixth Street. Streamers hang overhead between the wash-and-dry shop and the shish kebab shack, their shiny metallic fingers flapping in the wind. I pass the Kashkar Cafe and the sporting goods store, the small travel agency selling tentative trips to the homeland. Then I reach the ramp that leads to the boardwalk and the sky opens up, the ocean a metal sheet rippling.

A lone figure plods slowly down the beach dressed all in black, from the heavy shoes on their feet to the scarf over their head, kicking up sand. Outside the Tatiana Restaurant with its forest-green awning, two men sit at a table smoking silently, coffee cups in front of them. They watch me as I pass. Maloney's parting words drift back to me, about the new crop of criminals in Brighton Beach, unleashed from the USSR just a few months ago. Crock mentioned them, too. I wonder who they are and how they link up with Sergei and Solnikov's faction, if they do. Where they might be hiding in plain sight.

I eat my pirozhki, buttery dough sticking in my throat, then crumple the wax paper and throw it into a trash can. The rusted skeleton of what once was a bicycle hangs off the railing, chains and tires gone. Down the boardwalk, the amusements of Coney Island are just visible, the red tower of the old Parachute Jump rising up like a ruin. My mind returns to Junior, the cop back there at the scene, the way his voice went soft around the edges when he recognized my name. He knew the story—about the young women I tried to help, convinced it was within my journalistic power. And, well. Junior knows about how well that went.

That's the thing about being a reporter. Most of the time you're desperately trying to remember as much as possible. And then there are the things that, try as you might, you can't forget.

I let my eyes be drawn downward, falling into the boardwalk's hypnotic rhythm. The scent of damp wood rises from the crosshatched planks and joins with the sea spray. The boards are worn and uneven and stuck here and there with rusty nails. Every few steps one pops up under my heel, loosed by the phantom crowds of summer. As if at any moment the whole thing might crumble. Out of the corner of my eye I see the train creeping by in parallel on the elevated track. Something's always creeping by in parallel. Another story, another life. If you keep your eyes down, you might not even see it.

I take the ring out of my coat pocket and hold it up, letting the gray sky seep through. Someone's very long engagement, abruptly cut short. Or perhaps a promise someone never got to give. Or maybe even a decoy?

I return the ring to my pocket and take out the small orange bottle. I shake out two pills and swallow them like secrets.

###

By the time I get back to the Shack it's almost seven, which means I have an hour to make a few calls, bang out my article, and call it a day. The office is empty, everyone either out at a scene or just out. At my desk, I call over to the Brighton Beach precinct and ask to speak to the detective. Grudgingly, I'm put through.

"I'm writing a story about the truck containing a cargo of chocolate found on Shore Parkway and Coney Island Ave," I say. "What can you tell me?"

"I can't tell you anything about that. It's with OCCB," the detective says.

"And there it will remain until the end of time," I say. "Thanks for all your help."

I call the number I have for OCCB—the NYPD's Organized Crime Control Bureau—and announce who I am. As soon as I mention my affiliation with *The New York Street* they get clammy. I've been trying to make friends there since I was put on this beat, but it's like trying to dig my way out of prison with a spoon. Finally, I'm put through to the only one I've managed to make any inroads with—one of those tough-as-nails cops who's been around for so many years that he's no longer antsy and is frankly happy to claim some of the credit to which the FBI usually helps itself. After a few minutes of holding, I get him on the line. As luck would have it, he's familiar with the case and ready to say a few words off the record. The details are still thin, but it's good enough for me, and it's going to have to be good enough for Crock and his eight o'clock deadline. I take out my notebook and start to type up what I jotted down on the subway, along with the quotes I've just wrangled from my source.

A few minutes later the door opens. I don't have to look up to see who it is. I know his long, loping gait, as if he never has to hurry for anything.

"Oh," comes Schultz's voice. "It's you."

"Don't sound so happy to see me."

"Crock put me on the lobster shift, that son of a bitch. It's gonna be a long night." I hear him open his desk drawer and riffle around. "Me and Mulligan are going out to get a few drinks before the action starts. Don't suppose you want to come."

"You don't suppose right," I say, my eyes still on the screen.

"Don't you ever do anything?" Schultz says. "I mean, anything fun?"

"This is how I have fun," I reply. "Doesn't this look like fun?"

He saunters over to my desk and leans against it, hitting his notebook against the opposite palm. "Why do you think those Russians put up with you anyway?" He reaches for the pack of cigarettes on my desk. I slap my left hand onto the pack and slide it out of his reach, still typing with my right. He scoffs.

"I don't know," I say after I finish the sentence I'm on. "I think they find me amusing. Some people do, you know."

I can feel him leaning over me. "You used to hate it when I read your copy over your shoulder," he says.

"That's when I was still under the impression you could read," I say. "Speaking of which. I have to reread this and file. I'm not blowing deadline because of you."

I see his smug reflection in the screen as he runs a hand through his crop of sandy blond hair. "I'm sure you'll find some other way to blow it."

He walks away, whistling off-key. I sit stock-still, eyes narrowed at the screen, until I hear the door shut. Then I pull the sheet from my typewriter and head to the fax machine to file.

###

ABANDONED TRUCK HOLDS SWEET CONTRABAND

By Parker Snow

March 25, 1992

A truck was found abandoned near Ocean Parkway in Brooklyn's Brighton Beach neighborhood on Wednesday. Its contents? Hundreds of bars of foil-wrapped chocolate.

Local precinct police investigated the mysterious find before turning the case over to the NYPD's Organized Crime Control Bureau. While the force has yet to issue a formal comment, an officer familiar with the case told the *Street*: "This has all the markers of a case of trafficked, or perhaps hijacked, goods that, for one reason or another, didn't make it to their intended destination." When asked whether it could be a matter of a driver taking a break, with the intention of returning to his freight, the source replied, "It's doubtful he's still taking a leak."

The neighborhood, no stranger to organized crime, has seen a renewed wave of illicit activity in recent years with the loosening of restrictions in the now-former Soviet Union. Much of this is in the form of organized gangs demanding *krysha*, or a "roof"—protection from competing crime groups. A local business owner, a hairdresser on Brighton Beach Avenue who declined to be named, alluded to recent trouble, though was reticent to discuss the exact demands made on her business. She had tried calling a dedicated police hotline number to report the strong-arming, she said, but no one at the desk spoke Russian.

With translation help offered by her nine-year-old granddaughter, she told the *Street*: "Everything is different now. It's not like the seventies. This is the nineties."

4

Kid from the projects . . .

It's sometime after midnight when I bolt upright in bed, Nellie starting and jumping to the floor with a discontented hiss.

The face appears to me in a flash, clean and cold as a movie scene, from that evening in Bensonhurst. A pale, shell-shocked moon of a face surrounded by red-brown curls. She's talking to the guy who gave off the nervous energy—Carla's brother, Detective Maloney said. I see him more clearly now: tall, with dark, slicked-back hair. I'd thought she was a cop, but I realize now she's just a regular young woman, about the same age as the one on the ground. *At the J&V,* she's saying.

"J&V," I tell Nellie. Her eyes are shining in the dark. "Sounds like a corner store. Or a diner."

I lie back down, stare at the ceiling, and wait for the light to seep, gray and thin, through the window.

—

When morning comes, I brew strong black coffee in the cheap aluminum Moka pot I picked up for a song in Little Italy and wash down two blue pills for breakfast. I need to call OCCB again to see where they're at with the chocolate truck investigation, but first I need to close the loop on my memory of the night that Carla Russo died. Crock warned me off the story, but I can't drop something I haven't fully grasped. If I can just go back to Bensonhurst and ask a few questions of my own, I reason, I'll be able to shake off this feeling and put my focus back where it's supposed to be.

I call Crock and tell him I'll be out all day working a big follow-up story on the truck. We both pretend to believe it.

On the landing I meet my across-the-way neighbor, a Vietnam vet named Terry, preparing for another day selling whatever odds and ends he's gotten his hands on. One day it's Indian sarongs; another, cassette tapes by bands from the seventies that no one liked then and no one likes now. He has short white hair that's long receded from his forehead, though he can't be more than forty, and an air of absence offset by bright blue eyes that always look a little bit stunned. He's busily dragging cardboard boxes into the hall, which he'll stack into a rickety cart and wheel all the way to SoHo or the Village for a day of vending. His apartment door is propped open with one of them, and I catch a glimpse inside at a sagging couch against a water-stained wall, a worn-down breakfast table, and a small TV. The walls are bare save one brown picture frame and a service medal on a yellow ribbon, the only spot of color in the place.

"Terry," I greet him. "How's the knee?"

"Worse every day," he says. It's not nine a.m. and already he's enveloped in a cloud of malty perfume.

"Sorry to hear it," I say. "What's on offer today?"

"Just got a load of these," he says, kicking an open box toward me with a booted toe. It's filled with folded white I <3 New York t-shirts. "Gonna bring 'em down to Washington Square and get the early tourist crowd. I'll let you snag one before they go if you want it."

"I would, but I'm cash poor until payday," I say. "Then I'll just be regular poor."

"I hear you, Parker," he says. "VA missed my last two checks. Bunch of worthless paper pushers. No respect for those who died for their country."

I happen to know that Terry spends those checks on dollar beers at the American Legion on Canal, but that's neither here nor there. "Hope they get here soon, Terry."

"Maybe you can write an article about it," he suggests. "You could interview me."

"I'll run it by my editor," I say. I'm moving toward the stairs when something occurs to me. "You're from South Brooklyn, right?"

"Bay Ridge born and raised," he says. "Moved here after the service to be closer to the good breaks."

"Know a place called J&V?"

"Sure," he says. "Pizza joint over in Bensonhurst. Eighteenth Ave. Think it's around Sixty-Sixth, Sixty-Seventh."

"You're better than the yellow pages," I say. "Thanks a million."

"Sure, sure," he says. "Hey, Parker, the knee's really bothering me something terrible today. You know I wouldn't ask if I didn't really need it . . ." He gestures toward his cart, already piled high with boxes.

I help Terry load the rest and then drag the cart down the stairs, almost tripping and splattering on my way down. We wish each other luck and then I catch the N at Canal, Brooklyn bound. It's a familiar journey, but strange in the bald light of day. Usually it's a twilight sojourn, a somewhat solemn weekly pilgrimage toward the source of all good and evil in my life. I notice all the things that have escaped me in the faltering evening light: the light glittering off the cargo containers atop the freighters banked on the industrial shores of the East River, the undulating blue graffiti as we enter the underground tunnel, the vine-covered house with the burnt-out windows as we exit it.

I get out at Eighteenth Avenue and start down the block lined with green-lettered storefronts: grocer, baker, hair salon, pork store, the latter decorated with a cheerfully waving pig draped with sausage links. Kind of perverse when you think about it. A few people walk down the sidewalks with their shopping, each door chiming softly as it opens or shuts. Other than that, the block is quiet, the morning cool and bright. A spray of broken glass glints off the sidewalk, catching the sun.

A group of six or seven young toughs in wife-beaters and patchy adolescent mustaches is hanging out on the next corner by an orange construction barricade set up next to an empty lot. One of them, pale and lanky, with enough gel in his hair to stopper the leak in the Titanic, hops off the barricade as I approach. He saunters over to the metal trash can on the corner and kicks it over. Dog tags bounce off his skinny chest as trash cascades onto the pavement.

The can rolls into the path of the person walking a few paces in front of me—an East Asian kid in a black track jacket who looks a few years older than they are. They greet him with a chorus of unimaginative racist slurs about the shape of his eyes and his political leanings.

Their intended victim does some quick footwork and manages to avoid the can. Almost as if he was expecting this. It rolls off the sidewalk, leaving bottles and wrappers in its wake, and settles next to the curb. He steps gingerly around the trash that's spewed out and keeps walking, jaw set.

A laugh escapes me. "Don't you have anything better to do?"

The posse's gazes swing over to me all at once, hard little eyes set in babyish faces. The sight just makes me laugh harder. I take a step and my boot makes inadvertent contact with an empty soda can, sending it flying across the pavement and into the feet of the ringleader.

He raises his lips over his gums and snarls at me. His gang follows suit. I can almost feel the effort of their brain cells rubbing together as I pass. Then I hear the distinct sound of a wad of spit being collected and hocked, but I'm much too far away for it to make contact and I just keep chuckling.

On the next block I smell the slice shop before I see it, doughy plumes wafting out beneath the sign with the green swoopy letters reading J&V PIZZERIA. I push the door open and am instantly enveloped in the residual heat of pizza ovens and the warm familiarity of the neighborhood slice joint: the grease-printed oregano and red pepper shakers on the green Formica countertop, the slow, easy conversation between the guys behind it. A man with a black goatee deftly stretches a round of pizza dough across his knuckles, lays it on the counter, and spreads it with red sauce using the bottom of the ladle, all with virtuosic grace. I suddenly realize how hungry I am and order a slice. A man with a name tag that reads LENNY hands it to me on a paper plate in exchange for two singles. I confetti it with a little oregano and a lot of crushed red pepper and then extinguish it in a few bites, leaving only a slick burn on the roof of my mouth.

"Anyone hear anything new about what happened to the Russo girl?"

It's the goateed pizza maker who says it. Just as he does, a girl in jeans and a lighter denim shirt with a mane of curly hair appears from the back carrying a stack of empty pizza boxes. She pauses for a moment, then dumps them summarily onto the counter.

Lenny swats Goatee upside the head and gestures toward the girl. "Hey, Richie. Come on."

For a moment, everyone is quiet. Then the phone rings and the girl picks it up. "J&V." She slams it back onto the cradle a minute later and loudly announces, "Hey, Len, we got a big delivery to P.S. 186. They got an assembly or somethin'." She rips a ticket from the dispenser and turns toward Lenny.

Hers is the face that floated into my dreams last night: green eyes, copper hair, round moon of a face. When she sees me, she freezes.

"I'm gonna take my break, okay?" she says, eyes still on me.

"Okay, Gi, no problem. Take your time." Lenny takes the ticket from her and squints at it, then shakes his head and mutters, "Twelve pies? How am I supposed to make twelve pies just like that? Unbelievable."

I turn and walk out the doors and around the corner onto a quieter side street, stopping next to two stone lions on pillars guarding a white clapboard house. A moment later she appears, eyes wary. "You a reporter?" she says. "I saw you the other night. Talkin' to the cops."

I shiver involuntarily. I don't like when I talk to people and have no recollection of doing it. "Parker Snow. *New York Street.*" I show her my press badge. "What's your name?"

She says nothing, just produces a pack of Marlboro 100's from her pocket. I take out my silver lighter and flick it in front of the long cigarette she's eyeing me over.

"How's everyone doing around here?" I ask. "Pretty shaken up?"

She takes a drag. "Of course we're shaken up. Can't even have a funeral until they decide to—to give her back." She grimaces. "Italian Catholic neighborhood like this? It's killing everyone."

"I'm sorry."

"Sure you are. Why you here, anyway?"

"I was hoping you could tell me a few things about what happened that night, to help illuminate the story." *The story.* Until the words left my mouth, I didn't know I was writing one.

Did, too, says the voice in my head. *You've been writing this story in your head since you learned the name Carla Russo.*

She shakes her head curtly and blows out a stream of smoke. "I don't know shit."

"But you knew Carla."

The steeliness melts from her face. "Yeah, I knew her," she says, voice wavering. She swallows. "Born one month apart. We grew up together."

"So, you were close."

"Best friends," she says. "People used to call us Betty and Veronica 'cause she was the quiet type, and I was always a loudmouth."

"Not what you'd call a troublemaker, then."

"Carla? Nah." She shakes her head. "She was training to be a nurse. Just wanted to help people."

"Did she work? Go to school?"

"Both. She was finishing the nursing program at SUNY, and she worked as a nurse's aide at two hospitals. One in Downtown Brooklyn, one in the city." She says it with the pride of someone talking about her own daughter.

"Where would she have been coming from on Monday?" I ask.

She bristles. "You sure ask a lot of questions."

"You still haven't answered my first."

That elicits the ghost of a smile. "Giovanna Maldonato. They call me Gia."

I nod. "So. Monday."

She sighs. "Mondays she worked in Manhattan. When she got back to Brooklyn, she always stopped by home first to help with her dad, then she'd come here to say hi and chat for a few before going to study at the bakery down the block. That was her routine."

"Help with her dad?"

"Yeah. He's in a wheelchair now. Got some disease that keeps getting worse."

"Okay," I say. "So, that evening, considering where she was found, she was probably on her way home."

"Right. I was here, just standing at the counter, riffin' with one of the guys, when I heard a scream." She looks out at the street and grimaces. "I knew it was her. Somehow, I just knew."

I hear it again then, too: the sharpened point of her scream piercing the night. I take the ring out of my pocket. "Does this mean anything to you? I found it on the street near the scene."

At the sight of the ring, Gia's eyes widen, then harden ever so slightly. "That was Carla's," she says. "They must've taken it and dropped it. Whoever . . . did this to her."

An engagement ring pulled off by a spurned fiancé, dropped in the heat of the retreat, adrenaline reddening his vision and making the blood pump in his ears. Something sizzles white-hot through me.

Gia must see something on my face because she says quickly: "Listen, I know what you're thinking, but it wasn't him. He's not that kind of guy."

I raise an eyebrow. Gia looks at me sidelong as the silence stretches out. Then she exhales a plume of smoke and sighs. "I guess you're gonna find out anyway. Probably better you than the cops. Anthony Jones. Kid from the projects. East New York."

That takes me by surprise. "That must have gone over real well around here," I say.

She laughs bitterly. "Yeah, you guessed it. We're a real welcoming bunch." She shakes her head, a curl falling over her forehead. "I told her. I told her *so many times* not to keep seeing him. Of course, she didn't listen. She never did when she had her heart set on something."

"How long had they been together?"

She tosses the curl out of her face. "Almost two years. They met at Coney Island, in line for the Cyclone or some shit. She came knocking on my window afterward, the way we did when we were kids. Had me come out to the driveway at god knows what hour so she could tell me about it." She rolls her eyes. "She said he wasn't like the guys in our neighborhood. Said he had *a good soul.* When I heard that I said, 'Girl, you got it bad.'" She puts her hand on the stone lion. It seems to jog a memory because she smiles. "They even had a way of signaling each other without him having to call her house. When she wanted to tell him the coast was clear and she could meet up, she'd turn the Mary statue in their front yard around. Then she'd sneak out and meet him at their spot. If it was facing the right way, that meant he should get the hell out, because Sal was around."

"Sal?"

"Carla's brother."

Maloney's words echo in my ears. *Victim's brother. Not a suspect.* "He opposed Carla and Anthony's relationship?" I ask.

"That's one way to put it," she says drily. "This place is stuck in 1963. He's not a bad guy. Just a hothead, you know?"

A hothead who didn't like the guy his sister was dating. I think about the boys on the corner, the ones who seemed to be thirsting for a fight. The quiet violence that pervades this neighborhood, so intent on its normalcy.

Then I notice Gia looking at me closely. When she speaks, a note of desperation has crept into her voice. "He loved her. But you know how it is with cops. They're gonna *think* it was him. They always do, don't they?"

It takes me a moment to realize she's talking about Carla's boyfriend.

"Kid like him?" she says. "He don't stand a chance."

I can't say she's wrong—or that it wasn't my first thought, too. And so I don't say anything.

"I still can't really believe it," Gia says, her eyes fixed at some point in the distance. "That she's really gone."

Her voice trails off for a moment, and I wish that whatever she's seeing was visible to me. Then she blinks and looks at me. "Are you really gonna write about this?" she says. "I mean, everyone, her poor ma . . ."

"It could make a difference," I say. "Most cases are solved within twenty-four hours, which has now passed. So, we need to do what we can. You'd be surprised by how a well-timed newspaper story can get people out of the woodwork. It's helped catch more than one criminal before."

Gia looks strangely blank for a moment, the cigarette wafting prettily between her fingers. Then she nods. "If you think it'll help."

"It might," I amend. "Where would I find Sal?"

"Body shop on Sixteenth Ave and Sixty-Third. Otto's Auto," she says. "Just, you know, don't expect a welcome party."

"Noted. What about Carla's address? I was thinking I might go see her mom."

She flicks her cigarette onto the curb and grinds it out with a sneakered foot. "1825 Sixty-Sixth Street, between this ave and Nineteenth. But don't tell her I sent you, okay?"

"Thanks. And I won't." I look back at the pizza shop, the profile of the raised green sign visible. "Twelve pizzas. I guess you better get back. They ever have you throw the dough?"

She laughs, and for a moment she's just another Italian girl from Bensonhurst, nothing to worry about but the next half of her shift. "Girl, you don't want me makin' pies."

###

I leave Gia and head back out onto the avenue. I figure I'll pay a visit to this hothead brother, the one I remember from the scene, to see what I can glean from him. I know I'm getting further and further off piste from my Russian story, but once new tracks are laid, it's hard to stop following them. And my conversation with Gia has only made me realize how badly I want to figure it out: What happened to the girl I saw, her life brutally arrested in the prime of it?

On the way I pass my doctor's office. Since I'm in the neighborhood, I reason, I might as well ask for a top-off. Save myself a trip. But I'm surprised to see that it's dark, the shades pulled down. I've never seen it closed before. But then again, I'm not usually here at this time of day. Still, it makes my stomach flutter, even the thought of the conduit closing.

The yellow sign makes the auto shop easy to spot: OTTO'S AUTO. FOREIGN AND DOMESTIC CARS. OPEN *6 DAYS*. WE MAKE IT GO! A few heads turn as I walk by the mechanics in the process of making it go, who seem unused to seeing the fairer sex pass through their domain. The concrete floor is spotted with motor oil, red ladders leaning haphazardly against the wall as an overhead AC unit whiffles. The shop appears to specialize in little Italian sports cars that haven't gone zero to ninety in ten in a long time, if they ever did—much like their owners, whom I suspect to be middle-aged, early bald, and out of touch. There's a red Miata with a busted-up fender that's sloping toward the ground like it's given up on life and a Fiat that looks straight out of the sixties, neither design nor upkeep having aged well. A yellow cab suspended between the bright blue posts of a lift is the one reminder of the practical world, standing out like a bagel on a plate of pâte à choux. Something seems to be wrong with the lift because the cab keeps dropping down a foot or two before being sent back up with a windy screech, its front and tail ends wavering uneasily each time.

I spot Sal working on a lovelorn Alfa Romeo, crouched by its front left tire with a wrench in his hand. The back of his head—thick, dark hair slicked back—makes him easy to spot, but more than that is the feeling I get, the same one I remember from that night. An uneasy energy charging the molecules around him with a volatile electricity.

"They still have you changing tires?"

He straightens up and wipes his hand with a towel. "I know you?" The Brooklyn in his voice rings loud, clear, and a touch bellicose. With his high cheekbones and dark eyes rimmed with long lashes, he's handsome by any objective measure—except for the sneer that pulls his lips up over his teeth.

"Parker Snow," I say. "I'm a reporter for *The New York Street*. First of all, I wanted to say that I'm very sorry for your loss."

His lip curls further. "You got a lotta nerve, coming around here."

"Maybe," I say. "But actually, I think you want to talk to me. I think you'd like nothing more."

He rolls the oil-stained towel between his fingers, eyes narrowed. "And why would I want to talk to you?"

"Because you want to find the son of a bitch who murdered your sister."

Suddenly all the clinking of metal against metal ceases, the rough sound of the mechanics' voices still. Sal looks at me for a moment in disbelief. Then he tosses the rag onto the hood of the car and strides toward the open door of the garage. I follow him, the other mechanics exchanging looks as I pass.

Outside, the morning has turned breezy. Sal faces the street as he holds a cheap plastic lighter in a cupped hand, trying to coax a flame onto a cigarette.

"I got nothing to say to you," he says roughly when he sees me.

I take out my Zippo and spark it next to his cigarette. It catches. He looks at it as if he's not sure how it got into his hand.

"Do you have any idea who might have done it?" I ask.

He looks at me with the same disbelief, then shakes his head slightly. "Cops say it was a mugging gone wrong."

"But you don't think so."

"How do you know what I think?" he spits. Then he adds, "What about that guy she was hanging around with? You been interviewin' him?"

"I've heard that guy has a name," I say. "Hear it's Anthony Jones."

"Don't you say that name in front of me," Sal says. His eyes glitter with malice.

"Are you saying you think Anthony was involved in some way?"

"I got my suspicions."

"And have you shared those suspicions with the police?"

"Maybe I have, maybe I haven't. What's it your business?"

"Believe it or not, I'm trying to help you," I say. "From how Giovanna tells it, the feelings between Carla and Anthony were mutual."

"Gia," he says dismissively. "What does she know?"

"A lot more about your sister than you do, it seems," I say, and then I regret it when I see the pain screw up his eyes like they've been stung by smoke. He flicks the cigarette onto the ground and faces me.

"My sister," he says, "was naive. She didn't know what was good for her. She saw a poor soul in anyone with a sad face and sad past. Well, you know what I say? Who doesn't have a sad face and a sad past? This is *Brooklyn*."

"Can you at least tell me where you were on Monday evening, when it happened?" I ask. "Just so I don't have to stay up all night thinking about it."

"I was *here*," he spits. "*Working*. Giovanna called my ma and my ma called me and then I came out to find cops there and my sister dead in the street. Christ."

He puts the rag up to his face and wipes it, leaving a streak of grease across his cheek. Is his anguish that of grief, I wonder, or guilt?

"You shoulda heard them," he mutters. "The way he would go off on her."

"Anthony?" I say. "Going off on Carla?" That's a different sort of relationship than the one Gia described.

But Sal's made it clear that he's done talking. Wordlessly he grinds out his cigarette and stalks back into the garage.

I walk halfway down the block, then steal back to look at the faded sign listing the shop's business hours. Carla was killed around six thirty. Otto's Auto is open every day but the Lord's Day, from eight a.m. to eight p.m.—except for Mondays, when it closes at three.

###

On the train ride back to Manhattan my mind runs over my conversation with Gia, her speech thick with flat, no-nonsense vowels. She's all steely edges, forged and fired in the depths of Brooklyn, but I can tell she's an inch away from falling apart. I think about how young she looked in that last moment. How young Carla was.

We slide to a stop. Fort Hamilton Parkway. Seated across from me is a harried-looking woman with a child who stares at me skeptically. I return the look.

But there's no denying the truth about one thing Gia said: Sooner or later, the cops will glom on to the boyfriend, and the space between him and an all-expenses-paid trip to the Island of Rikers will be a hair's breadth. From the way she talked about his relationship with Carla, he doesn't sound like a prime suspect. But then there's the way her brother, Sal, talked about the same relationship. Supportive best friend versus protective brother. Without Carla to speak, whose account is true?

My mind starts to spin. *Anthony Jones. Kid from the projects. East New York.* That would be the Boulevard Houses, then. He wouldn't be too hard to find.

The train slides to a stop. Prospect Ave. The woman grabs the child's hand and bustles her off the train.

My pulse quickens. Crock isn't going to like this. I can hear him now, his voice hitting on every other word with the force of a Category 5: *This is exactly what I told you not to do! Goddammit, Snow! How many times do I have to . . .* et cetera, et cetera.

But then there's Carla. Her face, white and vacant. The total lack of witnesses or any suspects. How her death at—what? twenty?—is just another red point in the pattern, which isn't really a pattern, but a faceless, unreadable cluster. Souls condensed onto the red plastic head of a pin.

Maloney really isn't going to like this.

Crock and Maloney. Two men who know nothing about the darkness a young woman might, unknowingly, find herself hurtling toward.

Atlantic Avenue. The last stop before the bridge into Manhattan. The train jolts to a stop, and I jolt up with it.

5

Then he starts to run . . .

I go into a deli outside the station and ask for the phonebook. Jones comma Anthony yields seven results, one of whom is located in East New York. 828 Ashford Street, apartment 6E. Boulevard Houses. Also listed under that address: Jones comma Cynthia.

The train ride to New Lots Avenue is uneventful save for the heavy odor of reefer wafting potently through the car, gift of the blind Rastafarian smoking a joint with obvious pleasure on the other end. Just across from the New Lots station are the Boulevard Houses: identical brown brick buildings identically arranged in a star-shaped pattern around identical weed-choked courtyards, like everything else built by the New York City Housing Authority. They're even identically decorated, from the white hieroglyphs of graffiti to the signs declaring POSITIVELY NO BALL PLAYING ALLOWED right down to the bird shit that impastos the windowsills.

I walk through the complex, the sound of a basketball thudding on concrete reverberating through the air. The playgrounds are empty of children, their anemic jungle gyms stuck here and there with candy wrappers like bright bits of treasure. I find the building numbered 828. Next to a placard that reads NO PETS, a sick-looking orange cat is huddled in a window frame, eyes narrowed as if it can't keep them open but can't make up its mind to close them.

The small foyer is unlocked, the door hanging slightly open on its hinges. I walk past the metal mail slots and take the airless elevator up to the sixth floor, then step out into a long, drab hallway lined with dun-colored carpet. In front of the elevator hangs a painting, a thrift- store reproduction of some eighteenth-century pastoral scene, three cows traipsing down a green slope to reach a brownish stream. The canvas is so cracked, the sky more resembles a moon rock. I look to my right down the hall. Apartment 6E stares at me narrowly from the very end.

The door sounds hard and hollow underneath my knuckles. No answer. I knock again. Silence.

I'm turning to leave when I hear a latch click behind me. The closed door has been replaced by a petite, Black woman dressed in ankle-length navy slacks and a white cardigan. I'd put her age somewhere between forty and ninety. Hers is a face that seems to waver, split, and recombine every nanosecond, first youthful and serene, then ancient and etched with worry.

"Yes?"

"Mrs. Jones?" I ask. "My name is Parker Snow. I'm a reporter for *The New York Street*." I take out my press badge.

She glances at it. "How can I help you?"

"I was hoping for just a few minutes of your time," I say. "I apologize for not calling first, but it's something of a sensitive subject."

Her eyes dart around the hall behind me. Then she sighs, opens the door, and takes a small step back. "I suppose you might as well come in."

"Is this about that shooting last month?" she asks as I follow her into a short entryway. I detect the faint hint of a Southern accent in her voice. "I was at work when it happened. Today just happens to be my day off."

"Sorry to interrupt it," I say. The living room is small and pin neat: a periwinkle couch and matching accent chair and ottoman, glass coffee table, end tables decorated with framed photos of smiling faces. It smells faintly of wisteria. "But no. It's not about the shooting last month."

"Couple of bad apples," she says, shaking her head and adjusting a pillow on the sofa. "Always ruining the bunch." She straightens and looks up at me. "Where I come from, we believe in hospitality, even when we're not sure exactly who's come to call. Or why. Can I offer you some coffee?"

"I wouldn't want to trouble you."

She fixes me with the appraising gaze of a mother, then announces: "You look like you could use a cup."

While she's in the kitchen I take a closer look around. All the sharp corners of the apartment have been carefully softened, the institutional windows mellowed by iridescent cream curtains. Across the courtyard is a building that exactly mirrors this one—as if to say, in case you've forgotten where you are, don't. A keyboard takes up a not insubstantial amount of the room's real estate. On the stand is a sheaf of music, a Gershwin piece. I lay my fingers around it as carefully as I can so as not to rustle the pages, then tuck them into my coat.

When Mrs. Jones returns to the living room, she finds me on the couch, looking at a framed family photo set on the end table.

"Everyone says my oldest, Jeremiah, looks like me, and that my youngest, Anthony, looks like his father," she says, setting a cup of coffee down in front of me. "He got his talent, too."

"Is your husband a musician?"

"He was," she says. "He passed away several years ago. That keyboard belongs to Anthony."

"I'm sorry to hear that."

She nods. "So. What can I do for you?"

"I came here to ask you about Anthony, actually. In particular, about his relationship with Carla Russo. It was her best friend who gave me Anthony's name."

"Ask about what?" When I don't say anything for a moment, she says, "Something happen to Carla?" Her voice is tinged with dread.

I take a deep breath. "She died, Mrs. Jones. It seems to have been a violent crime."

She inhales and puts her hand to her heart, then drops down into the chair across from me. The silence simmers between us.

"When?" she asks finally.

"Monday evening, around six thirty," I say. "In Bensonhurst. Just a few blocks from her home."

"Poor girl," she says softly. She's looking off at the kitchen table, as if at an apparition of Carla sitting there. "But who would want to—?"

She breaks off suddenly, fixing me with a terrified look.

"They still don't have any suspects," I say quickly. "It could have been a random act of street violence. But I would be lying if I said that they won't inevitably question Anthony if they haven't already. Which is why I wanted to get to you first."

"Wait a minute. Are you writing about my son?"

"No. This is unofficial business. Off the record," I say. "I'm writing about the crime and trying to understand who she was, how this may have happened to her. I'll avoid bringing your son into it unless I have to."

She looks dubious. Then she glances back at the kitchen table. "She liked to sit there and look at photos of Anthony and his brother when they were growing up. Hear about how it was raising them after Joseph died. How it was growing up in the South. She liked to listen." She pauses, then says, softly, "He was so in love with her."

"Was there any trouble between them around here?" I venture. "From what I've heard, there was some tension between her crowd and his."

"Is that what you heard?" She looks back at me sharply. "Bensonhurst is the kind of neighborhood where kids from around here get beat up just for setting foot. For kids like mine, *that's* the wrong side of the tracks. One of them even died last year, they beat him up so bad." She shakes her head. "I used to think I'd left the worst racism behind in the South."

"Did anything like that ever happen to Anthony?" I ask.

"One day he came home roughed up. Supposedly some guys mugged him outside the subway."

"It sounds like you didn't believe that."

"When it's your own son, you can tell when he's not telling the truth," she says. "And it was right after he brought Carla by for the first time. The timing was just too strange. But I never got a word out of him."

"Where does he spend his days?" I ask.

"School. Brooklyn College. He's there on scholarship."

"He must be very talented."

"Whatever that's worth."

I take that as my cue and stand up. "Thank you for speaking with me and for answering my questions. I know this news is hard to hear, especially from a stranger. But I thought it might yield something useful. This case is still in its very early stages."

She doesn't say anything for a long moment, just continues to stare at the kitchen table, its empty chairs. I'm about to quietly take my leave when she speaks.

"Every day, it seems like someone else has to die in this place. Every day, I think it might be him. And I thank God that it's not." She looks up to meet my gaze. "Maybe this is worse."

###

Compared to the oil-stained interior of the auto shop and the stark concrete of the Boulevard Houses, the sweeping green lawns and stately red brick of Brooklyn College almost come as a shock. No wonder Anthony spends most of his time here. Students mill around like they're in a postcard of what's supposed to happen in America. I ask someone where the music department is, and after a few wrong turns, I find the sign and enter the first building I see.

The girl at the desk has a freckled face and long, curly hair, and is wearing a flowy, sea-green dress and about seven pounds of thrift-store jewelry. It takes a few tries to get her attention away from her Walkman. Music spills out of the headphones. It's opera.

"I'm looking for a friend of mine," I say. "Anthony Jones. He left some music at my place." I hold up the sheaf of papers that I slid off the music stand in the Jones apartment.

She gives it a bored glance. "Lemme see if I can find his schedule." She types something into the computer, the tips of her midnight-blue nails clacking against the keyboard. "Looks like he's comin' outta composition in ten."

"Which way would that be?"

"Out the door, turn left, follow the path around and it's to the right, past the quad."

I leave the office and follow her instructions, lingering a safe distance from the building until a group of students exits in a clump. As they dissipate, I spot him: the shy-looking kid from the photo on Cynthia Jones's end table, a few years older but unmistakably him. Lucky for me, he's not talking with friends—just walking alone, his head cast down.

"Anthony?" I say as I approach. "Mind if I talk to you for a second?"

He looks up at me and flinches, as if a bee had landed on the rim of his glasses. Then he starts to run.

"Goddammit," I say. And then I start to run, too.

I guess the five flights of stairs to my apartment is enough to keep me in some kind of shape, because after a few minutes of pursuit over the grass, I catch up to him. All I can do is grab him by the backpack, and when I do, the momentum jerks both of us back. I stumble backward and reach a hand out to break my fall. The sheets of music flutter to the ground like leaves in a fall wind.

Anthony takes a few stumbling steps, then whirls around to face me.

"What," I pant, staggering to my feet, "the fuck was that?"

"Who are you?" he demands. His glasses have flown off his face and his eyes are blinking madly. "What do you want from me?"

"Relax. I just want to talk to you," I say. I pick up his glasses and examine them. They appear to be intact. "My name's Parker. Parker Snow. I work for *The New York Street*." I wipe the glasses on my coat and hand them back to him.

He puts them on and blinks at me a few more times. "You're a reporter?"

"Yeah, but this is unofficial business. Off the record." More like a broken record. I'm on so much unofficial business these days it might as well be written on my badge.

His skinny chest is heaving beneath his plaid button-down. "I thought you were a cop," he says finally.

"If I were a cop, I wouldn't have asked you so nicely," I say, pushing the hair out of my eyes. "Anyways, what do you have to hide?"

He raises an eyebrow. "That's a cop thing to say."

I smile. "You're right." Then I look around at the pages scattered over the grass. "Sorry about this."

"How'd you get my music, anyway?"

"I took it from your apartment," I confess. "I went to see your mom. I wasn't sure how hard you'd be to find. I had to have something up my sleeve."

"You went to see my—" He stops, bewildered.

I put my hands up. "I just want to talk."

He looks around, as if checking for anyone he knows, then back at me. "There's a diner across the street," he says, his voice quiet and resigned. "It would be better than talking here."

Together we gather up the music, a little damp and most definitely out of order, but salvageable. He puts the sheaf in his backpack, and we start to walk. He keeps his eyes trained in front of him as we cross the lawn, and from my sidelong glances I can see that he's deciding what he's going to tell me. His silence hums with it.

We cross Bedford Avenue and enter a greasy spoon, the kind of place where the menu is thirteen pages long, your dollar cup of coffee goes on forever, and they ask you how you want your burger cooked and then always cook it the same way: charred on the outside and gray on the inside. We're seated in a booth across from an old couple stooped over plates of scrambled eggs and toast like the punctuation around a quote.

I ask for coffee. Anthony asks for the same. The waitress, mascara clumped around her tired eyes, plunks two mugs on the table and fills them, then delivers the sugar caddy and creamer jar with equal indifference. She's a woman who has long ago learned to be here without being here.

"You want something to eat?" I ask Anthony.

He shakes his head.

"Good," I say. "Because I can't afford it." I light a cigarette and sit back against the booth.

I sit and smoke and look at Anthony. With his plaid shirt and glasses and skinny limbs, his serious, unsmiling face, he looks like the sensitive type. The one who listened to jazz records when everyone else was listening to Run-D.M.C, who got his lunch money stolen, who struggled to talk to girls but who fell hard when he did. I'm having a hard time picturing his blood boiling with that red-hot jealousy and madness.

"Look, this is about Carla, isn't it?" he blurts out suddenly.

"In fact, it is," I say. "Who told you what happened to her?"

"Her friend Giovanna called me. Figured I'd—" He breathes in. "Figured I'd want to know."

I'm surprised. Gia didn't mention having talked to Anthony.

"Maybe she also figured the cops might call?" I venture. "And wanted to give you a heads-up?"

"Yeah, I guess that was part of it." He raises his hand up from the handle of his coffee cup, its contents still untouched, and wipes it over his eyes, sending his glasses askew.

"So, have they?" I ask.

He fixes his glasses, blinks a few times, and sighs. "Not yet."

"Good," I say. "We have some time. Where were you Monday evening between the hours of six and seven?"

"Jazz band rehearsal," he says. "I have it every Monday night."

"Great. Got someone who can confirm that?"

"Only the rest of the band."

I have to smile at the note of sarcasm in his voice. I wasn't expecting that.

"I'm not asking you for my own edification. I told you, we're off the record," I say. "I'm asking because that's what the cops are going to ask you. Their dance card's more than full these days, so they might take their time investigating. But when they start, they'll get to you. Fast."

Fear sparks in Anthony's eyes, but also suspicion.

"Your mom seems to think you ran into trouble in Carla's neck of the woods," I say, changing the subject. "Seems like it worried her."

"Oh yeah? What else did she say?" He picks up his coffee cup and finally takes a sip.

"She said you're a talented musician. That you take after your father that way," I answer. "She said you're here on a full scholarship. That she raised you and your brother pretty much on her own."

"Did she tell you where my brother is?"

"No."

"Attica," he says. "He started selling drugs when he was fifteen. Then someone in his crew shot a guy. He didn't have anything to do with it, but because he was there, they sent him up."

Shit. "No, she didn't tell me," I repeat.

He looks out the window at the redbrick buildings of Brooklyn College across the street. An empty shopping cart rambles down the avenue like it's making a getaway. "I met Carla and I thought, wow. Here's something better. Here's someone who believes in good in the world. Who believes in me." He shakes his head. "What a moron I was to think I could get out."

For a moment, the only sounds are the clink of a spoon against a cup, the low voices of the old couple, the waitress's litany to the line cook.

Anthony breaks the silence. "I used to come here with Carla. She would meet me here sometimes after class before she had to work a night shift. Just for an hour. We always sat there." He gestures at the booth diagonally across from us, empty and forlorn under the weak fluorescent light. "I just wish we could do it over again. That last time, I told her—"

I wait expectantly. Anthony chews on his lip, eyes still on the table as if searching for something there. Then he says, "Never mind."

I take the ring out of my pocket and place it down. His eyes widen at the sight of it, the way Gia's did. "I found this near the scene. Gia said you gave it to Carla."

He picks it up gingerly and brings it close to his eyes, like a relic from a lost civilization. Then he places it gently back down on the table and slumps backward into the booth, as if wishing it would swallow him whole.

"Where'd you get it, anyway?" I ask.

"Pawn shop on Atlantic," he says dully. "Charged me thirty bucks for the piece of junk." He looks at the empty booth across from us again. "I told her one day I'd buy her a real one."

"It's yours, then, I suppose," I say. "Do you want it back?"

"That ring is the last thing I want back."

I drop it into my pocket. "Well. You'll know where to find it if you change your mind."

Anthony turns his gaze down toward the spot on the table where the ring was. His eyes have that glazed-over look of the insomniac, of someone living in the darkest recesses of their mind.

Tread carefully, says a voice in my head as I regard the skinny, hunched-over figure across from me. Because sometimes it's the person you least expect. And sometimes it's exactly who you expect. Sometimes it's the person you trust the most.

"First my dad. Now Carla," he says, his voice almost a whisper. "And with Carla . . . You don't know what it's like. Someone like that leaves you and you can't even show your face."

Seeing him fighting back tears, I feel something in me give. "I know this isn't exactly what you want to hear right now," I say. "But if I were you, I'd get a lawyer."

He breathes in and seems to steel himself. When he looks at me, the old mistrust has returned. "Why are you helping me?"

I pause to consider that. The old couple has gone, the remains of their meal still on the table with the balled-up napkins and coffee-stained mugs.

"In my mind, everyone deserves a fair shake. Frankly, I doubt that's what you're going to get," I say. "Also, I don't think you killed her. And I want to find out who did."

###

Anthony leaves for his next class as I sit in the booth, drinking the last of my coffee. I check my watch. Still time to make deadline for tomorrow's paper.

I could just leave it here, I think. I found out the origins of the ring. I could just step away, go back to the job I'm supposed to be doing, and avoid stirring up more trouble with Crock.

Then an image flares up in my mind, unbidden. A young woman on an exam table. Hair sweat-stuck to her petrified face. The white paper beneath her going red.

I stand abruptly, coffee cup rattling against the table's mottled Formica. I go to the payphone in the back and slide a quarter into the slot, my fingers tracing their well-worn pattern over the keys.

"*New York Street*, copy desk."

"Jake," I say. "Guess who."

"Oh hey, Parker." The voice of my rewriter floats into my ear. Jake is my partner in reporting crime, the one who waits by the phone and a police radio at the *Street*'s Midtown headquarters and helps turn my stream-of-consciousness into a cohesive article when I'm out working a story. His voice is always softer than I expect. "Where are you?" he asks. "How are you?"

"Atlantic Ave. Listen, can you take down a couple of inches for me?"

"Sure. Just gimme a sec." I hear papers shuffling and, in the background, the usual newsroom mêlée. You can almost smell the rank cigarette smoke and stress through the phone line. "Okay. Ready."

I tell him what I can about Carla's murder, leaving out any mention of Anthony. When I'm done, he says, "Aren't you supposed to . . . I mean, Crock wants you staying out of these types of cases, right?"

"Maybe he does, maybe he doesn't," I say. "Does this mean you're not gonna file my story?"

"Of course I'll file it. I was just . . ."

"Suggest a real nice headline," I say. "I gotta go. Thanks."

His voice catches me before I can put the receiver down. "You didn't answer my second question."

Reluctantly, I bring it back to my ear. "Which one was that?"

"How are you."

I don't say anything for a moment. Through the restaurant's dirty front window, I see a homeless man rooting around a dumpster. He produces a loaf of brown bread and tears into it contentedly. A few months ago, he was probably selling bonds on Wall Street.

"You know," I say. "Same."

"Parker, I think maybe—"

I cut him off. "I gotta go. Thanks for the rewrite."

I place the receiver back into its cradle.

###

**WOMAN KILLED IN BROOKLYN;
NO-SUSPECT STILL AT LARGE**

By Parker Snow and Jake Grandor
March 27, 1992

A twenty-year-old woman identified as Carla Russo was found dead in the Bensonhurst neighborhood of Brooklyn on Monday. While full autopsy results have not yet been released, the initial cause of death appears to be blunt force trauma to the head, according to authorities, who believe Russo to have been the victim of a mugging gone wrong.

People close to the victim described her as a promising young woman, friendly and well-liked in the neighborhood.

"She was studying to be a nurse," said Giovanna Maldonato, Bensonhurst resident and childhood friend of the victim. "Just wanted to help people."

No suspects have emerged, nor have any witnesses come forward following police questioning. While the mysterious circumstances surrounding Carla's death are unusual, the neighborhood is no stranger to crime. "There's been more and more violence in the area," lamented NYPD Homicide chief Declan Maloney, in so many words.

Homicides in New York City have reached 506 so far this year, according to the most recent numbers—a strong first quarter that puts the city at a pace to fall just slightly below last year's all-time high of 2,235. Officials attribute the city's somewhat softer streets to recent community policing efforts and tougher law enforcement for minor crimes; others insist that the homeless, mentally ill, and delinquent are being rounded up and sent to Staten Island. For more fear-mongering, sensationalism, and rank speculation, look to your friends at *The Daily News*.

6

The deck is stacked . . .

I get down to the Shack as early as I can the next day, determined to make a good showing. I know I need to get back on the chocolate truck story with some sort of follow-up if I'm going to keep Crock happy; we have a reputation of serialized smeardom to uphold, after all. But I also want to go back to Bensonhurst, maybe try to speak to Carla's mother and get her take on her daughter's relationship with Anthony, if she'll give it to me. I'll bet it won't take long for the cops to close in on him, the victim's boyfriend. Not that it matters what I bet. In a case like this, as I've seen from Sergei's poker games, the deck is stacked.

"The deck is always stacked," I muse out loud.

The office door swings open and Schultz saunters in. "Talking to yourself? God, you're sad."

"Why?" I reply. "I'm the only one worth listening to."

He takes me in from head to toe, and I find myself taking mental inventory, too: muddy boots, frayed coat, dirty hair fringing my eyes. "Tell me, were you always like this?" he says.

"No," I say. "I used to be so good. Please and thank you and my hair in waves."

He smirks. "Then what happened?"

"Then I realized that life was a pile of dirty dishes I didn't feel like doing."

Crock's voice barks out from the open door of his office. "Snow! Get in here!"

"Busted," Schultz says with a sneer.

I walk into Crock's office, thinking about what I'm going to say when he mentions the Carla Russo article, byline Parker Snow and Jake Grandor. Nothing leaps to mind.

"Heya, Crock," I say.

"Oh, hey, Parker," he says, in the friendly tone of a county corrections officer. "Long time no see."

"Well, it's just that I've been busy researching the—"

"I know what you've been busy researching," he says, picking up the day's paper from his desk. He flips to the article and reads the headline out loud, then looks at me incredulously. "Did we not *just talk about* you sticking to your beat?"

"Well, yes, but—"

"Parker. Come on. There's a reason you don't cover this type of stuff anymore. You know it and I know it."

"This is an important story, Crock. For her and for me." As I say it, I realize how true it is: That helping bring Carla Russo justice would equal some kind of redemption in my own eyes, after my last street crime story failed another young woman so spectacularly.

The thought seems to occur to Crock at the same time, because I see something in him relent. He sighs. "If you really think you can do both, do both. But you have to get something even close to the quality of your last daisy-chain story on the Russian front, or else things here are not going to look good for you."

"I'm trying, Crock," I assure him. "It's just that my sources out in Brighton aren't exactly loose with the gab."

He thrusts a torn scrap of paper across his desk at me. I pick it up. It's an address: *57 W. 47th St.*

"It's your lucky day, reporter, because we got another tip. Guy said you should talk to someone named Petrowski in the Diamond District. That it's related to your story on the chocolate truck in Brighton. Probably horseshit but seeing as the last one paid off, why don't you go see for yourself. And for once, please, bring your friggin' *pager.*"

I sigh and pick up the crumpled bit of paper. "You got it, Crock."

###

No need for a street sign on Forty-Seventh Street: The hustler's madrigal lets you know you've arrived. It's a ballad in three parts, starting with affronted protest: *Are you kidding me? I could get four times that price on Canal! Forget about it. My three-year-old daughter would laugh at that price.* Which segues into a mewling argument: *I have a family to feed. I'll starve if I sell at that price. My children will starve. My wife won't let me in the house. Please. This is the very lowest I can do, and believe me, it's practically giving it away.* Which then melts into flattery: *I am just doing it for you, because you seem like a good guy, a mensch—my wife, though, if she found out!* The conversations are as identical as the storefronts, each smudgeless vitrine displaying the same array of grandma's silver, the wife-to-be's diamond, and promises of untold riches at rock-bottom prices.

I watch a beleaguered middle-aged woman in a cheap shearling coat speaking to the man behind the counter in one of the pawn shops, a small velvet jewelry box open in front of her. The distance between most people and total destitution is as thin as a silver chain, I realize then. Especially in these tough times. Not to say I'm any different. As a matter of fact, I'm a whole lot worse—I'd have nothing of value to pawn if I wanted to. But I don't depend on anyone, and no one depends on me. When you live like that, you walk a whole lot lighter in this world.

I'm looking for number 57. I find 55, and then the building numbers jump to 59. I do an about-face and walk past it again, searching the doorways for a sign.

"Looking for Petrowski?" a reedy voice says.

A small, weaselly guy in a long coat of scuffed brown leather is leaning against a streetlight. Dark glasses obscure the upper half of his pointy face, while the lower half is covered with a patchy goatee. He jerks his chin up at me. "Number 57?"

"That's right," I say.

"Through there. Up the stairs. Third floor."

I look where he's pointing. Barely visible, so that if the light hits it wrong, you'd miss it, is a painted-over glass door wedged between two more significant buildings. No number. No light shining through to announce it.

"Thanks," I say. The weasel shifts his weight and puts his hands in his pockets. I half expect him to take out a large diamond and gnaw it like an acorn.

I open the door and start up the narrow staircase, dark save for a patch of dusty light filtering in from some window at the top that I can't see. It smells inky and liquorish, the stairs made of hard brown rubber. On each narrow landing are two unmarked doors, one on either side. As I ascend, I think about what I'm going to ask when I get there. I'll keep it vague, I decide. Move in slow and let him come to me with whatever he knows about the stalled truck out in Brighton Beach.

On the third floor, like the weasel promised, there's a door with a placard reading PETROWSKI CUSTOM JEWELERS. I turn the handle and open it.

The room is as dark as the stairwell. The only illumination comes from the display case, small white lights set at angles to reflect the jeweled facets of the array of necklaces and bracelets, strings of pinkish pearls, rings set with rubies, amethysts, garnets. A pair of diamond earrings twinkles madly in its cone of white light.

"Hello," I call out.

"Can I help you?" a gruff voice responds. The voice moves toward the light, illuminating a stooped old man with a weathered face and a shock of white hair.

I'm about to ask him if he's had any trouble at his shop or in the neighborhood lately. Instead, I hear different words exiting my mouth. "I'm looking for a gift for my sister."

"What is it you're looking for?"

"I'm not sure, exactly. Something . . . simple," I say. "Is there something I can get, for, say two hundred?"

"Gold? Silver?"

"Silver," I tell him. "She doesn't like gold."

He sets a velvet cloth on top of the display case, takes a key ring from his pocket, and opens the case with a tiny key. From it he retrieves a pair of stud earrings inlaid with an opalescent stone, a bracelet of two braided silver strands, and a bone-white pearl on a sterling chain. His bony hands move with unexpected grace, like a conductor's.

He lays these out on the velvet, and begins to tell me about them, one by one—the metal, the number of karats, the origin of the semiprecious stones. I look them over. At first the interest is feigned, but then I find myself wanting to touch them, to feel their cold, metallic atoms vibrate against my skin. I pick up the bracelet and drape it over my wrist.

"How did you find my shop?" the jeweler asks. His tone is still rough, but now it's at least sanded down.

"My mother always told me never to shop antique jewelry at the street level," I say. "The best quality, the best deals are up top, in the places that aren't so loud and obvious."

"Your mother is a smart woman," he murmurs.

"When it comes to the material world, yes."

The buzzer sounds. The grooves in his forehead deepen as he turns to look at a small intercom screen behind him. He hesitates for just a moment before pressing a button.

"A customer," he tells me, his former gruffness returned. "With an appointment. That's how I do things here."

"I'm sorry," I say. I put the bracelet down. "I didn't know."

"No matter." He waves a hand. "You can keep looking, just move down." Distractedly, he picks up the velvet cloth and slides it a few feet down the counter. I follow.

The door opens and a short Hasidic man walks in with quick little steps, black payos side curls bouncing up and down his bearded cheeks.

"Hello, hello." The jeweler's bony head bobs up and down in greeting. His tone has changed completely. Now he sounds syrupy, deferential, almost pandering. "Welcome, welcome. Please come in. And you are—"

"Good afternoon." The man nods. "I am Abel."

"So good of you to come," the shopkeeper says, still nodding like he's being guided by a puppeteer with a hand tremor. He is already taking out more velvet cloths and laying them on the glass case. "Please tell me in more detail what you're interested in. What sizes, types of stones?"

"Rubies," the customer says. "Garnets. A sapphire, if you have it. Diamonds, of course." His accent is Williamsburg Yiddish, tinged with something else.

"Of course, of course," the shopkeeper says. He wheezes a laugh, which sounds so painfully forced it makes the hairs on my arm stand up. "Anything you want, I have."

The newcomer picks up a few of the stones and looks at them without interest as the jeweler monologues about karat size, clarity, the quality of the cut, speaking faster and with mounting desperation.

"These are very small," the customer says finally. "Do you have some that are—a little more impressive?"

"More impressive?" the jeweler says, his voice drifting off. "Well, yes, of course. I have a few in the safe that are truly special pieces. Let me just get them." His smile is stitched onto his face, and now the seams are failing. His eyes rest on the gems laid out in front of the man, who stares ahead expressionlessly. Then he turns to fiddle with a small safe set into the wall next to the intercom.

I look at the customer sidelong, his rounded woolen back obscuring the velvet cloth from my view. He doesn't seem to have noticed me in the dimness at the other end of the counter.

After a few short moments, the jeweler turns back and carefully lays down a luminescent blue stone set in platinum and surrounded by white diamonds. "This is a very special, rare blue diamond, of which there are only a few examples of this—"

"Thank you, but I have seen enough," Abel cuts him off. "We will be in touch."

The smile falls to shreds. "I—I—I assure you these are the finest stones, the *finest* stones you can find in the Diamond District," Petrowski stammers. "I've been in this business for forty years, I am a certified Master Bench Jeweler, I *know* the best—"

"We will be in touch," the Hasid repeats. "Good day."

As he turns to the door, the hem of his black wool coat brushes against me lightly, and I catch a glimpse of bright blue eyes over a long black beard.

I listen as his footfall recedes down the staircase.

A fraught stillness descends. I take a few tentative steps to where the jeweler is standing behind the counter. "I wanted to ask. Have you had any trouble here lately? Any unusual activity around your shop?"

"Are you buying anything?" he says harshly.

"Well, no," I falter. "Not today."

"Then please leave."

I move toward the exit. "Next time I'll make an appointment," I say over my shoulder.

But the man isn't looking at me. He's sitting on his stool, his chin in his hands, as if he's just watched his last hope walk out the door.

Out on the landing, I see that the customer is already near the bottom of the steps, his somber shape illuminated by the weak light seeping through the doorframe. And he's moving fast—too fast.

I take the steps two at a time. The door swings shut behind him. I push it open and look around.

"He went that-a-way." It's the same weaselly guy who was standing there before, with the sunglasses and the long leather coat. He jerks his head to the right. "The yarmulke. If that's who you're looking for."

I look down the block. Sure enough, he's already making impressive progress on his short legs toward Fifth Avenue, almost lost in the throng of people. The way he hustled in and out of the shop . . . it didn't feel right. As if, despite his request to see all those gems, he'd never planned to buy anything at all. As if he'd been there for information, just like me. Or for something else. I watch as he opens the back door of a waiting blue sedan and jumps inside.

Suddenly a door opens with a *bang* and someone is shouting in a shrill, wheezy voice.

"Cheap fakes!" the old jeweler is yelling. "She took my gems and replaced them with cheap fakes!"

It takes me what feels like a full minute to realize he's talking about me. A small crowd is already forming, all the hustlers and passersby having stopped what they're doing to watch.

"I didn't take anything," I protest.

A patrol car blips by. There's never one far from here, between the Diamond District and Rockefeller Center. "Police!" the jeweler yells, running to the car and banging on the window.

The car slides to a stop, the door opens, and out steps a mean-looking rookie with a premature beer belly and an angry spray of acne along his jawline.

"This woman, this *thief*," the jeweler pants, jabbing a long, skinny finger my way, "took my stones. On her way out of my shop, on the back of a reputable customer. She replaced them with *cut-glass fakes*." He takes these from his pocket and tosses them onto the sidewalk, where they wink dully against the dirty concrete like rhinestones on the tiara of a small-town beauty queen.

"That true, lady?" the cop asks me.

"No, it's not," I huff. "I didn't steal any of his precious jewels. What the hell would I have done with them, if I had? Swallowed them?"

"We'll find out, won't we?" he sneers. "Empty your pockets."

I reach into the pockets of my coat and turn them out. There's my thin billfold, an orange pill bottle, a pocket notebook, a pen—and a thumbnail-sized ruby, bloodred and glinting.

"That lowdown piece of trash," I say. "Of all the lowdown—"

"There's more! She has more!" The jeweler is practically jumping up and down.

"There's no more," I say roughly. "It was that *reputable customer*. I felt him brush against me on the way out. He must have stuck this one into my pocket. Small price to pay for a clean getaway. He must be halfway to Brooklyn by now and no one but me and this guy even saw him leave." I turn to gesture to the weasel. But he's nowhere to be seen—vanished into thin air.

I turn back. The cop is looking at me with triumph stamped into his beefy face.

"Alright." I sigh. "Let's go."

###

He slaps the bracelets on me and stuffs me into the back of his car like a bag of mixed recycling and takes me to the precinct, smirking in the rearview the whole way. His patrol car smells like a llama farm after the rain, and I tell him so.

When we get there, the booking sergeant tells me I'm there on one count of grand theft. That makes me laugh.

"Really? I have a few skills, but sleight of hand isn't one of them," I say. "The jeweler, Petrowski—he was standing there the whole time, except for the moment he turned his back to open the safe when the Hasid was looking at his inventory."

"Get her pedigree," the sergeant instructs his lackey, ignoring me.

"Dogs have pedigrees," I sneer.

Then he calls me a choice word and I really lose it.

They throw me into a holding cell. It's even more chilly and damp than outside, with all that concrete and metal. On my left, a fellow prisoner is hammering away at the bars of his cell, trying to get the attention of a cop sitting at a table doing paperwork.

"Come on, man," he's saying. "I didn't assault no one. I wasn't even *there*."

From his voice, I peg him at no more than eighteen or nineteen—just barely the age the law refers to as an adult. The cop at the table—who looks about the same age himself—is trying his best to maintain a tough face, impassively scrawling on his forms.

"That ain't gonna help so why don't you just save your breath?" he says.

I hear a low laugh from the guy on my right, whom I passed when they brought me in. Skinny and lanky in a t-shirt and jeans he was practically swimming in, he was stretched out on the bench in his cell like it was a feather-stuffed divan.

"It wasn't *me*, man," the kid on my left tries again. "I wasn't anywhere near Upper West. I was at Tower Records. *Downtown*. You gotta believe me."

"Save it for the judge," the cop says. "They picked you up, they got reason to pick you up."

The kid scoffs. "You think we all look the same, huh?"

The cop springs up, red in the face. "You're not gonna go around accusing me of shit, you punk. I can make things easy or hard for you. Which way do you want it?"

Now it's my turn to laugh. The cop looks at me, as if noticing me for the first time. He's clearly surprised by what he sees.

"What the hell are you laughing at?" he growls.

"Your made-for-TV movie lines," I say. "Anyways, whatever you think he did, he did it," I say, jerking my head to the right. Then I tilt it to the left. "He didn't."

He narrows his eyes. "What the hell do you know about what they did and didn't do?"

"Real perps don't bother maintaining their innocence," I say. "They just take a nap, like Slim Jim over here. The innocent ones, they stand at the gate raising hell and high water to make sure you know it."

"Oh yeah?" he says. He's trying to maintain his tough guy act, but the unsure kid is showing through beneath it. "And where does that put you?"

I shrug. "Somewhere in between." And I sit down, back propped against the wall of my cell, to ride it out.

Ironic that this beat was supposed to keep me off the streets. *But in a way*, I think, looking around me, *it has.*

Nothing about this feels right. Who really wanted me to go to that shop, and why? Someone angry about the chocolate truck story who wanted to issue me a warning? But then I remember what the hairdresser in Brighton Beach told me about the police hotline where no one spoke Russian. Maybe this was someone's way of offering a piece of knowledge the cops couldn't receive? But what? And most importantly—who was the crook that ripped off the jeweler and framed me?

I'll call Crock when I get out of here, I think, *and find out any details he can tell me about the tipster, even if it's not a name.*

But my mind quickly drifts from that to some other, more pressing calculations. I took my last dose around ten this morning. At this point, it has to be close to three o'clock. Usually, I'd be taking another right now. I tell myself that it's just force of habit that's making my palms itch and my heart skitter like a caged animal. The kid on my left keeps pleading with the cop while on my right, Slim Jim has begun to snore.

Forty-five or so minutes later another cop comes in, an older one with a benign air about him. He distributes rations: one cigarette apiece, which he lights, a can of soda, and a bag of chips. When he gets to me, I take the cigarette and the Coke and wave away the chips. "Give mine to that guy," I say, gesturing to my left. He shrugs and gives the kid both bags of chips.

"I don't smoke." I hear the kid say. "She can have mine."

I smoke the cigarettes, one in each hand. They help a little. Then I go back to tallying each unpleasant sensation now occurring in my body. My head is pounding, and I feel like every drop of liquid in my body has evaporated. The Coke feels like it was hours ago. I start to pace, too edgy to sit.

The door opens again, and in comes Officer Shepherd. I know it's him because he doesn't walk; it's something in between a saunter and a waddle. He stops in front of my cell, beady eyes bright below the hard fluorescent light.

"If it isn't Parker Snow, girl reporter," he sneers. "Heard you were paying us a visit. Thought it only polite for me to stop by and say hello."

"Where's your boyfriend? Out doing your dirty work for you?" My voice sounds like it's scratching its way out of a Saharan sand dune. "Ruining lives in the name of the law?"

He doesn't react; just keeps staring at me with the same smirking look. "I found something that I thought you might be missing," he says, and produces something from his pocket—a small orange pill bottle. The smile on his face has turned positively gleeful. He gives it a shake. The sound of jangling pills kaleidoscopes in my skull like a thousand maracas.

I go to the bench and sit on my hands.

"Baby has to stop herself from making a grab for her candy," he mocks. I'm not looking at him, but I can see it out of the corner of my eye—a glowing orange spot against the stone-gray wall.

The spot gets closer. Shepherd is pushing the bottle through the bars of my cell. "You must be itching something ba-a-a-d."

I turn to look at him. "I'm stopping myself from grabbing you by the collar and putting an imprint of these bars on your ugly fucking face."

Immediately the smirk drops from his face. His meaty hand closes hard around the pill bottle, and I can almost feel the plastic splintering. I know he's picturing my neck. "That's threatening a police officer."

"You're a genius," I say.

He unfurls his fist. The bottle hits the concrete floor with a tiny *plunk*, rolls in an arc, and comes to a stop a few inches away from the bars of my cell. It might as well be a mile.

I turn away. He exchanges a few words with the cop on duty, then leaves. I stare hard at the blank wall of the cell, where I now notice a brownish water stain the approximate size and shape of Mother Teresa, on one of Mother Teresa's bad days. The sounds around me seem to fade—Slim Jim's snoring on one side, the kid's droning pleas to the guard on the other, the drip of a leak that seems to be making its way closer and closer to the inside of my skull. I won't let myself look at the orange pill bottle on the floor, but still, it haloes my vision like a migraine. An orange stain burning and burning and burning.

Sometime later—it could be an hour, could be three—the cop with the gentle demeanor who delivered our rations reenters the cell block. He unlocks my door and tells me I'm free to go.

I pick my stiff limbs up off the floor. I can't tell if I'm shaking or if the room is. "May I ask whose benevolence I have to thank for my liberation?" I croak.

He holds the door open. "Just be glad somebody up there likes you," he says, raising his eyebrows toward the upper floor. "And it ain't our Lord, Jesus Christ."

As he leads me out, I cast a glance back to the kid on my left. He's just as young as I expected, slumped down on the bench with his arms crossed, staring at a spot on the floor.

The cop gingerly picks the orange pill bottle off the floor. "Yours?"

A few minutes later I walk out the swinging precinct doors, the pills I swallowed dry sticking in my throat. The cool evening air might as well be an Alpine forest instead of Midtown Manhattan. I breathe it in deep, and it sends my head swimming. I check my watch—5:17. Five hours behind bars that felt like an eternity.

###

Before I go home, I go downtown to Tower Records and talk the guy working the floor into showing me the CCTV of the afternoon. Anything to help a brother, he says. The video clearly shows the jumpy kid from the precinct holding cell browsing the hip-hop aisle. Time stamp: 1:34 p.m. The employee gives me the tape—they reuse them anyway, he says—and I go back to the precinct to give it to the desk officer, telling him it'll clear the kid locked up for the Upper West Side assault. No sign of Shepherd—probably out on foot post, braying and bashing heads. Then there's nothing else for me to do, so I go home.

I buy two hot dogs at a stand on Fourteenth Street—ketchup, mustard, and onions, no sweet relish—and eat them as I go. I stop in my bodega for a six-pack of Red Stripe. The streets feel emptier than usual, as if everyone has unanimously decided to pack it in for the night. When I open the door to my apartment Nellie is still sitting in the same place she was this morning, looking exactly as she did when I left, except that now the sunlight is gone.

"Nice to know I've been missed," I say. "No, no, don't get up on my account."

I crack open a can of cat food and sprinkle a few pieces of kibble on top. Nellie appears on the countertop like a phantom. *How do you like that*, I think. "How do you like that," I say. I place the dish onto the floor.

Then I sit on the couch and drink a beer, then another one, then another one, while Nellie's quiet crunching drifts in from the kitchen. I feel like I've aged twenty years in the space of a day.

The sound of violin scales floats down through the ceiling. Then they turn into a tune, something lilting and cheerful. Then that falters and stops. At some point Nellie finishes her dinner and returns to the living room, where she sinks into a pocket of shadow next to me on the couch. Street sounds seep in: the Dopplered scream of a siren, the caterwaul of a neighborhood cat. Both of us sit there, silent and watchful, as the last scraps of daylight fade from the sky and darkness steals into the room.

7

No witnesses. No suspects . . .

The next morning, I don't so much wake up as drift to the surface from a strange and shallow dream. I'm still on the couch. I get off of it and put the coffee on, then go into the bathroom and splash a few handfuls of cold water on my face. When I meet my eyes in the mirror, they look strangely shiny, the skin around them too taut.

Schultz's words come floating back to me: *Why do you think those Russians put up with you?* The deal I struck with Sergei—am I just being foolish, putting any kind of trust into a low-rank Russian mobster? Maybe he was the one who didn't like that story I wrote about the chocolate truck, and so he called the paper to set me up.

Or maybe what happened yesterday in the Diamond District is unconnected entirely. Had *Shepherd*—a cop with a reciprocal vendetta against this reporter—had something to do with it? I don't like how he knew I'd been booked and then came down to the holding cell just to fuck with me. Considering his record and his feelings about me, I don't doubt the lengths he'd go to make sure I know who holds the reins.

And finally, the age-old question: Am I just being paranoid?

Nellie slinks between my feet, affectionate as ever before breakfast. I go to the kitchen and dump a can of food into her dish. The air of the apartment is too still, every sound—the dull *thwack* of the can hitting the counter, the metallic twist of the opener, the *squelch* of the cat food around the spoon—digging into my skin. My pills are running low.

The coffee pot hisses. I drink a scalding cup over the stove, staring vaguely out the window, then pour another.

A brash ring slices through the silence. I start and put the cup down on the stove's white surface.

"Parker. I'm glad you're there," says the voice on the other end of the line. Soft. Clear. Quiet. Somehow still audible over the bluster of the newsroom.

"Oh," I say. "It's you. That's just jake, Jake. Calling to check up on me again?"

"Well, it's just that—"

"Because you really need to stop doing that. I told you I'm fine," I say. "Well, sort of. *Fine* is a relative word, isn't it?"

"It's just that I wanted to tell you—"

"Although I could have used a check-in yesterday," I acknowledge, twining the phone cord between my fingers. "Yesterday was a very strange day indeed."

"I'm sure it was. But actually, that's what I wanted to—"

"It started off in the Diamond District," I say. "Continued in a holding cell in Midtown, and ended—"

"There was another murder," he cuts in. "And it sounds just like the Russo case."

The room glazes over. "Where?" I manage. "Who?"

"Chinatown," he says. "Nineteen-year-old Asian female found dead in an entryway on Doyers Street. Looks to be foul play. No witnesses.

No suspects. I heard it on the police radio and tried to call you to let you know, but you didn't pick up. So, I called over to Morgan after. She said she didn't see you at the scene."

Another murder. Another young woman. No witnesses or suspects. And all the while I was locked in a six-by-eight cell in Midtown. An alarm bell has gone off in my cerebellum, making my ears ring.

I hang up and call Morgan at the ME's office.

"Got an ID, at least," she tells me. "Meilin 'Elizabeth' Lau, age nineteen. She still had her wallet on her."

So, it wasn't a mugging. That leaves another possible motive. "Any evidence of sexual assault?" I ask.

"None that I found in my first examination," she replies.

The alarm bell gets louder. "Cause of death?"

"Unclear," Morgan answers. "When I signed the death certificate, I wrote blunt force trauma, pending autopsy. There was an obvious skull fracture."

Then the alarm turns into a siren. Blunt force trauma—just like Carla Russo. "You say there was a skull fracture. So, what was unclear?"

"There wasn't much blood or pronounced bruising. In fact, there wasn't any."

"What do you mean?"

"Imagine," she says. "You get hit in the head with something, let's say a gun, or a brick. Hard enough to cause acute trauma to your brain and kill you."

"I'm imagining," I say with a grimace.

"You're going to get a lot of contusions and bruising in that spot. Oftentimes lacerations, depending on the object. Unless . . ."

"Unless?"

"Unless you get hit *after* you die."

I hold the phone receiver out and look at it, stunned.

"Parker?" comes Morgan's voice. "Are you still there?"

I bring the phone back to my ear. "But why would someone hit a person after they'd died?"

"If I speculated about why people do the things they do, I wouldn't get much work done," Morgan says. "As far as I'm concerned, the real question isn't why—"

"But how," I finish grimly.

"Exactly," Morgan says. "If it wasn't a whack to the head, then how was she actually killed?"

"Any ideas?" I ask.

"Not yet. I'll be doing a full autopsy shortly, after which I'll send tissue samples to toxicology. And you know how they are these days. Black hole. But hopefully I'll get the results back soon enough and they'll reveal something."

I watch a squirrel run across a power line like it's being pursued. "Morgan," I say. "I'm worried."

"Worried the powers that be will tell me to keep the cause of death as blunt force trauma and call it a day?"

"Yes," I answer.

"Me, too," Morgan says. "But I'm going to do my best to find out what actually happened to Elizabeth Lau."

###

Elizabeth Lau. Another young woman's life cut short for no apparent reason. Just like Carla Russo's.

I'm still reeling from the events of the day before, my head buzzing with unanswered questions. But now they've largely been replaced by another, which repeats itself in my mind like the ticking of a clock: *Why? Why? Why?* While Morgan is working on the *how*, I'm going to do my best to find out the answer.

I take the J train out to Chinatown, swallowing two pills on my way. By the time I arrive, I feel my head floating away from my feet, and in this disembodied way I fight my way through the crowds on Canal, souvenir shops full of bamboo plants and red string ornaments and those eternally waving porcelain cats, and then turn onto Mott Street, marked by a red-and-yellow pagoda with its spire reaching up toward the sky. The briny, otherworldly odor of seafood hits my nostrils as I pass the seafood market on the corner, bedecked with trays of fish and shrimp and scallops and squid on ice, white buckets of crabs on the ground. Their claws are rubber-banded together, except for some that have come free. They pinch at the naked air like they're trying to escape from a dream, crawling over each other only to be buried again.

I turn onto Pell and follow it to the crooked knee of Doyers, a curving slip of a street that all but disappears into the twisted knot of Chinatown. Though in fact it's a storied location to be found dead—I've heard they used to call it "murder alley" for all the Chinese gang warfare that took place here at the beginning of the century. A few doors down from the Nam Wah Tea Parlor, with its hand-painted yellow-on-red sign, between two tenement apartments, a few shreds of yellow caution tape flutter in the breeze in front of a doorframe. And that's all that marks the death of a nineteen-year-old Asian female.

There's a beat cop standing in front of it, shifting his weight and looking bored. They usually put one on the scene after someone's been killed because useful people tend to drift back in the days that follow—the curious, the knowledgeable, the grieving. The guilty.

I'm about to approach him to ask if he's had any action so far that day when someone else emerges from the other side, where Doyers connects with Bowery. He's a young Chinese guy, maybe eighteen, wearing dog tag necklaces over a white New York Dolls t-shirt with the sleeves cut off to reveal tanned arms, ropy with muscle. One is wrapped around a bunch of two-by-fours that rest on his shoulder. A long, mottled scar runs diagonally down one side of his face. He looks over at the cop, hesitates, then looks over at me.

We lock eyes.

Suddenly and swiftly, he turns around and begins walking back the way he came.

"Hey," I call out. He doesn't look back. "Hey!" I call again. He's retreating quickly.

The beat cop looks nonplussed as I dash past. I can tell we're both thinking the same thing: *What the hell?* Who is this kid, and why the abrupt about-face when he saw me and the law on the scene?

He must know something. Or maybe he did something.

As I start toward him my path is quickly marred by a stooped old woman wearing a plaid jacket and bright blue sneakers pushing a granny cart. I do a little soft shoe to get past her just as the guy is crossing Mott. I nearly get knocked flat by a silver sedan zooming around a blue tourist bus, but I regain my pace and start to close the gap between us.

I scurry up and tap him on the shoulder as he's walking briskly down the sidewalk. He stops and turns so fast I have to duck to avoid getting nailed by the end of the two-by-fours.

"Listen," I say, hands up. "I'm not a cop. I'm a reporter for *The New York Street* and I just want to talk to you for a minute. Please."

He gives me a hostile glance, still saying nothing.

I take my cigarettes from my coat and light one hopefully. "Smoke?" I offer.

He stares at the cigarette hard for a moment, a frown knitting his features. Then he dumps his load of lumber on the sidewalk, where it lands with a clatter.

"Ah, fuck it." He takes the proffered cigarette and leans against the wall, drawing a satisfied drag.

He notices me taking him in and raises an eyebrow. "How does it feel? Buzzing around murder scenes like a vulture?"

I raise an eyebrow right back. "I could ask you the same question."

A whisper of a smile drags up one side of his scowl. "You win."

"Did you know Elizabeth Lau?"

The smile disappears. "She was my friend."

"How'd you know she died?"

He shrugs and exhales a plume of smoke. "Word spreads fast around here." Then he turns to look at me with narrowed eyes. "Am I on the record? That's what you call it, right?"

"That is what you call it," I say. "But I'm just trying to get some information on background. I won't quote you if you don't want me to."

He nods but he doesn't look convinced. He's absently rubbing a black-and-tan rabbit's foot that's clipped to his belt loop, as if his thoughts were several steps ahead. Somewhere I wish I could see.

"What's your name, anyway?" I ask. Then repeat, "On background."

He releases the rabbit's foot. "You can call me Leon."

"Nice to meet you, Leon. I'm Parker. So, word spreads fast. You make it sound like an incident like this isn't so unusual."

Just then a clique of young men in their late teens or early twenties passes by, all wearing leather jackets and cuffed jeans like they've walked off the set of a fifties sitcom. One of them says something with the force of an epithet, then hocks through his nose and ejects a phlegmy ball of spit on the sidewalk at Leon's feet. I watch their retreating backs as they continue down the block, still talking loudly as if nothing had happened.

Leon watches for a moment, too, then turns back to me and says drily, "That means *fag* in Cantonese. In case you wanted a language lesson."

"Friends of yours?"

"Flying Dragons."

I look at him questioningly. He smirks. "You're a reporter. You've never heard of the Flying Dragons?"

"Can't say I've had the pleasure." *Too busy working on murder cases, when I'm supposed to be on organized crime*, is my next involuntary thought. Crock's words echo in my mind: *That's not your beat anymore.* I smoke them out with another draw from my Lucky Strike.

"Street muscle for the Hip Sing Tong, one of our local *fraternal organizations*. Rivals of the Ghost Shadows, who are muscle for the On Leong," he says. "The Flying Dragons are the reason I have this." He gestures to the scar running from cheekbone to chin. "They tried to recruit me back in middle school. I think they wanted more American-born guys to talk on the phone without an accent, help them do deals. One guy works you over, while another guy tells you how good you'll have it if you just join up. All the money you want. You can hang out and play video games all day. You can get any pretty girl you like. The rest of them just watch." He runs his thumb down the rabbit's foot at his hip again, his face dark. "Still, I refused. That really steamed them up. So, one day, they came at me with a knife instead of fists. I was just lucky the science teacher happened to come by, or they probably would have done a lot worse than this." He looks down gloomily at the pile of lumber at his feet. "I hate this neighborhood."

A delivery man on a green bicycle zooms by, his basket laden with plastic take-out bags printed with crude, yellow smiling faces.

"So, why doesn't anyone ask for help?" I ask.

"You ever seen a cop speak Chinese? They can't even keep track of our names," he scoffs. "Not to mention, we have a saying that translates to something like: 'No good Chinese person joins the army or the police.' Nah. We prefer to solve our problems ourselves, our own way."

I think back to my walk down Brighton Beach Avenue, all the tight-lipped shop owners who were either too scared or too stubborn or too embarrassed to talk about the *krysha* they were paying out to petty Russian mobsters.

"It's not true, by the way. I'm not a fag," he says abruptly, looking up at me. "Not that it matters."

"You and Liz," I begin.

"Not like that," he says.

"But you were close."

He nods. "We're the same age. We were always friends, even when we weren't. It's hard to explain. We were both quiet, sort of outcasts. We felt . . . different," he says. "I think we recognized that in each other. Plus, our dads worked together. They knew each other from the village back home. Mine got here first and got hers a job at one of the laundries. Back in China, a man wouldn't be caught dead doing laundry. Something my dad likes to frequently bring up."

"Do you think Liz could have gotten involved with the wrong crowd? Or that the Flying Dragons could have used Liz to get to you?"

He shakes his head. "Liz wasn't with the Dragons or anyone else, believe me. And I don't think their grudge against me goes that deep."

I think for a minute. "It sounds like you know her family pretty well. Can you take me to see them?"

He shrugs. "Sure. It's not exactly out of the way. They're over on Elizabeth Street—that's how Liz got her American name. They probably won't want to talk to you, though."

"Maybe not," I say. "But it's worth a shot."

I follow Leon back onto the clamor of Mott Street, then to Elizabeth via Bayard. Past the alleyway leading to Bowery and next to an antiques and jade shop, he opens a heavy steel door, its green paint peeling. I follow him up dingy flights of stairs that reek of old fry oil, peppers, and the remains of a million meals. The clanging of pots and pans and the pointy clatter of conversation emanate from the shut doors. Despite the fact that the day outside is cool, inside it's sweltering—the old damnation of the New York City heating system.

After three flights he stops at one of the doors and knocks. It opens a crack. He says something in Chinese, and the door opens a little wider. A small woman in a knee-length white skirt and a light blue top is standing there. Her face has few wrinkles but looks irreparably exhausted in a way sleep can't touch. She lets us in without looking at me.

The apartment consists of one room with a small alcove kitchen. There's an industrial sink stuck into the crumbling tile; the rest of the counter space is taken up by a metal dish rack. Clothes dry on hangers next to the pans, strainers, and cooking implements hanging by hooks from the ceiling. At a small table, a man sits in a worn but pressed button-down, reading a Chinese newspaper and smoking, a cup of tea and a thermos next to him. He doesn't look at us.

"Shoes," Leon instructs, removing his at the threshold. I follow suit. My dirty black boots stand out like a pair of goths at a cotillion.

"My name is Parker Snow," I tell Liz's mother. "I'm a reporter for *The New York Street*. I'm trying to learn more about your daughter, so I can help find out what happened." Then I add, "I'm very sorry for your loss."

Leon translates for me. The woman says something to Leon, and Leon back to her.

"She thinks it's strange that you're here," he murmurs to me. "They're not used to having *low faan*. White barbarians. She thinks you're a cop or a tax lady."

"So, what'd you tell her?"

"I said that you were with the paper but that you wouldn't use her name. Honestly, I think she's still in shock."

Leon says something else to her, then gestures at me to follow him as he walks toward the back of the apartment. Part of it is sectioned off by a screen. "Liz and her sister sleep here," he says, then amends, "slept here."

Her sister. I feel a pang spasm through my chest. "Older or younger?"

"Older. Four years."

"Where is she now?"

"School, I guess. Or work. She's studying at Hunter, and she also works part-time at a Buddhist temple off East Broadway."

I take in Liz's things. There aren't many—a couple of plastic hair clips and scrunchies, a glittery star-shaped key chain, some schoolbooks, a few cheap novels and glossy magazines, the perfume samples torn out and emanating a sweet, artificial smell. The things any teenage girl would have.

And one notebook. I pick it up. It's a small, cheap, spiral number with a purple plastic cover, the kind of thing you get at the drugstore for a dollar. I flip open the cover and blink with surprise. Each page is veritably covered with blue ballpoint. There are paragraphs of writing, angry and fluid, all the entries undated. The margins are crammed with drawings—doodles, really—but there's something unsettling about them. One seems to depict a tree on a sidewalk. Looking closer, I see it: Within the tree's branches is a face, its mouth twisted into a scream. On one page there's just a circle, but the circle has been outlined and outlined so many times that the pen has ripped through the page, like it's a hole that you could fall right into.

While Leon is saying something to Liz's mom, I slip the notebook into the inside of my coat.

I step out from behind the screen and back into the living area. "Could I ask them a few questions?" I ask Leon, gesturing to Liz's mother and father.

But before he can translate, her father bursts out of his chair, his face contorted into a mask of anger. He's yelling words I don't understand, looking both at me and through me. Then he slumps down onto the chair and puts his face in his hands, gnarled and scarred as old tree roots.

"I'm sorry," I say. I take a step back and glance at Leon.

Liz's mother says something quietly to her husband, then she and Leon exchange a few words. I follow him toward the door and my shoes, glancing back at the kitchen before I leave. Liz's father is still slumped at the table, her mother standing next to it, neither of them looking at each other but deep inside, at their own private miseries.

It's a relief to be out on the sidewalk on Elizabeth Street and its unreserved clamor after that apartment, dense with silences, with despair.

I let out a long breath. "I'm sorry I had to go and upset them like that. What was her dad saying?"

"Her dad said they made a mistake, having their daughter here. He said that this country is cursed," says Leon. He shakes his head. "Man. It's weird seeing him like that. I never saw the guy show one ounce of emotion. They didn't talk much. That's why Liz's Cantonese was so shitty. But none of us really do. Our moms feed us, our dads work, and we get good grades. Confucius says." He laughs joylessly. "That probably seems weird to you. Families not talking."

"It doesn't seem weird," I say. I look up at the apartment building. It feels a world apart from Bensonhurst instead of just a borough. "By the way—do you know if Liz had a friend named Carla?"

His brow furrows. "Carla? Doesn't sound familiar. Someone who went to Seward High?"

"No," I say. "Never mind."

"Like I said, Liz didn't have a lot of friends," he says. "Actually, she sometimes said that you should never tell anybody anything, because then you'll start missing everybody."

"Big Salinger fan?"

"Is that from a book?"

"Yeah," I say. "Sure is."

As if remembering something, he puts his hand in his back pocket and pulls out a money clip, similar to mine. He extracts a Polaroid and hands it to me. "That's her, by the way. That's Liz."

I take the photo. A girl is standing in front of an arcade game, twisting toward the camera as if someone has just said her name. Her dark eyes are intent, a slash of bright orange lipstick on her unsmiling mouth.

I try handing it back, but Leon waves it away. "You can keep it. I have more."

I clip it carefully into my notebook. There's something about the photo that tells me more about Liz than anything else has so far.

Something occurs to me. "One last question. Why did you show up on Doyers Street this morning?" I ask. "It seemed like maybe you were thinking about talking to that cop before I scared you off."

He considers that for a minute, grinding his heel against the pavement. "You know what I said about us solving our problems our own way? Most of the time, nothing gets solved. I can't say if I'll ever get out of this place. But at least I don't have to become this place." He toys with the rabbit's foot, then blurts out: "You can quote me. If you want. Just say I'm a friend of hers."

"Thanks, Leon. For everything."

He shrugs and puts his hands in his pockets.

"Where'd you say Liz's sister works?" I ask.

"At the Sung Tak Buddhist Temple on Pike Street," he says.

"Would she be there now?"

"Probably. I think she's there most afternoons. Her name's Yan. She looks . . . well, she looks a lot like Liz."

8

Snow White in mourning . . .

A giant white Buddha smiles down at me from the Sun Tak Buddhist Temple, peace fingers raised. He looks like he knows a lot of things I don't. The Buddha is set on a balcony a floor above street level, accessible via two sets of stone stairs carved into the building, below which is a sign painted with Chinese characters and the English words EASTERN BOOKS. I walk up one of the flights and pull open a heavy red door.

Empty rows of padded benches for kneeling face another Buddha statue at the head of the room, this one gold, which genuflects underneath a Chinese scroll. To the right of this area is a small gift shop with Buddha statuettes, books, candles, jewelry, and other items. Standing behind the counter is a woman in a light pink button-down, hair cut to a sensible shoulder length, who bears a striking resemblance to the photo of Liz.

"Pardon me," I say as I approach. "Are you Yan?"

She looks up at me from the bracelets she's arranging on a display stand. "That's me," she says. "Can I help you?"

I take out my press badge. "My name is Parker Snow. I'm a reporter for *The New York Street*. I was wondering if I could ask you a few questions about your sister, Liz."

"Why would you come here?" she says, outrage quaking her voice. "This is supposed to be a place of peace and contemplation."

"I'm sorry," I say. "Your friend Leon said I could find you here. He was just trying to help."

She hesitates and I seize my moment. "I'll just wait outside," I tell her. "If you get a break."

She shakes her head quickly, her eyes now shined over with tears. "I don't have breaks," she says. "Please go. I can't—I can't talk about this right now."

I look over the goods displayed on the counter. "How much are these?" I ask, gesturing toward the bracelets.

The pain in her face is replaced with surprise. "Ten dollars."

I pick one up at random, jade green with a gold disk charm engraved with a Chinese character. I take out my billfold and, as if by a miracle, find two fives wedged into the bottom. "I could use some peace and contemplation."

She takes the money I'm handing her and puts it in the register. I start for the exit.

"Take this one."

I turn back to see Yan removing a pale pink beaded bracelet from the rack. "It's Guan Yin. Goddess of mercy."

I hand her the green bracelet, slip the pink one over my wrist, and leave.

It feels disrespectful to smoke in front of the Buddha, so instead I just sit on the steps and hum, twirling the bracelet around my wrist. I think about everything Leon told me, about his father working with Liz and Yan's father in the laundromat, about the Flying Dragons, the tongs, the rival gangs, and everything I don't know about Chinatown. I notice Stars of David set into the Moorish arches of the temple. That's New York for you. Everything always becoming something else.

A quarter hour later, Yan sits down on the steps beside me.

"You got a break," I say.

She eyes the bracelet around my wrist, saying nothing.

"Worked here long?" I ask.

"A few years," she says.

"Like it?"

She shrugs. "It's not about liking it," she says. "I just feel better when I'm here than anywhere else."

I nod. "I'll be straight with you. I'm hoping to write an article about your sister. I just spoke to Leon, and briefly to your parents. But sisters often know things that others don't."

Her next question surprises me. "Is this something people care about? I mean, enough to write about in the newspaper?"

We'll see, I think. I want to tell her about Carla, to let her know that her sister may not be alone. But it's premature. I don't want to make a connection I can't yet back up. "It helps to share some personal details about the victim," I explain. "People care more when they feel like they know them."

Yan looks out at the street. "I don't really know what to say. Liz was a hard person to get close to."

"In what way?"

"I loved her, of course, but I always felt sort of awkward around her, even though I'm older. Like I wasn't sure what to say, how to reach her." She pauses. "Don't write this or anything, but I was always sort of jealous of her."

"Why is that?"

She shrugs. "She was born here. She lived with our parents her whole life. They had to leave me in China with my grandparents when they emigrated. It wasn't until I was six that they got this lady from the village who was coming here to join her family to bring me along," she says. "So, I get here, and there's this baby in the apartment. They didn't even bother telling me about her." She gives a short, wry laugh.

A chorus of honking starts on Pike Street, passing from car to car like a game of telephone. I feel there's more she wants to say, and I'm going to be quiet and let her.

"I always cared so much about what my parents thought. Liz, though, she always had this . . . this freedom about her," Yan says, a smile blooming on her face. "When we were kids, my mom had us go to this art class at the community center by Columbus Park. They'd put out a vase of carnations and tell us to draw them. There I'd be, you know, sweating bullets, trying to replicate them as perfectly as possible. And at the end of the class, Liz's paper would have a bunch of faces staring at you from their stems, crazy faces with crazy looks. And she'd just be sitting there, this tiny girl with this dead-serious expression on her face, not saying a word. The teacher didn't know what to say, either." She shakes her head with a mixture of dismay and admiration. "I don't know where she got this stuff. She wanted to be an artist, but my parents always discouraged it. Not practical enough."

That brings my mind back to the picture of the tree with the screaming face I saw in Liz's notebook—the one in my coat pocket now. I silently remind myself to make sure Yan gets the notebook back.

Yan interprets my silence as boredom. "Sorry. I don't know why I'm going on like this. I guess I wanted to talk after all," she says.

"Not at all. I'm glad you feel like talking," I say, then take a quick breath. "Speaking of which. I'm guessing you've spoken to the police?"

Her smile drops. "Yeah. They came here to look for me. As soon as they showed up, I just knew. It was . . . it was awful." She looks at me. "They seemed to think it was just some random thug who did it."

"Do you?"

"I guess it would have to be. I can't think of anyone else who would do this to Liz. She didn't have any enemies. Mostly kept to herself."

"That's what Leon said."

Yan nods and glances up at the towering Buddha. The pedestal from which he beams is piled high with flowers and mandarins. "You asked if I like my job. Our parents didn't have any religion back in China. So, it wasn't a thing we were raised with. But then I found this temple, or more like, it found me. We had a service late last night for Liz, to chant sutras and help ease her soul into its next life. My parents didn't even come." She contemplates the statue sadly. "I wish they had, even if they don't believe."

I thank Yan for her time, and the bracelet, and walk down the steps back onto Pike.

I walk along East Broadway under the Manhattan Bridge, the one I see each day from my kitchen window, listening to the train rattle above me. I deliberately avoid walking past the clinic where I spent so much time reporting on my last street-crime story, even though it makes my route longer and a thin rain has started to fall. Drops mosaic the dirty, gum-stained sidewalk.

I think of a young woman's body going into the black OCME bag to be taken to the morgue, rain spattering the outside as it's loaded into the van, the one that the cops sometimes call the *meat wagon* when they're feeling particularly lyric. I think about the crabs outside the seafood market, their wet, rust-red bodies moving blindly in the white bucket in a slow, continuous struggle to get out. As if they would meet something better if they did.

###

"How are you feeling?" the doctor asks. "Any new symptoms?"

I'm back in Bensonhurst again, at the doctor's office with the worn treatment table where no one is ever treated, the last of the evening light filtering through the dusty blinds. Not a detour I wanted to take, but I didn't have a choice. Not really.

"About the same," I say. Always about the same.

I'm relieved to see that he's already writing out my prescription. I take it gratefully and stand up to leave. But then I feel myself pause on the threshold of the exam room, trading the paper between my hands.

"How's business?" I ask. It's an absurd question, maybe even a perverse one, and yet I have to know. Because if he's not going to continue doling out these particular services, I'll need to find someone else who will. "I happened to walk by the other day, and you didn't seem to be open."

He takes his time to answer, his drawn face waxy underneath the filmy fluorescent light. The moment sits heavy in that bleak examination room, small and airless and stale, along with the other thing that ties us, even more than these visits: the secret we share, and the shame. The reason he's here pushing pills and the reason I'm here getting them.

"It's fine," he says finally. "I do a bit of moonlighting."

I nod. "Well. Goodnight."

He doesn't offer to see me out. He just sits there and waits, staring at the file in which he wrote nothing down, for his next patient.

I pause on my way out the door and look back. The waiting room is empty save for a couple of hapless souls occupying the worn blue chairs, awaiting their turn with The Good Doctor. Why is it that I remember seeing someone here recently—someone I knew?

But none of the worn faces look familiar. It must just be the aftermath of the pills again, hazing up what was, shuffling the memories like playing cards and making them reappear in the wrong places.

I go to the pharmacy next door to fill my prescription. It's one of those places that only sells old, decrepit things that no one would ever want to buy: yellowing cervical collars, brittle orthopedics in decades-old packaging, scoliosis braces that look like torture devices. You'd wonder how it stayed in business if you didn't know better.

###

On the way home I visit Sunny's bodega for cigarettes and buy a sandwich for Geronimo. His favorite: bologna, American, pickles, mustard, and black pepper on rye, lightly toasted.

"Geronimo," I say, tossing it his way. "Do you believe that you should never tell anyone anything, because if you do, you'll start to miss everybody?"

He turns a few times, sandwich in hand, ruminating. Then he says, "I don't, I don't, I don't know Parker. Way I s-s-see it, better to miss them than not tell them at all."

When I get back to my apartment, I don't feel hungry so much as recognize that I should be. My cup of coffee is still sitting on the stove where I left it, now ice-cold. Still wearing my coat, I peel the orange that's languishing on the countertop and eat it without tasting, pulling the shreds of membrane from my mouth with mounting disgust before throwing the whole thing in the trash. In the back of the cabinet, I find a stale box of stoned wheat crackers. "Stoned wheat," I say. "Ha, ha." I eat five, dry as bones, and, for dessert, one Mallomar that I can't recall ever having bought. I could turn my attention to the organized crime groups in Chinatown that Leon told me about—that would be on my beat, at least—but all I can think about is the dead, their agelessness. Black hair and porcelain skin. Snow White in mourning with orange lipstick on her mouth.

I think about what Yan said—that she never quite knew how to reach her younger sister. The part she didn't say and didn't have to: That now it's too late. I think about how much you can know someone, in ineffable, unspoken ways, a look or a gesture or the weight that you both carry. And yet there are folded-up corners, parts of themselves they hide so well because, really, it's you who doesn't want to see.

I get Nellie's food into her dish and start to take off my coat when I feel Liz's notebook in my pocket. I open the kitchen window and climb out onto the fire escape. The neighborhood is settling into night, apartment windows announcing themselves like portals in the dark. An ambulance's lights wash red against the dirty white brick of the building next door. Someone screams somewhere, whether in terror or delight, it's impossible to say. A trash truck clatters and bleats its chalky wail.

I sit and smoke one slow cigarette after another, reading Liz's journal until the night lightens imperceptibly and faces appear in the windows of subway cars coming over the bridge. Another day beginning. And now her face is with me, too.

###

Money. That's all I ever hear about. Day and night, when I get up and when I go to bed, over breakfast and lunch and dinner. I've heard Chinatown has something like 33 banks, all for our tiny little urban province, similar in size and significance to a grain of rice. Everyone here is always saving. To buy anything that's not an absolute necessity is seen as an extravagance. A large bag of rice: $7. A package of tofu: $4. Vegetables for the week from Mr. Kong on Mott Street: $17, unless he decides to gouge you, in which case, $19. Rent on our shitty tenement apartment: $850/mo, which includes water, but which does not include electricity—which, if you're careful, can come to less than $30/mo. The number of times I heard it: Meilin, turn off the lights! Meilin, why are the lights still on so late? For our parents, going to bed is a matter of frugality. If you're not working, you might as well be sleeping. A little cooking and cleaning fills the hours in between. Everyone thinks that once they've saved enough to open a souvenir shop or a laundromat or a restaurant, they'll have made it. All their toil will have been worth it.

But the fact is, no one really gets out of Chinatown.

I hate the way the toilet runs, I hate the landlords, I hate the endless winter. I look outside and think, This again? Barren trees, gray buildings, gray concrete. I look down at my hands, so scaly and red, and think, whose hands are these? I feel like one of the dried octopus at the Thai grocery store on Bayard, the ones with their suckers all shriveled up. Blech!

And the rats! God help you if you find yourself walking on Pell Street late at night. You'd think it was the goddamn Middle Ages. I hate these cramped old tenements, the way we've accepted that it's okay to live like this—men sleeping ten to a room in putrid gong si fong, the bachelors apartments, little brown roaches running around every drawer and cabinet.

Everyone here is fleeing something, often something terrible. But they all act like none of it ever happened. The hunger, the torture. Yan said that our Yeh Yeh was imprisoned back in the '30s for speaking ill about his boss. Then dad was imprisoned for refusing to speak ill about his boss. The irony. All they gave him to eat in prison were corncobs, and when he got pneumonia and almost died, he had a vision of the spirit leaving his body as he sat there in a cold, dank cell by some mountain in Guangdong. He said it was the image of my mom that got him through it. Imagine that.

The American teachers at Seward Park don't get it at all. To them, this is a free country. Can't we get it through our minds?

No, apparently, we can't. And so, silence persists.

I was always the quiet one in the corner that nobody paid attention to. Of course, in a school full of Chinese kids, there are lots of quiet ones. For some, it's because they don't speak any English. They just stare, wide-eyed, like they've been stranded on some bizarre outer planet with no idea how they got here. It's only a matter of time before the bad kids get to them—the ones that slick their hair back and roll up their jeans like they're on Happy Days. The Flying Dragons. The Ghost Shadows. They prey on kids like that. The ones who will do anything to feel like they belong somewhere, for a moment of escape in a back room with some skunky weed and some sketchy pills. Even if they don't know they want it yet. Especially if they don't know it yet.

I've been to those rooms. So smoky and stuffy your hair carries the stink of it for days. The TV always playing kung fu movies. Tapes and VCR stolen from some guy on the corner of forty-deuce, the one who looks like he's still being shot at in Vietnam. What's the point of trying to buy it? You'll never be able to, and anyways, anything you want is yours if you can get your hands on it and run faster and look scarier than whoever's selling.

That's the other kind of silence. Not because we don't have anything to say, but because we fear what would happen if we were to open our mouths.

There's that expression, Time heals all wounds. Well, for me, for us, time hasn't healed shit. It's made the wounds darker and wider and deeper, so that every day they're harder to seal up. And you figure, if there's no way to climb out of all this, you might as well see what it's like in the sewers and tunnels and darkness—the darkness we never truly get out here with these constant city lights. One time, Leon showed me a photo he took for his photography class, of the Manhattan Bridge at night from his fire escape. I never really saw it before then—how even at night, the city is filled with so much light.

So, you go down, and down, and down. Part of you is ashamed of what you find there. And part of you knows that this was you, the real you, all along.

9

A little bit of insurance . . .

The next day I wake up with Liz's words rolling around in my head. The darkness she wrote about feels like it's overtaken me. I pull my stiff limbs out of bed one by one and get ready, my clothes feeling like someone else's. Even the coffee tastes like ash.

I take the bracelet her sister, Yan, chose for me off my wrist and roll the cool glass beads in my palms. Liz Lau: a perhaps troubled, but not troublesome, young woman. Someone who felt the stifling boundaries of her neighborhood, who kept to herself and absorbed the pain around her. Just like Carla.

Then I can't help it. I go to the oven and open the door. I pull the paper out and look at it: the front-page photo that sends me to hell and back every time I see it. And yet I can't throw it away.

I think about what Geronimo said yesterday. *Better to miss them than not tell them at all.*

I pick up the phone and call Jake.

"It's me," I say when he answers.

"Oh, hi, Parker," he says. "What's up?"

"Just sitting here in my own truth and dread."

"I won't tell you where the place is," he quotes. "I already know who wants to buy it, sell it, make it disappear."

"Adrienne Rich," I say, surprised.

"I read, too, you know."

I smile. "I was just wondering," I say, my eyes still on the paper in my hands, "where do they put reporters past their prime?"

"PR agencies, I think."

"How do I join one of those?"

"I don't know, but I'm pretty sure you'd hate it."

"Probably."

"You're still thinking about it, aren't you," he says after a pause. "What happened at the clinic last year."

I look at the front-page photo for a moment longer, at the image that's been so hard to remove from my mind. "You know, the baby has become a literal poster child in a way I never intended."

"I know," he says. "But what can you do? When you write something and put it in the world, it's no longer in your hands."

"So, how do you know when you're actually helping, or when you're doing nothing?" I say. "Or when you're actually doing the opposite?"

He pauses for a moment, in that thoughtful way of his. "I guess you never know."

That's what I like about Jake. He never says something phony just to make you feel better.

I fold up the paper, open the oven door, and place it gently back inside.

"Thanks for calling yesterday to tell me about the Elizabeth Lau homicide," I say. "And sorry I cut you off. I was anxious to call Morgan and get down to the scene."

"That's okay," he says. "I figured I'd hear from you eventually. So, how'd it go? What'd you find out?"

I fill him in on my time in Chinatown, my run-in with Liz's friend Leon, our trip to her apartment, and my visit to the Buddhist temple where I met her sister.

"Basically, Elizabeth—Liz—was someone who didn't feel like she fit in, but didn't have any real enemies," I conclude. "She wasn't really happy with life in Chinatown, but she didn't try to escape it by running with the bad crowd. Her friend made that very clear." I pause. "It's strange."

"What is?"

"She was just left there on the street in her own neighborhood, with blunt force trauma to her head, and no one seems to have seen anything," I say. "Just like with Carla Russo."

"Is there any connection between them?"

"No," I admit. "It doesn't seem like they knew each other."

"So, maybe they really were just at the wrong place at the wrong time," he says. "Ran into a crazy or a perp out on parole and things got ugly. It happens in this city."

I sigh. "You're probably right." There's part of me that wants to believe it—that these two deaths are random, unrelated, and not part of some larger, looming threat.

Except . . . what if they're not? What if Liz and Carla are both victims of the same malevolent hand, like there are sure to be others? Maybe even now—a young woman walking in the streetlights of her gloom, unaware of the evil lurking at the next corner, intent on snatching her away from the life she's still trying to understand.

Jake speaks again, as if reading my thoughts in the silence. "But you don't believe it." He says it as a statement, not a question.

"No," I say. "I don't. The MO just feels too similar. And the fact that they *didn't* know each other almost unnerves me more."

"So, talk to Maloney. See if you can make him see it."

"Do you think I . . ." I trail off. My eyes are drifting back to the oven door, the one that contains the written proof of my deficiencies.

"I know you can," Jake says. "And anyways, what choice do you have? It's you. You're going to try to figure it out regardless."

He's right, of course.

We say goodbye. I slip the bracelet back on and leave.

###

I arrive at the Detective Bureau to find Maloney's door ajar, the man himself at his desk buried in a pile of paper a foot deep.

He looks up when I walk in. "What are you doing here?"

"Don't look so happy to see me. You'll break your face." I pull back one of the wooden chairs on the other side of the desk and sit down. "Two days ago, the body of Elizabeth Lau, nineteen years old, was found on Doyers Street in Chinatown. Blunt force trauma to the head. No witnesses or suspects. The circumstances are too similar to the Carla Russo case to be a coincidence."

"Thanks for the information," he says. "Did you think about reporting it to the police?"

"Just think about it for a minute," I continue, ignoring his sarcasm. "Young women around the same age, killed with what appears to be the same method. No evidence of sexual assault or any other obvious motive. No apparent connection between the two victims." When he says nothing, I press, "Come on. You have to see it."

He throws the file down on the desk and looks at me, his blue eyes wide with exasperation. "I've got twelve cases on my hands. Twelve. I have a pile of DD5s tall enough to circle the island. Twice. I don't have time to have you waltzing in here and telling me what I *have to see*. And anyways," he adds. "I thought you were supposed to be on organized crime."

I ignore that and lean forward, trying to seize his gaze. "Maloney, I think we have a serial killer on our hands."

"Listen, Parker, we don't have anything on *our* hands—"

I get up, my chair scraping across the tile, and start to pace.

"Rufus Domingo," I begin. "The cat-burglar killer. He scaled fire escapes, opened unlocked windows, then raped and murdered the inhabitants. Specialized in single women, any age would do."

Maloney opens his mouth to cut in. But now I'm on a roll.

"Julian Gates," I continue. "The post office perp. Learned about his victims through their mail and his daily stops to their homes. Had a particular affinity for married women of advancing years. It was his own wife, when her suspicions got too strong to ignore, who gave him up."

I look at the crime pattern bulletin board, its cluster of red pins, thinking. Then I turn back swiftly to face him.

"Frank Thorwald. The prostitute killer. Murdered sixteen women over the span of ten years until he was finally apprehended. Parking ticket. The cop who wrote it up noticed a foul smell coming from the trunk of his car."

"And that's what you get for not reading the signs," Maloney says. "Whatever it is that you're covering or not covering, you need to learn to stay on the right side of the crimes. You write about them. We solve them."

"You're not going to solve anything until you see the connection," I exclaim. "When you don't have a description and a composite on every precinct desk, it's like the thing never even happened. You guys don't talk to each other. A mugger in the Fifth can walk around scot-free in the Seventh before sticking up an old lady in front of a beat cop on his meal break in the Third."

"You watch it," he growls.

"I'm tired of watching," I say. "Watching is what you do when you've given up on finding the truth."

That hangs there for a long, tense moment. Then Maloney sighs, puts down the pen, and says, "You have five—you have *three* minutes."

I sit back down.

"It feels like the same perpetrator," I say. "The fact that no one's even gotten a look at the guy in either case is a problem. It means that he's good. Really good. Not just that—Morgan told me that Liz Lau was hit on the head post-mortem. Why would someone do that if this were just your average mugging?"

"If you want to have a little coffee klatch with the medical examiner, that's your business and I can't stop you," he says. "But your theories don't suffice as evidence. We've combed both scenes and there just isn't anything to work off of. Clean as a whistle."

"But isn't that how the best ones work?" I say. "They lure their victims away and do their dirty work elsewhere."

"They don't usually dump them back in their own neighborhoods," he replies.

I pause and think about that. "So, he killed them at the scene. He would have had to get close to them. They had to trust him, for some reason." I remember Morgan's words from the other day. "He must have left *something*. Every crime leaves a trace."

"Like I said, nothing that we've been able to find," he says. "Most likely they were just what they look like—muggings gone wrong."

"What about Liz Lau? She still had her wallet on her," I shoot back.

"She also had track marks up and down her arms."

Now I'm the one to be stunned into silence.

"She was an addict," Maloney continues. "When the tox screen comes back, we'll probably see that she had a fatal dose of heroin in her system."

I try to put this together with what Morgan said about examining Liz: That she had a fractured skull, though not the bruising usually associated with head trauma. She was trying to square it. Why wouldn't she mention that Liz did heroin? Why hadn't Leon, her friend, or Yan, her sister? Was it possible that Liz could have hidden it? And is it me, or is Maloney looking at me a little too closely?

I try to collect myself and think like Morgan, cool and clinical. "What about the head wound?"

"So, she nodded off. She fell. Hit her head. Happens all the time."

"And in the meantime, you'll just sit back," I say. "Chalk another one up to thugs and drugs."

He waits for what feels like a long time before answering. "You know as well as I do that most of those drug-related cases never get solved." Then, out of nowhere, he adds, "How is it that you just happened to be in Bensonhurst the night of Carla Russo's death?" His look has suddenly gone shrewd and sharp, the way only a detective's can, when you suddenly feel all the acuity behind the world-weary act. I don't like it.

"I had an appointment," I say simply.

"An appointment," he says. "Uh-huh." He takes a moment to study me, not saying anything. I know this trick. The one with the silence. But I won't give in.

Eventually he caves. "You didn't think it was worth mentioning it when you barged into my office the next morning?"

"It didn't seem relevant," I reply, a tad archly. Maloney doesn't know about my pill habit, and I'd like to keep it that way. God knows he thinks I'm unreliable enough already.

I hasten back to the subject at hand. "In most random acts of violence, the perp is usually too dumb to get away. Two such murders in the span of one week should raise serious red flags."

"Two is a coincidence," he says. "Three is a pattern."

The blood thrums hot in my veins. "So, that means you're going to sit back and wait for another woman to die to establish your *pattern*?"

He signs his name on the bottom of the form in front of him, closes the folder, and throws it onto the pile on his right, then picks up the next one from the pile on his left. He looks up at me wearily. "If you wanted to be a detective, Parker, you should've become a cop."

###

It would be a beautiful day in Tompkins Square Park if it weren't so filled with drugs and rage. The park has been the site of protests for all of its history, many of them violent, from the Civil War Draft Riots to the bloodbath that ensued when the police tried to clear out the undesirables just a few years ago. Maybe it's because it was a swamp before it was a park, but something about the place just feels cursed.

Maloney made it clear that he isn't taking my questions and concerns seriously. Funny how when a detective brings up such things it's a *hunch*. It's *intuition*. When it's a reporter—or at least a reporter like me—it's a *coincidence*. But I can't bother myself with what Maloney thinks. It's now become abundantly clear that if Liz Lau's death wasn't random—if there really is someone out there killing girls like her and Carla and who knows who'll be next—then there may not be anyone *but* a reporter like me to find out.

Right in the middle of the park, by Avenue A and the Ninth Street transverse, is a four-poster monument topped with a lady in robes—a nineteenth-century Temperance Fountain. Irony of ironies. It's the hangout of the Tompkins Square punks, who stand there every day smoking and drinking bottles of malt liquor and fighting anyone unlucky enough to walk by. There's the rail-skinny one with the green mohawk and the safety pin in his face, the big one with the square fighter's face lined with ropy scars, and the smirking one on the skateboard who always wears the same worn-out leather jacket, no matter the weather. Black, white, Dominican—they could be on a poster for the UN, if you took out the brass knuckles and cigarette burns. If I'm going to find out anything about Liz and her downtown habit, this fine bunch would be the place to start.

"Hey," I call out as I approach. "I have a question for you."

"Yo, Tricks," the big one says to Leather Jacket, who's crouched low on his board, making circles around the fountain. "This lady's got a question. I think she's trying to find her way to Times Square." He leers at me.

Leather Jacket does a little flip and catches the board, then takes a few steps toward me. With his hazel eyes and tawny hair cut choppy around his face, he looks like an underfed lion. "Oh, yeah? What makes you think we have any interest in answering your questions?"

"Just thought you looked like helpful types," I say. Then they seem to lose all interest in me, going back to their shoving and shit-talking as if I had never approached them.

Except for Leather Jacket, who still stands there, spinning a wheel of his board with a pale hand as he looks at me. "What do you want to know?" he asks.

Time to take my chances. I take a step closer and ask, voice lowered: "If someone wanted to shoot up around here, where would they go?"

"You wanna score?" he asks. "I got some I can sell you."

"I'm sure it's pure as the driven snow," I say. "No, thanks. I'm not in the mood for a helping of battery acid."

"You think we give out hot shots to a nice lady like you?" A wicked grin passes over his face. "Never. Unless it's a mix-up, of course."

"Sure," I say. "Thanks, anyway."

He eyes me, still spinning the wheel. "You live around here, don't you?"

"Towards Avenue C."

"I seen you in the park before," he says. "Most girls are scared to walk through here at night."

"Sometimes it's the quickest way to get where I want to go," I reply. "Why should I let a bunch of punks like you stop me?" I start for the path that leads out to Avenue B.

I hear his voice behind me. "Why you asking where to score?"

I turn back. He's looking at me with something like curiosity on his little lion's face. He's not more than fourteen if he's a day.

"I'm looking for someone I know," I tell him. "Someone from Chinatown. I've heard she likes to shoot up around here. So, I'm asking around hoping someone can help me find her."

"Haven't seen her in a while?"

"You could say that."

He puts the skateboard on the ground and places a sneakered foot on top, sliding it back and forth over the asphalt. "There's a loft over on Rivington, above Petey's Bar. A lot of the neighborhood junkies go there."

"Okay," I say.

"Tell them you're looking for the meaning of life."

"The what?" I ask, sure I've misheard. But he's already pushed off and rolled away to rejoin his pack of glue-huffing delinquents as they cross the park, only pausing to pivot into the path of an old man leaning on a cane as he limps by.

###

Through the dirty window of Petey's Bar, I watch a woman with arms tattooed like a church's stained-glass window draw a beer and place it in front of a bulky Hell's Angel with a shoulder-length tangle of dirty blond hair. Suddenly he twists around on his bar stool and throws something, hard, that was concealed inside his big ham fist. The dart lands squarely on the circular target, not a centimeter from the bull's eye or a foot from the group of nearly identical men standing next to it holding beers and cigarettes. Not one of them flinches—not the bikers and not the weary-looking bartender.

The Angel turns back toward the bar, and, as if he could feel me watching him, swivels his head toward the window. His eyes land straight on mine.

I push the door open, walk up to the bar, and sit down, leaving an empty stool between me and the dart thrower. The place smells like old cigarettes and cheap whiskey and spent youth. I ask for a Ten High, straight.

I drink it and lay five dollars on the bar. "I'm looking," I say, "for the meaning of life."

The bartender looks at me expressionlessly. Then she picks up the whiskey bottle and refills my glass.

"That's okay, I—"

"On the house." She pushes it toward me and walks down the bar toward the lone customer sitting at the other end.

I drink the drink and stand up, unsure what to do next. The bartender appears in front of me to collect my glass. Without making eye contact, she mutters, "Stairs in the back. Next to the bathroom."

In the shadows at the back of the bar, past a graffiti-covered bathroom door and a broken cigarette machine, is a narrow stairwell. I place a foot on the first step, then look over my shoulder, at the gang of bikers inside and the ghost of the street outside the grimy window. Nerves prickle over my skin.

Then I start to ascend. After two flights, I get to a landing. Dust motes float in the air like grains of sand falling through seawater. On the left side is a door. I try it, heart thudding in the cavity of my chest. It's locked.

I ascend another two flights to the next landing. The stairwell is only illuminated by the light from the bar, which is only illuminated by the light from the street, and up here, little of it makes it. For a breath-catching moment, I think I see something move in the shadows of the landing. But no one appears from the gloom.

I try the knob. It opens, smoothly and somberly, into a long, empty hallway.

I take a few cautious steps inside, leaving the door open behind me. The linoleum is partly pried up, the concrete walls looped with black graffiti, like an abandoned bomb shelter. I wonder whether I should announce myself, but my voice seems to falter and die in my throat.

I follow the hallway to where it opens into a squalid loft. The windows have all been painted black, the room's only light emanating from a few naked bulbs hanging from the ceiling. The air feels turgid and sweaty, like the inside of a car on a hot day.

All over the floor are bodies. Passed out under coats or filthy blankets, sharing sleeping bags, some murmuring and coughing, but mostly shunted into a comatose silence. There's a large hole in the middle of the ceiling from which drips a dirty, brown liquid. No one seems to notice.

I venture a few steps forward. The floor underneath my feet is sticky with the accrued layers of dirt, sweat, blood, and bad dreams, the air heavy with the dried chemical sweat of the addict. It feels like moving through melted rubber. By one wall, a blanket is spread with black shopping bags, neatly arranged and tied at the top with precise little bows.

The loft gives on to a few smaller rooms. I pass what once was a bathroom. The walls are yellowed, the sink covered in black grime, and the toilet missing its seat. Someone stares at me dully from the tub, eyes vacant and feral like those of a sedated animal. The ceiling leak drips behind me.

I walk back to the main room. The eerie silence is broken by a shudder coming from the corner on my left. I turn to see a woman removing a needle from her arm. It makes my stomach flip.

I swallow and take a few steps toward her. She's conscious, at the very least. Dirty cotton shorts and tank top reveal angry red sores covering her rail-thin limbs. She's leaning against the wall, eyes fluttering closed, the hand that holds the needle now lying by her side like it carries the weight of god. On her parchment-paper face is the drawn satisfaction of a corpse.

I take the photo of Liz that Leon gave me out of my pocket. "Did you know this woman?"

Her eyes flutter open a fraction. "Don't know."

"She died," I say.

The woman shrugs. She leans her head back against the wall, dirty hair falling over her face as it shuts down like a condemned building.

I straighten up. The other figures are all in various stages of nodding out; I won't be finding any help here. I turn around and walk back the way I came.

I'm almost at the door when a voice, deep and accented with drawn country vowels, calls me back. "You're looking for Tiny."

I turn. Standing next to the blanket spread with plastic shopping bags is a man wearing a pair of faded Levi's and a plaid flannel shirt, his hair the color of summer hay. His presence is looming and unnaturally large. For a moment, I wonder if I could be imagining him; if this place has spread its nightmare visions through the air.

But then he speaks again. "That's what I called her," he says, gesturing to the photo in my hand. "On account of she was so skinny. Delicate, like." Slowly he removes something from his pocket. A loose cigarette. A lighter. "They call me the Cowboy."

I feel sweat blooming on the back of my neck. There's something dangerously lucid about the man. What, I wonder, is inside those many plastic bags.

"You knew Liz," I say. My voice sounds strange here, like a copy of itself.

"Yeah. Sure did," he says. Then he adds, "Know her."

I don't like the way he says it. And I don't like his too-bright blue eyes, the menace that emanates from his hulking frame. One word beats like a headache against my temple: *Run. Run. Run.*

I turn, as calmly as possible, toward the door.

Footsteps sound behind me. With sinking dread, I realize he's following me out.

"We shot up together," he's saying. "Is that what you want to hear? That I got her hooked? Forced corruption into her veins? Led her to the devil?"

I open the door and step out onto the stairwell. The temperature feels, mercifully, about twenty degrees cooler. I look back to see the man standing in the doorway. It's not lost on me that he's been referring to Liz in the past tense—meaning he knows that she's dead.

"The truth is all I'm interested in," I say. "Specifically, the truth that leads her to a doorframe on Doyers Street."

"You think I killed her?" His voice goes rough.

"No," I say. "Should I?"

"No, ma'am, you should not, because I did not have a blessed thing to do with it." He takes another drag of the cigarette, and I see that his hand is shaking. Track marks covering his waxy forearm glow like sutures in the wan light. He glowers at me. "I'll just say this. She didn't need anyone leadin' her to the devil. She was heading to him fast all by herself."

"What does that mean?" I say.

He doesn't answer. I start back toward the stairs when his hand darts out with a speed I didn't think possible. I look at it around my wrist, then up at his face. In an instant his expression has gone from sullen to manic, the face of someone liable to do anything. I feel all the air being sucked out of that airless stairwell.

"It means that maybe she was just looking for a little bit of assurance," he says. His eyes are shining madly. "A little bit of insurance. The needle in the haystack."

I wrench my hand away and the bracelet that Liz's sister gave me breaks, sending pink glass beads spilling over the landing and down the stairs like a million tiny pin pricks.

I start to run. My feet roll and slip over the beads. I catch myself before I fall and keep running, down the four flights of stairs, through the bar, and out onto the street, where I stumble out, gasping, the smell of burnt vinegar hanging around me like a black cloud.

###

I open the door to my apartment, drop my coat onto the floor and collapse onto the couch. I feel like I've taken a trip to Hades and back instead of ten blocks south. The dripping of the ceiling leak in the loft seems to have bored its way into my brain, the twitching shadows lingering in the sides of my vision. I don't know how long I've been sitting there, melting into the frayed cushions, before the sound fades. I go to feed Nellie, then put the can opener back in the drawer and take out the white bottle. The sun is setting over the river and orange light pours through the narrow kitchen window, coloring the pills in my palm so they glow with a strange and beatific warmth.

###

Liz's face comes to me in my dreams that night, floating in a room with black walls painted with white graffiti. But then the features melt and change, until I realize I'm looking at the girl sitting on the exam table covered in bloody white paper. She's trying to speak to me except I can't understand her words. She holds her hands to the dark pit where her stomach should be.

Then the face morphs into Carla's. The face is stuck all over with safety pins. The graffiti on the walls becomes thick and material. I try to claw my way through it, but the more I struggle, the more I get caught in its ropy curves, tripping over the loops and whorls. I hear a voice—someone trying to tell me something. I am trying to understand it, it is crucial that I understand it, but everything that sounds like a word falls to pieces before it reaches my ears. Then I'm back in the loft with its close gloom and ocherous air, forcing its way into my mouth, up into my throat, so that I can't breathe. My doctor appears.

How are you feeling, he says.

I don't know, I manage.

He says nothing. I can barely discern his face out of the gloom. When he speaks again, it's with the Cowboy's drawl.

Any new symptoms?

I try to tell him no, I just want to get my pills and leave. He's holding them out to me. But then the bottle turns into a needle, silver and glinting. When I reach for it, I see a skeleton's hand, and the needle falls through my fine bones.

10

Tattoos on his knees . . .

I feel thick and slow as I dress and commute downtown the next day, residue of my nightmare lingering like the burnt-vinegar smell of the loft, which I'm convinced is still clinging to my coat. I want to know what Liz was doing in a place like that. I want to talk to her friend and her sister again to see if either had any kind of inkling about Liz's addiction, and if they'd seen or heard anything about the mad-eyed man who called himself the Cowboy.

I'm still sniffing at my collar when I arrive at the Shack, Schultz and the rest of the reporters already installed at their desks. I find Crock waiting at mine.

I set down my coffee cup. "Hey, Crock."

"Look who decided to grace us with her presence." He glares. That's when I realize, with a guilty glance at the wall clock, that it's well past noon. "Got any plans for today?"

"There was a murder down in Chinatown three days ago. Everything about it bears a striking resemblance to Carla Russo's," I say. "I'm getting a story together about it."

"No, you're not," he growls.

"Crock, another girl was *murdered*," I protest.

"And what does that have to do with you?"

The Shack goes silent. Conversations subside. Typewriter keys still.

"You're on organized crime now, may I remind you for the umpteenth goddamn time!" From my desk, he plucks up the newspaper that contains my Brighton Beach article. "What about the chocolate truck? Where's our follow-up?"

The truck full of candy bars that was abandoned outside the Land-O-Fun in Brighton Beach—and the investigation I abandoned the same way. Even for a reporter, there's no other way to spin it.

"I'm working on it," I say lamely. "You just have to give me time."

"I have to do no such thing," he says, pronouncing the words with dangerous precision. "*You* have gotta get *me* something besides this backwash." He hits the paper with a hairy hand. "Something even close to the level of your daisy-chain story. Come on, Snow. I shouldn't have to tell you that."

"There's no big story there, Crock," I protest. "And anyways, the people out in Brighton are all zipped up. Can't get a word out of anyone."

"Hit the streets!" he roars. "You're a reporter! Figure it out!"

He turns away in a huff and I hear his office door close. A moment passes as I stare at the spot where he'd stood.

Then it starts. A low whistle. A tongue cluck. I close my eyes and feel my ears go hot.

"Job getting a little over your head, Snow?" Schultz says.

"Need some help with research?" One of the other reporters chimes in. "I can ask my grandma. She's got some spare time on her hands over at the nursing home."

"Or maybe my sister's kid?" pipes up a third. "She's had it up to here with kindergarten, but I'm sure she'd be happy to make some calls."

"Fuck off," I mutter. I stalk out of the room, the door cutting off their laughter. The quiet of the hallway thrums in my ears.

Not my most cutting retort. It's because I know Crock is right.

###

The New York Supreme Court is located at 60 Centre Street, catty-corner to the old Hall of Records in all its Beaux Arts glory. You can't really miss it, with its neoclassical columns, white steps, and frieze that austerely proclaims: THE TRUE ADMINISTRATION OF JUSTICE IS THE FIRMEST PILLAR OF GOOD GOVERNMENT. Around the back, half underground, is the County Clerk's office, where the ideals are somewhat less lofty. There the cockroaches in the crevices move faster than the bored sinecures who file and hand out records, chips in their shoulders so deep you can see the marks.

It doesn't feel right to let go of Liz's case right when I feel like I was starting to get somewhere. What it feels like is that I'm letting her down—a young woman's death chalked up to H, when I just don't think that's all there is to it. But the fact is that I told Crock I'd be able to work both stories and I haven't exactly held up my end of the deal. I have to pick my organized crime work back up if I'm going to stay in my boss's good graces. Such as they are.

Black Sea Holdings: the name on the sticker at the back of the chocolate truck, and as close to a lead as I have at this point. If I'm going to find out more about the mysterious truck and its stalled cargo, I'll have to start here. Maybe it'll even be good for me. A good, old-fashioned paper trail instead of a mysterious murder. Something solid. Safe.

I heave a sigh as I contemplate the imperious-looking building looming above me, two large, stone women with shields lounging outside. The women look cold, but maybe I'm just projecting.

I pass through a black filigree door, then the metal detector, and shiver as I enter the drafty hall. The County Clerk's office is a circular, dungeon-like building of institutional, tiled floor and Roman numeral wall clocks, whose few windows look out on oddly shaped interior courtyards that feel faintly medieval. All around the curving hall are archways that lead to double doors, each with worn gold lettering at the top: Room 141, Marriage Bureau. Room 125, Vital Records. Room 116, Notary Public. Room 119, Court Records. And my destination, room 109B, Business Records and Liens.

I breeze through the swinging double doors, then pause in the foyer to glance over the shelves stacked with crumbling leather-bound minute books and corporate indices, lien dockets and maps going back to the 1920s. Then I continue to the help desk, where a guy with a face like an English bulldog is sitting looking extremely occupied with a cup of coffee and powdered donut. I stand there and project politeness. He makes no sign of noticing me, but I don't mind. I can wait.

Finally, he wipes his mouth with the back of his hand and says, "Can I help you?" in a tone that indicates that help is the last thing he intends to do.

"I sure hope so," I say with my best *oh, golly, gee* smile. All that's on the wall behind him is a State of New York Unified Court System calendar. Not much for office decor. "I'm looking for some information about a corporation. When it was incorporated, names of officers listed, anything of that nature that's available."

"You can look it up in those books," he says, lifting his chin toward the wall behind me.

I go to the shelf. "These are all organized by year," I say. "Can't you look it up by name? The business is called Black Sea Holdings."

"Depends."

"On what?"

"If it got a DBA."

"What happens if it got a DBA?"

"If it's a real business, could be up at the Secretary of State office in Albany."

"Albany?" I repeat.

"Yeah." He glares at me. "Ya know, the *capital*?"

"So I'm told," I say. "But don't you have that information here, if the business is operating in New York City?"

"Depends."

"On what?"

"On if it got processed yet."

"How does it get processed?"

He heaves a long, tortured sigh. "First it goes to Albany. Then they send us all the DBAs in batches," he says, as if explaining something to a very obtuse five-year-old. "We give 'em an index number and then we put 'em in those books over there. Then we match the DBAs to the number."

"How long does that take?"

"Can take a week. Can take a month," he says. When he sees I'm not moving, he adds, "Can take three."

"I don't really have a week or a month," I say. "Or three."

He shrugs. "Can't help ya."

"But that means you *could* have the DBA certificate," I say. "From Albany."

"Depends."

"On what?"

"On when it was incorporated."

"Well, I don't know when it was incorporated."

"Listen, lady, I'm about to go on my break," he says, as if that settles it.

"Assuming it was incorporated recently," I cut in as he's turning away, "and you have the original filings, is that something I can try and find myself? This is all public record, and seeing as you work for the public records office, Mr. . . ." I look at his badge. "deLucca, you must have some kind of obligation to help me find what I'm looking for. No?"

He spends a leisurely half minute giving me a deeply hateful glare. Finally, he says, "We just got a box of DBAs from the last two months. You can sort through it yourself."

"Much obliged," I say.

He gives me a look like I've just said something grossly insulting about his mother. "Wait right here."

He vacates his chair, which I now see is covered in pilling maroon fabric and a suspicious dark stain. I turn and lean my elbows against the desk. I wish I could whistle. It would come in handy in moments like this. Never learned how, though.

A few minutes later he reappears holding a cardboard banker's box in his two hairy hands. He gestures with his head. "Come on. You can look through it in here."

I follow him out the arched doorway to a small alcove, where he elbows the box onto a wooden ledge. The alcove looks like something out of Melville, complete with a placard admonishing workers, in no uncertain terms, not to use the mailbox for non-work-related memos and the humming sound issuing from the white metal grate above the NO SMOKING sign.

He walks away, leaving me alone. I light a cigarette and hold it in my right hand, sorting through the files with my left.

The papers register the incorporation of fast-food franchises, a café, a florist, a photographer on Fifty-Seventh Street, a record label on 108th. So many dreams scattered around the city. The only sound besides the rustling of papers is the humming from the grate and the occasional muffled footsteps from the hallway behind me.

Some time later, when all the names have started to blend together, I seize it triumphantly, almost ripping the paper in the process. Typed out on the top of the Articles of Incorporation for a new entity formed in New York State: Raknost Inc., DBA Black Sea Holdings.

"Gotcha," I say under my breath. I pull it out and set it on the table.

It purports to be in imports and exports, was incorporated in September of last year, and is owned by someone named Ildar Batryshkin. There isn't much else that stands out except for the name of the lawyer who notarized the document: James Forrester, Esq.

"Doesn't sound too Russian to me," I say out loud. "So, Mr. Forrester. What might you be able to tell me about all this?"

"Hey!" I hear old man donut's voice behind me, and it's mad. "No smoking. Didn't you see the sign?"

I glance over my shoulder. "Must have escaped me." The cigarette has already burned down to the butt. I put it out on the windowsill and then flick it into the wastebasket. I turn to him and hold up the paper. "Can I have a copy of this?"

He holds his hand out and snatches it, the small, hard eyes under his chimpy brow never leaving mine.

###

I look up James Forrester in the phonebook and find that he works for a personal injuries firm—and not just any, but one of the city's more notorious for spinning up large and ethically questionable class-action suits. Not what I was expecting. I call and introduce myself to the receptionist, telling her I'm covering victims of negligence due to our city's poor oversight, and would simply covet Mr. Forrester's valuable perspective on the matter. She connects me immediately. These types are always looking for a place to spout their righteous indignation on behalf of their grievously wronged clientele, and the pages of our paper are as good a place as any. Within five minutes we've arranged a meeting in thirty, at a bar near his downtown office.

The bar is already crowded when I arrive at five minutes to six: finance guys in identical Brooks Brothers suits clustered around tables and talking too loudly at the bar with the women who help them forget how shallow and empty their lives are. Lesson #1 of doing an interview: When you're meeting on neutral territory, always get there first. Better to guard the fortress than to breach the city walls.

I slot myself in at the bar, letting my eyes roam the room. I don't know what Forrester looks like, but soon enough, I know he'll surface.

"Vodka grapefruit," a voice yells into my ear. "*Vodka grapefruit.*"

At my elbow is an icy-looking blonde standing next to a typical Wall Street Nick, a cardboard cutout down to the blue Oxford button-down and the blazer slung over his briefcase. The bartender acknowledges her with the barest nod, hands continuing their work. Two minutes later he sets a highball glass of pink, murky liquid on the bar, which she grabs and immediately begins sucking down. "Put it on my tab," her date instructs. He puts his hand on the girl's back and then uses her like a navigation device to steer through the crowd.

I turn around. "Whiskey neat," I tell the bartender, then jerk my head in Blue Oxford's direction. "Put it on his tab."

A minute later I see a broad-shouldered man in his late forties walk through the door solo: expensive trench, expensive shoes, hairline receding behind a face that once was good-looking and still thinks it is. More than his appearance is the air about him, one of a man who mentally annexes every place he walks into. He looks around but his eyes don't land on me.

"James Forrester?" I say, taking a step out. "The barrister?"

"Parker! Nice to see you." He gives my hand a hearty shake, like we're family friends on the Fourth of July, before commanding a beer from the bartender. "Forrester the Barrister. That's funny. That's a good one."

"Stand-up comic is my other job."

"That right?" he says.

"No," I say.

"Hey, you never know in this town," he says, taking a sip from his beer. "Everyone's got a side hustle. Just ask my ex-wife. You good? You all set with your drink? Why don't we move somewhere a little quieter?" Already he's walking toward a table, his hand outstretched like a maître d' guiding a lady. The patter, the grin, the crack about the ex-wife—this guy's a pro.

I let myself be led toward a banquette near the back. "So," he says, folding his hands on the table once we've settled. "What's the angle of the story?"

I let him prattle on for a while about torts and negligence and the ultimate righteousness of our great legal system while I pretend to take notes, giving the requisite *hmm*s and *is that right*s. I don't even have to ask a question. He makes it that easy.

Eventually he's run himself out and he leans against the booth back, pleased with his narrative. "Any follow-up questions," he assures me, "I'm here to answer." He takes a card from his wallet and passes it across the table.

I take it and study it, nodding as if I'm reflecting on what he's just said. Then I look up. "There's just one more thing I wanted to get your thoughts on."

He spreads his hands magnanimously, Rolex catching the light. "Anything I can do to help."

"Well," I say, trying to suppress the delight creeping into my voice. "I got a call the other day about a truck full of what looked to be contraband goods out in Brighton Beach. I was wondering if you knew anything about that?"

Instantly Forrester's manner changes. His hands slip off the table and his gaze hardens. "I'm afraid I don't know what you're talking about."

"I'm afraid you do." I can't help it; I'm smiling now. "Let's try another *angle*, to use your word. The truck had a decal with the name of a certain enterprise—a Raknost Inc., DBA Black Sea Holdings, owned by one Ildar Batryshkin. This business filing, which describes the company as an import-export operation—as I'm sure I don't have to tell you—was notarized by you." I take the photocopy from the County

Clerk's office from my coat and lay it on the table. "This is all public record, naturally. Care to explain?"

He pauses for a moment, as if sizing me up. Then he takes a sip of his beer and places it down on the table with deliberate gentleness. "I notarized the filing at the behest of a longtime client, a friend of Ildar's. Just a favor. That's where my involvement starts and ends. I have no insight into their operations and no idea what incident you're referring to."

"Sounds awfully charitable of you."

"It's hardly unusual for lawyers to offer clients help on those types of formalities," he says.

"Even Russian ones?" I ask.

He looks surprised. "Of course. Are they not also entitled to legal counsel?"

I change my tone, back to Suzy Q, reporting for the school paper with her notebook and pen. I cock my head and let my invisible pigtails swing. "I guess I didn't understand that part. The legal counsel."

He pauses for a moment and squints at me slightly, as if trying to decide if I'm earnest or bullshitting. Then he says, "You have to remember, the Russians are coming out of a system that's completely different from ours. This is all very new to them. They don't understand the finer points of the American capitalist system, what's legal, what's not. To them, it's a matter of technicalities."

"Sure," I say. "But isn't it also true that there's been a spate of Russian émigré activity of the extralegal variety leading up to and following the fall of the Soviet Union? Much of which relies on the cooperation of legitimate lawyers and others in our corporate system?"

Alright, so I'm not really sure this is true. But it sounds true. And sometimes the truth has to get a bit flexible when the situation calls for it.

"I don't know anything about that," he says. "But I can tell you that there are a number of perfectly legitimate business operations out of Brighton Beach started by recent émigrés."

"Real enterprising lot, aren't they?"

"That's right."

I pause for a moment, nodding, as if we're in perfect accord. Then I add, "But isn't it *also* true that there have been several such legitimate professionals, even those coming out of your precise line of work—class-action suits—implicated in abetting the enterprises of the Russian mafia, to mutually beneficial return?"

Now the truth is really getting warmed up. She's doing toe-touches, getting limber, preparing for her big move.

"If that were true, I wouldn't know it," he says crisply. He's keeping his cool, but there's red creeping onto his face. "I didn't advise them on anything related to their legal affairs. I simply acted as a notary. A friendly favor. I have no other knowledge and nothing more to say about it."

I don't say anything. He's getting hot around the collar, and I'm going to let him. Sure enough, he makes to pick up his beer, then puts it down again. "Anyways, there's no such *thing* as the Russian mafia. It's made up. A fantasy of reporters like you, scrounging for a story."

"Often the people who say there's no such thing are the people who stand to gain the most from it."

"Is that an accusation?"

"Not an accusation," I reply. "An observation. I'm sure you can appreciate the difference."

"I don't have anything left to tell you." He starts to get up.

"No? Nothing about the recent brush with the law that the proprietors of Black Sea Holdings had even before the recent candy caper?"

Alright, so I took a flier on that one.

"Those charges were dropped," he snaps. "From lack of evidence."

I raise my eyebrows. I'm actually surprised it worked.

As the man across from me silently fumes, I pick up my whiskey and drain it. "You're a very well-informed notary, Mr. Forrester," I say, setting down my glass. "Thanks for taking the time to meet. You've been a big help."

He narrows his eyes. "Luring someone to an interview under false pretenses is not an ethical way to do journalism. Even at a two-bit rag like yours."

I feel my smile broaden to a snicker. "I'll pass your feedback along to the complaint department."

I watch him weave his way through the crowd, wielding his briefcase like a shield. For a minute I just sit, whiskey glass empty in front of me, next to the business card Forrester gave me.

Some people think this job is about putting the pieces together. But what I do is find a thread. I pull. I watch it all unravel.

I take out my notebook.

###

Sergei is at a table near the back when I arrive at Skovorodka in Brighton Beach the next day, looking every inch the young Moscow businessman between meetings in a well-cut navy blazer over a snow-white button-down. The effect is somewhat ruined by the screeching stereo in the background playing Soviet pop songs. And the two men at the only other occupied table singing along, loudly and poorly.

"Sergei," I say, sliding into the booth opposite him. "*Privyet*. I must say, capitalism looks good on you."

He smiles coolly. "Something to drink?"

"Coffee," I say. "*Spasibo*."

He looks over my shoulder, raising a finger. "Oi, Masha. *Dva kofe, bystro*."

I'd set this meeting with Sergei with the simple goal of learning more about his organization and his boss, Solnikov, but things have become quite different in the past few days. I need to know if Ildar Batryshkin, the owner of Black Sea Holdings, is part of the new group of criminals Maloney was talking about—and how a lawyer like Forrester, with his veneer of legitimacy, fits into all of it. And I need to find a subtle way of asking if Sergei knows anything about the Diamond District business and my arrest without out-and-out accusing him, which, in my experience, is never a good way to build relationships with low-level organized crime figures.

"Thanks for taking the time to meet with me, once again," I start out.

"Anytime," he says. "You know, the ways of the American press are quite fascinating to me. It is not often one has the pleasure of meeting with a member of its esteemed ranks."

A woman approaches the table with two cups of coffee and accoutrements on a tray—the willowy one with the light brown skin and the watchful gaze.

Masha, I think. A Russian name on a woman who hardly looks Russian, but who also seems to understand the language.

She says nothing, doesn't look up to meet my gaze, but I see that one of her eyebrows is raised just slightly, a whisper of a smile on her face. Sergei removes the items from the tray and shoos her away. I watch her disappear into the kitchen, leaving the door swinging back and forth behind her. Like a question or a reproach. I shift my gaze back to Sergei.

"So," he says. "What is it you would like to know?"

"Let's start with you," I say. "Seeing as we've never had a chance to have a nice, civil conversation. When did you come stateside?"

"Three years ago. With the big wave. I had just finished at MGU studying international markets and finance."

"And then?"

"And then I was bored." He shrugs. "I found a job at a bank, but it was not interesting for me. Some of my contacts here in Brighton introduced me to Kolya—to Solnikov—one night, here during a cabaret. He needed someone with a head for numbers. And the rest, as you say, is history." *Isss hisssstory*. He reveals his pointy-toothed smile.

"So, there's no other relation between the two of you?"

Sergei shakes his head, blond fringe swaying boyishly. "We don't work like the Italians. Families, bosses. We have groups. Connections. Mutually beneficial arrangements. It is a shame, I think."

"Why's that?"

"Because I believe that the one thing they have over us," he says, "is loyalty. I am Nikolai's right hand, you see?" He waggles his, then plucks a cigarette from the open pack on the table and sticks it between his lips. Lights up, leans back, exhales. "I understand him. But I also bring new ideas. Things are changing here. Since the Soviet Union fell, many more are trying to edge into our territory, bringing their own ideas and schemes, their connections elsewhere in the world. That's why I am so important to Solnikov. We need to keep up."

"What's he like?" I ask. "Solnikov?"

"He is a classic *vor v zakone*," Sergei says. "A 'thief-in-law,' I think is how you translate it. Tattoos on his knees." I look at him questioningly. "Because he does not bow down to anyone," he says with something like pride. "He was in the *gulag* back home. The authorities needed to clean the house, so to speak. So, there you have it. Welcome to Brighton Beach."

Just then a short, round man with a round face and a blond comb-over appears at the edge of our table.

"Sergei! *Kak dela?* How are you?" He grabs Sergei's hand from the table and pumps it, then turns to me. His bright blue eyes widen. I feel like I've met him before—and from the way he's staring at me, I'm wondering if he recognizes me, too. But then he says to Sergei, "And who is your most lovely friend?"

"Oleg." Sergei sighs. "What are you doing here?"

Baby-faced Oleg is now squinting at me. Unsure what else to do, I squint back. Finally, he says, "You are thinking of a song."

"I am?" I say in surprise.

"Yes," he says. "Think of a song. And watch. I will guess the song you are thinking of."

That's when the song playing over the restaurant's speakers changes, and Oleg seems to forget all about the one I'm supposed to be thinking of. He grips his heart with tortured passion. "This is beautiful ballad," he sighs. "About a man separated from his love by the *gulag*. Terribly, terribly sad is life, is it not? Oh, *gospodi*."

"I was just thinking, Sergei." Oleg suddenly drops his hand to his side and puts on a serious expression. "Perhaps the cabaret show could benefit from my act—song telepathy plus performances of the standards. It would be a lovely way to spend an evening." He hums a few bars, does a little dance, snaps his fingers.

Sergei says something under his breath in Russian, eyes narrowed, staring straight ahead. I take it from his intonation that he's not inviting Oleg to tea.

"Okay, *nyet problema*, I am on my way. It was very nice to meet you, I hope we will see you again sometime. Perhaps at the cabaret? You really must to come," he simpers, but his eyes are nervous now, skipping back and forth between me and Sergei. "But, Sergei, just think about it, *pozhaluysta, ya proshu tebye* . . ."

Sergei begins to stand up, and as he does, Oleg skitters away, his hands still flapping in front of him, the smile twitching helplessly at the corners of his mouth.

"What's the deal with the lounge singer?" I ask, watching Oleg make for the exit with quick, jerky steps. Masha the waitress, who has reappeared from the kitchen and is clearing a table, exchanges a few words with him before he disappears out the door.

"He is just a flea," Sergei says, brushing a hand dismissively. "There are many such types who have come to America with the delusion that fame and fortune will soon be theirs. They lived in the clouds in Russia, and they live in the clouds here." He picks up his coffee and murmurs, "I have no patience for weakness."

I pick up my own cup and take a sip. It's murky and gritty. "I guess we have that in common." I realize that the men over at the next table have stopped singing and are now speaking to each other in low, growling tones. Sergei looks at me curiously.

I gesture behind me. "Your waitress, Masha. She was at the poker game, wasn't she?"

"You are very observant," he says, tipping his chin in a nod. "Yes. Masha is a friend of ours."

"But not a friend of the family," I say. "A friend of the group?"

He smiles. "*Khorosho*, Parker Snow."

I place my empty espresso cup down on my saucer. "Speaking of friends," I say. "Do you know anyone by the name of Ildar Batryshkin?"

He releases a disdainful cloud of smoke. "One of many new arrivals attempting to elbow their way in."

"There was a truck full of chocolate that was abandoned by Shore Parkway last week with no papers or way to identify it," I say. "He seems to be behind it."

"Chocolate?" he repeats.

"Yeah, chocolate," I say. "You know. Willy Wonka."

He gives me a confused look. "Candy bars are not our concern. But there is something else I can tell you about that may be of interest."

"What's that?"

"Cars."

"Cars?"

"Yes. As you know, there was some trouble last year. The fuel tax business. We had to *lay low* for a while. Isn't that the expression?" He pauses to light a fresh cigarette, blowing the smoke up toward the ceiling. "Luckily, Solnikov is a businessman. He knows how to diversify. So, he has been sending cars back to Russia. A little Toyota here can fetch five times the price over there. Of course, they pay no export tax. They simply hide the cars in shipping containers and label them as household goods."

"Through a company also owned by Solnikov, I imagine?"

He grins. "There is a new twist to the plot, you can say. Now, they are simply stealing the cars off the street. They have learned this new skill, thanks to the help of some neighborhood friends."

"Hot cars, no tax, and a fivefold selling price. Not bad."

"Not bad at all." His grin widens, saliva glinting off his viperish teeth.

"One last thing," I say, stubbing out my own cigarette. "Why are you telling me all this?"

"We have a deal, after all," says Sergei. "And anyways, all charges against Nikolai have so far been dropped. It is much easier to accuse than to prove, especially with the help of a good lawyer." Then he adds, "And there are some advantages to being known. To being feared."

"Advantages," I say. "Or maybe you just like it?"

He smirks. "You know, last month, someone was killed in this restaurant." He's looking at the two men at the other table. "A dispute over some protection fees owed. And the funny thing was, no one in the restaurant could recall anything about it. When the police questioned them, none of them had seen a thing."

I follow his gaze. The men's voices are raised now, grunting yells punctuated by dense fists hitting the table. No one seems alarmed. I look back at Sergei. He's giving me a cool, blank smile. "You should come," he says, "as Oleg said, to our next cabaret night. It would be my pleasure to have you as my guest. It will be Saturday, here, at nine o'clock."

"Thanks for the invitation," I say. "I'll do my best. This lawyer you mentioned, the one who helped Solnikov get the fuel tax charges dropped. You wouldn't happen to know his name, would you?"

"I do, in fact," he says. "I have met him here many times. He has come to the cabaret shows often as Solnikov's guest. He gave me his card, in fact." He takes out his wallet and hands me a cream-colored business card. I know the name before I look at it: *James Forrester, Attorney-at-Law*, printed in green, raised type.

"Mind if I take this?" I ask.

"Not at all," he says. "I can always find him, if I need him."

I take the card and slip it into my pocket. I'm not going to mention what I learned about Forrester notarizing a business filing for Batryshkin. Better to keep that card close, too.

"I went to jail this week," I say, conversationally.

Sergei's only reaction is to be totally unimpressed. "Jail here is like garden for babies. Nothing like Soviet prison."

No reaction, except . . . is it me, or is there something menacing in that pointed smile that I hadn't noticed before?

"I have to ask," I say. "Cheating bettors out of their money, skimming money off gas companies, that's one thing. But the petty extortion. Shaking your neighbors down for cash, just ordinary people trying to run a grocery or a hair salon. Doesn't it ever seem wrong to you?"

"What interest do I have in ordinary people?" he says disdainfully. "If they were smart, they would be like me."

11

A very well-informed notary . . .

Daylight makes its faltering way through the window as I stand over the notes splashed across my desk, hoping some kind of sense will emerge from the chicken scratch. After my meeting with Sergei the day before, I'd written down everything I'd learned about Solnikov's operations thus far. But not before stopping by the Brighton Beach station house to inquire about the status of the wayward chocolate truck—only to find out that it had rolled right out of evidence and back to its rightful owner, no longer under investigation by OCCB, according to the tight-lipped and tired-eyed detective. Meaning someone with or representing the company has some serious pull.

Nellie is splashed over the desk, too, tail swinging insouciantly over the side. She's indifferent to the ring lying next to her on its pocked wooden surface. I pick it up and twirl it on my pointer finger. Technically, it's evidence and, technically, I'm withholding it. It's not my intention to be withholding; I just can't seem to be forthcoming. It's not in my nature. Not to mention that by this point, any telling fingerprints that may have existed on its surface have long since been replaced by my own.

"Right, Nellie?" I look to her for validation. She responds by jumping off the desk and slinking into the bedroom, where the late morning light is better.

I glance at my watch. Almost lunchtime. Carla, Liz, and all that relates to murdered girls will have to wait, if I want to keep my job and have a chance at seeing their stories through. I put the ring back in my pocket for safekeeping and take out the other object buried deep: a small, rectangular business card with a certain Midtown address. An address it would be most unforthcoming not to visit.

The day is sodden and gray when I emerge from the subway at Bryant Park. The fountain is dry, the grass neglected, and the carousel empty of riders, painted horses glistening garishly under droplets of rain. A figure is huddled in a pile of blankets at its center, giving the unsettling impression of being impaled by its metal axis.

I climb the steps that rise from the lawn and walk around the flank of the New York Public Library building. Salty steam from the hot dog carts parked outside briefly warms the air as I pass. One step onto Fifth Avenue and I'm immediately swept into the current of the midtown lunch rush: Identical suits pouring out of office buildings, some of them snarling into gray antennaed bricks held glued to their ears. Two women walk by me wearing suits in an identical shade of beige, one in a skirt and one in pants. Skirt says to Pants: "I don't care if he won't listen. You have to grab him by the balls and *make* him listen." Pigeons swarm the sidewalk, pecking savagely at the remains of a fallen hot dog bun.

It's approaching one o'clock when I enter the foyer of the building on Forty-Fifth and Lexington and ride up the short escalator to the lobby. I pace up to the security turnstiles in my best hurried dash, rummaging in my pockets the whole time. Next to it, a security guard with a shaved head and neck rolls is standing in an ill-fitting suit looking bored. As I dig through my pockets, a line of people queue up behind me.

"I'm so sorry," I say, glancing back and taking a step out of the way as if I've just noticed I'm stopping up traffic. "I must have left my badge on my desk when I went out for lunch. Shall I—"

Before I can finish, he's swiped his badge on top of the turnstile without giving me so much as a glance. The wings swing open.

I thank him with the right measure of entitlement and punch the elevator keypad. I ascend and then stroll across the quiet office floor, past backs bent over desks and the low hum of the copy machine. I find the name plate I'm looking for, slide the glass door open, and step inside.

The office is spacious, one wall covered in built-in mahogany bookshelves, bankers boxes of files stacked against the other. The walls are decorated with a few of the usual prints: a foggy Waterloo Bridge, a Klimtian garden, a candy-colored Renoir. A mahogany executive desk hulks in the middle.

I settle into the brown leather chair and swivel it toward the shelves. The leather is unpleasantly soft, like skin. A blazer thrown over its back emanates an aggressive, piney cologne. He'd been in shirtsleeves when he'd met me at the bar that first time, so this must be a Trial Blazer—only worn for showtime. My eyes rove over the books on the shelves. Along with the volumes of case law, there's *Fundamentals of Litigation*, *Tactics for Trial*, *Winning in Court*. He might seem like a shark from the outside, but really, he's a big softie.

I'm laughing to myself about that one when I hear the door open. I swivel around.

"Jesus Christ." The Barrister takes a step back. The door closes behind him with a faint *whoosh*. "What the hell are you doing here?"

I smile pleasantly, or what I think is pleasantly.

"Nice to see you, too," I say. "You gave me your card. I sort of took it as an open invitation."

"How'd you get in here?"

"I work here," I say. "Auditing corporate files is my other job."

He gives me a withering look, or what he thinks is a withering look. "I'm going to have to ask you to leave."

"You say you don't represent clients involved in the so-called Russian mafia," I say. "Which may or may not exist, I know. But the funny thing is, I took a trip out to Skovorodka—where I hear you're a frequent guest—to see a certain Sergei about certain shady dealings, including but not limited to back room gambling operations, extortion, and fuel-tax skimming. He handed me this card." I produce it from my pocket. "It looked awfully familiar. Can't mistake that embossing. Or is it debossing? I can never remember the difference."

His expression doesn't change. I smirk. "Everyone's got a side hustle, right?"

"That's just a business card," he spits. "It means nothing. Proves nothing. Even you must know that."

"You're right." I nod. "Absolutely correct. But what about the fact that you were listed as additional counsel to Nikolai Solnikov in last year's fuel-tax suit?"

If looks could kill, the one he gives me would be a ballistic missile. "I don't comment on past cases," he says in a low voice. "Of any kind. Now I need to ask you to leave. You're trespassing."

I look around the office. "You ambulance chasers really have the perfect cover. You can talk to any lowlife you want without anyone looking twice. You could be discussing a slip and fall as much as a crime syndicate."

"You have no idea what you're talking about," he snaps.

"I'm just trying to do my job, Forrester," I say. "That is, turning over rocks and showing the world all the worms underneath."

"You're just a lousy reporter trying to dredge up a story to save her pitiful excuse for a byline."

"And you're just a mobbed-up lawyer playing savior."

His scowl transforms into a wolfish smile. The kind that gives you a sinking feeling and makes you miss the scowl.

"I know what happened to you last time you tried to break a big story, Parker Snow. Like everyone else in this city who's ever read that smoldering pile of slander and shit you call a paper."

My chest tightens.

"Next time," he says, in a voice hard and precise as granite, "I ask that you please show your ID to security in the lobby so they can call me. Whatever little ruse got you in here, I wouldn't suggest repeating it."

"So, you can be in a meeting or tied up or not in?" I say. "Sure. Anyways, I don't think I'll be dropping by any time soon. You've been quite helpful."

I'm almost at the door when he steps in front of it. Casual, like he's just about to open it and wave me out with a chivalrous bow. From my vantage point, though, it's clear. His suited arm grips the handle tight, his body square as a boxer's, blocking my exit. I look him in the face. His eyes are napalm brown.

"I'd be careful if I were you," he says, voice low. "Push your luck too hard, you might find yourself in rooms it won't be so easy to get out of."

There's not five inches between us. I sense movement out of the corner of my eye, people and suits moving to and fro like black flies. A lone speck of dust drifts through the air. I force myself to count to five. Then, slowly, in between the poundings of my heart, I say: "I'll keep that in mind."

For a moment, he does nothing. The poison leeches out of him like a dark cloud, making my head feel light and ill. Just when I think I can't stand it anymore he opens the door and steps to the side, letting me pass like a faint spring breeze.

###

My watch reads 9:37 p.m. The afternoon's gray mizzle has turned into a moody rain that worries the sidewalk with cold, plunking drops. I'm standing in the pool of fluorescent light given off by the building on Forty-Fifth and Lexington, having spent the last several hours trying to dig up more about Black Sea Holdings, which didn't yield anything besides a headache. I'm holding the badge I swiped from an unoccupied desk on my way off of Forrester's floor that afternoon. It belongs to one Rebecca Porter, who is blond and blue-eyed and smiling. Not exactly my mirror image. At some point tonight, or at the latest, tomorrow morning, Rebecca will realize it's gone, report the badge missing, and ask for a new one. For all I know, it won't even work at the turnstile—and then things could get ugly. Instead of thinking about that, I grind out my cigarette and enter the building.

A man in a trench coat and briefcase rides down the escalator as I ascend, staring straight ahead of him like a zombie with a head cold. The place is nearly deserted. Two security guards make murmuring conversation behind the desk and a pair of heels click against the tile. I watch their owner, a woman in a purple skirt suit, crossing the lobby. Her steps echo in its hangar-like emptiness.

I nod hello to the guard by the elevator bank. He's not the same one who swiped me in earlier, which is good—there aren't many people coming into the building at this time of night, and I don't need two unusual incidents to help place me in someone's memory. I swipe the badge against the reader. It flashes red and lets out a loud, unhappy blat.

The guard grabs the badge out of my hand. I stifle a yell of protest before it escapes my lips.

"This thing actin' up again?" He wipes it against his trousers and slides it against the turnstile closest to him. The light flashes green and the wings swing open.

"They gotta fix that damn thing," he says. "I keep tellin' 'em."

I thank him and pass through, my heart still fizzing like I missed a stair step. Rule of Dissembling #27: Never say a word more than you have to.

I get to the elevator and freeze. I can't remember the floor of Forrester's office. I can feel the security guard milling around a few paces behind my back. Then I watch my hand reach out and press the button for thirty-three.

The elevator doors part when I reach it. The office floor is quiet, the cubicles mostly dark beneath the overhead lights. I hug the wall that leads to Forrester's office. When I met him the first time, at the bar downtown, it was promptly at six. I'll just have to hope he doesn't choose tonight to burn the midnight oil.

From somewhere across the floor, I hear a snatch of conversation between two male voices, one rising in a laugh. Neither is Forrester's, and they're both a safe distance away. They bid each other goodnight and then the voices cut off as the door to the elevator bank opens and shuts.

Forrester's office is unlocked. I take out the flashlight I've brought and splash the beam around the room. It looks just like it did earlier in the day: the looming desk and bookshelf, the stacked bankers boxes. The faint hint of his piney cologne still lingers in the air along with the smell of ink and paper and the chemical orange tinge of whatever the cleaning staff must have used.

Christ. There are so many boxes of papers in here, it's like the Library of Alexandria. There's no way I can possibly go through them all. On the other hand, these have to be the files for his workaday class action cases—he wouldn't keep anything compromising out in the open.

The wheels of a yellow cleaning trolley followed by a set of white sneakered feet pass. I slink down behind the behemoth executive desk.

The orange chemical scent makes me think the office has already been cleaned. I stand up slowly. No one outside. I face the desk and open the top drawer. Inside are pencils and paper clips, an invitation to a long-past business lunch. I try the top drawer on the side, a larger one. Inside is a bottle of whiskey and a set of glasses. The drawer below it is locked.

I cast the beam of my flashlight around the desk, hoping against hope that the key might magically be lying there. Then I hear the door open behind me. Hastily I switch my flashlight off. A petite Latina woman in a white cleaning uniform and sneakers, dark hair pulled back with a bandana, appears in the doorframe and switches on the office light.

"Mr. Forrester, he asked me to deliver some papers for him," I say quickly, picking up a file folder and giving a sheepish smile. "He forgot them."

"Always asking for *some*thing, that one," she says, shaking her head. She spritzes the window with a spray bottle, gives it a cursory wipe, then wheels her cart away like someone who's not paid enough to care.

I put the flashlight in my pocket and run my hands over the desk blotter. I open a box of cigars that contains nothing but cigars, a stapler that contains nothing but staples. I go to the wall and run my fingers over the tops of the framed prints. Nothing. Could it be in one of the books on the shelf? Or not in this office at all? Maybe Forrester takes the key with him.

Then something occurs to me. I go back to the desk and sit in the chair, then put my hands in the pockets of the blazer still hanging on its back. From the right one I produce a slim silver key.

I slide it into the keyhole in the bottom drawer. The lock gives.

Inside is a filing system filled with manilla folders, each labeled with the name of a case that means nothing to me. *Mack Fiorello and John Does v. Cheese-'Ems*, *Barbara Barrel and Plaintiffs v. Unlimited Amusements Ltd.* I flick through them until one of the labels catches my eye. *Druzya*—friends. I smirk. Clever boy.

Inside the folder are a few pieces of paper, each titled "Bill of Lading." I flip through them. They're shipping forms, evidently for loads that left New York bound for Riga, mostly, but also for Helsinki, Tallinn, and a few for Saint Petersburg. The shipper is labeled as Black Sea Holdings, LLC.

They're also in chronological order. Say what you will about Forrester the Barrister, but he's nothing if not organized. I skip to the front. The first sheet is a Bill of Lading for a shipment due to go out on April eighth from Pier 9 in Red Hook, Brooklyn—one week from today.

A very well-informed notary, indeed.

I pull the paper carefully from the file and peer out the office window. Other than the cleaning lady, whose cart is stationed three offices down, there's no one in sight. I'd seen a copier in the alcove by the window. It'll make noise, but I'll have to risk it.

I slide the door open and steal over to the alcove, feeling like a phantom in Chelsea boots. I lift the cover from the copier, slide the paper in, and push the green button that sets the machine whirring. Outside, Lexington Avenue is a canyon of lights bouncing coldly off the buildings' glass curtain walls. My reflection shimmers in between. In it I see the person I could have been: the woman in the purple skirt suit and heels who commutes every day from Connecticut to put in her pound of flesh. All of it—the wan fluorescent light, the speckled ceiling panels, the office-y smell of paper and ink underscored by stale coffee—gives me a strange, sweaty-palmed sense of existential absurdity.

I take the bill and copy and steal back to Forrester's office. I've just opened the drawer when I hear the sound of the elevator opening—a *ding* that resounds like a gong on the near-empty floor. Then I hear Forrester's voice, oilier than ever, answered by another man's voice. And they're headed this way. There's no way I'll be able to slip out without them seeing me.

I dive under the desk and curl up into a tight ball. But before I do, I steal a glance at the two figures walking up to the clear office door. One is Forrester. He's accompanied by a man I don't recognize: middle-aged, his hair shot through with gray, with a certain aristocratic bearing. He's wearing an expensive-looking wool coat and a maroon scarf.

I hear the door open. "We can talk privately here," comes Forrester's voice. "But first, can I offer you a nightcap? I have an excellent bottle of single malt in my drawer."

I can hear him moving toward the desk as he says it. The blood freezes in my veins.

"None for me, thank you," says the other man. His voice is refined, educated, with a trace of an accent, something cosmopolitan and hard to place. "My countrymen have a well-earned reputation for appreciating their drink, but I prefer to keep a clear head."

"Well," says Forrester, and with relief I hear his voice moving away. "Down to business, then. Everything is set for Sunday morning. I found someone who has the . . . expertise you were looking for."

"This man is good?"

"I have it on good authority that he's the best."

"It is difficult to form a network when one first breaks new ground," the other voice muses. "But I am quite sure the rewards will be worth it."

"Glad to be in business with you," says Forrester in a milky tone that makes me stifle a gag. "I trust that in resolving this little problem, we're clearing the way to work together for a very long time."

They speak for a few minutes longer, but it's nothing of substance—attempts at small talk on Forrester's part that his companion seems to have little use for. Then the light switches off and I hear the office door close, followed by two sets of quietly receding footsteps.

I relax my hands, which I realize have balled up into fists, as I try to parse the conversation still echoing in my head. Could his companion have been Solnikov? But that doesn't feel right. Sergei implied that Forrester and Solnikov went way back, and Forrester was clearly trying to impress this guy. Like he wasn't quite sure where he stood. Not to mention Solnikov's been the boss of Brighton Beach for years. He wouldn't need to ask Forrester for any help besides legal. So, could it be Ildar Batryshkin?

One thing I know for sure: I'm going to wait until the coast is definitively clear before I make my exit. That would make for an awkward elevator ride.

It's cramped but also strangely cozy underneath the desk. It gives me a moment to take stock of my life. Parker Snow, twenty-seven-year-old crime reporter, stuffed underneath a crooked lawyer's mahogany desk like an undertaker's dirty suit. No space too small, no indignity too great to feed the snapping jaws of the Crock. My neck starts to cramp up. I manage to shift and crook my elbow sufficiently to reach into my pocket, pull out the small orange bottle, and swallow two pills.

I wait for five minutes, then ten, before crawling out from under the desk and rolling my aching shoulders back. I open the desk drawer, stuff one of the papers back into the front of the file, then shut it and lock it with the tiny silver key, which I then drop back into the blazer pocket where I found it. The office is dark now, overhead lights extinguished, the cleaning lady and her cart gone. My watch reads 10:23.

By the time I unlock the door to my apartment, the grip is loosening and a pleasant lightness is settling into the space behind my eyes. I take the paper from my coat pocket and place it on the desk, then remove my coat and hang it over the back of the chair. The typewriter text labeling the details of shipper and consignee, consent and certification, surfaces in the wan light of the street.

"Hey, Nellie," I call softly. "Nellie, Nellie, Nellie girl—"

And then I see it.

No. Please, no. With shaking hands I switch on the desk lamp and shove the paper underneath. My heart quickens, then sinks like a lead anchor. There it is, thumping up from the corner of the page: a lacy beat of blue. The stamp.

Which means this is the original.

Which means the one I put back in Forrester's drawer was the photocopy.

Shit.

12

There are no perfect victims . . .

The next morning I stand over my desk, cup of Café Bustelo in hand, the Bill of Lading with its blue stamp mocking me from its surface.

"Well, Nellie," I say. "We've certainly gotten ourselves into a fix now."

She ignores me, preferring to bat at a stray ray of sunlight falling onto the floor in the kitchen. And so I dial the newsroom. "You busy?" I ask when Jake picks up.

"A bit," he says. The background is rife with shouting voices and ringing phones. "But I can talk for a minute. How'd it go with Maloney?"

"Not great," I say. "He still doesn't want to see the possibility of a serial killer on the loose. Plus, I learned that Elizabeth Lau shot up. Which basically means her death is being chalked up as an OD."

"She did *heroin*?" he says. "Wow. I wasn't expecting that."

"Not to sound like a D.A.R.E. poster," I say, "but it really does affect all kinds."

"Have you ever done it?"

"No," I answer. "Needles freak me out. And after what I've seen . . ." I think back to the filthy loft above Petey's Bar, its resident zombies. "I'm a live and let live kind of person but suffice to say it's not pretty."

"So, what are you going to do now?" he asks.

It pains me to tell him I won't be doing anything more on Liz's story for the moment. "Crock's chomping at the bit for a follow-up on my Brighton Beach mob story and I have to get him something. Actually, that's why I'm calling. I was kind of hoping you could help me sort through some of the pieces."

"Catch me up."

Gratefully, I do. I fill him in on Black Sea Holdings; Forrester, the accident lawyer who also seems to be the shadow counsel for the mob of Brighton Beach; and the fact that the chocolate truck was taken out of evidence before any real investigation could take place. I get to the conversation I overheard in Forrester's office last night when he cuts me off.

"Wait a minute. You stole an employee's badge and snuck into this guy's office?"

I pause. ". . . yes?"

After a long moment he says, "Okay. Keep going."

I finish by telling him about the Bill of Lading I found in Forrester's desk, for a shipment of goods set to leave Red Hook next week.

"So, that seems to be your next lead," Jake says.

"I think so," I say. "We'll just hope Forrester isn't monitoring his records too closely."

"Want me to help you write something up?"

I think for a moment. "No. Not yet. I don't have anything concrete." I can almost hear the sigh Jake is withholding. "I know, I know. But

I don't know anything about this shipment. Not even what the cargo is. And I need a little more time to learn more about Ildar Batryshkin. I feel like I have a pretty good handle on Solnikov's operation, but the new guy is still a mystery. Maybe I can wheedle something out of OCCB."

I hear an impatient voice next to Jake. "One sec," he says, followed by something muffled I can't hear. He returns to the receiver. "Parker, I gotta go. There's another story coming through for a rewrite and it's— Well, anyways. I gotta go."

"Must you remind me that I'm not your only reporter?" I say. "No, no, I'm not jealous. Go ahead. It's fine."

"One thing," Jake says. "The other day when I called to tell you about Elizabeth Lau—did you say something about winding up in a holding cell?"

"I got arrested. But then I got let go," I say. "It's a long story."

"And this chocolate truck, which is apparently property of Black Sea Holdings, to which this lawyer Forrester has a connection, as notary or otherwise, magically rolls out of evidence."

"Yes."

"And then he mentions some business he and his partner are *clearing the way for*."

"That's what I overheard."

"Do you think . . . Is it possible this Forrester might actually be dangerous?"

I think about Forrester's veiled threats, the barely contained aggression I felt when he blocked his office door. A thug in a tailored suit. "I don't know," I say truthfully.

Jake tells me to be careful and I tell him I will before letting him attend to his other story. I'm just dipping the end of a fresh cigarette into the blue flame of my Zippo, contemplating my next move, when the phone rings. It's Morgan.

"I have some news," she says.

I'm probably the only one happy to hear that from the Office of the Chief Medical Examiner. *"Dis-moi."*

"You know how I asked who the ME was on that Carla Russo scene, and you couldn't remember?"

"Yes," I say carefully.

"Well, that's probably because there *was* no ME at the scene."

"What?"

Nellie has wandered her way into the room to see what all the fuss is about. I pick her up and sling her over my shoulder, a gesture I am convinced she will one day come to appreciate.

"You heard right. When there's any evidence that a death's not natural there's supposed to be an ME there, but they've got so many homicides in Brooklyn these days and so few MEs, I guess they didn't have someone to send out," Morgan says. "Apparently, some local doctor who happened to be around signed the death certificate."

I flinch. Nellie scrambles off and jumps to the floor, her needly little claws digging into my shoulder. "You don't say."

"And then when the body did reach the office," Morgan continues, "some per-diem tech fresh out of med school did the autopsy. I guess that's all this murder warranted."

"So, what was the cause of death?"

"Blunt force trauma. Like Maloney said," she replies. "However. I did something I technically shouldn't have . . ."

"You *didn't.*"

"I did. I went over to the Brooklyn house where they're keeping her and asked to speak to the ME in charge there. He kind of owed me one from a case I helped with when they were overloaded."

"And?"

"And he obliged. I took a look at the autopsy report along with the body, and it bears a striking resemblance to Elizabeth Lau's."

The lit cigarette stutters in my other hand. "Meaning . . ."

"No sexual assault in her case, either. More importantly, she was certainly struck in the head—the skull was fractured—but there was the same unusual lack of bruising. In my opinion, she had to have been struck after death, too."

I take a moment to let that sink in. So, I was right in my hunch that the murders seemed too similar. Except—"Hang on," I say. "Maloney told me Liz was a heroin addict."

"It's evident that she used. She'd probably shot up recently, judging from the fresh needle marks," Morgan says. "She had them in some weird places, too. Pocket shots. She must have been getting really desperate."

"Pocket shots?"

"Yeah. Injections into big veins, like the jugular or subclavian. Sometimes addicts get other people to administer them for them."

Immediately my mind goes to the Cowboy. *She didn't need anyone leadin' her to the devil. She was heading to him fast all by herself.* My heart sinks. "So, you think she OD'd?"

"No."

My heart gets up and does a somersault. "Explain."

"Heroin overdoses are basically drowning from the inside. Fluid seeps out of the blood vessels and fills the lungs. Liz's lungs were clear," Morgan says. "I can't conclusively state the cause of death yet, but I'm sure she didn't die of an overdose. No, I think both Carla and Liz were killed some other way. The head trauma was there to misdirect, to hide the actual cause of death. Or maybe just to make sure they were really dead. Icing on the cake sort of thing."

I wince. "Some icing."

"But the thing is, I still can't say what *did* kill them," she continues. "At least not yet. I still don't have results back from tox, on either of them. But it is odd. Nothing about them looks amiss. I mean, besides the fractured skulls."

I take a fortifying pull from my cigarette and let it out with a sigh. "Okay. Keep me posted."

"Every body tells a story," she says. "This one just happens to be a lot more mysterious than most."

I bid Morgan *au revoir* and sign off.

"What kind of sick game was Carla and Liz's murderer playing? What was the last thing they saw and thought before they died?" I wonder out loud to Nellie. "And is Maloney going to listen now?" Nellie gives me her one-eyed stare back. Women overpowered, women subdued, women's last duty to serve the sick whims of men. It all has a distastefully familiar ring to it.

I know I should do what I told Jake I'd do—look into the Bill of Lading and this Batryshkin character, see if there's any news from OCCB—but suddenly a truck full of chocolate bars feels insignificant compared to two lives lost.

Because now I can't let go of the question: Did Carla have secrets like Liz?

There are no perfect victims any more than there are perfect crimes. I weigh this theory in my mind as I sit with my now-empty cup, trying to push away nagging thoughts of the mystery doctor Morgan mentioned. So far, Carla Russo's character is shallow, slippery, a tin pan running bright with cold water. A caring, kind, promising young woman. But that can't be it. Surely there must be something else. Like I've learned with Liz Lau, there's always more than meets the eye.

Maybe if I go back to Bensonhurst, walk the path I walked from the subway station to her inert body on the sidewalk, some clue will reveal itself. If I ask around, I may even find something in common between her and Liz, some hidden thread that will help weave together how they encountered the evil that ended their lives. Gia told me where Carla lived, still in the house she grew up in. Since I'd wanted to try and speak to her mother, that would be a good place to pick things up.

I can feel it happening: the momentum pushing me there as if by its own volition, what I *should* do quickly losing the race. Now that I have the idea in my head, I may as well already be there.

Leaving the bill on my desk, I put on my coat, give Nellie a scritch behind the ears, and start for the subway.

###

When I finally emerge from the subway station on Brooklyn's Eighteenth Avenue, the same group of teenage ne'er-do-wells is hanging around outside, leaning against the same construction barricade. They fall silent as I pass, their eyes snagging me like tiny hooks.

I cross the avenue and start down Sixty-Fourth. It's the first time I've been on the street since that night. I thought it might feel eerie, but in fact, it just feels like any other residential Brooklyn street. The houses are mostly neat, modest, single-family homes, white siding on red brick, well-trimmed scraps of yard kept with a reduced suburban pride. Mary statues on the half shell, deer-shaped planters filled with carnations. No trace of Carla's ghost that I can sense.

I walk two blocks down Nineteenth Avenue and then turn onto Sixty-Sixth—the Russos' street. I find number 1825, the address Gia gave me. It looks like all the other houses on the block except that it has a bay window. A short path of stepping stones leads from the sidewalk through the small front yard, bushes on either side flowering with bright orange day lilies and purple hydrangeas. Everything appears to be in order, but there's something off that I can't put my finger on.

I pause and consider going to the door. I want to talk to her mother. But I also don't trust myself to be faced with it, that barrage of grief. I reach out a hand to touch the hydrangea blooms, so round and purple and bright, and my fingertip is met by the rough tongue of weatherproof fabric. Fake.

Then the decision is made for me. The door swings open and a woman appears, gray hair framing a middle-aged face and making it look older than its years. I drop my hand from the flowers and take a step back.

"I'm sorry to bother you," I say. "My name is Parker Snow. I'm a reporter for *The New York Street*."

In my experience, people have two reactions to someone asking questions after a tragedy. One is anger. Those types slam the door in your face, appalled that you'd come darken their doorstep in their hour of grief. The other can be even worse: the ones who want to talk endlessly about the one they lost, and to anyone who will listen, as if in doing so, they might not have to let go. The old cheat-death filibuster.

But Carla's mother doesn't do either of those things. She doesn't even ask what I'm doing in her bushes. She just stands there, silent, arms hanging at her sides.

I'm about to walk away when she speaks, her voice struggling its way out of her throat. "You're the one who wrote about Carla."

"Yes," I say, somewhat taken aback. "That's right."

"Why did you do it?"

"Why did I—"

"How could you do this to us?"

She's staring straight at me now, but there's no anger in her stare. There's just a bareness so complete and unadorned that I have to look away.

Then she shakes her head and seems to come back to herself. "I'm sorry," she says.

"That's alright," I say. My voice sounds like a strange echo of itself.

She glances behind her into the depths of the house. "I'm sorry," she repeats. "My husband's not well."

"Please give him my best," I say, because I'm not sure what else to say. But she doesn't seem to be listening; instead, she's looking through me, as if seeing someone else in my place. A spray of freckles over pale skin. A shimmer of long, dark hair. Goosebumps creep up my arms.

She closes the door. Through the bay window I see her cross the living room, wringing her hands.

I'm turning back to the sidewalk when I see it—what's off about this scene. The Mary statue is turned away, staring at the house's white siding.

I walk slowly down the sidewalk and away from the house, the strangeness of it all still vibrating off of me. Where to go from here? Gia had said that Carla's after-work routine was to go home, drop by the pizzeria—then go to a neighborhood bakery to work. I'd seen an Italian bakery close to the subway. It would almost certainly have to be the one.

I step back onto the avenue and walk toward the bakery, passing by the group of felons-in-training who are still leaning against the barricade with cigarettes and soda bottles.

"Hey!" one of them yells—the ringleader, who pushed the trash can into the Asian kid's path.

"Hey!" he repeats. "I'm talkin' to you."

I turn around. "Yeah?"

"You're not from around here," he says.

"Very observant," I reply.

"You're not from around here, but you always come here." He hops from the barricade and walks over to me, his buddies falling into place behind him. They're all wearing wifebeaters and dog tags on chains that bounce off their skinny chests, their hair gelled back.

"Is this the part where you all break out in song?" I ask.

He narrows his eyes. "We don't like people nosing here who don't belong here." He has a bat in his hands that I hadn't noticed before, and he's swinging it lazily, like he's ambling up to the plate for summer softball practice.

"You need a passport to go to Brooklyn now?"

"You do on our watch." He drags the bat across a length of chain link. The gnashing sound of metal against metal sets my teeth on edge. "And we think you've been spending way too much time around here."

I don't have to glance to my right to remember the empty lot that's there—the one they're trying to corner me into. They're closing the distance fast, and it doesn't look like they're angling for an analysis on whatever went wrong in their childhoods.

A doorbell tinkles and a door swings open. A portly man wearing a forest-green apron over white shirt sleeves steps out. "Hey!" he shouts. "What are you brats doing bothering this young lady?"

"We weren't *bothering* no one," the ringleader says. But the bat is now hanging at his side. "We were just walkin' down the sidewalk. You own the sidewalk now?"

"Get home, Ruggiero," the baker commands. "Or I'm gonna call up your old man and tell him you've been getting your dirty nose dirtier."

The ringleader, Ruggiero, mutters something obscene under his breath. But then he starts walking. His friends slump along after him, leveling both me and the old man with their most malevolent looks.

I turn to the baker once they've passed. "Real charming bunch."

"Nothing to do but make a menace," he says, shaking his head as he stares at their retreating backs. He looks back at me. "You look like you could use a cup of coffee."

"I've been hearing that a lot lately."

I follow him in through the door he's holding open. Inside, glass cases are piled high with scalloped-edged butter cookies blitzed with rainbow sprinkles, thumbprints spotted with red jam, cannoli shells waiting to be piped with ricotta cream. On the countertop a La Marzocco espresso machine chromely gleams.

"Have a seat," the baker says. "They call me GP, by the way. That's my granddaughter, Martina. Helps me around the store, keeps the accounts. She's an angel."

There's only one other person there: a young woman sitting at a laminate wood table with a stack of receipts and a ledger book. Martina the Angel doesn't look up.

"I don't want to keep you if you're closed," I say.

"No trouble, no trouble at all. I've got to put up the dough for tomorrow." He shuffles behind the counter and takes the coffee pot off the warmer. "Those kids. They all think they're pretty tough, even if they are mostly bark. I remember when they were all little babies stumbling over themselves in their front yards. Now they're killing themselves to get to the back of Lupino's Fruit Stand." He shakes his head. "What the neighborhood's coming to. Cream and sugar?"

"Black," I say. "What's in the back of Lupino's Fruit Stand?"

"Neighborhood trouble. You know—the kind those brats think they wanna be." He pours the coffee. "Sports betting, mostly. Loans at sky-high interest rates to cover them, and god help you if you don't pay back. Their parents were all good, hardworking people, just doing their best. I look back and I try to find where it went bad. And I just can't figure it out."

"Some people have bad in them from the start," I say. "And they're the ones who infect everyone too weak to think their way out of it."

The young woman at the table suddenly speaks. "Danny Ruggiero's the weakest of all."

She hasn't looked up from her work, but she's not moving the receipts, her pen no longer going down the ledger. I go to the table and sit down across from her. The baker puts a white cup and saucer in front of me along with a plate of rainbow cookies. He pats his granddaughter's shoulder with a weathered hand and her face softens. Then he ambles back behind the counter and disappears through the swinging kitchen doors.

Martina looks up at me. "Who are you?"

"My name's Parker Snow," I say. "I'm a reporter for *The New York Street*."

She doesn't say anything for a moment, just taps her pen against the ledger book. "What my granddad says about how they're mostly bark. He wants to think it's true. It's not."

I turn the cup slowly in my hands. It says GIAMPIERO BAKERY in faded green letters.

"I made the mistake of going with them in a car one night when I was fifteen," she continues, her eyes looking distantly over my shoulder. "We were gonna drive over to Belt Parkway and head to the beach.

We only got as far as the overpass." She shakes her head, as if trying to throw off the memory. "When my mom always said not to get into cars with boys, I just thought she was being square."

"Did you tell anyone what happened?"

"No point," she says. "Not how things work around here. I was a dumb kid then, anyway. I guess I thought it was my own damn fault."

I take a sip of coffee. It tastes round and simple and hot, the way a cup of bakery coffee should, but it goes down like ice.

"What are you doing knocking around this part of town, anyway?" she asks.

"I'm reporting on the murder of Carla Russo," I reply. "Did you know her well?"

She shakes her head slowly. "We were close when we were kids. But I haven't exactly been close with anyone these past few years. I'm just helping my grandfather until I graduate. Then I'm getting the hell out."

"Sometimes one foot in and one foot out is the best vantage point."

She tips her head in agreement. "I'll say that none of the boys liked her. I mean, not like they thought she was a skag, or something. She wasn't. In fact, she was sort of . . . aloof. Not like everyone else." She pauses. "Carla knew the dark places."

"Did she . . ." I pause, trying to find a delicate way to say it. "Do you happen to know if Carla might have been involved with drugs?"

Martina blinks, her brow furrowing. "No. I mean, not that I know of. I would be very surprised, to say the least," she says. "Why do you ask?"

I sigh. "Just asking." I figured it was a long shot, but I had to check. So far, I haven't learned anything that illuminates Carla Russo's dark side. In fact, I haven't learned much about her at all. "Is this the bakery where Carla used to study?" I ask.

"Yep. She kind of made that table in the back her office," Martina says, pointing behind me. "GP didn't mind. Actually, her stuff's still there. No one can bring themselves to move it."

I automatically start to stand up, then stop and look at Martina. She looks back at me and shrugs.

I rise and walk through the row of tables. Sure enough, at the table in the very back corner, almost invisible outside the warm circle cast by the overhead lights, is a neat stack of textbooks. I move closer to read their titles: *The Pediatric Handbook. Essentials of Nursing. Caring for the Chronically Ill.* Next to them are a spiral notebook and two ballpoint pens, everything perfectly aligned. On the notebook's cover the words Carla Russo are written in tidy black letters.

I pick up the notebook and leaf through. It's filled with lecture notes, each page dated and followed by meticulous bullet points beneath underlined sections, until about two-thirds of the way through, when the pages go blank.

"How's it been, trying to find the facts?" Martina asks behind me. "I mean, besides Ruggiero and his wannabe wiseguys."

I flip the notebook closed. I'm not sure what I expected to find—a list titled People of Interest in My Murder?

"Not great," I say. "No true witnesses, no physical evidence, not even a good suspect. And no one's exactly helping. You all close rank pretty tight around here, don't you?"

She rolls her eyes. "Don't get me started. That's one of the reasons I'm getting out. This place is worse than a cult." She looks at the notebook in my hand, then says, "She actually wrote me letters."

"Carla?" I ask, surprised. "I thought you said you weren't close."

"We weren't," she says. "We barely spoke out loud. I don't even remember who started it, but it was like passing notes—like we used to do in class, when we were kids." She opens the flap of the messenger bag on the seat next to her and starts fishing around.

"But she had Gia," I say. "They were best friends. At least that's what Gia told me."

"Oh, yeah. Those two have been inseparable since birth. But I guess sometimes it's easier telling things to someone you don't know that well, who doesn't have a certain idea about you. Plus, she was questioning her faith, which she couldn't talk about with Gia, good Catholic that she is. Like everyone else in this neighborhood. But she knew I'd stopped going to church when I was, like, twelve." She produces a folded piece of paper and holds it out to me. "I still have the last letter she wrote me. You can read it, if you want."

I place the notebook on the table and reach for the letter, unfolding it with unsteady hands. It's written on the same paper, in the same careful blue ballpoint as her class notes, but there's an urgency that threatens to spill out over the neat college rule. I catch a few words as I skim—*dad*, *Anthony*, *Brighton Beach*, *hospital*. But it's the date at the top that hits me like a speeding subway car: 3/22/92. The day before Carla was killed.

My heart leaps to my throat. "Can I have this?"

"Not sure how useful it'll be, but go ahead," Martina replies. "I'm glad someone's trying to find out what really happened. I might not believe in God anymore, but I still want Carla to rest in peace. You know?"

I nod. "I know."

I refold the letter and tuck it carefully in the inside pocket of my coat. I pick up my cup for a final sip, place it back in its saucer, and get ready to holler my thanks back to GP, for the coffee and for saving my hide.

But something still gnaws at me. "You said you thought it was your fault, what happened to you back then," I say to Martina. "What do you think now?"

She looks out the window, dark eyes narrowed. "Now I think you're better off not thinking too hard about anything."

###

I'm back at home now, a lit cigarette wafting comfortingly from between my fingers. Nellie leans back on her haunches, then jumps onto the bookshelf and settles in front of the French philosophers. Nellie has always been particularly influenced by the works of Camus. Piano scales filter down from the apartment above, then a bravura attempt at Rachmaninov that quickly fades. The Bill of Lading is still on my desk next to Liz's journal, its typewritten logistics exerting a weak pull compared to the last recorded thoughts of a flesh-and-blood being.

"Leon said Liz didn't have any friends named Carla. And when Martina said that Carla didn't do drugs, I'm inclined to believe her," I ponder out loud. "Of course, people can hide habits like that," I acknowledge. My pill bottle winks dully from my desk.

Nellie looks at me from the shelf, unimpressed. I stub out my cigarette and heave a sigh. "Why can't one thing, just one thing, be easy?"

Nellie twitches her tail and cocks her head slightly. Then she jumps off the shelf with a contemptuous meow and pads out of the room.

I think about everything that happened that afternoon with the bat boys, the bakery, Martina. What all that has to do with a pizza parlor, or a music student, or a body shop that specializes in nice things past their prime. But what stays with me is the image of Carla's mother wringing her hands behind the bay window.

Carla knew the dark places.

I take the square folded sheet of paper from my pocket and smooth it out on my desk. Carla's last letter to Martina. It looks sad and strange there, vibrating white against the scuffed wood. Like a wedding guest at a funeral.

Nellie springs up into the tattered old armchair by the window, watching me. I pull out the desk chair and sit down to read.

3/22/92

Martina,

I think it's sweet, the way your grandfather is always calling you angel. We always have to be angels here, don't we? It seems like men are always trying to control us, even if it's with how much they love us.

Like my dad. He had all these pet names for me, too—sugar and princess and sweetheart. But then if you did something stupid, or something he thought was wrong, his eyes would get dark and angry and the yelling would start. If he was really heated, you'd get a belt to your bottom or, later, a hand to your face. Sal, me, it didn't matter. The only one he never touched or raised his voice at was our mom. With her, he was always meek. We always knew she was upset with him when he'd show up with a bouquet of peonies—her favorite. My favorite, too. After a bad spell, our house would suddenly be filled with them. "See?" Mom would say. "Things aren't so bad. It'll be okay."

"It'll be okay." Have you ever noticed how often people say that? As if saying it will make it so? When you're a kid you think they must know something you don't. The biggest shock of my life was realizing that there were some things that aren't, that will never be, okay.

Like when it started with my dad. Stumbling, tripping, slurring his words. My mom thought he'd started drinking, though that's one thing he'd never done before. He got even moodier. Then he curled up into himself, like a cicada that year they swarmed in and left their nasty husks on every tree branch and mailbox. This person who always seemed so powerful. And there was Mom, still spending her days cleaning the house, as if it even mattered. Insisting everything would be fine. "It's not fine," I wanted to yell at her. "Stop pretending. Nothing is fine."

I think about it too long and it makes me feel the same way. I start to chew, can't swallow. I feel it gripping me by the throat, constricting my airways. Some days I feel like one of those dried-out fishes they sell in stacks over at Brighton Beach, my lips peeled back against my skull, my eyes wide and gaping. The fear gets me like the blade of a hand right where my shoulder meets my neck, sending a jolt all through me. Like something stalking me.

When Dad got too sick to control me, Sal filled his place. He thinks he's being protective when really, he's suffocating me. Especially when we both know the reason he fights and thrashes and gives off so much sound and fury. Because life is a wave going over his head.

And of course, Anthony. In normal life he's quiet and pensive. The kind of person you don't even notice on the sidewalk or in the subway, who'd rather live in music than here, in the real world. But when we're alone, just the two of us, it's different. A side other people don't see, that Gia or Sal could never understand. It scares me sometimes, the fierceness of it. What someone can do if they love you that much. How it's too much and still not enough.

It's nice talking to you like this. Almost like writing in a journal, except that there's someone on the other side asking why? Or how? Or, did it feel like this, or like that? It's helped me a lot, in ways you won't ever know. In ways I can't really share with Gia, as much as I love and admire her. I always envied her confidence, the way she always said exactly what she felt. Whereas I didn't even know exactly what I felt.

Anthony thinks he knows more than I do. That I should just listen to him and believe.

What he doesn't know is that it will destroy me.

13

A woman fading into herself . . .

The next day, I open the door to the office a crack. Then I open it another crack, enough to peer at Crock's door. It's open and the light is off. I step inside and exhale.

That's when I see Schultz, his chair leaned back and his feet stacked on his desk, face hidden by yesterday's paper. A corner of the paper lowers. He's staring straight at me with a smirk on his face, as if I was just the person he'd been waiting for.

"Avoiding the Crock?" he says. "Whyever could that be?"

"I'm not avoiding anyone," I say pointedly. "Though I could do with a little less of you."

"Hey, no need to get squirrely. I liked your article. I mean, I enjoyed it." He swings his legs off the desk and leans onto an elbow. "Parker Snow, righteous defender of the innocent. But tell me, like—is it really worth your ass getting canned? Especially when it was probably just the boyfriend who did it?" He leans on the other elbow. "Isn't it always?"

"Why don't you worry about your own ass and leave mine be?" I reach my desk and start to empty out my pockets.

"Just trying to look out for you," he says. "I mean, do you *really* think you could get yourself another job in this town?"

I ignore him, flouncing my coat over the back of my chair. One less collar for me to get hot under.

But he's not giving up that easy. "I'm just saying. It just seems to me that you got a pretty good thing going now. Crock letting you stay on as organized crime reporter, what with everything that happened with your story about those immigrant girls—"

"Shove it, Schultz," I growl.

He picks up the paper again and flicks it open. "No need to get defensive."

I sit down and start flipping through my notebook. One thing he's right about: I have to get down to business on this Russian stuff. I find the number for my contact at the Organized Crime Control Bureau and am just picking up the phone to call when Schultz pipes up again, right on cue.

"Oh, I almost forgot," he says, lowering the paper again. "Someone called for you earlier."

I put the phone down, exasperated. "What? Who?"

"Some lady. Says she has some kind of information about the girl."

"What girl?"

"You know, Snow. The one who got bumped," he says lazily. "Carla what's-her-face."

I know he's being obtuse to infuriate me. As devil-may-care as he plays it, Schultz has a mind for details like a steel trap.

He puts the paper down and riffles through some scraps on his desk, then extends one of them to me. "Candace something-or-other. Says she wants to see you. Doesn't want to talk over the phone."

I stand up and take the paper. On it is scrawled *Candace Gracen, 908 Park Avenue*, in Schultz's crabbed script.

"What could a woman with an uptown address possibly know about the murder of a twenty-year-old girl in Bensonhurst, Brooklyn?" I wonder out loud. But I'm already picking up the things I put down on my desk not a moment ago.

"Probably a quack," he says. "One of those poor little rich ladies trying to get some attention."

"Shall I let her know your prices by the hour?" I say as I shrug my coat back on. The look on Schultz's face gives me the first real laugh I've had in weeks.

###

The maid lets me in. I know she's the maid because she's actually wearing a maid's uniform, with the white apron and the starched collar. I didn't think they even made those anymore, but I guess I wasn't being let into the right apartments. This one starts with a foyer that could comfortably accommodate my entire one-bedroom. Right in the middle is a circular table of Italian marble laden with a flower arrangement fit for a palazzo, which leads to a hallway lined with more closed doors than Versailles. The maid, a dark-eyed and unsmiling woman, leads me down it and deposits me in the parlor without a word.

A woman is standing, looking out of a set of large windows that overlook Madison Avenue, her back to me. I'm first struck by how thin she is, her shoulder blades cutting knife-like through the green silk of her dress. Her arms are crossed, a hand clutching each elbow.

She turns to me then, though I haven't said anything and neither has the maid. It's as if they're both playing parts in a well-rehearsed play, and I'm the one who hasn't gotten her stage directions. She's around fifty, with white-blonde, shoulder-length hair and pale blue eyes. A woman fading into herself.

"Parker Snow?"

"Ms. Gracen."

"Thank you for coming," she says. She gestures toward the divan. "Do sit down."

I do as I'm told. The divan is upholstered in cream-colored leather, so soft and supple I find myself rubbing the pads of my fingers against it. Everything about the parlor is tasteful and expensive, from the enamel-inlaid end tables to the silver bar cart to the gray drapes fluttering slightly in the breeze. And especially the woman now sitting opposite me in a high-backed mahogany chair. She's wearing taupe heels with the silk dress, emerald-and-diamond studs in her ears, and the kind of makeup that looks so apparently non-existent, it must take her an hour to put on. Well-kept and miserable. I know her type so well it hurts.

"Anna, will you bring us some water, please?" she calls.

The maid seems to materialize out of nowhere with a tray, pitcher, and two glasses. She sets them on the polished coffee table, pours the water, and leaves without a sound. I wonder if she's mute.

Candace Gracen and I sit for a moment in silence. I glance around at the walls, painted a light, periwinkle blue and hung with framed Impressionist watercolors that would make the Met curator jealous.

"Nice place," I offer.

"Thank you," she says, inclining her head with the privileged humility that comes with old money. "One of the things my ex-husband was kind enough to leave me."

She attempts a smile, but it quickly fades. Silence again. I catch a whiff of her perfume—something green and violety, peppery. She fingers the platinum tennis bracelet around her wrist, and I notice that her hands are trembling.

I clear my throat. "My colleague indicated you had something you wanted to discuss regarding the story I wrote about Carla Russo."

Her hand darts out to the glass of water on the table and she takes a sip, as if steadying herself. Then she draws a deep breath and looks at me.

"I knew her," she says. "Not well. But I knew her."

"How?"

"I run a philanthropic circle for children with cancer," she says. "It's a cause particularly close to my heart. My youngest brother passed away from it when he was only twelve years old."

"I'm sorry to hear that."

"Yes. Well." She gets up and starts to pace. "The girl, she was a nursing student. She volunteered for us at Mount Sinai, providing assistance when we'd go to visit the children and their families, bringing them toys and such. That's just one part of it, of course. We're also funding a research program in pediatric oncology." Her eyes dart back to me.

I wait.

"I met her several times through the course of these visits," she continues. "We were friendly. I always admired the way the children just seemed to relax around her. A manner I never had myself, with my own children, if you ask them." She gives a quavery laugh.

"The last time I saw her, it was the weekend before she . . . before she died. So, you can imagine my shock when I opened the paper and saw your story." She walks toward the windows again, as if she'd been making a study of something outside and must continue it. It strikes me that she doesn't look like the kind of person who would read a tabloid—more of a *New York Times* type—but I don't want to interrupt whatever revelation Gracen seems to be warming up to.

"We had another round of visits scheduled for the following Saturday," she continues, her back to me. "I can't describe how terrible it was to read, to know that her young life had been taken from her in such a brutal manner."

"Do you remember what you talked about, the last time you saw her?" I say. "Anything at all, even the slightest details, can be—"

"Yes. I remember." She turns suddenly to face me. "I had started to feel warmly toward her, almost like she was my own. So, I noticed right away how she looked. Pale. Troubled. I asked her what the matter was.

At first, she brushed it off. But I pressed her and eventually she told me. She said her brother was in some kind of trouble. She wouldn't tell me exactly what. But she mentioned a woman named Maria. Of course, I made my assumptions, but she was just so upset. She was . . . she was deeply agitated."

Sal's face springs up in my mind, his bristling energy, a spark plug searching for something to ignite. "Did she say anything else about this Maria?" I ask. "Or what it was her brother was involved in?"

"No. She didn't say anything else." She walks to the couch and sits down next to me, gripping my arm. "You'll do your best to find out, won't you?" Her eyes are blue and fathomless as glaciers.

I look down at her hand on my forearm. She follows my gaze and releases it.

"I just feel that someone who could do something so terrible is bound to do it again," she says.

"Of course," I murmur. Suddenly I feel the pill bottle blaze white-hot in my pocket. "I'll do my best to look into it."

"I hope you'll forgive the dramatics." Again she attempts the quavery laugh. "Things have been . . . difficult, recently. My father's been ill and it's putting quite a bit of stress on us all." She picks up her hands as if showing me something, but they fall down into her lap like shot doves.

Then all at once she changes, her tone becoming bland and bright as she leads me out with the light hand of a practiced hostess, thanking me for coming and hoping we'll stay in touch, like we've just finished afternoon tea. Her glacial eyes are now mirror glass, clear and unrevealing.

Anna the maid is standing silently in the hallway, like she's been waiting. She hands me my coat. Before I follow her back to the foyer, I glance back through the partially opened parlor door. Candace Gracen is standing at the silver bar cart, uncapping a bottle of vodka and pouring it into a crystal tumbler, sunlight glinting brilliantly off the shiny metal around her wrist. She gulps it down with a thirst that makes me sweat.

###

I go back to the office and find that Schultz is, blessedly, no longer there. I pick up the phone to call over to OCCB once again, only to find that my fingers are dialing another number.

"J&V Pizzeria."

The sound of the pizza shop jumps brightly into my ear, the voices of the guys behind the counter mingling with customers and the pizza oven shutting with a creak of hinges. "Gia," I say. "Parker Snow, from the *Street*."

"Hey," she says after a short pause. The kind of *hey* that's really an *Oh. It's you.*

"Sorry to bother you at work," I say. "I just have a quick question. Do you know someone named Maria?"

"Girl, this is Bensonhurst. You're gonna have to be more specific."

"Someone Carla knew, too, who might know something about the case?"

"About Carla getting killed?" She sounds surprised. "Nah. They're just regular neighborhood girls. Can't say nothin' worse than that."

I sigh and scrunch my fingers through the lock of hair that always falls into my face. "Okay. But if you think of anything, any possible connection, call me, okay?"

"Okay," she says. "Why do you ask, anyway?"

"I got a lead. It's probably nothing, but I had to check into it." I'm about to thank Gia and let her go when she says: "There is one thing."

The hair on my arms pricks up. "What's that?"

"It doesn't have to do with any Marias, but I thought it was weird." I hear Lenny's voice yelling at Gia to stop tying up the phone line and get back to the register. She yells something less than decorous back, then returns to the receiver. "Sal had been really nervous about something before Carla died. Like, he was terrified. Walking around the neighborhood pale as a ghost. But then . . ." She trails off.

"What is it, Gia?" I urge.

"I almost don't want to say it, because of how it sounds," she says, reluctance edging her voice. "But the thing is, just yesterday, he comes into the shop for a slice and it's like, some weight's been lifted. He's jokin' with the guys, almost like his old self again. It's almost like . . . he's relieved." I hear something clatter in the background. "Now I really gotta go. I'm tyin' up the line."

She hangs up, leaving me in a perplexed silence. What was Sal so scared of, and why did that change after Carla died? What weight could have been lifted with his sister's violent death?

"And who the hell is Maria?" I say out loud.

No one answers back. I try to get back on task; I start to call my Organized Crime Control Bureau contact again, but my fingers feel fat, my mind sludgy. Maybe I took one too many this morning. Or was it this afternoon? Suddenly I can't remember, and I feel very tired.

Random sentences come back to me from my book of Russian phrases. *The situation is very delicate. The arguments I referred to won't hold water. I'm afraid I shall have to cry off till Monday. The medical facilities at the plant are of a very high standard indeed.*

Medical facilities. The dark scene from the clinic enters my mind again, the scene from last year—the girl on the exam table, scared and vulnerable. The life that leaves her. I try to push it away, but then there are Schultz's words, echoing annoyingly in the back of my mind: *Righteous defender of the innocent. Is it really worth your ass getting canned?*

I get up, throw on my coat, and leave.

###

Orange vesper light filters into Otto's Auto. The shop is empty save for Sal, who is standing over the open hood of a dented Maserati.

"Sal," I say. "Got a minute?"

He looks up so fast he almost hits his head on the top. He's clearly surprised to see me, and not in a pleasant way. "What the hell are you doing here again?"

"Sorry to show up unannounced. It's just that something's been bothering me."

"How's that my problem?"

"Because it's you that's bothering me," I say. "Let's cut to the chase. It's no secret you don't like Anthony Jones. You never did. Last year, a kid from the housing project where he lives was killed for walking into your neighborhood. You wouldn't know anything about that, would you?"

"No, I wouldn't," he says nastily. "I mind my own goddamn business."

"But this *was* your business," I say. "You didn't approve of Anthony, and you knew Carla was engaged to him."

"Are you saying I'd whack my own sister because she was dating the wrong guy?" he scoffs. "Jesus. This isn't Sicily. We don't kill our relatives because they ruined their honor."

"I don't think you killed your own sister," I say. "But I do think you know something you're not copping to. Anthony was not welcome in this neighborhood. He even got beat up here once, right after he started seeing Carla. Maybe someone decided to retaliate."

"I didn't— I wasn't—" His face has gone tight and red. "I never laid a finger on the guy."

"I also know you were lying about being at the garage that night," I continue. "I know it because the garage was closed. What's more, you were nervous about something right up until the day Carla died. And then something changed. You weren't scared anymore."

"You got it all wrong."

"So, where were you, then?" I demand. "That Monday evening when Carla was killed?"

He pulls the prop out from under the hood. It slams shut with a loud *clap*. "I was at Lupino's Fruit Stand, okay?"

Lupino's Fruit Stand. The place GP, the baker, had told me about, where the neighborhood wiseguys collect bets and break knees.

I take a step back to examine Sal's face. Shame and contrition are written all over it. I realize that he's telling the truth.

"Horses, baseball, or jai alai?"

He looks away, jaw set. Then he mutters: "Football."

"How deep?"

He throws the towel onto the hood of the car and sits down heavily on an overturned bucket. In a voice drained of any fight, he responds, "Ten grand. Before interest."

I kick another bucket over with my foot, slide it slowly across the floor, and lower myself down, facing Sal. The setting sun is squeezing its way through the garage's small windows, throwing the cars, the wall of tools, the stacks of tires into glowing relief.

"There was a moment when I . . ." he starts. He's looking away, talking more to himself than to me. "When I thought that the bookie and his crew were trying to send me a message. Like, maybe they didn't mean to kill Carla. Just rough her up, you know?" His eyes meet mine. "Because they knew that would scare me a lot more than roughin' me up. They knew how protective I was of her. I thought maybe it had gone further than they'd wanted, that it was maybe an accident. But then . . ." he trails off, looking searchingly toward the windows.

"Then what?"

He huffs a sigh. "After Carla dies, just this last week, the guy who'd been on me for the dough asks for a meeting. Naturally I'm scared. I decide to just be up-front. Own up to the situation and ask for more time. So, I start talking about the money I owe, and how I'm gonna pay it back, all that yada yada, and then he goes, don't worry about it." He shakes his head, incredulous. "Just like that. *Don't worry about it.*"

"Maybe they decided to forgive it," I say. "In light of what happened to your sister. I mean, ten grand. It's not the end of the world."

He looks at me scornfully. "You kidding? These guys would break your legs over a goddamn five spot."

"So, what do you think happened?"

He lifts a heavy shoulder. "I got no idea."

Carla's description of her brother in her letter to Martina comes back to me then—that life was a wave going over Sal's head. I realize that the electricity he gives off is coiled-up rage: rage at the life he lives and the one he doesn't, the troubled mother and the sick father, the sibling he had who he'll never have again.

Sal doesn't look at me when I get up to leave. He's off somewhere else, staring into another life, one that doesn't start in this garage and end in Lupino's Fruit Stand.

14

Just pure, honest grifting . . .

I get to work the next morning, coffee and bagel in hand. It's quiet and still at the midmorning hour, everyone off on assignments. I'm thinking about Sal and the mysterious forgiveness of his debts after his sister's death. It doesn't seem like a coincidence. I'm thinking about Candace Gracen—all her wealthy fragility, how eager she seemed to make sure I knew she was a good person—and all the other parts of this case I don't understand when a gruff voice yells my name.

I start. I didn't know Crock was there. *And how the hell did he know it was me out here?*

"Where's my follow-up?" he says by way of hello when I walk through his office door.

I feel my neck grow hot. Because what have I gotten him after he chewed me out, demanding *something close to your daisy-chain story*?

"I'm working on it," I say lamely.

Crock looks at me in disbelief. I look uncomfortably back. They're doing some work on another floor and a high-pitched scraping is emanating from somewhere in the guts of the building, a sound that sets my teeth on edge.

"That's what you said to me five days ago," he says once the wailing fades.

Five days ago? I think. *Was it really five?*

"I know," I say, trying to sound conciliatory. "I'm sorry. There have just been other things—"

"A lot of people in this office are lazy," he says, cutting my non-explanation short. "Schultz, the rest of them. They make it their mission to do as little as possible. That's not you and that's never been you. From the moment you walked in here seven years ago, even when you didn't know the first thing about how a paper gets made, you were smart. More than that, you were fearless.

"But you have a way of pushing things too far," Crock says, his voice rising. "And now you've pushed me too far. Every inch I give you, you take a goddamn avenue. You're on organized crime now. So, where's the big story you claimed to be working on?"

The scraping, or drilling, has started again, so I have to raise my voice over it. "I promise you, Crock, it's in the works—"

The building starts to vibrate, and as it does, a paper slips off the pile on his desk. He grabs for it, but he's not fast enough. I catch it before it lands on the floor and flip it right-side up. It's the proof for a story with the headline BABY ROSE FINDS NEW HOME, accompanied by a photo of a baby with one arm.

The baby who suffered a botched abortion. The baby who went from foster care to adoption because her mother is dead, the mother who never actually became one. The baby whose photo first made the front page on that paper I keep at home in my kitchen. To the public, that baby became a symbol of a failed system. But to me, the baby represents my worst mistake—my failed attempt to change that system.

I feel my heart squeeze like a wrung sponge.

As if on cue, all the noise and vibration stops, replaced with a sudden and complete silence. Carefully, I place the proof back on Crock's desk.

"I'm sorry, Parker," he says, his voice quiet now. "I know you have something to prove to yourself by reporting on these girls' murders. But street crime isn't your job anymore, and for good reason. At this point, I think it would be best if you stepped away from the paper for a bit."

It takes a moment to settle in—what he's really, actually saying. Anxiety swells inside me like a black balloon. All at once I'm back at the loft above Petey's Bar, looking at the woman with the corpse face and sores covering her twiggy limbs. "I need this, Crock," I say. "I need this job." I can hear the pleading in my voice, and I don't care. Because I no longer have illusions. The dragon the woman was chasing, the one that's really chasing her—I know, deep down, how little chance I'd have of outrunning it.

When I meet Crock's eyes, he's looking back at me with real sadness. But he just shakes his head. "You've broken the rules too many times, Parker. I can't."

The last two words settle down like a death knell. But then, careening past my better judgment, is the insistent monosyllable: *Pills. Pills. Pills.* The doctor's hand, writing the prescription. How long will it take to get to Brooklyn? How many will he give me? I can practically feel the paper in my hand, my thumb and forefinger rubbing it between them.

Paper. Signatures. Forms. It flashes before my eyes—the Bill of Lading. Sitting on my desk at home. The ship setting sail out of Red Hook harbor in just four days.

"I have something," I blurt out.

And then I start talking. I tell Crock I've been putting together a big story about the newest theft-and-export scheme the Russians are working on, stealing cargo and shipping it back to the old country for a fat profit. I leave out the part about sneaking into Forrester's office and stealing the bill; instead, I make it sound like I've been working hard behind the scenes investigating and all I need to do is get to the docks to put the final piece in place. It's going to be a real bombshell, I hint, this article. I might talk up how certain I am, just a little bit, but it's all in the name of journalism.

Crock pauses for an excruciating moment. Then he says, "Okay, go work it." I can tell that both of us are relieved.

###

I throw out my now-cold bagel and go home to get the Bill of Lading from my desk, then board a Brooklyn-bound D train. Now it's making painful, grinding process along the tracks, lurching forward a few feet only to come to a bone-jarring halt, as if its sole purpose is to make me feel the full extent of my mortal powerlessness. It's doing a very good job. I consider getting out to hail a cab I can't afford, but then we crawl out of the tunnel and onto the bridge, only to stop halfway suspended between Manhattan and Brooklyn. I look down at the glittering river and wonder what it would be like for the train to just tip over and fall into it. I imagine the sight of it from East River Park, the glint of the cars as they fall like links on a massive chain, the mammoth splash as they hit the water.

Catastrophe. Like the one I brought on at that downtown clinic.

There was an abortionist doing late-term operations on young women, most of whom were here without papers, who spoke little English and had no money. I think he felt he was doing something good. A service of sorts. I was working up a feature about it. I would wait outside the clinic every evening and talk to the girls, slowly earning their trust. They had so much to say, once they got going—about where they'd come from, how they'd gotten here, what they imagined this place would be and what it was. They were scared and overwhelmed but also hopeful that this could just be something in their past, something they could one day forget.

I realize now that I should have told someone about it who wanted to help them and had the power to do so. But I didn't. I kept hearing their stories, adding more and more to mine. I wanted to get it right in a way that felt impossible in a few hundred words churned out before the daily deadline to fill out space on page eighteen.

Well, I guess I held out a little too long, because the cops ended up finding out about the place before I published. I'm not sure what or who tipped them off. They raided it during an operation—a complicated one—and the girl on the table bled to death before they could save her. The baby survived, though she lost an arm.

So, that's what happened last year.

The train once again lurches and we haul forward, wheels scraping along the tracks. I take two pills and close my eyes, trying to get the image out of my head, the shame out of my body, to burn out the sadness and replace it with smooth pharmacological white noise. I still have my job, I remind myself. I still have this story. I still have a chance.

###

As neighborhoods go, Red Hook would be one of Brooklyn's loveliest if it didn't so much resemble hell on earth. At one point George Washington led his troops to fend off the British here, after the Dutch dug canals and gave them charming names like Buttermilk Channel for the cows they used to gently lead across the shallow waters. Now it's an isolated hamlet of crack, crime, and crevasses in the street so deep you could lose a fender. You can't even let a house cat run around unmolested because of the street dogs. I mean, dogs *literally* eat cats here.

Poor Nellie. I shudder to think of it.

I walk along its blighted byways, watching uneasy waves churn the slate-gray surface of the Erie Basin, where, in warm weather, kids swim out to the White Rock soda company to nick cases, ferrying them back to shore on inner tubes. My mood starts to lift. *Oh, Forrester, I'll get you yet*, I think as I skip past the busted-out windows of once-thriving factories and the empty lot by the water that serves as an open-air brothel for the city's more errant tastes, once the sun goes down.

I stroll toward the pier. In front of a boat stacked with brightly colored metal shipping containers, a man leans on a wooden pillar, a rope in his hands and a cigarette in his mouth. He looks to be in his late forties, with a weathered face, bulldog eyes, and a red beanie pulled over curly brown hair.

I make a show of looking the ship and its cargo up and down, pretending not to notice his annoyed and bewildered stare, as if one of the three-eyed fish from the Gowanus Canal had just decided to flop onto the dock and into his rigging.

"Can I help ya with somethin'?" he asks finally.

"Oh, I don't know," I say, turning to face him. "I think I'm a little lost. I'm looking for . . ." I make a show of pulling the Bill of Lading out of my pocket and unfolding it. "Pier 9."

"You found it, lady," he says, looking curiously at me and the paper in my hand. He's trying to put two and two together and I can't say I'm not enjoying the spectacle.

"Not much to see, is there?" I say, looking around. "Well, thanks anyway." I start to turn away.

"Hey," he calls. "Who you workin' for?"

I look over my shoulder and smile. "Oh, just doing a little research for my boss. He's thinking of investing in his colleague's business." I flap the paper around. "Sort of a joint venture." I want to keep things vague, imply I'm working for some shady new figure on the scene. If I tie myself too directly to Solnikov or Forrester, I figure, there's a chance this could get back to them.

"May I?" He gestures toward the paper.

"Of course," I say, handing it to him.

He studies it for a moment, then hands it back. A little light has sparked in his eyes. "I know your boss?"

"By name, you might," I say. "But he's rather new to this particular industry. Just getting his bearings. That's why he sent me here. You can never do enough research, that's what he always tells me."

"He on the same side as the company he's investing in?" he asks casually. He flicks his spent butt into the water and roots around in his pockets for a rumpled pack of Marlboros. He shakes one out and offers me one, which I decline with a demure raise of the hand.

"Black Sea Holdings?" I say, thinking fast. "No. He's part of a different organization, with mutual interests. Some here on the waterfront, in fact."

I can see him figuring, his bulging eyes darting right and left.

"The thing is," I continue, before he can get too much thinking done, "before he invests, he'd really like to know whether the party he's dealing with is doing what they say they're doing. Naturally this is all part of the regular due diligence process. We like to think our potential partners are trustworthy, but you never can be too careful." I pause, then add, "There may be something rather lucrative in it for anyone that can help raise his confidence."

The gleam grows a notch brighter. "Well," he says, with a pathetic attempt at nonchalance. "I'd be happy to give a nice young lady like yourself a tour of the vessel. If that would help with his *confidence*."

"How very kind," I say amiably. "I think that would help very much."

I follow him across the metal gangway and onto the ship.

"So, we just got boxes of stuff labeled as mattresses in these here containers, but I'm sure you already know about their biggest export," he says, raising his left hand and wiggling his fingers. "Girl's best friend, and such. Things a little lady like you might like, am I right?"

That afternoon at the Diamond District—the mysterious tip, the stolen gems. So, the Russians are in on that, too.

Either way, I can't let on that this is news. "You certainly are," I say, stirring up a frothy little laugh.

We get to one of the containers that looks just like the rest, and he produces a set of keys from his pocket. "I'm your man on the inside, see," he says in a low tone, like a wannabe gangster. "We work it real smooth. I under-weigh the Russian freight, then add the weight to someone else's cargo. They got some guy in customs over in Riga receivin' 'em, for a sweetener. That's the capital of Latvia, ya know."

"Fascinating," I say. "You clearly are a man who knows his business. But why the under-weighing?"

"Leaves extra room for the cars."

"Cars?" Then I remember what Sergei mentioned during our meeting at Skovorodka—a new business they were getting into, stealing cars off the streets and selling them as new.

"You got it, sis. That's the other racket they're in." He leans in confidentially. "From what I hear, they pinch the cars off the street, store 'em for a while until the owner gives 'em up for stolen. Then they send 'em to their places in Brooklyn, one to do a new paint job, one to do a phony license plate, all that. Make 'em up to look different, ya know? They have it done in different shops so's no one shop knows the whole story. Safer for everyone."

"You said they store the cars somewhere before they fix them up," I say. "Where would that be?"

He's already walking off the boat, tucking the key back in his pocket. I dodge a glance back at the shipping container and then I skip a little to follow him. We cross the gangway, and he leans again against the same wooden pillar. "Now don't take my word for it, 'cause I never seen it for myself," he says, looking around him furtively though there's no one around but me and the gulls. "It's just the name I's heard, from one of them Russians likes to talk. Generally, I mind my own onions."

"Understood," I say, trying to hide my impatience. "What's the place called?"

"Gravesend Auto," he says. "Junker joint. Somewhere near Avenue U, god knows. Not a place anyone would ever think to look, I guess."

"Any idea who runs it?"

He shrugs. "Heard them mention some guy named Jazzy D. Sounds like a fake name to me. But what do I care? I don't ask questions. Worry about yourself and you won't have to worry. That's what I always say."

"Indeed." I nod, as if this were god's wisdom being brought to light. "Indeed. Well, you've been very helpful. Thank you for your time."

He swipes a dirty thumb across his nose. "If you see the boss, tell him he owes me what he said."

"If I see him, I'll tell him," I say.

"Bunch a commie bastards." He shakes his head and turns back to his rigging. "Think they can come here and take advantage of all we got without doing a damn thing. That ain't what made this country what it is, I tell ya."

"Nope," I say. "Just pure, honest grifting." I pick up the pack of Marlboros and the lighter from the pillar, light one up, and flash him a grin. "Thanks for your help."

In that glorious moment, all of it, the Business Records dust and smoke-filled poker games and hiding beneath desks, is worth it to see the look on his face.

I'm halfway down the dock when I hear him yelling. "Hey! Who you really work for?"

I stop and look back at him. The face under the red beanie says he's not sure if he's just walked into the biggest trap of his life. Or if the trap walked into him.

"Don't worry," I call back. "You've never heard of her."

###

The car yard is located in a no man's land between Bay Ridge and Gravesend, a bleak and featureless neighborhood with nothing to recommend it besides dusty, industrial blocks of glass fabrication, metal framing, and other similarly mysterious activities taking place behind windowless brick walls. All corners, no people, a flat vacuum at midday. And leagues away from the subway.

Sergei mentioned the stolen-car scheme. But now it's become clear that Batryshkin's Black Sea Holdings is in on it, too. Maybe the two of them are working it together—Solnikov, the boss incumbent, and Batryshkin, the new arrival. Or maybe they've both arrived at it independently, and yet another turf war is in the offing. Maybe that's the story, I think.

Finally, I find it: Gravesend Auto Yard, the name written in weathered blue paint on a particle-board sign above a metal roll-down door, at present rolled down. On either side are cinder block walls topped by three lines of flat barbed wire, metal ties glinting austerely in the afternoon sun. Outside the roll-down door a tough-looking number is sitting on a lone bar stool, smoking a lackadaisical cigarette.

"Jazzy D available?" I ask.

He looks me up and down. He doesn't seem to like what he finds. "Who's askin'?"

"A friend," I say. "Call it a welfare check."

"You're gonna have to do better than that, sweetheart."

"Alright," I say. "My friend's car went missing. They have reason to believe that he might know the whereabouts of the vehicle. My friend just wants to know where it is. And how they might be able to get it back."

He gets up from the stool, eyes still on me, and goes to the metal door. He brings it up halfway, then ducks and disappears into the darkness. I try to get a look inside, but all that reaches me is a rush of cool, damp air and murmuring voices. Somewhere in the distance I hear the sharp, sweet ring of shattering glass.

Toughie reemerges, slamming the door down behind him. "Jazzy ain't here," he says, his look more menacing than before. "And you can tell your *friend* that they should quit lookin'."

I feel his gaze like two nails in my back as I walk away. I keep my pace casual and I don't look back.

Nothing about this situation feels good. My instinct is telling me to flee the scene, to leave this creep and his car lot and let this investigation die on the pavement. But I can't give up that easily—not without at least getting a look inside. Not after getting this far.

I turn the corner and slow down, letting my eyes rove over the walls on my right. The place is sealed off like a mausoleum: walls constructed from twelve feet of cinder block bricks, not counting the parting gift at the top. I turn the next corner. On this side, a few pieces of green-painted particle board have replaced a section of the cinder block, the kind hastily nailed up at construction sites. Weeds and white flowers grow along the bottom. No barbed wire at the top. One of the boards is already rotting out, the wood damp and soft. I give it a kick. It splinters and gives way. I wedge myself in through the hole and fall onto the crumbling pile of asphalt on the other side, then scramble to my feet.

There's a high pyramid of tires stacked against the wall next to where I've landed, some worn almost smooth, others having hardly seen the road. A few yards away on my left is the low building where Toughie guarded the street entrance. The door leading to the car yard is shut. No one in sight.

I start to walk, the heels of my boots making dull clicks against the paint-flecked asphalt. It smells of sunbaked rubber and engine oil. The yard is filled with vehicles in various states of decomposition. I pause by a pile of rusted-out metal parts, next to which an old transmission sits by itself like it's in time-out. Another car, brown with rust the color of dried blood, is parked with its hood open, guts swarmed with flies. In stark contrast is the one a few feet away: A new blue Toyota that looks like it could be driven off the lot right now, except that the license plates have been removed. I go to inspect it more closely.

Then I hear the whip crack of a gunshot.

15

Now you see it . . .

First I jump. Then I duck and scramble, hands over head, to take cover behind the blue Toyota.

There's a moment of silence when all I can hear is my own wild breathing. I tilt my head up to see if I can catch a reflection of anything in the car's side-view mirror, but all it shows is the pile of rusted-out parts.

Then I see a flash of movement. Footsteps crunch over the asphalt—not close but coming closer.

Another shot rings out.

I look across the lot to the construction wall I slipped through. It can't be more than thirty feet away. I bite my lip hard. I don't want to cross that open expanse, but I sure as hell don't want to stay here.

I rise from my crouch and start to run, daring a glance behind me. Toughie is walking, slowly, almost leisurely, a small silver revolver at his hip. With a burst of terror, I realize he's not walking toward me—he's heading toward the hole in the construction wall.

I change course. Now I'm weaving behind the cars parked throughout the lot, heading toward the far end of the tire pyramid. I hear two more pops, one followed by the sound of metal ricocheting off metal, then that of breaking glass.

I reach the tires and start to scramble up. The worn-down soles of my boots slide on the rubber. One of them slips out from under me and I almost lose my footing. With sudden inspiration, I wedge another tire loose, sending it rolling in my wake. Then another. I hear them tumbling down behind me.

I get to the top and cast one last look back. Toughie is making his way around the pyramid's base, dodging the rolling tires. I gaze down the other side of the wall. It's about an eight-foot drop. I swing myself over and hang onto the edge, then drop down the rest of the way. The sidewalk's hard concrete reverberates painfully in my soles and up through my shins. But I don't care; I start to run and I don't stop until I'm in front of the subway station. My heart is walloping in my chest, my lip bleeding where I bit it, feet blistering in my boots. I feel like a filly at the finish line. I'm just glad it wasn't me that was finished.

"You alright, lady?" A man is standing there with a grocery cart loaded with opaque plastic bags filled with cans. He looks concerned.

"Sure," I gasp, leaning against the railing. My pulse is still pounding against my skull, my hairline wet with sweat. "Sure, I'm alright."

He shrugs and pushes the cart away. Eventually my heartbeat slows, and I make my way down the subway steps.

###

Back at my apartment I pace and think about what I'm going to write for Crock's follow-up, trying to tamp down the little fireworks of panic that keep shooting off inside my gut. What did this afternoon's misadventures get me, besides shin splints? If I'd been able to get something more specific—a car that had been stolen that I could trace back to an owner, an actual look at the goods in the shipping containers—I might have something. But I don't. How to even begin this follow-up? *Reporter visits Gravesend Auto; customer service lacking*, I think. *Reporter unwisely follows tip from shady longshoreman. Reporter attends target practice; is target.*

"Reporter not paid enough for this shit," I say out loud. "How's that for a fuckin' *wood*?"

Jake asked if Forrester might be dangerous. I'm starting to fear that he was right. Considering the forms I found in his desk, Forrester seems to be presiding over these smuggled shipments, which means he must also have a hand in the car operation. Could he have actually ordered Toughie to shoot at me? Or was that just routine thuggery? I think about his parting words when I was leaving his office that first time: *Push your luck too hard, you might find yourself in rooms it won't be so easy to get out of.* He must have found the photocopy of the Bill of Lading and figured it was me who'd taken the original. *He must be onto me*, I think with fresh dread.

As I'm emptying a can of cat food into Nellie's bowl, I glance at the calendar tacked up by the window. Tonight is the cabaret at Skovorodka that Sergei invited me to. After the day I've had, I'm hardly in the mood to go. But there's Crock's bombshell story, and my job, on the line. One lackey deckhand's word isn't going to be enough for an article, or to bring up to OCCB. I need something more concrete. It was Sergei who told me about the stolen-car scheme during our sit-down at Skovorodka; maybe he'll give me a few more specifics off the record. Though now I'm starting to wonder how much Sergei really knows about his boss's dealings.

But Sergei knows Forrester, which means he might even know what the lawyer was talking about that night in his office with his mystery companion. He'd even said Forrester liked to frequent the cabarets. He might be there that very night. I could confront him, maybe even surprise him into revealing some part of the truth, like I'd managed before. Not that I relish being face-to-face with the guy now. Especially considering the other thing Sergei told me during our meeting. *Last month, someone was killed in this restaurant . . . No one in the restaurant could recall anything about it . . . When the police questioned them, none of them had seen a thing.*

Unfortunately for me, reporters can't call for back-up.

Oh, well. "In for a penny," I tell Nellie. I grab my pill bottle and swallow one for fortitude. Then I go get my coat.

###

Skovorodka is much livelier than it was during my preceding visit. In fact, I have to fight my way in through the crowds swelling out the front door. A woman is holding court near the coat check: tall and slender with light brown skin, wearing a red dress that weds itself closely to her willowy figure. When she turns, I'm surprised to see that it's the waitress, Masha. A string of slanted Slavic vowels come out when she opens her mouth. All the men walking in seem to know her; they chat with her and she chats and laughs back, but even as she dots their cheeks with airy kisses and smiles a smile that seems manufactured especially for each of them, she holds them at a distance.

I see Sergei approach her and put a hand on her arm, whispering something in her ear. Her smile falters for just a fraction of a second before she nods, and he starts making his way smoothly toward me. I'm not even sure when he clocked me.

He thanks me for coming and leads me with a hand on my back toward a round table occupied by women in heavy makeup and Swarovski-studded evening gowns seated next to men in sport coats. We exchange nods.

"I must say it's a surprise to see you here. With the schedule you keep," Sergei says, pulling out the chair next to his and filling my glass with wine the color of rubies. I'm still wearing my coat—I never trust a coat check—and so he helps me out of it, hanging it over the back of my chair. "It's a pleasure to be able to show you a bit more of our culture."

I take a sip. The wine is thick and sweet. "Would that be *russkaya kultura* or *Brighton Beach-naya*?" I look around—no sign of Forrester. I'm not sure if I'm relieved or disappointed.

He smiles his sharp-toothed smile. "You know, this is a privileged seat. One time, a somewhat infamous Russian boxing baron came to visit Brighton. He wanted to see the cabaret, but that night it was all sold out. Not a seat left. So, he offered someone a giant sum for theirs, and still he had to raise the price in order to get a taker."

"How much are we talking?"

"More than would fit in your bank account, ten or twenty times over."

"Reporters don't have bank accounts," I say. "We have small drinking funds."

Sergei pours us each a thimble-sized glass of vodka. "*Za zdorov'ye*," he says, picking up his. To your health.

I do the same. "*Poyekhali*." Let's go.

I'm about to ask if he knows anything about the ship setting sail from Red Hook next week, when he gets a question off first: "So. Have you looked into the car business I told you about?"

"As a matter of fact, I have," I say, surprised. "Just today."

"And did you learn anything interesting for your newspaper?"

Sergei had played it cool that day we had coffee in this same restaurant and he told me about the hot-car scheme, but now he looks eager, almost hungry. "Well, that's part of what I wanted to ask you about," I say. "I tried following the lead today, but it led to something of a dead end. So to speak."

"A dead end?" he repeats. A small, polite smile plays on his face.

I'm studying him like a hand of cards, determining my next move, when the lights go down, the music changes, and a swirl of green-and-yellow lights twirl and pivot over the stage. Then the show begins. Singers in feathery headdresses and knee-high sharkskin boots perform a kitschy song-and-dance number to a Russian radio tune everyone in the audience seems to know, because they sing and clap along enthusiastically. They exit, and a short blond man with bright blue eyes takes over. The one who dropped by my meeting with Sergei here a few days ago, who I thought looked familiar. He'd claimed he could do song telepathy and begged for the chance to perform. I guess Sergei must have relented, because he's now singing a heavily accented version of "Can't Take My Eyes Off You," gamboling about in a white suit and top hat and a sequined red tie. *What was his name?* He does a few magic tricks, classic "now you see it, now you don't," but not without finesse. A daisy. A bottle of champagne. A tiara, rhinestones glinting in the swirling lights. It's on the tip of my tongue. *Igor? Olav?* The waiters seem to be continuously whisking away plates and glasses and bottles and bringing out more plates and glasses and bottles. Crystal bowls of potato salad, plates of pickled vegetables and herring, quail eggs, pelmeni served with ramekins of sour cream, platters of smoky grilled meat. I hate when I can't remember a name. But then I let it slip away, watching the proceedings and sipping slowly on my glass of vodka, which I can only assume Sergei is continuously refilling from the chilly bottle in the ice bucket between us because I never seem to reach the bottom. I drink so much it begins to taste like water.

"Sergei, *dobryy vecher*, thank you for giving me the chance to perform," says a voice behind me. It's him—the little round-eyed man, still in his white tuxedo. Sergei gives a dismissive reply I don't catch, his eyes on the stage. The man tries again, letting loose a fast spate of Russian and wild gesticulation. A flap of his hand sends Sergei's glass of wine tumbling. It splashes onto the champagne satin of the woman next to him and leaves bleeding spots of crimson all over the white tablecloth. The woman shrieks, hands flying off the table as Sergei and her companion bluster over her with water-moistened napkins.

"*Oleg*," I say out loud. That was his name. But he's already scurrying around the tables toward the door. He must hear me, because he darts a glance back, eyes wide and furtive, like a mouse afraid of getting stomped.

Suddenly the house lights go down another degree, so that the stage gleams diamond-white. When I return my eyes to it, I let out a *huh* of surprise. Masha, the waitress, is emerging from the wings. At the sight of her, the noise in the audience stops, like so many snuffed-out candles. Not a cough or a clink of a fork. Even the wine-spattered woman seems to have forgotten all about her ruined gown.

Masha walks to the microphone, eyes down. Pauses. The pianist ripples a dramatic opening chord. She opens her mouth and the voice that emanates into the stilled banquet hall is strange and sad and brooding. As she sings, I catch the phrase *bokalo kholodnogo brendi*—a glass of cold brandy. The pianist's hands run up and down the keyboard like they're trying to trap something, and her voice picks up strength, betraying a grief, even an anger, that shakes the hall to the very last table.

Then there's the sudden, rude report of a gunshot. I start. But it's just the pianist, a palm on the top of his instrument.

The singer gazes up at the audience, hands electrified on either side of her face, an expression of inner storms and suffering that her words can only outline. Then it crescendos, becomes fragile again, and is gone.

For a long moment, the entire cabaret is silent. Then the crowd breaks into the most explosive applause I've ever witnessed in my life, the hypnosis giving way to cheers and whistles and stamping feet. With that, Masha is the waitress again, the woman in the foyer, bowing, smiling graciously, bowing again, then exiting the stage.

When the cold night air hits me on the boardwalk outside I become acutely aware of the dizziness swirling in my head. People are filtering out of the restaurant, Russian sentences and laughter pealing off into the dark. The moon hangs low and bloomy, a nail's edge away from full. I'm about to make my weaving way toward the train when Masha emerges. She extricates herself from her cloud of admirers, men with bloated faces and bellies. When she sees me, she smiles.

"You again," she says. She has a black shawl wrapped around her red dress, much too thin for the brisk night.

"Me again," I say. "Quite the show. I wasn't expecting to see you grace the stage."

"First time?" Her speaking voice is lower than I expected, and accentless.

I nod and take out my cigarettes, extending the pack to her.

"No, thanks," she says. "Bad for the vocal cords."

After a few attempts I get mine lit and take a long drag. "If mine were anything like yours, I might be more concerned."

She dips her head demurely. I notice that there are tiny crystals at the ends of her false eyelashes. "I also play violin," she says. "You should hear my Shostakovich. It would make you weep."

"I truly don't think I could stand it," I say. "How is it you speak Russian, anyway?"

"Unexpected, I know," she says. "My dad's from Cuba. He was a musical prodigy. They sent him to Russia to study with the masters and bring some culture back to the island. He ended up defecting to the island of Manhattan. Met my mom at a dry cleaner's in Harlem. Rest is history."

"All that talent, and they still have you hostessing poker games?"

A shadow passes over her face. "That's New York for you," she says. "Nightlife *chanteuse* doesn't exactly pay the bills."

Something strange and tense rears itself up in the pause that follows. "That song you were singing," I say finally. "It was like nothing I've ever heard."

"Oh, that one? It's one of the old folk songs, the ones they call *russkiy shanson*. An émigré poet wrote it while in exile in Paris in the thirties. Someone set it to music sometime after, though no one's really sure who," she says, real enthusiasm entering her voice for the first time. "Personally, I like it pared back like that, with just a little piano accompaniment, so you can really hear the raw emotion come through."

"What's it called?"

"*Chërnaya mol'*—the black moth." A breeze picks up off the beach, and she draws her shawl around her tighter. "It's about a nice college girl who has to flee Russia during the October Revolution. So, she goes to Paris and lives the dissolute and miserable life of a prostitute."

"One thing I love about Russians," I say, "is their eternal sunny optimism."

She smiles. "They love this stuff. They find it utterly romantic."

"Even the criminal element?"

"Especially them."

"What's it like working for them?" I venture. "Sergei and his lot?"

"A girl can do worse," she says, then adds, quieter, "oh, yes. A girl can do much worse."

A dull thud echoes from down the boardwalk where Coney Island starts, followed by a cry. I squint. In the weak glow of streetlights, I can just make out the shadow of dark figures tussling.

"Don't know what you're doing," I hear Masha say, quieter still, the words slipping away with the dark updraft.

I turn back to her. "What was that?"

"I said, I should be going," she says. But she's not looking at me, and she's making no move to leave, looking out past the empty boardwalk, the only sound the waves that surge and crash against the dark shore.

"Which way does the moon go?" she asks suddenly.

I don't understand and I tell her so.

"Where does it start? How does it fill itself in?"

I give it a hard look, but the subject resists study, bobbing and undulating on the surface of the waves. I squint, trying to bring it into focus. "By my best unscientific approximation," I say, "that would be a waning gibbous. But then again, it could be a waxing crescent."

"Do you want to go to the water?"

"What?" I say, sure I've misheard. My ears are still cottony with the cabaret noise, the vodka.

"Sometimes I go in late at night," she says. Her eyes glow under the sodium lights, crystal-tipped lashes making shadows on her cheeks.

"Bit chilly for a dip, isn't it?"

But she's already walking to the edge of the boardwalk, then down the steps that lead to the beach. I follow her down, stopping midway to the shore. She keeps walking until she's just a figure in the darkness. She dips her hand into the water, splashes it upward. I don't see it in the air, but I hear it fall.

I lie down on the cold sand. Waxing, waning. Gibbous, crescent. Which way does the moon go? The vodka surges up through my head like the waves, tossing and spinning me before pulling me under. *I never seem to reach the bottom*, I think. *I never reach bottom.*

###

I wake up to find that my head is pounding, my phone is ringing, Nellie is mewling her graceless head off, and my problems haven't had the decency to go away overnight.

"Parker," Jake's voice, filled with quiet urgency, lands in my ear when I pick up. "I've been trying you for an hour. Where have you been?"

I unstick my tongue from the roof of my mouth. "Chasing my morning wheatgrass shot around Central Park." I sound like I've swallowed a pint of sand instead. "Where the hell should I be? I was sleeping and I'd like to get back to it."

"You know I wouldn't be calling if it wasn't serious."

"What is it then? Spit it out," I growl. Nellie weaves in between my ankles, taking the opportunity of finding me vertical to try a new tactic. I hardly remember the train ride home last night, or how I got up the stairs and into my bed, but the evidence indicates that those events indeed occurred.

His voice travels a long, slow trajectory before it penetrates the gauzy depths of my skull. "Candace Gracen is dead."

16

The body speaks volumes . . .

I get dressed and within six minutes I'm in a cab heading uptown. The day is gray and drizzly, and the cab has that forlorn, damp smell all cabs have on rainy days. I stare out the window as it makes its way west, then bumps up Lexington Avenue, the words playing themselves over and over in my mind until they're empty of emotion, intonation, meaning. *Candace Gracen is dead. Candace Gracen is dead.* All I can think about is my last glimpse of her through the parlor door that afternoon when she'd called me to her apartment to tell me what she knew about Carla. The image of her standing by the bar cart, reaching for the vodka bottle.

Then I have another rude realization: I've forgotten my pills. There's grit between my teeth and a sharp, bitter taste in the back of my throat. I feel the sea sloshing in the pit of my stomach, as if I'd swallowed it whole.

Outside Gracen's building I see a familiar motorcycle parked out front, squeezed deftly between two boxy town cars: a black Honda Nighthawk. I enter the lobby to find Morgan Delacroix arguing with the doorman, a spotty eighteen-year-old in an oversized cap that makes him look like a kid playing bellboy.

"I can't let you up there, miss," he's saying to her. "I'm not authorized to let anyone in."

"You have to. I'm the medical examiner."

He glances at the badge she's holding out. "Why don't we wait for your boss to arrive."

"She *is* the goddamn boss," I say, reaching the desk. "Can't you see her badge says OCME? And every second that you don't let her up there is another second she's losing in figuring out how one of your very protected tenants managed to get very murdered in her own apartment. I don't think *your* boss would be too happy to hear that, do you?"

The kid goes white. "Murdered?"

"Sure looks like it," I say. "Now are you going to keep sitting there or are you going to let us up?"

His mouth moves around fishily for a minute. Finally, he comes out with: "Who are you?"

"Parker Snow. *New York Street*," I say, flashing my press badge. "We're going up to Candace Gracen's apartment."

"I can't let you up there," he repeats. Panicky now. "Who's coming in next, the chief of police?"

"Are you kidding?" I say. "That guy's got better things to do than work. Come on, Morgan. Sixth floor."

On the ride up, Morgan stares at the door, strain pulling at the edges of her pale face. I know it has nothing to do with touching dead bodies.

"It won't always be like this," I say.

She looks at me. "It won't?"

The elevator opens and I'm greeted by a strange sense of déjà vu. The flower arrangement in the foyer is the same as the last time I was here, and still looking fresh. Today the maid is nowhere to be seen. I walk down the hallway toward the parlor, Morgan following behind. It feels both familiar and utterly foreign, like a dream about your childhood home.

I turn into the parlor and see Maloney with a couple of detectives and CSU guys, the EMS team on their way out after taking their obligatory turn, the crime-scene photographer snapping photos. Candace Gracen is lying stomach-down on the floor near the window, one arm splayed out in the direction of the bar, face turned away. She looks underfed and pitiful in a gray, knee-length dress and the same tennis bracelet she was wearing when I met her, except now it looks more like a handcuff.

Morgan crosses the room to the body, sets down her bag, and pulls out a pair of rubber gloves. I survey the room. Everything else looks almost exactly as it did the week before, except for a few subtle differences: an overturned ottoman, a broken glass on the floor, on which the photographer now has his camera trained. I raise my eyes to the bar. The vodka bottle is uncapped. I wonder if anyone's noticed.

Maloney has his back to me, talking to one of his deputies. "Phone was off the hook. Looks like she started to dial. Phone records might give us a lead."

"Looks like you've got your pattern," I say.

He turns and looks at me like I'm a bee buzzing around his picnic, the kind that returns mercilessly to hook its bifurcated body over your cup. That just seems to keep coming back every time you swat it away. Someone's going to have to move, and it's not going to be the bee.

"Parker," he says, and closes his eyes briefly as if he hopes that when he opens them, I won't be there. It doesn't work. "What the *hell* are you doing here?"

"Was anyone else here today? The maid?"

"Maid was off," says the deputy.

"What timing. Who else came in?"

"We'll find out who else was in today, okay?" Maloney interjects.

"Anything stolen?"

He throws up his hands, resigned. "Looks like some jewelry. The box in the bedroom was left open and some of the items appear to be missing."

Shepherd shuffles in from the hallway, his skinny sidekick Szybist in tow. He sees me and smirks. "Nice to see you, Snow. Steal anything lately?"

"Great to see you, too," I say. "Solve anything lately?"

Shepherd sneers, ugly lips lifting around his ugly mouth. Then he clocks Morgan, bent over Candace Gracen. "This girl again. When are you going to get a real ME on a scene?"

Morgan continues her examination, hands assured, eyes laser focused. Her lips form a tight, white dash.

"Hey, Tinkerbell," Shepherd says loudly, crossing the room to lean over her shoulder. "What time this dame kick it?"

Morgan looks up. "I can't say exactly."

"Waddaya mean, you can't *say*?"

She reddens. "I mean, it doesn't really work like—"

"Waddaya mean, it don't work like that? The other guy, Sorens, he always says exactly when the pulse stopped, I'm telling you, *exactly when*."

"Stop cutting the woman off," I say. "And back off. How do you expect her to do her job while you're breathing down her neck? Anyways, Sorens is a lush. Actually, worse. He's a lush with an ego. They keep him on ice because that's easier than trying to kick him off the city dole."

Morgan stands up and takes her gloves off with a snap. "The cause of death is unclear. There are no exit wounds. No blood. She doesn't appear to have been struck, in fact, in any way."

There's a long pause. The breeze riffles the sheer curtains the way it did the day I sat in this room across from Gracen, alive if not somehow already fading away.

Szybist breaks the silence. "But she's dead, ain't she?"

Morgan looks at him sharply. "She's dead."

"Natural?" asks Maloney.

"Could be," Morgan says. "Stroke or cardiac arrest. She might have been struggling to breathe and knocked these things over as she was trying to get help. Only an autopsy will tell that."

"Explains the phone being off the hook," Maloney says, his eyes roving the room like a chess master examining a board. "But not the jewelry going missing."

As they're talking, I take the opportunity to slip out of the room. Down the hall, two doors are ajar across from each other. I peer into the room on the right. It's a bathroom, though it would also make a fine study, breakfast nook, or studio apartment. I walk in to find a hand hovering in the medicine cabinet mirror. I scold the hand and it falls back down to my side. I step back out into the hallway.

The door on the left leads to what can only be Candace's bedroom. The bed seems massive for such a small person, a king-sized cruise ship with cream-covered pillows set neatly against the headboard on top of a heather-gray duvet. The same gray as the dead woman's dress. The jewelry box on the dresser is open, and a few items appear to be missing from the velvet lining. Other than that, everything is spare and clean and tidy—the dresser drawers unopened, the closet doors shut tight. In the air is a familiar hint of the perfume I smelled last time, cut grass and verbena mixed with the gasoline edge of violet flower.

The only thing rumpling the scene is a crumpled slip of paper on the vanity. I pick it up. On it is a phone number, scrawled in cobwebby blue ink. I flip it over. No name. Just ten digits beginning with our new city area code. I fold it and slip it into my pocket.

Back in the parlor, no one seems to have noticed I've gone, standing and conferring in the same positions they were in before. Even the photographer seems to have forgotten his job, having put his camera down to offer his two cents.

"It's an open and shut case, boss," he's saying. "Someone came in here, stole stuff, and knocked the lady off when she tried to put up a fight. Same thing happened last week in Midtown."

"And this 'someone' just happened to know it was the maid's day off?" I say.

Everyone turns to look at me. They make a weird little party, in their baggy suits and police uniforms, gathered around the wasted body of a rich, dead woman.

Then Shepherd pipes up. "Sure, why not? The most knuckleheaded fire-escape scalers get luckier than that every day."

Always ready to support any theory that's not mine.

"There is one thing I noticed," Morgan says. She's flipped the body over, so that Candace Gracen is now facing the ceiling. "A small puncture wound right next to her clavicle."

"Huh," says Maloney. "Weird spot for a puncture."

Morgan nods. "Usually, we'll only see those if someone had recently had a central line."

"We'll check her medical records," says Maloney. "Provided the family will release them. Let's get going. Crime scene took what they need. Shepherd, I want you to check those phone records. Szybist, get all the CCTV they have in the building so we can see who went in and out in the past twenty-four hours. These buildings always have it. Once the autopsy results are in, we'll know more."

"The OCME truck should be outside in a minute," says Morgan. "I'll go out to meet them."

Everyone files out. I'm the last to go, lingering outside until CSU shuts the door and embellishes it with a strip of caution tape—tape that's mostly there to warn off the doorman and the super looking to help themselves to the deceased's unguarded goodies. I go down the elevator and exit the building, then find a payphone on the corner of

Eightieth and Madison. I take the slip of paper out of my pocket and dial.

"Doctor's office," says a cool female voice on the other end of the line.

"Hello," I say. "I wrote down your address, but I seem to have misplaced it. What is it, please?"

"It's 1595 York Avenue, between Eighty-Fifth and Eighty-Sixth Streets. Do you have an appointment?"

"Yes," I say. "Only the doctor doesn't know it yet."

After a short walk, I arrive at a stately red brownstone with a plaque on the side of the door with a list of four names, followed by their alphabet cereal of credentials. I push the wooden door open and walk down a short hallway to a small, dim reception. In the middle are a green marble coffee table and a brown leather couch that look more like museum pieces than furniture. No pictures on the dark gray walls. No magazines on the table. It's a room that would be frightened by the idea of a magazine. A bunch of blinding white chrysanthemums glimmers from a black vase on the desk.

"You know, in Chinese culture, white chrysanthemums are a funeral flower," I say.

Also at the desk is a slim brunette in a cobalt blazer cut so sharply you could nick your hand on the collar. She looks up from the agenda she's been writing in. "May I help you?" Hers is a porcelain mask of a face, smooth and unyielding.

"Yes," I say. "We just spoke on the phone. I'm here to see the doctor."

She tilts her head, pointed chin jutting down. "I'm afraid that won't be possible." Her voice has that cool firmness that tells me this isn't the first time she's had a type like me in her reception, nor the first time she's gotten a type like me out of it. "He currently has a wait list of six months, and he doesn't take—"

I cut her off. "It's about one of his patients. Candace Gracen."

Her eyes widen, but barely. "Well, I'm afraid that I'm not at liberty to discuss his patients."

"Even dead ones?"

This seems to have something close to an effect, because she leans back a centimeter in her chair. "I'm sorry to hear that Ms. Gracen is no longer with us," she says. "I'll let the doctor know. May I ask, who are you?"

"I came here because I was curious why," I say, ignoring the question, "as a woman who seemed determined not to reveal anything about herself, she happened to have this office's phone number on her vanity table. And why she had a puncture mark right next to her clavicle." I take a few steps toward the desk. "Gracen had an alcohol problem. Something tells me that wasn't much of a secret. So was she taking a cure? One of those experimental treatments they're hustling these days?"

"I wouldn't know. And anyways, like I said, I'm not at liberty to discuss—"

"I got it the first time. Now would you let me talk to the doctor? What kind of doctor is he, anyway?"

"He's a wellness practitioner," she says smoothly. Butter wouldn't melt in this woman's lacquered mouth. "And as a matter of fact, he's not in. He was called away."

"'Called away,'" I say. "Uh-huh. If he happens to change his tune, have him give me a call. Parker Snow. He can find me at the police bureau of *The New York Street*."

"Parker Snow," she says, the slightest shadow crossing her brow. "Your name sounds familiar."

"Always nice to meet a fan," I say. "Speaking of names, there are four on the door. Which one is Gracen's doctor?"

After a long pause, she says, "His name is Dr. Winter. Dr. Roy Winter."

The name means nothing to me. Neither does the term *wellness practitioner*. I walk out of the reception and down the short hallway, open the front door, and shut it. Then I steal back along the hall and peek inside. Blue blazer isn't there. Or if she is, she's hiding.

###

I think for a moment about getting on the 6 train downtown, then decide to walk. The day is mild and I need to give this thing a good turning over in my mind, the way only many sequential steps down a long avenue affords. Not to mention that right now, hours from my last dose and with my skin starting to crawl, anything sounds better than the 6 train.

I pass a beauty parlor where a bored-looking woman sits having her blonde hair blow-dried. The Pekinese sitting on her lap is also having its hair blow-dried, tan wisps making a lion's mane around its tiny face. Maybe that's just how life is. Either you're getting the crap knocked out of you or you're bored stiff.

I get down to Sixtieth Street, which always feels like the seventies. It's too early for the working girls who usually hang around the bridge, but there are enough shady-looking blades in cheap suits and nice cars to indicate what the evening will bring. I walk over to Second and peer into the Subway Inn. They say Joe DiMaggio and Marilyn Monroe used to go there, but these days the stools are unglamorously occupied by neighborhood barflies. I briefly consider joining them, then decide against it. I haven't had the best luck in bars lately.

I find another payphone ten blocks south and call Jake. "Sorry for my tone earlier," I say when he picks up.

The crackling cacophony of the newsroom filters through the ant holes of the receiver for one long minute. "Rough night?"

"You could say that."

"How's the story going?"

"Like shit."

"Anything I can do?"

"Nah. It's my party and I'm staying till the end."

"Or until the cops break things up."

"Whichever comes first."

A silence ensues. Then he says, "Speaking of police. I heard about Gracen on the police radio. I called to tell you about it because I knew you'd want to know."

"I did want to know," I say. "I'm grateful, even if I didn't sound that way at ten this morning."

"I wasn't finished. I thought you'd want to know, but also, I don't think you should be chasing this one anymore. It's getting dangerous."

"I think that's a bit of an over—"

He cuts me off. "Gracen tries to tell you something about Russo, and then she dies. That feels like too much of a coincidence."

There's that feeling in my mouth again, the grit rolling between my molars. "Maybe," I say. "But that's what I need to figure out."

"And didn't you say something about going to jail?" Jake continues. "That would have been the day Liz Lau was murdered, right? That feels like too much of a coincidence, too."

"I went to jail because some pickpocket tried to frame me." I sigh. "Some petty jewel thief. There are probably dozens of them crawling the Diamond District." I'm not convinced it's true even as I say it, but right now I just want to get Jake off my back.

And still, he presses on. "I don't know, Parker. It feels like this is getting way too big. I just don't want this to become the same story as last year, when you got yourself into something that was more than you could—"

"I get it, Jake," I snap. "Point taken, okay? Loud and clear. I'll talk to you later."

I'm about to put the phone down when his voice surfaces again.

"Wait a minute, Parker. Don't you have something for me to file?"

"I'll file it with Crock," I say. "I don't have all the details yet anyway."

I hang up.

I know I shouldn't be irritated with Jake, but I am. So, I go where irritation always leads me: to the nearest egg cream. Today it's at Sarge's Deli on Third Avenue and Thirty-Sixth, where the same tired waitress greets you with the same shopworn hello, the way she has for decades, wearing the same apron and hat. She has shoulder-length hair dyed wine-red and eye and lip liner that aren't quite within the lines. She does her job with a soldier's sense of duty, mouth set as she slings bowls of matzo ball soup and plates of beet-red pastrami on rye and celery sodas and the ubiquitous plate of pickles, half and full sour, that arrives promptly at your table when you sit down. When I die, that's the food I want at my funeral.

I nibble my pickles and take in the evening's scene. The decor is all brown-maroon and yellow-ish wood, glass light fixtures hanging overhead. Next to me, two old men sit across from each other, eating their sandwiches in slow motion. One has bushy, wild eyebrows and very little hair left on his head; the other has Coke-bottle glasses on his raisin-wrinkled face and is very neatly dressed. The one with the eyebrows says something mordant to the other, who waves it aside with a bony hand before turning back to his sauerkraut. You can tell they've been having this same argument for decades.

The thing is, I would've liked to talk it over with Jake. He knows how to listen, really listen, how to ask the right questions, to work the thing over with me. But he seemed more intent on getting me to drop the whole thing.

I can't say that I don't understand his concerns. But if I think about them too hard, if I allow his doubts to wheedle their way into my brain like termites, chewing holes in my resolve to figure this thing out—then maybe I will drop it. Maybe I will walk away. And that is one thing I absolutely cannot allow.

So, I'll just have to talk it over with myself. I take out my notebook and flip to a fresh page.

"Gracen was afraid of something, or someone. That much was clear from the day we met," I say out loud, tapping my pen against the blank paper. "But what? And who was the *Maria* she mentioned, who Carla told her about?

"Her doctor's—that is, her *wellness practitioner's*—receptionist didn't seem surprised by the news," I continue. "Not surprised enough, anyway. And she was obviously lying about her boss being gone.

"Unless he wasn't really her doctor," I add to the previous thought. "Unless they were involved in some other way. Continuing along this thread . . ."

I try to explain the case again. I put on a very confident tone. "In effect," I say. But nothing follows.

"In effect . . ." I try again.

But all I can think about is the glass on the floor. The glass she must have filled, and filled, and filled. How she was the day I met her. The wavering voice. The unrevealing face. The remark about her children, how they never liked her.

"So dramatic," I say. "So self-pitying. Maybe she didn't deserve to be liked."

She was in distress, though, wasn't she? says a quiet voice inside me. *She had her own demons following her around. She was scared. She was—*

"She was unhappy," I say out loud.

"You waiting for someone?" The waitress is looking at me suspiciously, her arms loaded with plates of sandwich crusts and coleslaw shreds.

"No," I say. "No one."

She drops the check. I think back to the night before, my strange conversation with Masha, which has all the hazy unreality of a dream. I close the notebook, put a small wad of cash on the table, and leave.

My feet drag over the pavement on Third Avenue as I make my way toward the subway, the hangover I'd managed to ignore all day now pressing on my sinuses. I'm exhausted. Sometime while I was drowning in vodka and swirling cabaret lights, night breeze sweeping the shadowy boardwalk outside, Candace Gracen was killed. What was it that she knew, and what was she trying to tell me?

Cut grass and violet flowers. Sand in my shoes. Which way does the moon go?

The body speaks volumes, but it doesn't talk back.

###

I'm back in Bensonhurst again. After a desperate search of my apartment, under the bed and between the couch cushions, I couldn't find my pill bottle anywhere. It probably rolled out of my pocket when I was lying on the beach, one *bokal* of brandy away from blackout.

I don't tell my doctor about that. I simply enter the examination room and quietly close the door behind me.

"I believe your prescription isn't due to be refilled for another week," he says. Always with the politesse, as if our dealings here were standard procedure. It's theater and we both know it, but he plays it straight.

Lost them, I tell him. Unfortunate accident.

Unfortunate, he murmurs. You know, if controlled substances are stolen . . .

Maybe it's something in my look that does it because he breaks off then. He takes out his pad and drops it onto the table with a sigh that fills the small, close room. I notice that his hand is shaking as he writes. He looks gaunt and waxy under the light, like someone being slowly mummified. But he says nothing else, and neither do I, so that all that's left is the scratching of the pen   the prescription to be refilled right next door, the sham clinic next to the sham pharmacy, all of it designed to pick up the pieces of people like me.

17

Like the handle of a gun . . .

I wake up the next morning filled with a restless energy. Candace Gracen is dead, after trying to tell me something about Carla Russo. Her death could still be from natural causes—she didn't exactly radiate health—but still, it feels like too much of a coincidence. That much, Jake is right about. But I also feel like a revelation is right around the corner, so close I can hear it breathing. *If I can just talk to Maloney and get the right information*, I think, *I'll be able to run it down.*

I get down to 1PP and up to the eleventh floor as fast as I can. When I arrive, I find Maloney, as usual, head bent over a stack of reports. I wait for a couple of uniforms to file out of the room before I sit down and whip out my notebook.

"Candace Gracen. What else have you found out? Security tapes? Call logs? Anything new from forensics? By the way, you're really going to have to watch out for the doorman, the one who looks like the last in line at the junior prom. That guy will contaminate your crime scene faster than rat poison at a corner bodega."

His left eyelid twitches the way it does when he's especially tired. Or especially mad. "Parker, you have no idea what kind of morning I've had. Please."

"Come on, Baloney. What about the CCTV?"

"Nothing."

"Nothing?"

"They had an outage that night. Doorman says it's been happening a lot lately."

"In that Park Avenue palace? That's convenient," I say. "What about the phone records?"

"Also nothing. Just calls to her kids, her doctor."

"Her doctor?" I say. "Roy Winter?"

"Yeah," he says, looking at me suspiciously. "How did you know that?"

Oops. "Never mind. Did he give you anything useful?"

"We haven't been able to reach him," he says. "His receptionist said he didn't come in this morning, and he's not answering his home phone. We'll send someone over there later."

"What about the missing jewelry?" I ask.

"We found it earlier this morning, in her safety deposit box," he replies. "The autopsy results haven't come back, but there's no indication of foul play. And now will you kindly get out of my office?"

Just then a head pops into the doorframe, with flame-red hair and an acne-scarred face. "Hey, boss. Just wanted to let you know that we got a formal statement from Solnikov. She just left. We offered to put an undercover on her, but she said no."

"*Solnikov?*" I repeat, nearly jumping out of my chair. "As in, Nikolai Solnikov?"

"Yeah. That was his wife, Lilia." The head disappears, then reappears again. "Solnikov got shot."

I turn back to Maloney in disbelief. "When did this happen?"

"This morning around eight o'clock."

"And you weren't even going to *tell* me about it?" I can hear the punctuation in my voice.

"You didn't exactly give me a chance," he says drily.

"Dead?"

"Nope."

I scoot my chair in a little closer. Suddenly everything related to Candace Gracen and broken vodka glasses and porcelain-faced receptionists has disappeared like vapor. "Tell me everything."

Maloney stands up and cracks his neck, then starts to pace. "Solnikov keeps his family at his house in Sea Gate, but he still uses the Brighton Beach apartment for business. On this occasion he brings his wife, Lilia. He's meeting with some associates, who leave a few minutes before they do. The Solnikovs exit the building and bullets start raining. Nikolai goes down, Lilia picks up his gun and returns fire. The hit man floors it. Somehow, she gets out without a scratch. Tough broad."

"Mob business," I say.

"Sure looks like it," he says tiredly. "When it comes to narrowing down Solnikov's enemies, it's not exactly a short list."

I'm thinking back to the conversation I'd overheard from underneath Forrester's desk about the *little problem* he and his mystery companion were resolving so they could do business together. Now I can be fairly certain who that person was.

"Ildar Batryshkin," I say. "Look into him."

Maloney looks at me pointedly. "What do you know about Batryshkin?"

I tell him about Black Sea Holdings and what I've gleaned about him and Forrester, leaving out the part where I snuck into the lawyer's office. Maloney looks disgruntled, but he listens. "Solnikov's gang were dismissive of him, but it seems that they shouldn't have been," I finish.

"He's one of the new crop we've had our eye on," he acquiesces. "He seems to be into heavier stuff. Not just poker games and shakedowns. We've even heard some rumblings that Solnikov's guys are defecting to his side, but it's not confirmed." Then he quickly adds, "This is off the record."

I know what he's really saying, without saying it. The city is up in flames. The department is understaffed. We've entered a new era on Brighton Beach, and they're having trouble keeping up.

"How about the hit man?" I ask. "Lilia get a good look at him?"

Maloney shakes his head. "Guy was wearing a mask, and he barely got out of the car. Just sort of popped the door and leaned out. Used a Krinkov. Real Soviet cowboy stuff. Good shot, though."

"Apparently not good enough," I say. "How's Solnikov doing?"

"Hanging in, I guess," he says, sitting back down in the chair and picking up the DD5 he'd been filling out. "It's serious, but it looks like he'll pull through. The shooter got a good one to his upper thigh. Another barely missed his lung. Then a graze on the arm, probably happened when he was trying to draw his piece."

"Coney Island?" I ask.

He gives a brief nod.

"You got guys on his room?"

He looks at me scornfully. "Of course I got guys on his room. What am I gonna do, let someone else come finish the job?" Then it dawns on him. "Parker, don't even *think* about going over there."

"This is news, Maloney. It's my right to cover it," I say. "I'm the organized crime reporter for *The New York Street*. I shouldn't sully the affairs of Nikolai Solnikov with my poison pen?" He lifts a hand to speak. I beat him to it. "Listen, I'm gonna go there whether you like it or not. And I'll find some way to get near the guy's room. You know I will. If I don't, I'll have no choice but to call on the long-suffering Lilia for her thoughts on the illustrious work of the NYPD in preventing lawless gangsters from making an attempt on the life of her law-abiding, entrepreneurial, immigrant husband. I'll have no choice but to ask other people in the building about how safe they feel living there, and on the increasingly violent streets of Brighton Beach. I'll have no choice but to—"

"I get the point," he snaps.

"So, why don't you just make things easy and let me hear his account of what went on?" I finish.

He closes his eyes. I see his eyeballs moving behind the lids. I almost feel bad for the guy.

He opens them. "Ten minutes."

"You won't regret it," I say, jumping up out of my chair.

He looks at me wearily as he dials the number, phone receiver cradled under his ear. "I already do."

###

After a brutally long train ride and a tart exchange with a sour-faced receptionist who insists my name isn't on the visitor's list, I find myself standing outside the room of Nikolai Solnikov, fist grazing the door. This is the closest I've gotten to the man himself, the boss of Brighton Beach. At least for now.

The detective to whom I showed my press badge is leaning against the wall drinking coffee from a paper cup, gun handle protruding coolly from its holster. I take one last look down the river of scuzzy gray tiles stretching between liver-colored walls, then knock twice and enter.

The bedside table is overflowing with gaudy bouquets, carnations dyed orange and purple and stuck with Mylar balloons that sway gently in an unseen breeze. Solnikov is lying on the hospital bed, alone. He doesn't look especially surprised to see me; in fact, his face betrays no expression at all. He's shaped like a series of ovals, a bald head on top of round shoulders with a portly stomach protruding from the blue hospital blanket. Six beeping machines surround him like hovering nursemaids.

"Mr. Solnikov," I say. "My name is Parker Snow. I'm a reporter for

The New York Street." His eyes, small and pebble dark, rove over me silently. "I've spoken many times with your associate Sergei, but you and I haven't yet had a chance to meet."

For a long moment he's quiet, eyes slitted so narrowly I wonder if he's asleep. Then he says, "Quite a time you've chosen." His gravelly voice is intoned with the flattened vowels of Russian, but clear and precise.

"I apologize for intruding during your recovery. I won't be here long." It feels strange, after so much circling, to now have Solnikov captive. I remember what Sergei said—*Tattoos on his knees. Because he does not bow down to anyone.*

I gesture to the empty chair pulled close to his bed. "Do you mind if I sit down?"

He doesn't so much nod as ever so slightly incline his egg-shaped head, which I take as an invitation.

"Thank you." I sit. "Mr. Solnikov, as you may know, I've taken quite an interest in your operations."

"What is there to be interested in?"

"Well," I say carefully. "You seem to have diversified your business quite a lot in recent months."

"I am a simple man. I keep a simple business," says Solnikov. "I am from a village, back home. Brighton Beach is a village, too. I just try to keep the peace."

He lifts a hand, its fingers heavy with gaudy rings. It travels over to the end table, takes one of the stuffed animals that's perched there, and brings it to rest on top of his elliptical belly.

I get right to the point. "Do you know who did this to you?"

He looks at the stuffed animal, eyes narrowed, and says nothing.

"I'm guessing this person—wants some piece of your business?" I venture.

"This *person* thinks they can come in here and take over everything I've built," Solnikov says.

"Had he approached you before?" I say. And then I risk it. "Batryshkin?"

"Of course," he says simply. I blink with surprise. "With our fuel tax operations," he continues, "of which I understand you are quite the expert." He throws me a look like a dart, and I almost start from my chair. "Now, I've already had to give a cut to the Italians. Same thing. Same conversation. Either we play nice and split the difference or they muscle their way in. I've done it once before. Saw my profits cut in half." He shakes his head bitterly, eyes back on the plush toy. "*Bozhe moy.* No way to make a living like this."

I nod sympathetically. "So, you said no. I take it that's not a word he's accustomed to hearing."

"Of course I said no. You give them something, then they ask for something else. More and more. He has since managed to shoulder his way into some of my most valuable exports," he says. "No way that *suka* can come in and take my place. I am not easy to kill, you see."

It's true that despite his small stature, and his weakened and confined state, he radiates a certain power. Like the handle of a gun.

"Your most valuable exports," I say carefully. "Would that include jewels?"

"Jewels." He waves a hand. "Not since potato-bag days."

"Potato-bag days?" I repeat.

"Yes. First scheme that put me on the map. Selling antique rubles. Really bags of potatoes." He shrugs. "Now too much attention. Police here, they are Mickey Mouse. Nothing compared to Soviet *militsiya*. But still, they are catching on. So, I say, let Batryshkin and his people have it. They will take rap. This was my wife, Lilia's, advice."

"Where's Lilia now?" I ask.

"She is at home," he says quietly. "Protecting our interests."

I start to reach out to touch one of the bouquets on the table, but something about Solnikov's look makes me think better of it. I let my hand drop. "She sounds like quite a woman."

"She is," he says, his voice warming a degree for the first time. "She is stronger, more loyal, than any of those who profess to be my brothers."

There's a rap on the door. A slice of the detective's face appears. "Ten minutes," he says politely. He leaves the door ajar.

I stand up. Maloney bent the rules for me, and I'm going to uphold my end of the deal. "I'll let you rest," I tell Solnikov. "Thank you for speaking with me."

He says nothing. His mind seems to be elsewhere, ruminating about subjects I'd rather not consider. So, I leave him with the stuffed bear on his chest, reminding myself that this is a man connected with untold extortions, defraudings, and murders, and whose true talent may lie in the fact that none of these has ever been proven.

###

Twenty minutes later, I'm standing in front of Solnikov's Brighton Beach apartment building, having extracted the address from the detective at the hospital in exchange for a fresh cup of coffee. The building is about twenty floors high and has the look of a once-proud piece of new real estate now starting to wear around the edges. The area has already been swept for shell casings and clues; now you wouldn't even know that anything had happened there, except for an almost invisible spray of dried blood on the white-gray brick, near the door.

I want to see what I can get from the residents—someone who heard or witnessed the shooting, maybe, or who was used to seeing Solnikov and his so-called associates. I push the lobby door open. There's an empty desk where a doorman would be, a few packages lying around the mailboxes like roadkill. My plan is to talk to tenants as they're coming and going. When drama of this level happens, there's always someone eager to grace the paper with their take.

I wait around restlessly for a few moments. No one comes, and no one goes. Patience is a virtue in this business, but it's never been mine.

I'm heading out the door for a cigarette break when I crash into two large paper grocery bags. They're being carried by a short woman with dark hair, her other hand occupied by that of a skinny child in a plaid jumper, two braids running down her back. As we collide a red cabbage flies from the top of the bag, which I catch before it falls to the floor.

"I'm so sorry," I say, handing it back to her. The girl jumps up and intercepts it, running across the lobby. I seize my opportunity. "I can see you're busy, but could I trouble you for a few moments of your time? I'm a reporter for *The New York Street*. I've been covering organized crime in the neighborhood."

"Are you writing about the shooting?" the woman asks as she takes a few careful steps toward the elevator. Her daughter starts dancing in circles, tossing the cabbage into the air and catching it. "Terrible. Just awful. Luckily we were all out when it happened. Dana, quit it! Your grandma's going to have a fit if you get her cabbage all bruised up." Then she turns back to me. "Do you mind hitting the button?"

I hit it. "Can I help you with that?" I ask, gesturing toward the bags, which look like they're one wrong move away from bursting.

"I'd hate to trouble you."

"It's no trouble," I say, collecting one of the paper sacks in my arms. No trouble at all.

The elevator arrives. "Dana, hit fourteen. And *only* fourteen." She instructs the girl.

As the three of us ride up, I ask, "Do you know Nikolai Solnikov?"

The woman shakes her head. "I've never seen him. From what I've heard from the building gossip, he didn't live here. Just uses his place for meetings."

The elevator opens and I walk the pair to their door. "I can bring this in for you," I offer.

"You're a lifesaver," she says. "I'm Miriam, by the way. Miriam Melka."

"Parker Snow."

I follow her inside and into a small kitchen, which is warm with savory aromas tinged with something sweet and cinnamony, pale yellow challah dough rising on the counter, and a pot of something savory bubbling on the stove. I set the bag on the kitchen table as Miriam starts banging things into the refrigerator. Across from the kitchen is a bathroom, the door open. A flash of movement shimmies in the bathtub.

"I don't mean to be rude," I say, "but I think there's something swimming in your bathtub."

"Carp," Miriam says, straightening up.

"Pardon?"

"Fish. For the gefilte. Mom makes it from scratch. Buys it live at the market on Brighton Beach Ave, cleans it, and hand chops it herself," she says. "As if the brisket and the chopped liver and apple cake weren't enough. It takes all day, and you should see the mess. But it is divine."

"What time's dinner?"

"Not until seven. But we still have plenty to do. I haven't even ironed the tablecloth. Ma!" she yells. "I got the stuff you wanted. They were out of sour pickles, so I got the half-sours." She turns back to me. "Mom's best friend Ida, she lives down the hall. It's her birthday today and we're hosting her dinner. Honestly, I think Mom just likes to show off."

"Does it make you nervous, your mom living here?" I ask.

"It does now," she says ruefully. "We've had this apartment in our family for generations, since my parents came over from Poland. I would hate to have to sell."

"What was it like growing up here?"

"It was wonderful," she says, a smile lighting up her face. "Growing up, I thought Brighton Beach was the absolute best place in the world. We never had any money but we never felt poor. Free rides at the Luna Park merry-go-round where my friend's father worked. Chocolate bars from the Yablochko Chocolate Factory, with the apple stamped on each of the squares. The salty crumbs on the bottom of a cup of Nathan's fries. Sleeping on the beach on summer nights."

"It sounds nice."

"I couldn't imagine living anywhere else. But now . . ." She returns from her memories, her smile fading. "You seem like a nice girl. I don't know why you'd want to be mixed up in this."

"Believe it or not, it's supposed to keep me off the streets," I tell her.

"All I can say is to be careful," she says, shaking her head. "There were bad eggs in every wave, sure. I remember them back in the seventies. But this new generation is different. They don't seem to stop at anything."

Something sticks in my head about Miriam's childhood memories. "You mentioned a chocolate factory."

"With an apple," her daughter pipes up.

"Right," I say. "With an apple. Does it still exist?"

"It's been boarded up for years," says Miriam. "Though, funny you mention it, the other day I was passing the building, just down on Brightwater and Sixth, and I could have sworn I could smell the chocolate, just like when I was a little girl. But that's nostalgia for you."

I file that away. "Thanks for all your help. I'll let you go." I take in the spread that's materializing. "I don't think the neighborhood will go hungry tonight."

"You think this is a lot. Come back on the seventeenth," she says. "Passover."

"I just might," I say. I step into the hallway and glance back at the bathroom, slippery flashes of gray enjoying what they don't realize is their last swim. "Carpe diem."

Gently I close the apartment door behind me. The hallway is empty, a fragile stillness washing over the worn blue carpet. Quiet as Egypt must have been before the plagues.

###

RUSSIAN "BUSINESSMAN" SHOT IN FRONT OF BRIGHTON BEACH BUILDING

By Parker Snow

April 7, 1992

Nikolai Solnikov, a well-known if shadowy figure in Brooklyn's Brighton Beach, sustained grave but non-life-threatening injuries after being shot three times leaving the building in which he keeps an apartment. Police believe it to be the work of a hired gunman, who is still at large.

In an exclusive conversation with the *Street*, Solnikov professed to be a "simple man" presiding over a "simple business."

"I just try to keep the peace," he said from the confines of his hospital bed.

His condition was described as stable.

The shooting, which took place in broad daylight on Brighton Sixth Street and Ocean View Avenue, is a prime example of the type of bravado crime taking over the neighborhood's streets.

Miriam Melka, a former resident, was at the building a few hours after the incident to visit her aging mother. The apartment has been in her family of Polish immigrants for generations, she said.

"I would hate to have to sell," Melka lamented.

Echoing the sentiments of other longtime Brighton Beach residents, she has seen the crop of criminals change from the small-time seventies to the freewheeling nineties.

"This new generation is different," Melka said. "They don't seem to stop at anything."

While police have not yet released the name of the suspect behind the attempted hit, Solnikov believes it to be one of his business rivals. Owing to this paper's general distaste for libel suits, the name of that rival cannot be disclosed at this time but will be released as soon as the NYPD gets their act together and builds a case against the man whose name this reporter gave them.

18

My shadow stalks me . . .

The next night is another poker game. It's in Midwood this time, a neighborhood so ordinary in both name and character it probably doesn't even figure on Maloney's crime map—which is probably why the Russians chose it. I guess Brighton Beach may be getting a little too hot.

I feel strangely apprehensive as I ascend the subway stairs and start down the avenue, its surface oily with puddles, toward the address I was given in a gravelly, Slavic-intoned voice over the phone. I reach the corner and wait for the signal, the bright orange hand sending warning ripples over the rain-slicked street. That feeling doesn't visit me often, so when it does, I don't know whether to slam the door in its face or invite it in for a drink and a chat. My mind keeps returning to the attempt on Solnikov's life, the conversation I witnessed while under Forrester's desk—and the fact that by now, I'm pretty sure he sent his goons after me in that car lot. A man capable of that could be capable of much more. Not to mention the man he's working for, Ildar Batryshkin. I'd brushed off Maloney's warnings about the new order taking hold on Brighton Beach, but now I'm wondering if I've unwittingly placed myself right in the middle of a writhing pit of snakes.

And it all started with a quirky few inches of copy about a chocolate truck.

I cross the street. A white church stands on the corner behind a fenced-off garden, rhododendrons glowing from below, thanks to a strategically placed electric light. My shadow stalks me in long, loping steps, roiling over the brick walls of the pre-war apartment buildings and empty squares of sidewalk lit by the low glow of streetlights. The rain is falling in a slow patter, one cold syllable pronouncing itself on the nape of my neck and rolling below the collar of my coat. I glance over my shoulder, chased by the sudden feeling of someone behind me. But the quiet street is empty. Nearly eleven p.m. and everyone is already tucked in for the night.

Halfway down the darkened block, the streetlights faded to whispers, I find the address: a nondescript single-family home with stairs leading down to a basement apartment. A plaster copy of the Statue of Liberty about as tall as I am has been nailed, inscrutably, to a board on the corner of the L-shaped landing.

I descend the stairs and knock, and the door swings open. The same thuggish bouncer from the last time takes my fifty-dollar bill in silence.

The studio apartment is not more than fifteen by fifteen feet and dense with cigarette smoke. Off to the left is a sliver of a kitchen. At a scrap of countertop, Masha is uncapping bottles and placing them on a tray, tonight in all black—her waitressing uniform. She turns when she hears me walk in. We lock eyes for a moment. Quickly she breaks the gaze and goes back to her work.

A card table with six chairs is set up in the middle of the floor. Of the five that are occupied, I recognize three men from the last game. Or at least I think I do—these types have a way of blending together.

But unlike at the Peterhof, no one is laughing or carousing. The atmosphere stretches tight like a drum. Of the two unfamiliar faces, one looks like something from a Munch painting: gaunt, with thick gray hair, skin drawn hollowly over his cheekbones. The other is big and paunchy with the bloated look of the lifelong drunk, tiny eyes set in his swollen face. He's the only one attempting levity—trying for jokes, laughing at them himself and goading the others to join. But they stare straight down at the table, as if waiting for it to deliver the secret of life. Some smoke cigarettes, tamping them into one of the glass ashtrays on the table in a gesture you could almost describe as delicate and with an expression you could almost describe as thoughtful. A deck of cards sits in front of the empty seat, like a patient awaiting surgery.

Sergei's hard boys in their dark blue track suits are standing silently against the wall. No sign of Sergei. I lean against the counter and survey the room. Nothing decorates the white plaster walls, which are in need of a paint job and pocked with the holes and chinks of tenants come and gone. It's the kind of apartment rented in a moment of desperation and given up in one more desperate still.

The front door swings open and I'm surprised to see Oleg stumble in as if he'd been pushed—the one who did the vaudeville Penn and Teller act at the cabaret show, who spilled the glass of red wine at our table afterward. The one who said he could read my mind.

There's a long, protracted silence as he stares, bewildered, at the men assembled around the table. Then he goes to the empty seat, sits down, and looks at the deck.

I blink with surprise. *This guy, playing dealer?*

He pulls it toward him and shuffles, one tight riffle that a casino card shuffler couldn't have done smoother. His round blue eyes flit around underneath his lids, but his hands don't hesitate, unlike the mechanic at the last game. They're hands that work faster than the brain attached to them.

He deals out the pocket cards, and play begins.

Cards considered. Chips placed down. Another round of cards dealt out. The movements repeat themselves, grim, joyless, robotic. The faces of the men are yellow and lined in the cheap studio's tawdry light. The rain outside is picking up, droplets sliding down the pane like they're trying to get in.

Small Eyes is looking sweatier and sweatier as he stares at his hand. He keeps putting down chips, sliding them forward with less and less eagerness each time. The Scream stares at him coolly, then mutters something under his breath, his eyes sliding in the direction of the hard boys. The other men continue their play with no expressions on their faces. Small Eyes's bald head is growing shiny with sweat, a drop of it sliding down his temple, where an artery pulses like a small blue worm.

I'm watching tensely when I feel something cold and damp being pressed into my hand. It's a bottle of Russian beer with a brown-and-gold label. Masha is handing it to me.

"*Spasibo*," I say, and take a long sip.

"*Ne za chto*," she replies. I'm about to ask her if she got home okay the night of the cabaret after her late-night dip, when she says, slowly and distinctly: "You might want to leave."

I follow her eyes to the table.

"That guy," she murmurs, nodding toward Small Eyes. "The big one who looks nervous. He's been coming for months, playing, and losing a lot of money. He put up some jewelry as collateral, but—" she stops abruptly, her eyes flickering over my shoulder. I turn to find Sergei behind me.

"Masha," he says, with a small, sharp-toothed grin. "It is very kind of you to entertain our guest. But you see, Ms. Snow is not the only one here in need of your attention." *Misss Sssssnow.*

Masha's lips press closed like they've been sewn together. She gives a curt nod, then goes to the gambling table and begins collecting empty bottles.

When Sergei looks at me, his smile has become something lethal. "Lovely to have you here, as always." *Alwayssss.*

"Thanks for your hospitality, once again," I say. "And I'm sorry about Mr. Solnikov. It must have you all on edge."

His eyes narrow. "You know about this already?"

"It looks like he'll pull through, though," I say, hoping to strike an optimistic tone. "When I saw him at the hospital today, he seemed to be regaining his strength."

"He let you see him in hospital?" His voice has gone quiet and I don't like it. It makes me think that telling him about my visit to his boss might have been a major blunder.

"Well, he didn't really have a choice," I say hastily. "I just kind of walked in."

Sergei nods slowly. "We had a deal, though, no? You are not writing about this incident?"

"Well, of course I am," I say. "It's my beat. And anyways, by the time it hits tomorrow's paper it should be common knowledge. The other papers will probably cover it, too."

He holds my gaze for a long, disconcerting moment. Then he says, "Are you chilly? I thought it was getting quite warm outside."

I realize I have my coat clutched tight around me. "I fear a draft," I say. "As I'm sure you Russians understand."

He smirks and starts to walk away.

"Sergei," I call. He turns around. "Did you know that James Forrester was also working for Batryshkin?"

He shakes his head. "Some people," he says, "have no loyalty." As he turns to go, he adds, casually, "You should stay and watch the game until the end."

I watch him cross the room and whisper something to one of his hard boys, who gives a barely perceptible nod. Then he exits through the front door.

At the table, the final card is being dealt—the river. The room is stock-still, clammy and fraught with dread. Small Eyes is the buffalo at the watering hole, surrounded by lions. All that debt, and yet he still came back to drink.

I don't want to see how this ends. I get up and make for the door, past the table and its grim cadre of card sharks. When I do, Oleg gives a sort of start, as if he, like Sergei, is going to urge me to stay. But he says nothing. I stare straight ahead as I pass, ignoring the movements of his fast dealers' hands.

The door guard's face is impassive and unyielding as stone. My hand on the knob, I hear Small Eyes behind me, his voice wheedling in Russian. Then there's a loud *clap*. I turn to find him standing, hands on the table, his chair fallen to the floor behind him. The track suit boys surround him.

I open the door and walk into the alley and out onto the sidewalk. It's started raining harder now, the sky flashing with lightning. The apartment door opens, and Small Eyes tumbles out, the hard boys behind him, pushing him into the dark alleyway. I hear him first reasoning, then protesting, then pleading. All of this is met with silence. The gaunt man exits then. The skin of his forehead looks taut and sallow in the apartment's weak exterior light.

I've just started down the street when I hear the sick thud of a punch being landed. I turn to see Small Eyes gasping and grabbing his face, his nose blossomed red. Another punch and he falls heavily to the pavement. Raindrops fall on a diagonal in the white beam of a streetlight. The hard boys' fists fall methodically. The man's body jerks and writhes with each blow, his screams muffled by the heft of their bodies surrounding him and the driving rain.

The gaunt man lights a cigarette, takes a long drag, then turns and dissolves into the wet night.

Raindrops hit my nape with deadpan plunks as I make my way back the way I came. A wet branch brushes against the back of my neck as I skirt between a car and a garden gate, thunder cracking overhead.

By the time I descend into the dank-smelling station I'm thoroughly soaked. I go to the pay phones against the wall next to the ticket machines, pick up one of the black receivers, and dial three digits.

"I just witnessed an assault," I say to the bored voice asking me what my emergency is. "Twenty-Sixth Street and Avenue N in Brooklyn. It looked bad. And they're still at it."

I walk halfway back up the stairs, so I can see the street but remain sheltered by the roof of the subway station. A few minutes later, a patrol car cruises past. The siren is off, red-and-blue lights swimming silently in the mist. It turns onto the street with the church on the corner, blinking lights reflecting for a moment against its white exterior before disappearing. I'm sure the track suit boys and the rest will already be gone, leaving their quarry where he was: wet, bloody, unconscious. Hopefully just unconscious.

All the way home on the subway I shiver. The only other occupant of the car is a middle-aged man in a poncho, rocking back and forth and repeating like an incantation: "Did it shoulda done it everyone I told 'em I told 'em a hundred times I told 'em they didn't listen didn't want to listen I told 'em I told 'em all . . ." I scrape my wet hair over my forehead, lean my head back against the window, and close my eyes as we enter the tunnel. The sharp scree of the train's metal belly scraping against the rail fades into one long, oblique cry. A gust of wind over a canyon. An echo in an abyss.

I step into my apartment, boots squelching underfoot. Nellie is nowhere to be found—probably hiding in the closet, like she always does during storms. I strip off my wet coat and shoes and leave them in a heap by the door. The rain assaults the windows, slows, then picks up again with even more force. The image of the miniature Lady Liberty in front of the apartment bursts into my mind. The torch she holds that brings no light. Then the sound of the man falling as the kicks landed heavily on his soft body, over and over again.

Had Sergei meant for me to see it?

I go to the kitchen and pull open the drawer between the stove and the sink. I'm shivering with the cold that's soaked my skin, the rain pouring down like so many pouring-out eyes. I take out the white bottle.

###

When I wake up the next morning, the rain has stopped and clapped a lid of slate-gray cloud over the city. As I wait for my coffee to steam up through the holes of my espresso pot, I think about Sergei's look when I mentioned visiting Solnikov in the hospital. Clearly, he's not as close to his boss as he thinks. That, or he thinks *I'm* getting too close to him.

Then I remember Masha's words. Small Eyes had put up jewelry as collateral, but . . . but what? Sergei cut her off before she could finish. *Jewelry*, I think as I hear the coffee gurgling. *Diamond District*. I take my mug from the draining board. The anonymous tipster who brought me to that jeweler, Petrowski's, shop, where I was promptly framed for theft. I'd dismissed the incident to Jake as a petty con, but I can't dismiss the fact that the crony at the Red Hook shipyard had not-so-subtly hinted that diamonds were part of the boat's cargo. There's something going on here—a scheme that I keep getting in the middle of. But who's responsible for it?

Only one way to find out.

I drink my coffee, throw on my coat, and hustle off to the Shack. It's blessedly empty, Schultz and the rest probably still sleeping off their late deadline. I leave my notes on my desk in two piles to return to in the afternoon: one for the organized crime story I'm supposed to be researching, and one for the murder story I'm supposed to have nothing to do with. I'll pick up the Russian stuff after a little field trip, I decide. I'll check in on the connection between Candace Gracen and Carla Russo, inquire at Mount Sinai where she says they volunteered together. Maybe try to pay her *wellness practitioner* another visit.

Forty-Seventh Street is as loud and sad as ever when I arrive around ten. I watch an old woman in what was probably once a nice fur coat open the door to one of the pawn shops with an arthritic hand. On a whim, I follow her in. I hang around the back of the tiny shop as she completes her transaction with a grave sort of dignity, exchanging a pile of tarnished jewelry for a small wad of cash, which she tucks into an embroidered change purse that she then snaps closed.

The door whooshes quietly behind her, leaving me and the shopkeeper alone. He has hangdog eyes and a chin grizzled with white stubble and wears a blue button-down that looks like it hasn't seen an iron since it left the factory. He looks up at me with a question he doesn't ask.

I decide to play it straight. "I'm a reporter for *The New York Street*. I've gotten wind of a con sweeping the block." I take a step in closer. "Have you had anything stolen recently?"

His hangdog face droops further. "Only my best three diamonds."

I blink with surprise. "You were robbed?"

"Sure. Robbed," he says bitterly. "Right in front of my stupid face. Took the diamonds and replaced them with fakes. Jewish guy." He puts his hand to his chin to mimic a beard.

Sirens go off inside my head. "Did you tell the police?"

"What's the use? He'd never get caught," he says, waving his hand. "Almost had to give up the whole place because of it. Only reason we're hanging on is because people like that old lady keep coming in here. Everyone needs a buck these days."

"But what about the insurance?"

"They ain't insured."

"You have thousands of dollars' worth of jewelry in here," I sputter, looking at the display cases. "And no insurance?"

He glowers at me. "Lady, I know how it sounds," he says. "I have insurance on the shop, but not the individual pieces. Not most of them, anyway. I got behind on payments. I thought it would only be for a month or so, but then . . ."

“Hey, let me know if you find ’im!” he yells after me as I leave.

Out on the street, the same weaselly character who was there the last time is leaning against the same post, wearing the same floor-length brown leather coat and sunglasses.

“You again,” I say, wrinkling my nose. “You sure have a way of turning up at opportune moments. And disappearing at them, too.”

He shrugs. Apparently, the fact that he saw me get hauled away by the cops doesn’t bother him. Why should it?

“You get that guy?” he says. “The yarmulke? Haven’t seen him in a while.”

“I haven’t gotten anyone,” I say. “What’s your line, anyway? Why do you always hang around here?”

He grins and opens the flap of his coat. It’s lined with watches, glinting gold and silver and cheap.

“Rolex,” he says.

I scoff. “Sure. And I’m the prima ballerina for the New York City goddamn Ballet.”

He gives the same one-shouldered shrug. It says, *If I say they’re Rolex, if people think they’re Rolex, what difference does it make?* What special place does truth have if everyone believes the same lie?

I open the door to number 57. The gray daylight recedes behind me as I walk up the same narrow stairwell, the smell of it both liquor-y and bitter, like wine mixed with shoe polish. I reach the second floor and push open the door. The shop is empty of customers. Petrowski is sitting behind the counter, jeweler’s loupe to his eye, in a small cone of light. The shop is otherwise dark except for the illuminated jewelry cases.

“Thanks for the silver bracelets,” I say.

When he looks up and registers me, his face is stricken, but not surprised.

I walk toward him. “You know it wasn’t me who took your stones, right?”

"He promised to be a good, paying customer," he says.

I guess that's supposed to suffice as an apology. "That good, paying customer has been hitting up every place on the block, palming jewels and replacing them with fakes. And all of you sitting on tens', hundreds of thousands' worth of inventory with no insurance."

"Business has been poor lately, with the recession," he says quietly. "I got behind on the payments."

"People come here and hock their family heirlooms because they're a few bucks behind on rent for a few months too long. Because the job doesn't pay enough, or the pension or the alimony," I say. "But you're no different than the people you take from." I put my palms on the counter and lean forward. "So, let's hear it. Where's the insurance money going? Bar? Gambling table? Lady on the side?"

Slowly, he puts down the loupe, reaches into his pocket, and produces a shabby wallet. He pulls a photo from it and gently places it on the counter, where it's illuminated from underneath by the jewelry case lights: a young woman in a wheelchair, her limbs curled and wasted, looks up at me.

"My daughter," he says quietly. "Born disabled. Health insurance only pays so much, and she needs a lot. She can't talk and I don't know if she really understands anything at all. But she's ours."

After I've made my own apology, I leave and walk toward Fifth Avenue, hands jammed into my pockets. The clouds outside have only grown heavier and gloomier. I don't even say goodbye to the weasel. I'm just not really in the mood.

When I reach the corner of Forty-Second, I feel something rattling in my coat. My heart lifts like a zeppelin. I pull a cloudy orange pill bottle from my pocket like a magic trick. I look at the date. It's the bottle I thought I'd lost the night of the cabaret. It must have been here the whole time, hidden deep in my coat. I pop it open, trying to control the tide of hunger rising from my chest, and shake a couple loose. They skip down my throat like sugared almonds.

Almost instantly, the pills raise me to a new lightness. There's a spring in my step as I skip down the avenue, leaving the Diamond District behind. It's time to get it all out, I decide. The shipping containers, the pier at Red Hook, the lot in Gravesend full of stolen cars. I'll say what I can, quote who I can. From what I saw last night, enough is enough.

The three marble arches of the New York Public Library loom across the avenue. Those arches mean a pay phone, inside, private, with a bench. Just the place to tell my tale. I check my watch. Deadline is still a few hours away; Jake will have plenty of time to rewrite and file for me.

I cross and walk up the steps I hardly feel beneath my feet, stone lions goading me on. I pass under the hanging chandeliers, push open the door, and enter the lobby. The lights of the candelabras fog into filmy haloes on the high, Gothic ceilings. I rub my eyes, but the haloes remain. The stone brick walls remind me of the walls of a castle; they swim at the sides of my vision. I turn left and start down the hall of the east wing, where I know there's a phone booth no one ever uses, tucked away in the shadows at the end of the corridor. I sense that I'm stumbling a little, my feet running over themselves like small dogs. I'm on the deck of a listing ship, looking through a film of cellophane at an old photo negative, everything clashing and blurring at the edges. Above me, the baroque flowers of the filigreed bronze ceiling twist up into confused knots.

Then I see it, as if at the end of a very, very long corridor: the little wooden booth with the red NO SMOKING placard inside. I walk, and walk, and walk, and yet it seems to get no closer. Then, all of a sudden, it's right in front of my nose and I have to put my hands out not to crash into it. I get the folding door open and fall onto the little wooden seat. Hands trembling, I extract a quarter and dime from my pocket.

"Parker?" The voice rises, staticky, to my ear.

"It's me."

“Are you okay?” Jake says. “You don’t sound so good.”

“I’m fine,” I say. “I’m fine. Get this down . . .”

I get out the story haltingly, in pieces. I can hear him typing, feel the phone pressed against his ear, see his face knotted with the questions he wants to ask. I talk until I can’t talk anymore, and then I let the phone slip from my fingers. The walls of the phone booth fall away. Sentences from my book of Russian phrases float up through my consciousness.

Mr. H to Comrade X: “I am somewhat surprised to find that ‘Uncle Vanya’ still draws a capacity crowd: It has had such a long run.”

I only hope I’m not going to die, doctor. That would be in very bad taste indeed, after all the hospitality I was shown here.

Of one thing I am certain. Whatever one’s political complexion, there is no denying it: The Russian people long for peace.

19

It's unraveling now . . .

"Parker? Parker? Are you okay? Can you hear me?"

I'm swaddled deep in a gray cloud of ether, depthless and spaceless and dark. Then, slowly, senses start to enter: The faint smell of paint that always seems to linger. The low murmur of a TV through a wall. That particular slant of gray window light.

"Jake?" I croak. My voice is a fishhook being yanked out of my gut.

"It's me, Parker. It's Morgan."

I blink my eyes open. I'm at home, lying on my bed. Morgan is sitting at my side, her small face tight with worry.

"Did Nellie get fed?" is the next sentence that exits my mouth.

"I fed her. She's fine."

I struggle to sit up. Morgan puts a hand on my shoulder.

"Relax, okay? You probably don't feel so good."

If that isn't an understatement. I feel like you do in the worst moment on the worst night of the worst flu. Like you might actually die. And if you did, you might actually welcome it. My eyes flutter closed.

"Jake called me after he lost you," Morgan is saying from somewhere in the world of the living. "He said you didn't sound right. He thought you'd mentioned something about the library, so I went there to try and find you. It was almost closed. I was walking up and down the halls, calling your name. Then I noticed a pair of boots sticking out of the phone booth."

That's me, I want to say, the Wicked Witch of the East Village. But my lips still feel gummed together.

"You woke up, though," Morgan is saying. "I tried to take you to the hospital, but you said no. You were insistent. So, I brought you here."

I can't say I remember any of this. But it does sound like me.

"These were in your pocket," she continues. "How many did you take?"

A splash of slinky weight lands on my midsection. I open my eyes to see Nellie on my chest, looking at me with deep skepticism. I lift a hand that hardly looks or feels like my own and give her head a clumsy stroke. Her lip raises above her snaggletooth.

"Two," I croak. I manage to get myself sitting, knocking Nellie onto the bed in the process. The cinder block wall presses into my back behind the thin pillow. There's an ache in my hip where I must have hit the floor, and my head feels like it's stuffed with needles trying to make their way out through my eye sockets. "Just two."

Morgan opens the pill bottle, sniffs it, shakes a pill into her palm and squints. "Did something happen to these? Did you lose track of them, or get them somewhere different?"

"What do you mean?" I manage.

"They have some kind of powdery residue, and it's not blue like the pills. These must have been tampered with."

I feel questions forming, and they're deep in the ether cloud, too far away to grasp.

"I'll bring them to the lab and see what I can find. We'll figure it out," she says, trying to sound more reassuring than she looks. "In the meantime, you should really get some rest. Do you have an extra key? I'll come check on you, just in case."

"Desk drawer," I mutter because I don't have the strength to protest. "Thanks." Then my eyelids fall closed again, like the plastic eyes of a baby doll. I use my fingers to pluck them open. Morgan's still there, looking at me.

"Jake was stuck at the copy desk," she says, almost apologetically.

"Just wanted to make sure he got the story," I slur. I sink down flat again, feeling the dark veil of sleep beginning to overtake me again.

Morgan turns from the doorway. "Are you sure you're okay? I can stay longer if you—"

I wave her away, my cheek scrunched against the scratchy pillowcase. "Go save the world. I'll be fine."

She nods and her slight form disappears through the doorframe. I hear the sound of the desk drawer opening, the jangle of keys, then the front door quietly shutting. Somewhere across the concrete a siren makes its mechanical lament, the one that sounds so often I can never be sure if I'm hearing it here or in my dreams.

###

I emerge from another gauzy orbit in a strange and distal universe to the sound of ringing. I struggle out of bed, panicked. It sounds again. The light filtering in through the cracks in the blinds is grainy and blue. Groggily, I stumble into the living room and pick up the phone.

"Parker," says a smoke-rasped voice. "I've been tryin' to call you since yesterday. I even tried to *page* you, and guess where it buzzed? On your goddamn desk! Real helpful!"

I have to clear my throat a few times before I can choke out: "What day is it?"

"What day is it? What *day* is it? It's Friday! Fucking Friday! Jesus fucking Christ."

Friday. Even with a brain that feels like it's been shot through with BB pellets I can calculate that I've been out for almost forty-eight hours.

"Where the hell have you been?" Crock demands.

I close my eyes. "That's a long story."

"Know what else is a long story? The one you wrote about the Russians."

The Russians. For a second, I don't even know what he's talking about. Then it starts to come back to me: what I told Jake in the library phone booth. Except what had I told him, exactly? About the shipping containers, no doubt, and the Diamond District con.

"You told me to get you something better" is all I can manage.

"Something *better* that's also *accurate*," he roars.

"What are you talking about?" I croak.

I can hear the fire of Crock's anger crackling through the line as he composes himself. "Your story about the shipping containers we put out on late deadline for yesterday's paper? About how they're full of American cars and gems stolen from uninsured jewelers in the Diamond District?"

"Yes," I say, feeling the lead weight of dread starting to descend in my stomach.

"Well, guess what? On account of your story, plus the notes on your desk I had to look at in an attempt to fact-check said story by an apparently blacked-out reporter, the Organized Crime squad sent a whole team to swoop in on that boat scheduled to leave out of Red Hook," he spits. "Got a warrant, opened the whole damn thing up. And what'd they find! No goddamn jewels, Parker! Nothing but boxes of mattresses, a new Toyota, and more of that goddamn chocolate!"

The receiver goes hot against my ear. "How can that be?" I sputter. "They're stealing jewels and cars and shipping them out from Pier 9. I know they are. They have a whole operation set up. I saw it."

"You *saw* it?"

"Well, I saw the containers. The guy there, he told me the stuff is labeled as mattresses, but really, they're hiding cars and gems."

"Apparently you were misinformed," he says icily.

"I'm telling you, Crock—"

"Enough. You're done, Parker," he says, his voice both firm and resigned. "Come in tomorrow to pick up your last paycheck."

I'm about to protest, to plead, to ask for another chance, but I can tell from Crock's tone that my chances have gone the way of the Third Avenue El. I put the phone down.

What I want is an emergency. The sirens blaring. The shrill screech of alarms. I want to kick down a door. Put my fist through a dark window.

Instead, I go to the kitchen, where Nellie is perched on the counter as if awaiting my entrance. She cocks her head and gives me a look of curiosity mixed with contempt. But she's not pawing my eyes out for food. That's when I see a note on the counter next to her: "Came in to check on you. Out cold. Fed Nellie and refilled water. Call me when you wake up. —M."

Thank god for Morgan. I go to the window and shove it open. A jetty of cold air slinks in, sending a shiver through the lone potted plant on the sill. Someone bought it for me and now I have to take care of it. I resent that. If you asked me what kind of plant it was, I would answer the green kind. It used to have shiny dark leaves and one white, ear-shaped flower jutting up from the center. Now the flower is gone, and the leaves have a pruny, sickly look to them. Nellie used to chew on them before even she lost interest. Now they bow their heads as if they've given up. Sad.

I hate every word that comes out of my mouth. I hate every thought that enters my head. I'm angry at the trees, how steadfastly they refuse to blossom. I don't care what the Russians say. In New York City, winter is one long year.

I shut the window.

I go to the living room. It's that April limbo when the radiators have been turned off, but spring is only here by a technicality, and so the apartment is always cold. Balled-up socks are cast around the floor like mice. All of a sudden it makes me so miserable I can't stand to be there a moment longer. I grab my coat and leave, my feet against the stairs feeling loose and jelly-like and separate from the rest of me.

Avenue C looks like a bomb hit it. The broken windows, abandoned construction, litter-ravaged gutters, and graffitied brick suddenly reveal themselves to me with stark clarity. There's a square of sidewalk underneath a blue U.S. post box that has been pushed up by some act of weather or sewage, so that the box sits askew on its four legs like something out of the early draft of a Disney movie that didn't quite make the cut. I pull my collar close against the cold twilight, put my head down, and start off to nowhere in particular. I'm reeling from my conversation with Crock (am I really *fired*?) as much as the bad drugs, but nevertheless, the wheels of my mind are slowly starting to grind. Who tampered with those pills? Sergei, the night of the cabaret? But I would have noticed. *Or would I*, I wonder. But *why* would he do it? What could I have possibly done that so offended him that he'd want to get rid of me?

Then I pass a newsstand and nearly jump out of my skin.

There's just one copy of *The New York Street* left, though the stand is well-stocked with all the other papers. It's curling in on itself, just revealing the *wood* on the front page: LADY KILLER ON THE LOOSE. I yank it from the rack. There are photos of Carla Russo and Liz Lau, and, in smaller letters, the words: *City rocked by serial sicko.* I stare at it in cold shock.

"Please be careful, miss," says a lilting voice. It belongs to the man behind the newsstand counter. I look up at him, not comprehending. He has a thick black mustache and hair covered by a purple turban. He gestures to the newspaper. "Young ladies like you must watch out for yourselves."

"Yeah," I say. "Thanks." I dig out two quarters and leave them on the counter.

I walk down the street with my eyes glued to the article. There are ghosts of the details I've gathered throughout, but they're overshadowed by half-baked assumptions, empty generalities, glazed-over details, and misplaced context. Just the kind of thing that keeps a New York City tabloid in print.

But what hurts the most is the byline: Eric Schultz and Jake Grandor.

I pass by a man drinking a bottle of Modelo, eyes bright and glassy. He grins at me. "Smile, lady," he says.

I take the bottle from his hand and smash it against the ground.

I catch my reflection in the window of the bar as I pass, his screams in Spanish resounding behind me. I look like a hurricane meeting a tornado.

I walk into McSorley's and throw the paper on the bar. "What the fuck is this?"

A few grubby heads raise themselves from their drinks. They're all the characters I usually try my best to avoid—our city's third-rate fourth estate. Schultz looks up at me lazily from his beer and the conversation he's having with Carl Cabrera from the *News*: the very Cabrera he tore to shreds at the office for stealing his Matchstick Murphy story.

"Oh, hey, Parker. So nice of you to grace us with your presence." He looks at the bartender. "Beer for the lady. On me."

"I repeat," I say, my voice hard-edged as a diamond. "What. The fuck. Is this."

"Crock needed a story," he says with a shrug. "I'm a police reporter. I write stories. Sometimes they just happen to make the front page."

I'm stupefied into silence. Schultz is clearly enjoying it. He's looking at me with the smug satisfaction of the cheater who got an A on the test he didn't study for. "Doesn't feel too good, does it?" he says. "Getting scooped?"

"It doesn't count as *scooped* when it's for your own fucking *paper*." I say. I'm not about to tell him about my conversation with Crock—that I can't actually claim any paper at all. "And as if it weren't bad enough, you had to turn it into a total hack job. You're leaving the door wide open for all the copycats and nut jobs who feel like trying their hand at the same fucking thing. It's lazy. It's wrong. It's irresponsible."

"Irresponsible," he says, looking around the bar as if he's holding court. He repeats the word again, holding up his glass like a scepter. "Ir-re-*sponsible*. In the words of none other than Parker Snow. A retraction, please! An apology, posthaste!"

I bite my tongue because I know that if I don't, I might regret what I say. Two glasses of beer have been set in front of me, because that's how they serve one beer at McSorley's. I pour one down my throat. It's slightly warm and slightly flat and so it goes down easy.

"I heard your story about the Russians didn't turn out too well," Schultz says, affecting sympathy. "Crock was all steamed up when he got the call. Too bad. Maybe they'll start having you write the horoscopes instead. Your reporting is about as accurate." His fake pout dissolves into a grin I want to crack wide open with my beer glass.

I set it carefully down on the bar. "Fine," I say. "Have it your way. Go tell Crock I'm writing the society pages from now on and leaving all the crime reporting to you, since you're such a goddamn newsman. Tell me, when was the last time you got a story that wasn't fed to you, whether by me or the NYPD?"

He rolls his eyes, downs the last of his beer, and gets up from his stool. "I'm going home. See ya, Cabrera. Next round's on me."

I sit at the bar, not moving. But something is still bothering me. I get up and go outside, where I find Schultz with a cigarette between his lips and a lighter in his cupped palm.

"How did you know all this stuff anyway?" I demand. "Even Jake didn't have that level of detail."

He hands me the cigarette he just lit, and I take it without thinking. He lights another.

"Easy," he says, blowing smoke upward toward his shaggy crop of hair. "You left your notes on your desk. Damn hard to read, though. You should really work on your penmanship."

My mind flashes back to the last time I was at the Shack, when I'd dropped off my notes with the expectation of coming back to work later in the afternoon. One pile that Crock had seen, hoping to make sense of the Russia story I'd called in to Jake, and one pile . . .

"What makes you think it's okay to take notes off my desk?" I sputter.

"Come on, Parker," he says. "You were never gonna write that story. You were gonna keep pushing and pushing like you did last time, with those Mexican girls. You wanted to be the one to break the story more than you wanted them to be saved. I hate to say it, but—"

I cut him off. "You don't hate it at all."

Schultz raises an eyebrow but says nothing. For a moment both of us are quiet, lifting cigarettes to mouths in front of the bar windows in the fading evening light. Then he says, "Sometimes, Snow, you just gotta know when to quit."

I bristle. "And do what you do instead? Chat up two-bit lieutenants at titty bars in Midtown? Chase every story that the boys at 1 PP have edited and approved?"

"Come off it, would you?" His voice splinters. "You may act like you're too good for me and everyone else. But where did *too good* get you last time? Huh?"

"Wherever it got me, it's better than being like you."

He stares at me with a mixture of anger and bewilderment. "How did you get to be the way you are?"

"How did I," I say. "How does anyone."

I throw my cigarette on the ground and walk back into the bar.

When my would-be exposé about the abortion clinic shattered into a million terrible pieces, everyone threw the blame on someone else. Should I have said something? Alerted the authorities to what the doctor was doing? Then what? What would have happened to those girls? Would my story and the public sympathy it might've brought have led to a less hostile intervention? Was the doctor at fault? Or the cops? Wasn't everyone trying to do what they thought was right? Questions I can never answer. But the fact is, I had pushed too hard, like Schultz said.

The worst part was, I still had to write the article afterward, with every painful, terrible detail about the clinic and the girls and how the whole thing got botched. And it's not really true, that I got benched from street crime and put on organized crime. In fact—and this is a fact that only Crock and I know—after that story, I couldn't write another.

Until Carla Russo.

The paper is still sitting on the edge of the bar. Maybe I should just become another cop ass-kisser, I think as I start to flick through the local news, the national syndicated columns, the irate op-eds. Or write those society pages. That would be a nice, safe place for me. Why not? What's the point of all this? Why stick my neck out when this is what it gets me? First the Russian shipping fiasco, and now this. And Jake—Jake. I can't even think about it now, him writing the story with Schultz, because if I allow myself to think about it, it's all over. I'm liable to hunt him down and say things that neither of us will ever forget. And because of the knifing pain that thinking about it produces right through my heart.

I get to the obituary section. I always like reading obituaries; they have a way of calming me down. A minor expressionist painter has died, along with an octogenarian French Olympian and a beloved local pin-juggler. There's also a write-up on Candace Gracen, whose place on the social ladder was apparently high enough to warrant a whole inch. Philanthropist, pediatric cancer advocate, mother of two, late wife of James M. Forrester, Esq.

The words hit me like a slow ton of cement. I read them once, twice, three times. There it is, in starkest black and white: I've made one of the biggest mistakes you can make. I took someone's words as if they were true.

###

I leave the other glass untouched and race to the *Street*'s reference library. Fortunately, my badge still works; news of my recent unemployment doesn't seem to have reached them. There I learn that Candace Gracen—late wife of the personal injury attorney James Forrester, with whom she'd just started divorce proceedings—had plenty of money of her own, as the heir to the Gracen rare earth materials dynasty. And she didn't have any ailing father to worry about, either—he died in 1981. I also called over to Mount Sinai, where she claimed to have volunteered. They had no record of a Candace Gracen.

My head is reeling as I step into my apartment and shed my coat, laying notebook and pen on my desk. I pace the living room, trying to make it all make sense. What was Gracen trying to tell me that day she called the *Street*'s office to summon me to her apartment? Her fear was obvious, but why the story? What was she afraid of, and what could that possibly have to do with Carla Russo—if Candace really knew Carla at all? And then I wonder with a start: What's the connection between Forrester, mobbed-up lawyer, and Carla? And what about Liz Lau? What—or who—connects them?

I remember thinking it out of character for an Upper East Side blueblood to read a rag like the *Street*. But now I realize that she must have been looking everywhere she could for news about Carla, knowing she was in some kind of danger. But what exactly *did* she know?

It's finally unraveling, the long red thread of it, but it's tangling around my feet.

I know I won't be able to sleep now. The streetlights outside are now illuminated against the darkening sky, each its own accusation. Nellie looks at me meaningfully from where she's perched on my desk. I go to the kitchen and fill the Moka pot with Café Bustelo. Maybe I can write my way through this chaos—keep throwing the facts in the air until they land on the page in some sort of order.

I pick up my pen, flip open the spiral cover, and steel myself for a long night.

20

Eyes as blue as the Black Sea . . .

I'm standing on the platform at Eighth Street the next morning, waiting for the R to take me to 1PP to pick up my last paycheck because I still don't quite trust my legs, when I see someone getting their pocket picked.

It takes me a moment to recognize him—the pickpocket. He's good. His victim, a tall, dark-haired man in a long wool coat, is looking toward the tunnel and doesn't even notice. But recognize him, I do. Short, round, blond. I've had some time to study him, after all. Like when he was dealing out cards for an underground poker game, or cavorting about onstage at Skovorodka.

Or—and that's when it hits me—swapping jewels for cut-glass fakes at a Diamond District jeweler's shop.

"Oleg," I say.

He looks up. When he sees me, his eyes widen to the size of poker chips. Eyes as blue as the Black Sea.

In a flash, he's moving toward the Q train that's just pulled up, slightly stooped back to me, and enters with a small crowd via the door just ahead of where I'm standing. Before I can think twice, I dodge my way onto the car through the one closest to me.

Immediately he turns around, blinking like a small woodland animal who's sensed a predator.

Oleg edges to the end of the car, then, in a movement so fast and sudden I barely see it, flicks open the metal handle and darts between the train cars.

I swear under my breath. He's already in the next car, and hastily making his way to the end of it. I get to the end and flick the door open, stepping out onto the narrow metal coupling. It pivots and slides underneath my feet as the train careens through the tunnel.

I push open the door to the next car and step inside. Oleg turns around and shoots me a terrified glance. Then he's at the end of the car and passing through to the next.

Seconds elapse until I'm there, too, coat flapping around my knees as I dart through groups of straphangers and one upright bass, blood running scorching hot through my veins. In the next car, a group of teenagers waving Styrofoam cups of soda blocks the way. Oleg weaves through them easily. By the time I get around them, he's already onto the next car.

I open the door and step onto the next coupling. Oleg. The obsequious manner I'd been so dismissive of when he intruded on my meeting with Sergei at Skovorodka, when he asked me to think of a song. He never did guess it, and I never revealed it. As a matter of fact, it was "Luck Be a Lady."

The train grinds to a halt and I almost lose my footing. I manage to catch myself before I careen into the tracks, one hand landing on the edge of the two cars surrounding me like I'm preparing for a gymnastics routine. Oleg scuttles and then darts off the train through the now-open doors.

I jump off the coupling and onto the platform at Canal just as the train is starting to move again. Gray wind rushes through my hair as it exits the station, leaving a swirl of trash and the must of urine in its wake.

Oleg is a few paces in front of me. He looks over his shoulder and clocks me, then rushes toward the stairs. To his right against the platform wall is a nook about the size of an elevator car that leads to a door labeled MTA EMPLOYEES ONLY. I bound over, grab him by the back of his coat, and throw him into it. He stumbles back against the brick wall.

"Parker! So nice to see you!" he says, as if he hadn't just been running down the length of a subway train, and I hadn't just been chasing him. Sweat glazes his forehead. "Is there something, er, did you want to see me about something?"

"Oh, not much," I snarl. "You could just say I'm in a sentimental mood."

He attempts a smile, but I can see him furtively glancing around me. I put one hand to the wall and jam the opposite foot into the other corner, blocking his exit.

"I knew I recognized you when I saw you at Skovorodka, even without the beard—*Abel.* Wasn't that the name you gave the jeweler right before you slipped that ruby in my pocket?" I say, leaning toward him against my elbow. "Are you your brother's keeper? Sure wouldn't want to be him."

"Please, I don't know what—"

"And that Yiddish accent. Real middle school theater. You must've been a hit in show choir when you did *Fiddler on the Roof.*"

"I'm sorry, Parker, I really do not know what you're talking—"

"Don't worry about it," I snap. "Just something to amuse me. It helps to be able to amuse yourself when you keep getting stuck in the most inconvenient places. Like jail."

"I did not intend for you to go to jail," he says mournfully. "I was simply acting on orders. Yes, I will admit, I was told to call your paper and suggest you visit the jewelry shop. But it was just intended to cause some confusion, a temporary distraction. That is all."

But I'm already past that. Now I'm thinking about the pills—the ones that went missing the night of the cabaret, that I thought Sergei might have tampered with—and which mysteriously turned up in my coat pocket again the day after the poker game, the same but altered. The pills that nearly killed me.

"Sleight of hand," I say. "The deal." I stare at him, shaking my head in disbelief. "You took my pills the night of the cabaret when you walked past our table and spilled that wine. Then you put them back in my pocket the night of the poker game. The same way you slipped in that loose gem without me even noticing."

He winces. "Parker, I did not know those pills were dangerous, they assured me there was nothing lethal—"

"Shut up," I say gruffly. My mind is racing. Why was Oleg at Petrowski's shop that day? Solnikov said they were getting out of the jewelry business. Unless he was lying? Or unless Oleg's not working for Solnikov at all. Unless, just like Forrester, he was actually there for—

"Batryshkin," I say out loud. "You got them because you're not working for Sergei and Solnikov. You're working for Batryshkin."

I take a step back and look at him. He looks back at me sheepishly. Suddenly it all makes sense. Oleg, the one always trying so desperately hard to get into their good graces, the ones who treated him like a fly to be swatted—he'd be the first one to defect from Solnikov's gang and join his rival's. To play double agent. What did Sergei call him? *A flea.* But I remember the way he dealt those cards—the sharp eye, the canny hands. Slick as a dealing machine.

"You're sick," I say. I take a step out, leaving the way free. Oleg gives me one last darting glance, then scampers past me and up the subway stairs, nub of yellow hair bobbing as he disappears out of sight.

If you ever believe your first impression of anyone, you're the true sucker.

###

I finally get down to 1 PP and up to the Shack. I've been rehearsing a hurried speech to throw down like a parlay before Crock can start in on his *very disappointed* bit. That and all my new findings, including this last revelation about Oleg.

But when I get to Crock's office, I stop dead. The door is shut, and from what I can hear behind it, he's well warmed up already: *poorly researched, look like idiots, top brass*. I have my ear to the door, heart racing with adrenaline and blood thrumming in my ears, when it suddenly opens. I jump back as Schultz walks out, looking wounded and sulky.

"What the hell happened?" I ask him. I catch a glimpse of Crock before the door shuts, chuffing and whinnying and stamping the ground.

"Great research you did, Snow," Schultz glares at me. "That whole serial-killer theory of yours? Bullshit."

"What are you talking about?" I say, not bothering to point out that he's criticizing the research that he stole.

"They caught the guy who killed the Russo girl! And guess what? No ties to the other cases."

I turn to him so fast I feel something in my neck snap. "*What?*" My mind shuffles through the possibilities like cards in a tarot deck. The bat boys? Someone with a hidden connection to both Carla Russo and Liz Lau? Or a random mugger all along?

"Yeah. It was the boyfriend after all," Schultz says, raking a tangle of too-long hair out of his eyes. "Told you," he adds bitterly. He sinks down into his desk chair, muttering as he tries and fails to get the light on a cigarette. "Crock's got me on *probation*. Whatever that means. All thanks to you."

The room curdles red in front of my eyes, my palms going sweaty. I see Anthony sitting across from me at the coffee shop near Brooklyn College, walled off in some private misery. And then the face of his mother, her words when I told her about Carla: *Every day, it seems like someone else has to die in this place. Maybe this is worse.*

My talk with Crock about Oleg, and my job, will have to wait. I vault out of the room, over to the stairwell, and down three flights of stairs.

"Anthony Jones," I choke out to the desk sergeant filling out paperwork.

She looks up without interest. "Perp?"

"Suspect."

She moves the form to the side, glances at something beneath it, then resumes her work. "Gone."

"How?"

"Detained."

"When?"

"Noon."

"Where?"

"Tombs."

"Shit."

I sink down onto the bench near the wall, my vision blurring in front of me. The booking sergeant's pen continues scratching out its senseless scrawl. *There's no way this is right*, I think. *It can't be.*

The door to the hallway swings open. I look up to see Maloney, flanked by Shepherd and Szybist, entering the office.

"Maloney," I say, standing up with a jolt. "What the fuck?"

"Nice to see you, too, Parker." He eyes me warily.

"What the hell is she doing here again?" Shepherd says to him. I follow them as they walk toward the stairs.

"Why is Anthony Jones at the Tombs?" I demand.

"'Cause he *did* it, Parker," Shepherd bleats. "He killed her. Admitted to it."

"*Admitted* to it?"

"He admitted to being at the scene," Maloney amends. "Which is enough to pick him up. Not only that, a neighbor came forward and said they overheard him arguing with Russo earlier."

I'm so stunned I stop in my tracks on the landing. Then I scramble up the last flight after them. "How is this fair? The kid is, what, twenty?"

"He's an adult," Maloney says. "He'll be assigned a lawyer if he can't afford one, and he'll have his day in court just like anyone else. And if anything else comes through that absolves him before that, he'll be a free man. You know how it works."

We get to the top of the stairs. "What about Liz? The similarity between the two murders? Same time of day, same type of victim, and apparently the same method? Did you get him for that, too?"

"Elizabeth Lau? The ME found she had a lethal dose of heroin in her system."

"Morgan found a lethal dose of heroin in Liz's system?" I repeat the words back, uncomprehending. Why didn't she tell me?

"Not Morgan. The other guy," Szybist pipes up. "Sorens."

"*Sorens?*" I repeat. "No. This isn't right. The chain of custody was with Morgan. A body isn't supposed to move between one ME and—"

Shepherd cuts me off. "Give it up, Snow. It was all done by the book. Your girl was just another druggie."

"No chain of custody! No medical examiner present at the Carla Russo scene! On a homicide!" I exclaim. "How can you say it was all done by the book? What book?"

But Maloney and Szybist have both disappeared into the detective's office. Shepherd hangs around, gloating.

"This was because of you," I say, anger rising. "You wanted Icebox Sorens as the ME on the case instead because you have him in your pocket, and he's too drunk to think for himself anyways. This was your doing because you don't like Morgan and you wanted this case closed."

"He's a qualified medical examiner and he had the time. Wouldn't want to *overwhelm* your friend Ms. Delacroix. Overworked as she is." He smirks. "And hey, come to think of it—wouldn't want us to look too hard into the source of that *prescription* we found on you when you got booked yourself, now, would we?"

I close my eyes. The curdling red is back. I open them and Shepherd has also disappeared, the doorway to Maloney's office now closed.

I look down the empty hallway, the cold tile floor and worn office nameplates. Season of locked doors and malice. I can't help feeling like the revelation I thought was just around the corner has turned into a dead end.

###

The Manhattan Detention Complex, more commonly known as the Tombs after the supposed inspiration for its design, is situated a few blocks from both One Police Plaza and Chinatown. Across the table in a private visiting room, under harsh fluorescent lights and flanked by guards, Anthony is looking young and scared and totally out of place in an orange jumpsuit.

"He called me in for questioning," he's telling me. "One of Maloney's guys. The big one."

"Shepherd," I say. I feel the inside of my mouth pinch like I've just eaten something bitter.

"He backed me into a corner. He said someone from the neighborhood had seen me getting off the subway at Eighteenth Ave. He was probably just making it up. But he kept hammering away at it, asking what I was really doing that night, and then that other guy, the skinny one—"

"Szybist," I say, taking that bitter thing and spitting it out.

"Yeah. That one," he says. "They had their whole good cop/bad cop routine down, with him acting like he was on my side, like it was totally fine if I was there that night. So, then I admit it, and apparently, that's enough to send me here. Even though I didn't say I *did* it." He shakes his head. "I should have known. I should've *known*, after what happened to Jeremiah. But you're in that room for hours, and you're confused, and they keep coming at you, and you can't think straight."

I'm hearing his words, but they're not making their way into my brain. All of this is wrong. "I thought you said you were at rehearsal," I say. "I thought you said the whole band could corroborate it."

"I was," he says. "But we got out early. So, I went . . . I went to Bensonhurst."

"But why?" I demand. "What were you doing there?"

Anthony looks more wretched than ever, arms hanging limply at his sides, head tilted toward the table. "I can't say."

I press my fingertips to my forehead. "You can't say. And why is that?"

"I just can't," he says, looking up at me. He's not wearing his glasses, and without them, his eyes look mousey and frightened.

But then I remember the comment Sal made when I first went to see him. *You shoulda heard them. The way he would go off on her.* He, meaning Anthony. Going off on Carla.

And what Carla wrote in her letter to her neighborhood friend, Martina: *It scares me sometimes, the fierceness of it. What someone can do if they love you that much.*

I take a deep breath. "When you went to Bensonhurst that night, did you see Carla?"

When he says nothing, I ask again, louder. "*Did you?*"

"Now you believe it, too." His voice is hollow.

"Well, you gotta admit it, Anthony," I say. My voice rings shrill in the emptiness of the visiting room. "From the evidence presented, you're not winning any awards for world's least likely."

"I saw her, yeah, but only to talk to her. She was really upset. Her dad was sick, it wasn't going well, she was—" he breaks off, then starts again. "I know how it must look. But you just have to believe me when I say I didn't do it. If anything, I tried to—" he stops abruptly.

"Tried to what?" The silence that follows is so long it starts to vibrate and ring under the hard blue jailhouse light. "Anthony, you're not making sense." I put my palms down square on the table, trying to seize his eye. "Did you see something that night? Did you see the person who hurt Carla?"

He just shakes his head. He looks young and petrified, jazz head caught in a hard-edged world that doesn't belong to him. But there's a sense of resignation at the core of the fear that puzzles and scares me more.

"Look," I say, trying to tamp down my rising agitation. "I'm sure you have your reasons for this. Maybe you're scared. Or maybe you're trying to protect someone."

I give him a pleading look. He only looks back helplessly. Finally, he whispers, "You have to believe me."

I get up and walk out the door, not turning around to watch Anthony get cuffed and led back to his cell, to the vermin and violence. So far away from the music-filled halls of Brooklyn College, from his mother's soft-edged home.

On my way past the guards and the security checkpoint and the metal detectors, back out on the street on the edge of Chinatown that feels like paradise just by dint of being free, I think about Cynthia Jones and every hardship life has loaded on her—enough for a hundred lives. How naive it was of me to think I could spare her one more.

###

I get home and call Morgan. She's happy I'm alive, but just as distraught about the Liz outcome as I am.

"The tissue samples came back from tox," she tells me. "She did have a relatively high dose of heroin in her system, but not enough to kill someone who was used to it. Like I said, I looked at her lungs. There was no pulmonary edema. She didn't OD."

"Fucking Sorens," I say. "Fucking *Shepherd*."

"I'm sorry, Parker."

"That's okay," I say. "You did your best."

I hang up. It's Saturday, which is a convenient day to have a total moral and physical breakdown. I always do my laundry on Saturdays. It's the day the laundromat has free soap. They advertise it with a big yellow sign that says FREE SOAP SATURDAYS. I pile my dirty clothes into a trash bag and grab my book of Russian phrases to entertain me while I wait, because I'm too spent to choose anything else. Then I drag the bag downstairs and up the block.

I throw my clothes into a washing machine and sit down on one of the hard plastic benches. The sickish light of the overhead fluorescents dribbles wanly onto the dirty tile floor. Not the kind of floor where you want to drop a clean pair of underwear. But of course, you always do.

I want to go see my doctor and get a whole lot of whatever he'll give me. But now that last year's disaster is on my mind again, the idea gives me a queasy feeling in my stomach. Because the fact is, my knowledge of that back-alley abortionist didn't end when I published my story. The fact is, that doctor had a second career. A career pushing pills for anyone with desire and a few bucks to pay. And who was first in his appointment book?

It's all coming full circle now, the shame and the pain that I had been trying to hold off. The reason I hadn't even told Morgan about Crock firing me. Because it confirmed that, in fact, Maloney was right. I am unreliable.

I'll find another doctor, I decide. Or better yet, I'll quit altogether. After one last trip out to Bensonhurst. An emergency measure. Something to help me forget that all of this even happened, one last, numb hurrah before I start fresh. The thought is like a defibrillator on a corpse. It revives me, but barely.

As I wait for my laundry, I flip idly through the book of Russian phrases. There's a section on "The Role the Soviet Trade-Unions Play in Labour Protection." Topical vocabulary: *Promotion to a managerial post. Quota setting. Dismissal; to get the sack.* Topical, indeed. Another titled "Soviet Spacemen Win the Hearts of People."

I pause on the section on Russian diminutives, that most Slavic custom of shortening the first names of one's familiars. Explains Comrade P.: Vladimir may turn into Volodya, Vova, or even Vovochka under an affectionate tongue; both Aleksandr and Aleksandra claim Sascha as their diminutive; while women with the given name Maria are more frequently called . . .

I throw the book down as if I've been singed. I can feel the few other patrons in the laundromat looking over at me, but I hardly notice. The self-pitying stupor from a moment ago has washed away completely. *Could it be?* The voice in my head asks. And then answers, *Yes, it could.*

I stand up and dash outside, leaving my clothes spinning wetly in the washer drum. I have to get to a phone.

Geronimo is outside Sunny's bodega, holding a cup of coffee and turning his slow circles. The front door flies open. I jump out of the way and slam straight into Geronimo, his coffee spilling all down my front.

I yell my apologies as he stammers his, and then I get to my building and speed up the stairs. Terry is on our landing, pushing boxes into his apartment.

"Oh, hey, Parker," he says, looking at me benignly.

"Terry," I gasp. "Do you still have any more of those t-shirts?"

"Sure I do," he says, his face brightening. "What's your size?"

I go into my apartment, new white shirt in hand. Before I change, I go to the phone. My fingers are vibrating with nerves. I'm not sure what will happen after I make this call—what chain of events I'll stop or set off—but I know that if I don't, I'll regret it for the rest of my life.

21

Just where she said she would be . . .

I walk from the Brighton Beach subway station toward the boardwalk for what I hope will be the last time for a very long time. I don't meet anyone and nobody meets me. The air hangs foggily over the beach, the sand hard packed and ashen. The sky is a milky blank.

Masha—hostess, waitress, nightlife chanteuse—is standing under the covered picnic area, facing the sea. Just where she said she would be.

The Maria that Candace Gracen wanted me to find.

"Maria," I say. "Is that your real name?"

"Maria de Santos," she says, turning to face me. She holds my gaze without fear or apology. "Cuba by way of Little Odessa. That's what the Ukrainians call Brighton Beach, you know. They say it reminds them of home."

When I called over to Skovorodka to ask for her, I was miraculously put through. As luck would have it, Sergei was in New Jersey for the day on some sordid piece of business. She'd sounded almost relieved to hear from me.

"So," I say. "Let's start with Carla Russo."

We stand there for a moment in silence, Masha framed between two gray pillars, the waves behind her gnawing the cold shore.

"I used to see them coming in and out," she says finally. "Young women from Ukraine or Russia. Wide-eyed. Lost. Girls they promised a restaurant job with plenty of money to send back home. They thought they were coming here for something glamorous."

I furrow my brow, confused. *What does this have to do with Carla?*

"But of course, they weren't just expected to wait tables," Masha continues. "I didn't see it, but I heard the stories. Sergei pushing one into a bathtub, holding a hair dryer over it. I tried to ask him about it once. *Ssssssspokoino*, he said." She imitates his lisping speech. "*Calm down.*"

"But I never thought," she continues, "that it would happen to me."

I grimace. Women being trafficked from Eastern Europe, lied to, and abused—there's a story there, but not the one I'm here for. Yet something about Masha's manner tells me to be quiet and listen.

"I thought I'd gotten pretty lucky. Guaranteed audience at the cabaret shows almost every night, and an appreciative one at that. Good pay. Steady work. They tried to be nice about it at first. They said they'd pay extra if I would *keep the guests company*. I said no. I thought I actually had a choice." She gives a low, emotionless laugh. "Then one day, Sergei tells me to come to the back. There's a phone call for me. It was my grandmother back in Cuba. She said a man had come to 'visit' who said he knew me from New York. She had even asked him in for tea. And that's what really terrified me. They wanted me to know that they knew where she was, that they could find her whenever they wanted to."

I feel a hand clench around my esophagus. Sergei, with his cool smile and sharp little fangs, who had described Masha as *a friend of the group*.

"But why?" I begin. "I mean, why go to such lengths to . . . ?"

"You mean, why was I so special?" She shrugs. "I was the exotic flower. Something different. And by that point, I was part of the act. People came to see me, and they didn't just want to look. And don't men always want what they can't have?"

Carla Russo—pretty and young, an air of innocence, maybe, that might appeal to their tawdry clientele. Did she get herself mixed up in a world that may have seemed like an adventure or a little extra cash, only to find herself in way over her head? Before I can ask, Masha speaks again, her voice now almost too quiet to hear.

"One night, when I was leaving the restaurant, Batryshkin was waiting for me. He said he could help me, and I could help him. I wouldn't have to work for Sergei and Solnikov anymore, to do the things they asked me to do. That I would have a new job, *s dostoinstvom*. With dignity."

"You and Oleg," I say as her words sink in. I think of the two of them talking at Skovorodka just before Oleg dashed out the door, the air of furtiveness about their exchange. "You were both secretly working for Batryshkin."

She nods grimly. "Batryshkin, he instructed me to go to hospitals and clinics and the places addicts went and wait for vulnerable-looking women to come out. I was good at approaching them. I looked like a normal person, someone they might be friends with. But they could also sense, I think, that I knew something about the way they felt. Of being trapped."

I lean against the pillar closest to me, suddenly weak-kneed. The breeze stirs a fine scattering of sand around my ankles.

"I struck up a conversation, invited them for coffee," Masha is saying. "And I told them that there was another way out."

"Way out?" I repeat, uncomprehending.

"The instructions were simple." Masha is looking out at the water now, a tragedienne delivering the soliloquy she'd been reciting to herself for a long time. "Go to this agency and take out a life insurance policy. The agency was paid off not to report anything on their medical examinations. The cost for services was part of the payout of the policy. It would look like an accident, or a mugging. A random act of violence. But they wouldn't feel anything. It was very simple, very clean. And most importantly, they would have something left over for those in their lives who needed it."

A sudden breeze carries a dirty, salty smell, like the bad end of a fishing pier. A seagull shrills somewhere nearby. I let it wash over me, the gray tide of this misery. The murders were connected, like I'd thought. But the killer wasn't a random sociopath. It was a system of manipulation, of corruption, of greed. I think of the immigrant women on the operating table, at the breaking point of desperation. Women who didn't know a better choice existed.

"But why would they agree to this?" I ask, vocal cords constricted, voice tight.

"They each had their own reasons," Masha says. "I think Carla Russo was the first one you wrote about?"

The first one. The phrase gongs sickly in the walls of my skull. Because of course Carla wasn't the first. Of course there were others before her, and who knows how many?

"She had a hereditary illness," she continues. "Something that her grandmother had died of, and that her father had. She was already showing symptoms, but she hid them. She was studying nursing, so she knew more than most. The onset was early, and irreversible."

Carla's father—the one in the wheelchair who her mother was taking care of, who was getting worse and worse. Knowing that would be her fate. Anthony's confused words to me in the Tombs's visiting room. *Her dad was sick, it wasn't going well.* Her Italian Catholic neighborhood with its battalion of Mary statues, the fear of eternal damnation that remains when everything else fades. And Carla's brother Sal, whose debts suddenly disappeared. Except they didn't disappear. They were paid back.

"And Liz Lau?" I ask.

"HIV."

I breathe in sharply. All at once I'm back in that murky loft above Petey's Bar, its smell of burnt vinegar, the shudder and sick release. The words of the Cowboy—*She was just looking for a little bit of assurance. A little bit of insurance.*

"What about Candace Gracen?" I say. "Forrester's wife? Who died the night of—"

"The night you came to the cabaret," she finishes. "I didn't know that was the plan. Believe me, I would have tried to at least talk them out of it. I guess she knew too much. Enough for her to be dangerous."

It hits me then. Gracen was, in fact, murdered—and if not at her own husband's hand, then at least at his behest. "I met her," I say. "She asked me over, spun a fake story about knowing Carla, mentioned someone named Maria."

"From what I pieced together, she'd overheard Forrester talking to Batryshkin on the phone about Carla during the early planning stages," she says. "Forrester always called me Maria, my real name. Gracen knew he was up to something really bad, but she couldn't very well march him into the police station, you know? She would have seemed totally crazy."

So, Gracen hadn't asked for this. She had simply known too much about the husband she was trying to escape, his dealings with the rising power of Brighton Beach. She'd read my article about Carla's murder and known her husband was in some way behind it, or involved in it, but she didn't know why or how. Calling me to her apartment was a last, desperate attempt to get the help the police wouldn't give her—especially not with Forrester, with all his wiles and all his pull, on the other end. It strikes me then what courage it took for her to make that call to the paper, to even try and do something to stop a man as dangerous as he was.

There's a question, wide and glaring, at the center of it all: Liz's autopsy. Some heroin found in her body, but nothing else. "Did you . . ." I trail off.

She shakes her head vigorously. "I was never there for the actual . . . for the event itself."

"Who did it? How?"

"I never found out that part," she says. "I didn't want to know."

Part of me bristles at that. To avoid the details of what she was really involved in feels spineless. At the same time, I don't know what I would have done in her position. And the fact is, Masha is the first person involved in this story who's spoken to me with absolute honesty. "I'm just glad you told me this much," I say. "Thank you."

"I wasn't going to," she says. "I think Batryshkin actually brainwashed me into thinking that it was okay, what I was doing. Like it was a reasonable way to keep living one's life. Maybe even good. But I kept seeing you around, reading your articles. I saw the way you wouldn't let go. And then when you called, it was like . . . I woke up." When she looks at me, her eyes seem to have absorbed the color of the sea, gray-green and metallic. "Forget about my grandmother. They'll kill me one day, when I'm no longer of use to them," she says, voice flat. "But it won't matter. They'll keep doing this until they find something else. And it'll be worse."

A chill runs through me. Because I know she's right. She'd tried to escape Solnikov's faction only to find herself in the clutches of something even more evil—just like Oleg. The former sick of Sergei's and Solnikov's abuses, the latter tired of being made to feel like a flea and hungry for his piece of the pie. They made easy recruits. A failure in Solnikov's management philosophy.

Something dawns on me then. "Will you wait here a minute?" I ask. "I have to make a phone call."

I jog up to the boardwalk to the nearest pay phone.

"Parker," Crock says when I get him on the line. He sounds both worried and relieved to hear from me. "I thought you were coming in this morning for your last paycheck."

"I did come in," I say. "But then I had to leave. Listen, Crock: Who was it who called in the tip about the chocolate truck?"

"Huh?"

"Willy Wonka. Who called it in?"

"How should I remember? Why are you asking, anyways? What's going on?"

"I really need to know," I press. "You always note down the tips, right? Maybe there's something from that day you can dig up?"

He grunts and mutters some choice words under his breath. But I hear the sound of paper riffling, and I can picture him pawing through his wastebasket that hasn't been changed since the seventies. "Actually, I remember the guy's voice," he says suddenly. "Had an accent. Russian, I guess. It stood out because he had a lisp."

I close my eyes for a moment. Then I put the receiver slowly back in its cradle.

The line about how it's better to be feared, the one that sounded like it came from a two-bit gangster movie. Our so-called deal. Sergei and Solnikov knew their crew was defecting to Batryshkin's. So, they thought they'd use me. I'd bait the other side, reporting on *their* activities and taking the attention off of Solnikov. How easy, really, it all had been, to set me on a dangerous trail, one that would lead me to jail cells and car yards run by psychopaths. Meanwhile they could keep up their extortion and poker games and remain the barons of Brighton Beach. Sergei had put me out like a chicken for the wolf.

And I had fallen for it.

I walk back to the picnic area where Masha is still standing, watching me nervously, hands crossed over her chest.

"Did you do what I asked after we spoke on the phone?" I ask her.

She nods. "I called him. He said he'd see you on the roof of his building. This way, he says, you can speak without fear of being overheard."

"Sounds dramatic," I say. "Okay. Where is this building?"

"3109 Brighton Sixth Street."

"Isn't that where Solnikov has a place?" I say with surprise.

"That's the one," she says. "Batryshkin bought it."

"*Bought* it?"

"Yep. He bought the building."

I take a deep breath, unease rising in me like the churning surf. "Alright," I say. "On my way."

"I don't think you should go there alone," she says, taking a few panicked steps toward me. Her face is illuminated by the light on the boardwalk. "At least let me come with you. I know him pretty well at this point. I can read his moods, his signals. And if something happened to you, well, I would feel—" She pauses, then says quietly, "I wouldn't be able to forgive myself."

I shake my head. "I'm not involving you in this any further." I look past the boardwalk toward the apartment building, then back to Masha/Maria. "We're going to get you out of this."

From her look, though, she seems to think I'm not getting either of us out of anything.

I leave her and cross the boardwalk, then start up the street. My stomach lurches with every step I take toward that building and the person awaiting me there, if you could even call someone like Batryshkin human—someone sick enough to think up the scheme that Masha just described. You would never know how much violence exists underneath the surface of this out-of-the-way neighborhood. It feels especially rueful then, streets empty, evening quickly passing to night. On the corner of the brown-brick tenement buildings is the defunct Yablochko Chocolate Factory, the one that used to make the bars with the apple stamped into their waxy brown surfaces. The high-spirited hope of it. What this place could have been if not for—

The scent stops me in my tracks. Faint but sweet, warm and rich and mellow.

"I thought this wasn't operational anymore," I murmur. Then I remember what Miriam Melka said, how she thought she'd smelled it recently. She'd chalked it up to nostalgia. But she was right—there's a definite aroma of chocolate emanating from its boarded-up windows.

I try the front door. Locked. I pace back and forth, then walk around to the side of the building. The scent is emanating from a vent. Next to it is a window, opened slightly.

There's a pile of crates by the wall. I slide one over with my foot and step onto it. With a jump I'm able to catch the window ledge, feet dangling. I feel very stupid doing this. I swing myself onto an elbow and push the window open farther with the other hand. Then comes the hard part. I wedge my midsection through, the bottom of the windowsill scraping my stomach, then duck and dive forward. I roll onto my back like they taught us to do somersaults in the first grade, the hem of my coat flapping behind me like Charlie Chaplin's.

I straighten up and dust myself off. The smell of chocolate envelops me. Production is in full swing, equipment whirring over the unpainted concrete floor: the mixing drum full of melted chocolate, the white spouts filling trays with shiny, tempered liquid, the rolling metal cylinder stamping each finished bar with the apple insignia. At the end is a table neatly lined with cardboard boxes full of bars wrapped in gold foil, ready to be taped up and sent off. Bars that look just like those I saw on the errant chocolate truck.

I walk around slowly, my eyes roving over the line. Could it be that Batryshkin and his gang really are just exporting chocolate? That their Russian customers have gotten a taste for something better than the grainy, Soviet ersatz stuff? Maybe he bought the old factory and equipment and started it up in secret to avoid taxes, or a competitor leaping in. But it all seems too sweet and wholesome for the likes of him.

Unless . . .

With sudden inspiration, I pick up a handful of the unwrapped chocolate bars from the line and toss them into the mixing drum. I pick up some more. Then more. As the paddle turns, the bars begin to melt. A glimmer appears from the molten brown. Then another, and another. One ruby red. One garnet green. One bright, diamond white.

Just chocolate, Crock had said about the shipping container in the Red Hook dock the cops had pried open. Nothing to see here.

"Chto vy delayete? Kto vy?"

I turn around. A short, stout woman in a hairnet is standing with an irate expression on her face, holding a box of gold foil wrappers. The door behind her is open, revealing a small office where a man sits at a table. She yells something to him, gesturing toward me angrily. He continues examining the pile of jewels in front of him with slow precision, seemingly unmoved by any of this.

"I'm sorry," I say, my hands up. "I was just leaving."

I go to the window to go out the way I came. But it's too high to jump without the crate. So instead, I walk to the front door, slide the metal bolt from its plate, and leave.

###

When I push open the door to the roof some fifteen minutes later, Batryshkin is already there. He's wearing the same wool coat and maroon scarf he had on the night I saw him in Forrester's office, except now he's looking out over Brighton Beach, hands clasped behind his back, as if surveying his domain. The only sound is the faint swell and break of waves on the darkened beach below.

"Good move," I say, taking a few steps onto the roof. "Using the old chocolate factory, hiding the stolen gems in the bars. Very clever."

"Parker Snow." His cultivated voice surprises me again, the accent refined and almost florid. He takes his time turning around. "A pleasure to finally make your acquaintance."

Up close, his face is sharp and intelligent, very different from Sergei's dull-eyed muscle boys or Solnikov's village brutishness—or even Sergei himself, the schoolboy playing businessman. His eyes are a strange silvery gray.

My shudder is so slight that most people wouldn't notice it. But Batryshkin's mouth prickles in amusement. "Is it chilly?" he says mildly. "I haven't been cold since I came to this country."

"Let's make it brief with the 'you haven't seen cold' business," I say. "I've heard enough of it from you people, and frankly I'm tired of it."

He laughs, a low, quiet chuckle. "Yes, there is really no cold like winter in Saint Petersburg. A beautiful city. Have you been?" he asks politely. "No, I don't suppose you have. In winter, darkness falls on everything like a shroud. Even the banks of the Neva contract, the water locking itself up into black ice. Like a spirit has invaded the very nature of things. Except for certain nights when the snow falls and the city transforms into something folkloric. It recalls the time when women who spoke French in court were taken to grand balls in horse-drawn carriages. You can almost hear the hooves falling over snow-dusted Nevsky Prospect."

"An image Tolstoy would surely appreciate," I say. *Or maybe Dostoevsky.* I want to ask where he's going with this but decide it's safer to let him arrive at his point on his own. He turns again, slightly, to look out over the rooftop, at the buildings and sea beyond. I notice a high-rise is going up in Sea Gate, its skeleton lit up in the night. An elevator moves up and down like a finger along a spine.

He turns back to me. "Permit me to tell you a story."

I raise an eyebrow. As if I have a choice.

"On one such winter night, when I was not eight or nine, I was lying in my bed watching the snowflakes fall through the dark sky," he begins. "We lived on one of the grand boulevards in the old city. I was gazing outside at the flakes of snow falling in the light given by a streetlamp, hypnotized by the magic hush." A wistful smile appears on his face, then fades.

"I heard a terrible scream. It made my blood run cold. I sat up in bed. The first wail was followed by another, still worse. High-pitched, keening. Puncturing the stillness of the night," His gray eyes seem to recede down the canals of memory. "I looked out my window and saw a figure stumbling down the otherwise empty street. A young woman wearing only a thin dress, high heels on her feet. The night was punishingly cold, the sidewalks already covered in snow. She was screaming with cold, a cold that made my toes ache to look at.

"I ran to get my father, who was a very high Party official by that time. He was sitting in his study, looking over some papers. I still remember the distinctive smell of his cigarettes. Belomorkanal brand. He didn't seem to have even noticed the screams. We went together to the window. He looked down at the miserable creature, who had reached the corner of the block and looked ready to collapse. He shook his head and said, simply, '*Zhalko.*' A pity. Then he returned to his desk."

"I surmised later that she must have been a call girl entertaining some Party functionaries," Batryshkin says. "She must have drunk too much, grown too bold. Said something untoward. And then she found herself tossed out into the street without even a coat to cover her. And no one, no one in those days would open their doors."

I grimace. "A heartwarming tale. When does the picture book come out?"

Batryshkin's eyes glimmer in the dark. "It was a lesson," he says. "Sometimes it's better not to see things. Not to know too much."

"You couldn't have just let her in?" I say with dismay.

"And then what? You are thinking with your American mind, Ms. Snow, which maintains its steadfast belief in justice and righteousness," he says, with equal dismay. "If we had brought the girl inside, if she had told us things that were not for our ears to hear, if we'd had to involve ourselves in getting her home—which undoubtedly would have been the case—things could have become much, much worse. No. It is impossible to help someone without their pain and troubles bleeding onto you."

"Isn't that how you were raised?" I say. "The hammer and sickle, and all that?"

"Unfortunately, what one gains from ideology one quickly loses to experience. No. What my upbringing taught me most profoundly was how little indeed prevents us from being the ones out in the cold," he says. "And so, I vowed that I would do everything, anything and everything, to keep myself inside that window, looking out."

"What about Solnikov? Doesn't he worry you at all?" I say. "It looks like he and his apparatus may be harder to kill than you think."

He waves a hand. "A minor annoyance. Solnikov runs a petty operation, crass and unsophisticated. My organization is something quite different." He begins pacing again. "In addition to our exports and operations here, we have aluminum factories in Moscow, diamond mines in Sierra Leone, poppy fields in Thailand, weapons moving from Florida to Bulgaria, submarines flowing cocaine down to South America, women all over, and all of the money washed clean in Antigua."

"Sounds like I'll have plenty to write about," I say. I'm beginning to wish I hadn't come here.

"This country is sick, for all its evident plenty," he says, shaking his head. "How sad that the innocent must suffer while the guilty run free."

"You seem all torn up about it," I say. "Listen, I know what you did to those women. Carla Russo. Elizabeth Lau."

"*Did* to them?" He stops. "Oh, no. You have it wrong. They *asked.*"

The word makes me flinch, like the pop of a firecracker too close to my ear. "You manipulated them," I protest. "You made them feel their lives didn't have any worth." How many had been made to feel this way before and since?

"This is incorrect," he says. "It was a mutually beneficial arrangement. They themselves felt their lives didn't have any worth. But suicide would not be an option for them, for various reasons. Not the least of which is that life insurance policies don't pay out on suicides."

My throat goes tight and numb. It was a game for him. A setup he created just to see if he could. "I want to know how you did it," I manage. "At least tell me how you did it."

"Air embolism," he says, almost proudly. "An injection of air into the subclavian vein. Almost impossible to detect on autopsy unless you were looking for it. A savvy doctor could perform it with the tiniest of puncture marks. From there, it was easy to make it look like a murder. A blow to the head, which the patient wouldn't even feel. Random street crime," he says, then adds, "and so inexpensive."

Needle marks found on Candace Gracen. And on Liz Lau, but she was a junkie, so who cares? An overworked or inexperienced ME could easily miss the signs, anyway—like the one who performed the autopsy on Carla Russo. It was perfect, nearly perfect. Except . . .

"How did you find a doctor who would do this for you?"

"How?" Batryshkin says, smiling like a chef about to remove the cloche from his favorite dish. "Oh, Parker. You know the answer to that question."

Waiting on the subway platform. Pills in my pocket. The scream that tore through the night. Someone who had been waiting to scream her whole life.

"No," I choke out.

"The story you wrote about those girls looking for abortions and the doctor who operated on them—I read it in your little paper," he says. "That doctor was the perfect candidate. Someone medically proficient, but shamed, who had narrowly escaped a much more serious charge. Who had so little of his life left, and who needed money badly. And who, perhaps more than that, needed purpose. To be useful."

To be useful. Girls on the table, the ones who survived and the one who died. The baby without an arm. The doctor I returned to, who had lost his license and was driven even further downward in his fall from grace, and whom I was only too happy to meet there.

"Of course, at the time, we had no idea about this *habit* of yours. It made it so you were present at a rather inconvenient time," Batryshkin says. "That put a—what is the expression—a wrench in things?"

"I'm feeling a wrench in things," I say. "Between my spinal cord and my cranium, to be precise."

"You have a very colorful manner of speaking," Batryshkin remarks, as if we're two well-dressed guests in Empress Catherine's parlor.

But I'm thinking about the doctor. The change in our familiar script. The office closed when it was never closed. How nervous he'd been acting these last weeks when I'd gone to see him, those twilight appointments—

"Just after business closed for the day," Batryshkin says, as if reading my mind. "Yes. That is his preferred time to assist us. Of course, sometimes it gets late. Such as this evening." He pauses, then bares his teeth. "Doctor, your patient will see you now."

The door to the roof opens. It takes me a moment to recognize him, so out of context, except for the familiar slump of his shoulders. I so rarely even looked at him in those shadowy hours, it occurs to me now—my vision dimmed by what I knew was coming, that unnatural satisfaction. His face looks thirsty somehow, like staring at a picture of the sea.

The Good Doctor.

"English is an exceedingly transaction-driven language," Batryshkin is saying. "When you believe something, you *buy it*. When you're convinced of the merits of an idea, you're *sold*. You even have such an expression about dying—*buying the farm*. How quaint. If everything in this country has a price, can be bought and sold for a market rate, why not this, too?"

But I'm not listening to him. Because something is coming back to me. That evening in Bensonhurst. I'd left the doctor's office and gone to the pharmacy next door. The pill haze was already beginning its slow descent, blotting out the memories to come. But as I was walking out, she was walking in. Her hand on the doorknob. Something glinting in the early evening sunset light. We'd made eye contact.

All at once it falls into place. Why Carla's face in my mind was untouched by any visible trauma. Why I wanted to hang on to the ring for so long, like a talisman. Because I knew it was in there, the true memory in place of the false one. When I'd gotten to the scene, the crowd had already gathered, blocking my view. I didn't see Carla dead.

I saw her alive.

"In fact, we're getting out of this business. The insurance payouts are simply not worth it for the trouble," Batryshkin is saying. Like he's talking about clipping coupons. "But our dear doctor will be performing one last service for us tonight."

The doctor is looking at me silently, and I at him. He has grown extraordinarily skinny, as if his body has been consuming itself.

Suddenly I remember Candace Gracen's *wellness practitioner*—the one the blank-faced receptionist wouldn't let me meet. "Moonlighting," I say. "That's what you said you were doing when your office in Brooklyn was closed. Moonlighting as Dr. Roy Winter?"

"It helps to have eyes on all parts of your organization," Batryshkin cuts in. "Something my father taught me. You never know when you might need their . . . insight."

The doctor breaks my gaze, but not before I see the shame on his face. Then he finally speaks. "Mr. Batryshkin, really, I don't think this is necessary." I forgot how deep his voice was—a voice that still contains a shadow of authority.

"I'm afraid it is," Batryshkin replies. What a pity, his expression says. *Zhalko.*

The doctor takes a step toward me. I take a step back.

He removes a needle from his pocket.

Batryshkin reaches out and grabs my wrist, his hand closing around it with the force of a vise. All at once I'm sickly aware of the power underneath that well-cut suit, the grip there's no leaving, no way out, no way, no way. My own birdlike bones so frail underneath my faintly pulsing wrist.

"No need to worry, Ms. Snow," he says softly. "It will all be over soon."

The doctor is lifting the needle. He is bringing it down. It's happening in slow motion—the birds—the way they flew from one platform overhang toward the other, then returned, like so many warnings. They saw something. What? And only a matter of time until one would misjudge its U-turn and hit the opposite wall. Only a matter of time.

The metal tip of the needle glints like something precious in the scattering light. All I can do is shut my eyes, wait for the impact, the one that will be so light, that will carry me aloft like a balloon, fill me with air so that I float up and away from this place.

I hear a gruff yell, then a curse in Russian. Suddenly the viselike grip releases from my arm. I open my eyes to see Batryshkin staggering backward. The needle is sticking out of his neck. He reaches up to wrench it out, but then freezes. Blood is already pouring out from where the syringe is lodged in his jugular, the conduit already ruptured.

"I'm sorry," the doctor is saying. "I couldn't do it the painless way. You never would have stayed still long enough. There's precision in my work, you know."

Batryshkin is staring at him with an expression of pure shock. Then his eyes flutter. He staggers, drops to his knees, and falls forward, landing heavily on the side of his face. Everything is silent.

I turn to the doctor. My heart is jumping like a rabbit between my ribs. "We have to go," I choke out. "Now."

He gives me a sad smile. "I hope you know that it wasn't just for the reasons he said. I felt I was giving them—all of them—peace," he says. "I hope one day you'll find your own."

He's walked past me now, to the edge of the roof. He sits down gently, letting his legs swing over the edge, like a child looking out at the sea.

"No!" I scream, reaching my hands out instinctively. But it's too late—he's already pushed off and down. There's an awful moment of silence when my breath catches like a bubble in my throat and then I hear it, a sound I know I'll never forget: the dense meeting of flesh with ground. The moment when a person becomes a body.

###

I stare down over the edge for I'm not sure how long. Then I snap out of it and look back at Batryshkin. He's still lying on the floor of the roof, his dark form unmoving. I run to the door, and for a terrifying second, it won't open. I pull again, harder, and it flies forth, sending me stumbling back. I manage to save myself from the fall and dash into the foyer, jabbing the button for the elevator for an excruciating minute until the car rises and the doors part. I catch a glimpse of myself in their brushed metallic surface: The white I <3 New York t-shirt I forgot I was wearing is now striped with the dirt of the windowsill in the chocolate factory, damp with sea air and sweat.

When I get down, Brighton Sixth Street is still. The only sound is that of my heart, pounding at the wall of my chest like it's trying to escape. Then I hear a high, hysterical wail, like the wail of the girl Batryshkin described, the one who heard too much, who said too much, her bare toes and shoulders freezing in that ungodly Russian night. Is it coming from me?

Then I place it—the scree of a siren. Coming closer. Blue-and-red lights are suddenly being thrown in shimmering circles onto the side of the building, the sidewalk. A police car pulls up, then two. An ambulance. A telltale Ford Crown Victoria, from which Maloney steps. People in uniforms and suits and scrubs are rushing toward me, asking if I'm hurt, if I need help.

"I'm okay," I say. "I'm fine." I'm about to delve into the whole thing, to tell them about the doctor who just jumped off the building's ledge, about Batryshkin lying on the roof, dead, probably, maybe, hopefully dead, when another car pulls up—a brown sedan. The door opens. Crock hoists himself from the driver's seat in a wrinkled white shirt and slacks, strands of hair flying from his comb-over as he waddles toward me at a speed that, for Crock, may as well be a sprint.

"Parker," he gasps when he reaches me. "Why don't you ever carry your goddamn pager?"

22

There's spring in the air . . .

What they don't say is that it's not always a wish to die, so much as to no longer have to live. That there is a moment when the world doesn't consist of infinite possibilities waiting to unfold, but one drab, gray corridor, from which there is no exit and only one way to move. You walk alone there. Sometimes you hear sounds from the outside, you even see faces, but they can never reach you. There is another way out, but because of them, you can't take it. All their lives they would wonder: What could they have done, and why them, and why you? And they would enter their own dark corridor.

That's when you see a glint. A possibility. It's there at the tip of a needle, in a bubble of air, a tiny pocket of nothingness. And once you put that nothingness inside you, you can become nothing as well.

You, who have never had control, now cede it willingly.

Then everything is simple. It will all be gone in a moment, with the ease of a breath. One quiet, sharp exhale.

###

Some interesting things will happen in the days that follow.

Anthony will be released. We'll meet again by Brooklyn College, and in the weary light of the diner over cups of stale coffee, he'll tell me that he was indeed there the night Carla died, and that they did fight. It seems we just missed each other. He'd found her at the clinic, right before she went into the exam room with The Good Doctor. Convinced her to take one last walk around the block with him. She was sick and getting sicker, she told him, as she'd told him a dozen times before. She didn't want to be a burden, or worse, an embarrassment. She said it should be her choice, what she did with her own life, if she had any choice at all. She'd thrown the ring to the ground in her anger that was really grief.

He should have taken it, he realized later. But in the moment, he'd felt too helpless, too stunned. It didn't seem real, he said. He couldn't quite believe that she would actually go through with it. So, he'd left it there. Maybe some part of him wanted it all to lead back to him. If he got caught, he'd finally be doing something for her, giving her something he never could before.

I'll give that ring back to him. He'll take it to Petrowski in the Diamond District, hoping to get something for the metal. The latter will examine it under his jeweler's loupe and, to the great surprise of both of them, tell Anthony that the fugazi from the pawn shop on Atlantic is real.

Anthony will negotiate a sale because he still never wants to see the thing again.

He and his mom are using the money to get a better lawyer for his brother, the one doing time at Attica for a murder he didn't commit. They're preparing for an appeal, asking for his parole. They're hopeful.

###

I'll also go to three funerals.

The first will be in Chinatown. I'll stand across the street from the funeral parlor on Mulberry, watch the procession of white scrolls brushed with Chinese characters in black paint. I'll see Mr. and Mrs. Lau making their somber entrance. Leon will be standing by the door next to Liz's sister. He'll catch my eye for a moment, then look away. I'll watch him put his arm around Yan and guide her inside, a bouquet of white chrysanthemums clasped in her two pale hands.

The second will be in Brooklyn, at the Saint Athanasius church. When Gia sees me, she'll loop an arm around me and cry, her long curly hair falling into her face. I'll pay my respects to Carla's mother before leaving, a bouquet of peonies in my hand. Sal will accept these on her behalf, hands streaked with grease.

In between these I'll attend a Passover Seder in which an eight-year-old will beat me repeatedly at Go Fish.

The third won't be so much a funeral as a meeting at a cemetery, attended by a few society ladies visibly desperate for their afternoon martinis, as well as the son and daughter the deceased is convinced never liked her. The resemblance will be undeniable: two tall, bony figures in merino coats and cashmere scarves, a shade of their mother's neurotic beauty in her, a flicker of their father's smug self-assurance in him. They'll stand a foot apart, not speaking, as if they don't want to be near each other but also can't help it. I'll think I smell a hint of her perfume in the air—cut grass, the gasoline edge of violet flower.

Her doctor, Roy Winter, won't be there. In fact, no one's seen hide nor hair of him since that night on the Brighton Beach rooftop.

Candace's husband won't be present, either. He'll be out on bail, awaiting trial for counts of conspiracy to smuggling and aiding and abetting, which is all they've been able to pin on him so far. Most likely they won't be able to prove any of that. He'll be out scot-free and resuming his business in no time, talking hapless souls into a free trip to Pity City, a big chance at the big win, a pot he'll obligingly split.

Maybe he'll even put an ad in the paper.

###

That day at Brighton Beach, the darkness has turned to dazzling sun. The poplar trees that line the block are blooming, little pinwheels of white fuzz drifting down to the street like snow.

Masha was worried after I'd left to meet Batryshkin. I have to hand it to her. Without a thought for saving her own skin, she'd flagged down a squad car on patrol, and it happened to be driven by none other than my friend Junior, who remembered me from when he was minding the chocolate truck by the Land-O-Fun. It didn't take long for him to contact Maloney, who contacted Crock.

Now I'm standing with the detective in front of Solnikov's old building, now Batryshkin's. RIP. Cops, investigators, and crime scene techs swim around in the background. There was the doctor's body to take care of. The rooftop to gather evidence from. The chocolate factory to tear through, after a hasty warrant was issued.

"The federal boys got in this morning," Maloney tells me, gesturing toward the men in suits distinctly better cut than his own. "They've gotten the Coast Guard involved to call the ship carrying the chocolate back to port. And they've already got Sergei in for questioning, on tentative counts of money laundering, assault, and extortion. They're working on Solnikov, though he'll be a harder nut to crack. Seems we finally got their attention. Well, it seems you did."

I hear the edge of regret in his voice. There's nothing Maloney hates more than missing something.

"What about Masha?" I ask.

"They're talking to her now. Sounds like they're working out a deal."

I know what that means: If she testifies, she won't be charged. Her insight must be invaluable to those FBI guys. Come to think of it, Masha would be a great undercover agent. She's had enough practice.

"You did good work, Maloney," I say. "You were there when I needed you."

"We got there in the end," he says.

What we don't say is that even if we've caught the finger, the elbow is still wagging. That the giant, twisting body is still lurking underneath the rotted boardwalk, sliding in between the tables at Tatiana's and the National, between the women in sparkling dresses and the laughter and the bottles of booze, throwing its hulking shadow behind the honest shopkeepers and lawyers and doctors as they close up their storefronts and hurry home, hardly daring to glance over their shoulders. The old order is being unseated, but something newer, darker, keener is taking its place.

But for now, the sky is blue, the sun is mellow, and the air, despite the fact that we're standing between the parkway and the sea, is almost sweet.

"Until next time," I say. A bit of poplar fuzz floats down from the sky and lands on Maloney's shoulder. I pluck it off.

"Until next time," he repeats. His face is weary, estuaries of lines around his blue eyes, but the eyes themselves are bright and awake. Looking into them I feel, for a moment, safe.

I say goodbye and head to the train, tipping two fingers to Angelo, the *Street*'s photographer, who's arrived to snap a few photos. It's early still, and I'm a long way from 1 PP. There's copy to write, stories to file, deadlines to meet. Cats to feed. I'll get a coffee from my cart, have a shower, pick up the clothes I abandoned at the laundromat. Crock left at dawn and will already be back at the office by now, waiting for me with some new tip. Schultz will be there, too, with something else to razz me about. Another building on fire. For all I've been through, it's just another day reporting on my beat.

But first I stop at the payphone and dial Jake's number one more time.

When he answers, his voice is like the whitewater on a wave. "Parker. I heard what happened. Are you okay?"

I take a deep breath. "Still listening to the old brag of my heart," I say. "*I am, I am, I am.*"

"Oh no," he says. "Someone's been reading Plath again."

"Guilty," I say. "I am okay, though. I'm actually calling because, well . . . I know I haven't been the easiest to deal with recently—"

"You're always hard to deal with."

I'm about to take offense to that, to roundly and vehemently deny any such thing. But I find that I'm too tired. "Yeah, you're right," I say. And then we both laugh. "I just really wanted to get to the bottom of this thing. And it really got to me seeing your byline on Schultz's article about the serial murders, which wasn't ever his story to write."

"He told me that you'd asked him to write that story," he says in surprise. "Which, to be honest, didn't really sound like you, but since Morgan told me you were sick, I figured you just wanted the story out there."

Schultz. That goddamn son of a bitch. But in spite of myself, a smile is creeping onto my face. Because I might have done the same thing. "I didn't ask him to. But that's okay. I wanted to say that I'm sorry for getting annoyed when I know you're right and I . . ." I take a deep breath. "I appreciate you."

There's a quiet moment in which I can picture Jake, sitting still at his desk amid the chaos of the newsroom, smiling quietly, too. Then he says, "How about we grab a drink? Once the dust has settled and you're feeling up to it. You still haven't told me about getting yourself arrested."

I'm about to say no, I really don't have time. Because whenever I see Jake, one drink turns into hours of drinking and walking and talking and then I say too much and then I start to miss him. But then I sense something out of the corner of my eye—a shimmering outline. She's nodding at me, telling me it's okay. And then I feel myself nodding, too, and I hear myself saying, "I could use a drink. And it's a pretty good story."

After we hang up, I walk back to the Brighton Beach station. It runs the F and the D. I need the N. And it's Sunday—weekend service. I suspect it's going to be a long ride. As I slide my token into the slot, I hear the groan of a subway car stuttering to a stop on the platform above. I pass through the turnstile, Maloney's words playing over in my mind, like the last line in a poem, or the first. *We got there in the end.* It's hard to accept, what Batryshkin said—that even death has its own dollar value. I start for the stairs, hear the doors open with a mechanical wail, the conductor's murmuring voice announcing the stop. A few passengers exit, coming home from night shifts in the city, maybe, or parties that went till morning. Then two pings and the doors close, the cars wheezing back into motion. That's how it goes: The fabric of the city smooths over, stretches, and repairs itself, until something rends it again. Your feet are throbbing and your head is aching, but there's spring in the air, the tide's coming in on the Atlantic, and whatever train that was, you missed it.

■